Offline

Offline

Brian Adams

GREEN PLACE BOOKS | *Brattleboro, Vermont*

Printed in the United States

10 9 8 7 6 5 4 3 2 1

Green Writers Press is a Vermont-based publisher whose mission is to spread a message of hope and renewal through the words and images we publish. Throughout we will adhere to our commitment to preserving and protecting the natural resources of the earth. To that end, a percentage of our proceeds will be donated to environmental activist groups and The Southern Poverty Law Foundation. Green Writers Press gratefully acknowledges support from individual donors, friends, and readers to help support the environment and our publishing initiative. Green Place Books curates books that tell literary and compelling stories with a focus on writing about place—these books are more personal stories/memoir and biographies.

GREEN PLACE BOOKS   GReen wRiTers press

Giving Voice to Writers & Artists Who Will Make the World a Better Place
Green Writers Press | Brattleboro, Vermont
www.greenwriterspress.com

ISBN: 978-1-7327434-2-7

COVER DESIGN: Asha Hossain Design, LLC
AUTHOR PHOTO: Karen Gardner

PRINTED ON PAPER WITH PULP THAT COMES FROM FSC-CERTIFIED FORESTS, MANAGED FORESTS THAT GUARANTEE RESPONSIBLE ENVIRONMENTAL, SOCIAL, AND ECONOMIC PRACTICES. ALL WOOD PRODUCT COMPONENTS USED IN BLACK AND WHITE, STANDARD COLOR OR SELECT COLOR PAPERBACK BOOKS, UTILIZING EITHER CREAM OR WHITE BOOKBLOCK PAPER ARE SUSTAINABLE FORESTRY INITIATIVE (SFI) CERTIFIED SOURCING.

Acknowledgments

Many thanks to:

Morgan Phippen, Kate Gallagher, Carla Haddow, Casey Adams (the best daughter in the world!), Mairead Blatner, and Skye Young—my glorious readers, who good-naturedly suffered through a semi-coherent first draft of Offline and painstakingly pointed out the many glaring inconsistencies, stupidities, off-color jokes that weren't remotely funny, plot drops, plot flops . . . (the list goes on and on). You cannot begin to imagine how important your feedback was to me.

Audrey Bruell and Joanna Wilson for allowing me the opportunity, sketchy as it sounds, to cruise their dating sites with them. Thank God I'm not single! Women would take one look at my profile and swipe left faster than a tweet out of hell.

Donna and Will "Earth Badger" Elwell who, in a courageous act of community defiance and discontent, built a replica of Thoreau's cabin directly in the path of a proposed fracked-gas pipeline. How awesome an idea was that? Their work inspired the characters in my novel to attempt something similar. The days of fossil fuels are over! Climate action now!

Dede Cummings, my publisher extraordinaire, who has worked tirelessly to turn this book into an international bestseller and major Hollywood blockbuster starring Lupita Nyong'o and Chadwick Boseman. Wait a minute . . . my bad. I think I might be confusing my book with something else.

Michael Fleming, my editor extraordinaire, who told me, "Yes, we have a novel here! It's alive!" It is through his magic that this book actually came together. Don't ever leave me, bro.

Sarah Ellis, my wonderful line editor, for catching the gremlins that can creep into a manuscript, Asha Hossain for coming up with the fabulous cover design, and Ben Tanzer for working his magic with promotion and marketing.

Liza Harrington, the librarian at Greenfield Community College, for introducing me to the world of social media, about which I was totally clueless. Of course, by the time I had it somewhat figured out, everything had completely changed, so . . . what the hell. I'll never understand what is going on out there in Cyberland.

Taylor Adams (the best son in the world!), for his incessant texting during meals, which drove me to the brink of insanity and seeded the idea for this brilliant novel.

Karen Gardner, Dale Samoker, and all of the Verizon and Staple techies who have done their utmost to keep my piece-of-shit computer functioning as I write a broadside blasting everything to do with computers. Hypocrisy? *Moi?* How dare you!

Kirkpatrick Sale, whose wonderful book *Rebels Against the Future: The Luddites and Their War on the Industrial Revolution* inspired my interest in Luddites. My character Sheila's songs about the Luddites are taken directly from his work.

Green Writers Press for their good work in the world and their continuing efforts to publish books that will spread a message of hope and renewal. Support your small publishers!

Broadside Books in Northampton, Amherst Books in Amherst, Jabberwocky Books in Newburyport, Everyone's Books in Brattleboro, and all of the other independent bookstores who open up their hearts and stores to local writers. Buy local!

My wonderful wife, Queen Luddite herself, Morey Phippen. Oh. My. God. I can't imagine living with a writer and putting up with all of their ongoing angst, tantrums, and bullshit. Thank goodness she can and does. I love you so much!

King Ludd, for inspiring the common folk in England in the early 1800s to rage against the machine, wage a ferocious war of economic sabotage, smash the industrial looms, burn down factories, and threaten the new class of industrialists. Though their rebellion against the future was short-lived, they have inspired countless others in their ongoing protests against so-called progress. Luddites of the world, unite!

Donald J. Trump. Just kidding! Even though his offensive, incessant, narcissistic, terrifying tweets further fueled my desire to write a book trashing technology, I cannot and will not dedicate anything to that most loathsome of presidents. Unless of course he tweets about this book. My goodness, think what that would do for sales! Tweet away, you bastard!

Chapter 1

It was a Wednesday afternoon in early June, and Caleb's apartment windows were wide open. A warm, salty breeze was blowing in from Boston Harbor, rustling the curtains and whispering in my ear.

I didn't have a clue as to whether or not Caleb was the boy's real name. Guys on my dating site were making shit up all the time, so who knew what the truth really was. Maybe his name was Boris or Ernest or Fletcher. Maybe something even lamer than that.

But whoever he was, he had certainly done his best to romanticize the bedroom—candles on the bedside table in cute little glasses so the flames wouldn't flicker out in the breeze. Freshly cut flowers on the dresser. Soft, romantic, indie-pop music in the background.

He certainly hadn't lied about how he looked. The boy was even hotter in person than his online picture: tall, broad shouldered, curly hair, and big, pouty lips. Rock star lips. Lips and a sweet, hyperactive tongue that knew exactly where to go and what to do.

We were sitting on Caleb's bed making out. I hadn't yet made up my mind as to where to draw the line when it came to doing anything more than that. The condoms prominently displayed on his bedside table were a clear indication that, as far as Caleb was concerned, there were no lines to be drawn. My fuzzy lines, changing position by the second, were giving me a wicked case of vertigo. The whole bedroom was spinning round and round.

And *damn* if he wasn't being persuasive with that tongue of his. All I had to do was say the word.

I was dizzy. Dizzy and scared to death.

I had never been with a guy before. By *been* I mean, you know, done it. Actually, I had never done anything with a guy before, let alone *it*. Don't get me wrong—I had had oodles of opportunities. Practically every guy who swiped right on my profile on *Passion*, my go-to online dating site, seemed ready to do it at the drop of a hat. But this was the first time I had ever taken someone online offline. I was definitely wallowing in unchartered waters.

Caleb's kisses began straying south of my lips, and his fingers were fiddling with the back of my bra, when suddenly . . .

Ping!

My cell phone. I leaned over, just for the briefest of moments, to steal a quick glance.

Oh my God! It was another hit from *Passion*. Three more hits just since the last time I had checked, right before Caleb and I had started fooling around.

I liked Caleb. At least, I thought I did. I had met him online and we had cyber-flirted for a couple of weeks (a record for me) before I had made the first-of-its-kind truly momentous decision to actually hook up with a guy for real.

"Don't do it!" my best friend Sheila had texted me. "Bad things happen to girls offline. You gotta keep it safe. You gotta keep it virtual!"

But I hadn't listened. And now, here I was, sitting in some bedroom with a random guy's hands all over me, the room spinning like crazy.

I don't know what it was about Caleb that had convinced me to drop my hard-and-fast rule nixing all offline interactions. In the past, whenever a boy would start to get pushy online about taking it offline, I'd just ghost him and he'd be gone forever. But Caleb, the most persuasive texter *ever*, had caught me at a vulnerable moment. I had been binge-texting on my dating site and hadn't slept for days and what was left of my brain was all fuzzy and discombobulated and I really wasn't in my right mind and then, before I knew it, here I was. Offline. Alone. With a guy. In his bedroom!

Oh. My. God.

I had to admit, Caleb was quite the catch. A sophomore in college, a decent summer job, money to burn, a bright red sports car, his own apartment. (At least that's what he had texted me. But then again, who knew what the truth really was.)

This much was definitely true: that boy sure knew how to use his tongue. Not that I knew much of anything about tongues. Not that I knew much of anything about anything having to do with boys.

I hadn't lied to Caleb about myself all that much. Okay, maybe I *had* told him I was nineteen, not seventeen, that I was a freshman in college rather than a junior in high school, that I had lost my virginity years ago. That and a bunch of other diddly little crap—but hey, that's what you do on an online dating site, right? Invent any kind of self you want. That was the beauty of the whole thing. And I never thought in a million years I'd actually hook up with him.

Ping!

There went my phone again.

Caleb was way cute, but my phone . . . well . . . it was my phone! I *had* to pay attention to it. Given my longer-term relationship, I could tell it was jealous at being ignored, desperate for attention. My heart went out to the poor thing.

And three hits in the last ten minutes! A girl has to keep her options open, right? The dating scene on the net moves fast and furious. You snooze, you lose. Let a profile pass and it could be gone forever. Just like that. The hottest guy in the world, *poof*, disappeared, history. It made sense to be up-to-the-minute on who was available, just to cover my bases. Must have a Plan B, that's what my Gramps always said.

I gently took Caleb's hands out from under my sweater and twisted myself into a position where I could text a quick reply to one of the online guys. It was no big deal. It would only take a moment.

Caleb stopped in mid-grope and glared at me.

"Stephanie!" he said, a hurt, puppy dog look on his face. "Seriously? You're actually gonna text at a time like this?"

Full disclosure: Stephanie wasn't my real name. Meagan was. But hey, he didn't need to know that, right?

"Sorry," I said. "Gimme just a sec. Let me do just one quick thing here."

I wasn't trying to be rude or disrespectful. I really wasn't. It was just that three guys had hit on me in the last few minutes. What was I supposed to do? Not text them back? Leave them hanging? How rude and disrespectful would *that* be? I was definitely not that kind of girl.

And, truth be told, this whole in-the-flesh boy thing was totally freaking me out. Sexting was one thing. But *sex*? That was something else entirely.

Caleb sat up and swung his long legs over the edge of the bed.

"Where are you going?" I asked nervously.

"To the bathroom," he said. "Don't you worry. I'll be right back." He leaned in and kissed me again, and then reached over to the bedside table and deftly opened the pack of condoms.

"You make me crazy," he said, whispering in my ear.

"Um . . . thanks?" I replied.

I was an absolute wreck. Why had I come here? What was I thinking? What could possibly have possessed me to actually show up at a guy's apartment just because he text-begged me to?

How stupid was I?

I anxiously checked my phone again. Each guy I had just texted had immediately texted me back. And now there were two more hits, two new profiles to check out. And to top it off, Sheila was flooding me with texts demanding that I bail, bail, bail! Abandon ship! Get the hell out of there! Report back to her house immediately!

Ping! Ping! Ping! Second, third, and even fourth thoughts ricocheted off my brain like ping-pong balls. This whole fling thing was one enormous mistake. A total dumpster fire in the making. Sheila was right. I had to get out of here. Fast. It was now or never.

Caleb came sauntering out of the bathroom, hips swaying, lips smiling.

He took one look at me and stopped in his tracks.

"What's up?" he asked, his face falling. "Is everything okay?"

"I don't know," I said. I was sitting on the edge of the bed, my knees pressed tightly to my chest. "I'm thinking maybe I should . . ."

He leaned in and softly pressed his lips to the side of my neck.

"I'm thinking maybe you should, too." There went those kisses straying south again.

Ping!

There went my phone pinging again.

"Look," I said, stiffening up and pushing him away, a little less gently this time. "I like you, Fletcher. I mean Caleb. I really do. But I gotta go."

"Go?" He took a deep breath and exhaled softly in my ear. "Why? We were just getting started."

"I know. I'm sorry. My bad."

"Is it something I said? Something I did?"

"No, no." My mouth went dry and my voice quavered. I held on to the side of the bed to keep from spinning right off it. "It's nothing like that. It's just . . ."

Ping! Ping! Ping!

"I don't get it." Caleb said. There was that hurt puppydog look again. "I thought we had something going here. I thought we were—"

"We did. We were. But . . . I have to go. I just have to." I was practically shaking in my shoes. I couldn't even look him in the eye anymore.

"Can I call you?" Caleb asked.

"Call me? Um . . . well . . . I'm not so sure about that. Calling is so. . . you know. . . . Just text me instead. Okay?"

I stood up and quickly backed my way towards the door.

"You sure about this, Stephanie?" he asked.

"Caleb," I said, this time looking right at him. "I'm not sure about anything."

Chapter 2

"Where's my phone?" I asked, panicking. "I can't find my damn phone!"

"Right where you left it next to the zucchini, darling," Udder said.

Believe it or not, there I was weeding my grandparent's garden. Me. Weeding. Who knew that was even possible?

It had been two weeks since I had dumped Caleb for my cell phone. My junior year in high school had officially ended the Friday before. I was now a rising senior.

Huzzah and hooray for me!

Udder was killing bean beetles and Gramps was tying tomato plants to their wire cages, using cloth strips made from tattered T-shirts. Too holey or worn-out to have practical use, they were resurrected and given a new lease on life binding cucumbers and pole beans and tomatoes to their stakes and cages. Udder and Gramps's garden was dotted with these weathered strips, their political slogans still shouting out fragmented *Take it to the Man* messages.

Stop the War on the, one read.

U.S. out of Afghanis, screamed another.

In addition to a shit-ton of vegetables I had never even heard of, a bizarre collection of assorted oddities dotted the garden in a mythical, magical way. Three upside-down whiskey bottles were perched on posts to catch and trap the evil garden spirits that evidently lurked in zucchini plants, spirits that brought forth a holy host of pests and plague and pestilence to wreak havoc on Udder and Gramps's beautiful garden. Rusty pipes were set into the soil, a cell-free way for Udder and Gramps to communicate to the underground and offer up encouraging words to the worms and the root hairs and the beneficial microbes. *Grow, baby, grow*, I'd hear them whisper down the pipes, their eyes closed in silent, soothing plant prayer. Aluminum pie pans with pasted heads of revolutionary political figures, Che and Malcolm X and Gandhi, hung on a wire, banging and clanging with the wind in a fruitless attempt to scare away crows and jays and other assorted garden thieves. And in the very center of it all, watching over the garden with a benevolent gaze, perched a smiling Buddha on a rock, serene and calm and fat as a sumo wrestler, countless layers of birdshit splotched all over his cracked, bald head.

Truth be told, I barely knew a weed from a watermelon, and to be frank, I couldn't give a shit. Vegetation just wasn't my thing. I hated weeding their garden. I hated being outside. It was way too . . . nature-like. Way too offline. But gardening was Udder and Gramps's thing, and, given that I had been exiled there by my parents for the summer, I really had no choice.

Udder stopped killing beetles and looked right at me.

"I don't mean to be critical," he said, "but I think that your parents might be right. You really do have a problem."

"Earth to Udder," I said. "My parents have never been right. They never have been and they never will be."

"Nonetheless," Udder continued, "on this issue they may be onto something."

I fiddled with my cell and braced for the incoming: Yet another lecture detailing the deplorable depth of my technology addiction. A monologue on the severity of my Nature Deficit Disorder. A rant on the moral degradation of the text-not-talk culture. Even more psychobabble nonsense on the perilous blurring of my online and offline life.

"How many real relationships have you had in the last year?" Udder asked.

"Oh my God!" I shook my head and rolled my eyes. "I can't believe you're asking me that!"

"I don't mean to pry, but . . ."

"I know exactly where this conversation is going. Your definition of 'real' is totally different from mine."

"When I was your age—" Udder began.

I cut him off. "When you were my age there were no cell phones, laptops, or online dating sites. You and your Free Love generation were all about pot, protests, and penises. The three P's."

"What's wrong with the three P's?" Gramps asked, rolling yet another joint. "They still sound good to me."

Gramps gave Udder a wink, and reached over to caress his thigh.

I closed my eyes and looked away.

Old people sex. Yuck. It made me want to gag.

Gramps sat back down in his garden chair to take a breather and finish his rolling. Because of his medical issues, Gramps had the coveted medical marijuana card that allowed him to purchase weed from a certified dispensary. While marijuana use in Massachusetts had been legalized in the last election, recreational pot dispensaries had still not opened. My grandfather had a lot of physical crosses to bear, but it was also perfectly clear that the recreational nature of the drug seemed just as appealing to him.

"My point is this, darling . . . ," Udder continued.

I loved how Udder called me "darling." Once a guy texted me using that very same word. I had replied immediately with a "WTF!!!!!" and about sixty talk-to-the-hand and throwing-up emojis. When Udder used it, though, it seemed so genuine. So endearing. I really was, after all, his *darling*.

". . . It seems as though every single guy you connect with, you ditch. All for the same reason. Here you are—beautiful, smart, and pretty damn funny when you want to be—but you just can't seem to disconnect yourself from your damn phone long enough to get to the good stuff."

"What's the good stuff again?" I asked.

"Love. What else? A real relationship."

"For the fiftieth time—I have real relationships."

"Texting random guys you find online does not count as real relationships."

"It does to me."

"Meagan! Darling! It's become increasingly clear to your grandfather and me that you've let social media trump actually being *social*. Facebook has replaced face-to-face. You're tethered to the internet in an incredibly unhealthy way."

"Oh my God, Udder!" I ripped out a particularly long and loathsome weed and threw it hard into the compost pile. "What'd you just do? Google 'clichés for Y2K's'?"

"Don't be rude to your Udder," Gramps said.

I had told the two of them the entire sad story of my meltdown with Caleb without even cringing. I told my Udder and Gramps everything. Along with Sheila, they were my confidantes. My go-to two. For whatever reason, I found I could share things with them I'd never dream of sharing with my parents. Somehow a skipped generation made all the difference.

There was no way I'd ever tell my parents anything about boys, online or off. They were ridiculously clueless when it came to anything about my life, way too preoccupied with their own pointless and pathetic existences, it seemed, to even register that I was their own spawn. As long as I didn't totally flunk out of school, stayed off drugs, confined my dance music to my earbuds, and kept myself out of the police log, I had always been pretty much good to go.

But now, for whatever ridiculous and unfathomable reason, my mother and father had gotten it into their thick heads that I had "issues."

Me? Issues? The sheer audacity of it all!

"You're an addict," my father, in his infinite wisdom, had told me at breakfast one morning.

"Add what?" I asked, not even looking up from my phone. I had learned early on that to establish eye contact with a parent was the kiss of death. It was to be avoided at all costs.

"I don't believe I've seen you look up from your phone in the last year and a half," he blabbered on.

Duh! Why would I possibly trade a screen shot for my father's face?

"I've forgotten what you even look like," he continued.

"Look like who?" I replied, texting away. Was the man ever going to stop talking?

And anyway, who the hell were they to talk? The only time *they* ever looked up from *their* cell phones was to criticize *me* about how much I used *mine*. They were into screen time as much as I was.

I could barely remember a single, solitary moment in my entire life when I had ever had their undivided attention. They'd pick me from school without looking up from their phones. I'd gaze into the audience during my school play and see them, heads down, texting away. We never fought at dinner because we never talked, too busy with our phones to even know who we were eating with. It took my mother a year and a half to recognize that my boobs had come in because she never looked at me.

And now, here they were, going off on me as an online addict? Seriously? What a bunch of bullshit. Hypocrisy with a capital H. That was so the pot calling the kettle black.

It wasn't as if my parents and I had a bad relationship, going at it the way that Sheila did with her parents. It was more like we had no relationship at all.

Since I had arrived at Udder and Gramps's I didn't miss them a bit, but I had been thinking about them a lot. Not so much about what they did, but more like what they didn't do.

Take, for instance, the L word. Never once, in my entire life, do I remember my parents telling me that they loved me.

"Love," my father spat, in one of our very few conversations about that strangest of all four-letter words. "Nobody *loves* anybody else. They may say it, but they don't really mean it. You might love how someone makes you feel, but you don't love *them*. I hate to break it to you,

Meagan, but this myth of love is nonsense. Love yourself, that's all I can tell you, because no one else is going to."

Seriously? Thanks, Dad! Such comforting words for a girl just coming into her own.

My dad and mom were certainly not positive role models when it came to love. Their own relationship clearly was just not meant to be. After a series of sordid affairs on both their parts that traumatized all three of us, they finally divorced when I was eleven. Given their joint custody, I flip-flopped back and forth between their two houses in Boston, eyewitness to a series of failed attempts at new relationships. Serial monogamy was the name of the game, and I can't begin to remember how many "boyfriends" and "girlfriends" my parents had gone through by the time I was a junior in high school.

Their two houses had revolving doors, and, quick as a *ping* on my phone, it was out with the old and in with the new, again and again and again. I made out like it didn't bother me, like I didn't care, but the fact is, I thought it was actually pretty twisted. I don't know what the hell they were looking for, and I'm not sure they did either, but it seemed pretty clear that love had absolutely nothing to do with it.

"Did you love him?" I once asked my mother after she had broken up with yet another so-called boyfriend.

"Love?" she asked, putting her arms around me and giving me an awkward hug. "Of course not, Meagan. Why would you even think such a thing?"

Warped or what? Maybe this was just her way of reassuring me that everything would be okay, but still—*of course not*? Really? That was the best she could come up with? No wonder I was so damn disillusioned, so cynical, so totally confused about the whole love thing.

Given the chaos and confusion of their lives, I shouldn't be so hard on them. They probably did the best they could. So I got a little short-shrifted in the love department. What else is new? When I heard stories about other kids' childhoods with their helicopter parents monitoring their every move, I suppose I should have counted my blessings.

But still, it was much more satisfying to blame my parents for all of my issues. Make them the go-to scapegoats. Let them take the fall. After all, isn't that what parents are for? My mom and dad were the ones responsible for my genetic predisposition to reject the real self for the virtual one. It was their genes *and* their parenting that had made me hardwired to go wireless.

When I was a little girl and underfoot and my parents couldn't deal, which seemed to be most of the time, they'd tell me, "Why don't you go online and play?" Never "go outside" or "invite a friend over" or "draw something" or even "watch TV." Just "go online." I was groomed to be a raging net girl from the get-go.

I learned early on that real dolls were nothing compared to their computer counterparts. Why play with Barbie when the online version of the *Barbie Dreamtopia Adventure Games* was so much more thrilling? Real dolls were boring, lifeless, stupid. The easily uploadable *Pearl Princess Puzzle Party* or *Tutu Star* were what I lived for. By the second grade I was already consulting the online version of *Barbie's First Date Dress Up* and *Princess Barbie Facial Makeover* for inspiration.

It wasn't that I didn't have friends. It was just that sometimes they got old and in the way and hogged a lot of my time that could have been so much more enjoyably spent online.

The worst punishment my parents could give me was an online time-out. I remember clear as day Thanksgiving dinner in the fourth grade. I threw a temper tantrum and, for some bizarre reason, poked my cousin in the eye with a drumstick and rubbed mashed potatoes into his hair. My parents sent me to my room and took away my computer. I was beside myself. I wept, ripped a hole in my pillow, and blanketed the room with the feathers, threw all my stuffed animals out the window. Finally, I managed to break out and, still weeping, called 911. After all, what greater emergency could there possibly be than for someone to be deprived of their God-given right to be online?

That glorious day when my parents gave me my very first smart phone, an iPhone 4, it was love at first sight. Within minutes I couldn't live without it. With that phone in my hand, I felt invincible, complete, one with the universe, happy and whole. It touched me in a way nothing else did. When new cell phones came on the market and I was allowed an upgrade, I would be over the moon—but still, parting with the one I had already was like losing a loved one.

Maybe, just maybe, part of me knew I had issues, but I could easily rationalize it. After all, everyone else was doing just what I was doing. We were all *screen tweens* and then, when we came of age, *screenagers*. How could I possibly be an addict if everybody else I knew was just the same as me?

It wasn't like I was ostracized or ridiculed or bullied for my obsession. Just the opposite. It was the kids who didn't possess the latest in technology, who didn't have their selves buried in their phones, who were teased the most.

"Oh my God! Look at her!" a kid at school would smirk at someone walking down the hall texting away with an outdated phone. "She still has an iPhone 6. Hello? What century is she even living in?"

And anyway, so what if it *was* an addiction? It wasn't as if I was on drugs or anything.

True story: There was a senior at our high school who went partying one night and, for whatever screwed-up reason, tried heroin. Snap! Just like that, he was an opioid addict. One single fix was all that it took. The heavy stuff was all he began to care about, all he wanted to do. Everything else became irrelevant. Life was all about getting that next high.

The week before graduation he died of an overdose.

So hey, there were addicts and there were *addicts*. In the grand scheme of things, my affliction, even if I really had one (which I didn't), wasn't such a big deal. At least the highs wouldn't kill me. And the lows? All I had to do was exit and switch sites.

Armed with a computer and a cell phone, there was really only one additional, crucial weapon that I needed in my arsenal: a like-minded cellmate to obsessively text with. Not an anonymous plaything from the net, but someone actually real.

Voilà! As Lady Luck would have it, Sheila appeared.

It was seventh-grade science class with Mister Gimitri, who was perhaps the most boring human being ever to walk the planet. He was the type of teacher who made a zucchini seem clinically hyperactive. There were times when, motionless in front of the classroom, it was difficult to know whether or not the man was actually alive.

On one particular Monday morning (I even remember the day of the week), Mister G was slouched as usual, semicomatose at his desk. We were supposed to be reading the textbook, and, as always, I was surfing social media sites on my phone.

"Meagan, give me your phone."

I hadn't seen Mister G coming. I was shocked that he had the energy to even notice what I was doing, let alone physically make it to the back corner of the classroom. But there he was, holding out his hand, demanding I turn over to him my most prized possession.

"What?" I asked, incredulously. "What did I do?"

"I have asked you repeatedly to stop texting in class, and you clearly haven't gotten the message."

This may or may not have been true. Whenever that man actually did speak, I usually wasn't paying attention.

"I'm not texting," I told him. "I'm updating my profile."

"Meagan, give me your phone."

"Dude!" a voice from across the room yelled. "You can't make her give you her phone!"

I turned and saw a girl I barely knew defiantly waving her phone in the air.

"That's like, you know, against the law or something," she went on. "We have our rights."

It was Sheila! Coming to my rescue. Defender of all things handheld. Outraged on my behalf at this gravest of techno-tragedies.

"And we have our rules," Mister G persisted. "I will take your cell phone now, Meagan. Yours, too, Sheila. You may pick them up at the end of class."

"That's just wrong," Sheila said. "It's a total violation of, like, the Fourth Amendment. Our right to privacy. This is like an unreasonable search and seizure. You're breaking the law here, dude."

"The last time I checked, texting in the middle of my class is not covered under the Fourth Amendment."

"Then what about the First? Huh? The right to free speech?" Sheila demanded. "Are you going to take away that freedom too? This is how Hitler rose to power. First take away one right, then another, and before you know it the world is plunged into war and chaos and— "

"Sheila! Meagan! Give me your cell phones. Now!"

The whole class was riveted. No one had ever seen Mister G so animated about anything!

"He's alive!" I wanted to scream out. "The man's alive!" Thankfully, the vocal cords disengaged just in the nick of time.

"That dude needs to chill," Sheila said after class when, following a final stern rebuke, we repossessed our phones and headed down the hall to English.

"Thanks," I said. "For, you know, standing up for me and all."

"*De nada,*" Sheila said. "Can I see your profile?"

And the rest, as they say, is history.

My last week of school closing out my junior year hadn't exactly ended on a high note. It was sort of a repeat performance of the seventh-grade fiasco, only this time the outcome was a little bit worse.

My science teacher had accused me of using my cell phone to cheat during the last exam.

Me? Cheat? How dare she accuse me of such a thing! There was no way I could possibly have cared enough about science to stoop that low.

Following an escalating misunderstanding that could easily have been resolved amicably, I had been given an early vacation.

The school referred to it as a suspension.

Whatever.

The whole stupid thing was not the ginormous deal everyone made it out to be. It was barely worthy of a detention, not an involuntary leave of absence. After all, all I had been doing was the usual—checking the incoming on my dating site, something I did at school a hundred times a day—when Ms. Science began to totally freak. She demanded that I turn over my phone and I got a tad emotional (she called it "belligerent"), but it was, after all, *my phone* and I was right in the middle of an *important text*. Okay, maybe I did make a few smart-ass comments that I probably shouldn't have. And maybe whacking her hand when she tried to grab my phone wasn't my finest moment. But still, talk about losing your shit for no reason.

A suspension? Over that? Really?

To get to the point—the whole unfortunate incident did not go down well with my parents. It also didn't help that somehow I had mistakenly given some perv on *Passion* my address (whoops! my bad) and he had come knocking at the door at three in the morning, clearly looking to you-know-what. The guy must have been forty and he had on more tattoos than clothes. This did not exactly please my father who, after reading him the riot act and threatening to call the police, practically chased me back into my room. For once agreeing on something, my parents demanded that I go and live with my grandfathers for the summer, a complete digital exile to a godforsaken place with spotty cell reception at best. And no laptop allowed. I was to be at my grandfathers' beck and call, tending their garden, cleaning their house, doing whatever needed to be done. For the entire summer. No vacations. No days off. No nothing.

I floated the alternative idea of hiding out in the basement and doing absolutely nothing offline for two glorious months, but that didn't go down so well.

Parents! *Arghhh!!!!*

Chapter 3

Being a child of the unenlightened ages when homosexuality was still considered a psychological disorder, the *finding-who-he-really-was* thing had taken Gramps quite some time to come to grips with. Following two total train wreck marriages to women—the first to my grandmother, resulting in (hooray for me!) my dad—Gramps finally figured it all out, got his act together, and settled down with the great love of his life, Udder.

Udder wasn't Gramps's husband's real name. His given name was Francis Bacon Nightingale the Third, which suited him just about as well as slippers on an eel.

When I was little, my dad referred to Francis as "your other grandpa," but with my little lips I couldn't quite say the word *other* and what came bubbling out instead was *udder*. Everybody thought that was quite the hoot, particularly Francis Bacon Nightingale the Third himself, who from that day on insisted that everyone call him Udder.

The name suited him well, particularly now that he sported such an impressive set of man boobs.

So it was Udder and Gramps, although occasionally, just to mix it up a bit, I'd refer to Gramps as the udder Udder, or U-squared, or even just U-U.

It wasn't until I was in kindergarten that I realized that not all grandfathers were gay. Before then I had just assumed that that was the way of the world.

"Where's your other gramps?" I remember asking one of my friends when I was over at her house for a play date.

"What do you mean?" the friend asked.

"I mean, why's your grandpa holding hands with that wrinkled-up old lady? Where's his udder?"

My two grandfathers got a real kick out of that story.

The oldsters lived in a rambling farmhouse on five acres in Haydenville, one of the sleepy little hilltowns in the Berkshires in rural Western Massachusetts. It was a couple of hours west from where I lived in Boston, pretty much out in the middle of nowhere.

Before they had retired, Udder had been a therapist with a private practice and Gramps a grant writer at the University of Massachusetts. Now, as far as I could tell, they spent three seasons gardening and the fourth, winter, holed up in that drafty old farmhouse doing God only knows what.

It was clear from the get-go that Udder and Gramps could use all of the help they could get with their house and garden. Getting old sucked. Remind me never to do it. They both had major issues with arthritis, and some days they'd be stiffer than the wooden posts out in their garden. It was a wonder they could move at all. Just getting up off the couch was one of life's little victories. Through no fault of their own, they had let the housekeeping side of things slide for the past year or two. The old place was in dire need of a top-to-bottom deep cleaning.

And their garden. Oh my God! It had become a tangled, impenetrable jungle that was nearly impossible to walk into, not that I had the slightest desire to walk into it anyway.

It made sense for them to have someone there to help get things in order. Someone they could boss around for free. Someone like me.

Hence my sitting in the damn zucchini patch, covered in dirt, cursing my rotten luck, and weeding away.

I had unearthed a wickedly yucky earthworm, and the little bugger was freaking out. It was squirming this way and that, desperately trying to figure out which end was up. I scooped it over next to the zucchini and dumped a pile of soil on it. Thinking that worms were bad for the garden, I had launched the last one I had found up and over the garden fence, but now, following a lengthy reprimand from Gramps, I knew better.

"Worms," Gramps said, looking over at me. He took a hit off his joint and blew the pot smoke the worm's way.

"Yeah," I said. "They totally gross me out. So sad and always doing their own weird squirmy thing."

"I don't know about sad," Gramps said. "They've got quite the active sex life, you know."

"Seriously?"

"I kid you not."

Udder rolled his eyes. "For the love of God, Meagan, don't get the man started!"

Gramps fancied himself an amateur naturalist, a citizen scientist, a self-taught entomologist. He was forever lamenting the fact that he wasn't some fabulously wealthy English dude from the 1800s like Charles Darwin, who lived in an era when the discussion of worms' reproductive proclivities wasn't considered quite so eccentric.

To his credit, Gramps really did seem to know his shit. He'd go a little overboard on the sexual oddities of the natural world, but if you gave him half a chance and a little bit of weed, he could actually be quite fascinating. Much more so than my high school science teacher, who was a complete and utter MORON (remember the incident with my phone?) and could bore you to sleep just by walking through the door of the classroom. If the question of sex (which she did her absolute best to avoid) ever did come up, she'd get all red-faced and tongue-tied and reveal to the entire class how totally lame and stupid she really was.

"Hermaphrodites," Gramps said.

"Hermaphro-who?" I asked.

"Worms. They're hermaphrodites. They're both boys and girls at the same time. Each little wormie's got its very own sperm and eggs."

"You gotta be kidding me. Is that even possible? Do they actually *do* themselves?"

"No, no, no," Gramps said, shaking his head. "They come together. Literally. Both get sperm from the other and fertilize their own eggs. They make these slimy little cocoons, and out sallies forth the next generation."

"Wait a minute," I said anxiously, digging out the worm to get a closer look. There was nothing I could find bearing resemblance to any sort of reproductive part, so I buried it again in the soil and went back to rubbing my phone like a worry stone. (Even though there was no coverage in this digital wasteland of a garden, keeping my phone next to me at all times was still absolutely essential. Without it *I* felt sad and lonely.) "Why are you telling me this? Please don't say it has something to do with *my* relationships." I was beginning to think that Gramps was going somewhere with the sex-life-of-worms thing, and it was not looking pretty.

Gramps only laughed.

"Imagine a worm's dating profile on *Passion*," I said. "*W'sup? Wanna get down and dirty tonight? Flexible bundle of muscle looking for that special someone to slime with. You give me yours. I'll give you mine. We'll put the kink back in kinky!*"

Udder was right about one thing: I could actually be pretty damn funny sometimes.

There was, however, not a worm's worth of truth to the psychobabble bullshit that Udder was droning on and on about. His past life as a therapist could really be quite annoying. Next to Sheila, I loved my two grandfathers more than anyone else in the entire world, and generally I treasured the pearls of wisdom they'd impart to me. But on this issue, they were dead wrong.

Me?

An addict?

Humph!

Addicts' lives were out of control. Addicts' lives were totally fucked up. Just because I was way more comfortable online than off, like every single person my age in the entire world, did not mean I was an addict.

Don't get me wrong: I'm not saying everything in my life was perfect. I'm not saying I didn't have issues. Everyone has issues. But there is a ginormous difference between an *issue* and an *addiction.* My online life wasn't nearly the problem that the adults in my life seemed to make it out to be.

All right, so maybe I didn't sleep all that well at night. Truth be told, I didn't sleep much at all, except (if I wasn't texting) during the middle of class, which never seemed to go down so well with my teachers.

"Meagan!" they'd yell, standing over me and rudely shaking me by my shoulders. "You're nodding off again!"

"What?" I'd startle awake, totally zoned out, confused as to what planet I was even on. "Where's my phone? Who texted?"

That was bound to get a laugh from my peeps, but generally not from my teachers. How unfair was it that my grades would suffer so much just because of that one minor detail? Maybe everyone else managed to remain upright in class with their eyes partway open, but did that mean they were paying any attention at all to the drivel the teachers were spouting off about? I don't think so. And seriously, when else was I supposed to get a bit of the old shut-eye? Everybody knew that the real online action took place after the sun went down, so missing out on the midnight madness clearly wasn't an option.

And maybe I *had* just gone to the doctor's office with chronic pain, spasms, and occasional burning sensations that made my hands seem as though they were on fire ALL OF THE TIME.

"Radial styloid tenosynovitis," the doctor had told me.

"Typhoid?" I asked, completely freaking out. "Oh my God! Am I going to die?"

The doctor laughed.

"Styloid," he said. "Not typhoid. Also known as texting thumb. You've just got to lay off the phone a little."

Yeah. Right. As if *that* was going to happen.

And maybe I wasn't in the best of shape. I'd go to the Y to work out and end up standing stock still on the elliptical for an hour and a half without moving a single part of my body other than my thumbs. When I got home I'd continue to binge-text with one hand while binge-eating Dove Bars with the other. Neither of these activities did all that much to improve my muscle-mass-to-fat ratio.

And maybe it was true that, other than a couple of awkward grop- ing incidents in darkened basements at Sweet Sixteen parties, the only offline romantic relationship I had ever had was with that boy Caleb or Fletcher or whatever the hell his name was, and we all know how that one ended, don't we. But hey, every one-on-one in-the-flesh relationship I knew of inevitably ended in an explosive train wreck. Online guys were constantly texting to ask me out, but why would I possibly ever even *think* of saying yes? Once burned, twice learned. Why waste my precious time with a real guy when I knew what the end result would be? It just didn't make any sense.

Guys were way more appealing in their online profiles than they ever were in real life. Real-life guys, like the losers in my high school, spent the vast majority of their offline time in hand-to-hand combat, battling each other over the title of alpha male, way too hyper or narcissistic or brain-dead to be of any use to me.

It's a proven scientific fact: guys are developmentally delayed. It's like they're subhuman or something, more Neanderthal than *Homo sapiens*. Even the dorkiest sophomore girl is way more mature than any senior with a penis.

I could have easily made a hit reality TV show at my high school. I'd call it *Teen Girl Hell* or *Bozo Boy Bingo* or *Seriously, Four Years of This?* Let the camera roll and let the guys do their thing. The critics would rave.

"Cringe-worthy." — *The New York Times*

"A sad and pathetic look at what it's like to be male." — *People Magazine*

"Wow! Thank God *I'm* not a teenager." — *Teen Vogue*

But online? Oh my God! Online was a different story.

Swipe right if you like, swipe left if you don't. Relationships were just a finger-flick away.

No more cringe-worthy, sad, and pathetic real-time talk with those long, awkward pauses that made me nervous and jittery. No more spon- taneous conversation with unedited sentences coming out of nowhere that I knew I'd later regret. No more eye contact and body language and tone of voice so damn difficult to decipher. No more agonizing over how to end a real-time conversation without acting like the idiot.

Real-time conversations were like driving without Siri and GPS. You had absolutely no idea where the hell you'd end up and how lost you would be. I mean, seriously, how scary was that?

Online, you could be whoever you wanted, whenever you wanted. It was so much saner.

Plus, online, I could string along multiple guys at once, hopefully with one of them witty enough to hold my attention. And if I got bored texting, I'd just ghost them and that would be the end of that. *Adios*, dude. Later. As in: never.

Of course, the flip side was that the boys flirting away out there in Cyberland were swiping right back at me. I was not just the hunter, but the quarry as well. The predator and the prey. The rejector and the rejected.

It wasn't that I didn't get off on the idea of fooling around with real guys. My five minutes of fun with Caleb, painfully awkward as it was, had been quite the eye-opener. But the cons of offline totally outweighed the pros. Anyone with an ounce of sense could see that one-on-one was way too complicated.

The flirty messaging back and forth with boys I had never actually met seemed just as big a turn-on as doing the deed. And so much less terrifying. I was a pro at using my thumbs to sext and my fingers to do the rest. Online—the ultimate safe sex.

Plus, I had been taught by my parents at an early age never to get my hopes up around real-life boys, because those hopes were sure to get batted down fast. "*Expectation is the root of all heartache,*" my mom was fond of saying, quoting Shakespeare or Buddha or some other dead guy. "Especially when it comes to men," she'd be sure to add.

I learned that lesson early on. When I was in the fourth grade there was this sweet boy in my class named Jared, who I was really crushing on. All the other boys would tease the hell out of him because we'd play together at recess.

"*Ewww*," they'd groan. "You're playing with a girl!"

He was turning ten and he invited me to his big birthday bash the weekend of Halloween. Everyone was supposed to come in costume.

"I have an awesome idea," he whispered to me behind the climbing structure during recess, standing so close that we were almost touching. "I'll dress like a king and you dress like my queen."

You can just imagine what that did to my elementary little heart. Holy shit! I spent the entire week going nuts over my outfit, and on the day of the party I showed up in a poufy pink sparkly floor-length skirt and a cardboard crown with glittery tassels cascading off the sides. I was all set to marry that boy on the spot.

I walked into the party and there he was: dressed like a zombie, fake blood oozing all over him, pretend guts spewing out from his ripped-up shirt, no king in sight. He didn't talk to me. Not during the party or after, at school. We never again played together at recess. No explanation. No nothing.

I was heartbroken.

My early introduction to boys and expectations.

"Take a look at this," Gramps said, once more leaving his chair and getting down on his hands and knees to help me pull weeds. I could hear his bones creaking with the effort. "Francis found this down at the Food Co-op." He inhaled deeply and blew a cloud of cannabis smoke slowly over the zucchini (no wonder they grew so big!) and handed me a flyer.

Sometimes Gramps called Udder by his real name: Francis. Gramps's real name, by the way, was Curtis. Together they sounded like two pet hippos in a zoo.

"You never know," Gramps continued, "it might not be such a bad idea."

SCREENAGERS! the flyer read. *Technology controlling your life? Want to get off online?* (I laughed at that. Seriously? Was the writer of the flyer really that clueless?) *Texting thumbs aching from abuse? Has the cyber-world taken you over? Join us Wednesday nights at the Unitarian Church in Northampton. Netaholics Anonymous for teens. We can help!*

Oh my God! Was this some sort of a joke?

Netaholics Anonymous? Screenagers? Did people actually take this shit seriously?

Gramps started singing a stupid golden oldie song from the 1950s, changing the lyrics in a way that he and Udder thought hysterically funny:

Screen Angel, can you hear me?
Screen Angel, can you see me?
Are you somewhere up above?
Texting with your own true love?

I moved the soil away from the zucchini where I had dumped it, looking for my elusive hermaphroditic friend that I had oh-so-rudely relocated. Wormie was nowhere to be seen. Disappeared. Gone forever.

Worms.

Boys.

Who knows, maybe there really was a connection.

"It might be worth a try." Udder and Gramps were both staring at me, making me nervous. "What do you think?"

"In your dreams," I said, standing up, shaking my head, rolling my eyes, and storming back to the house in a huff.

Chapter 4

"You're kidding me!" Sheila said, laughing away at the other end of the phone.

I had called Sheila on the landline rather than walk down the road to try and find service. Udder and Gramps had been shooed onto the porch so I could have at least a little bit of privacy.

"'Netaholics Anonymous'?" she said, snorting away. "For real? That's like the lamest thing I've ever heard."

"I know, right? Totally ridiculous."

"It's probably some back-to-the-Bible, God-squad, lunatic-fringe cult thing. You know the drill: they suck you in with this 'netaholics' crap, and before you know it, you're shackled by the ankles hanging upside down in a church cellar while some pasty-faced geek in an oversized robe with a rope for a belt recites scripture at you."

Sheila wasn't one to hold religion in high regard. Her grandparents were from Lebanon and she had heard way too much about the damage religion had done to their country to want to have anything to do with it. Muslim, Jew, Christian—she was pretty much fed up with the whole lot of them.

"Exactly," I said to her. Sometimes, even when I disagreed with Sheila, it was easier to agree.

"Or, worse yet—they really *are* serious," she went on. "Can you imagine people actually thinking that being online is some sort of problem?"

"I know. It's beyond lame."

"It makes lame look tame."

"Totally."

"So what'd you say?" Sheila asked. "'Fuck off'? In a nice way, I hope."

"Well . . . um . . . not exactly."

There was a long pause on the other end of the phone. "What do you mean 'not exactly'? What *did* you say?"

"It's just that . . . you see . . ."

"Meagan! You can't be serious! Please don't tell me you're actually going!"

You know the classic line: *Houston, we have a problem?*

Well, I definitely had a problem.

Monday night, I had borrowed Gramps's car to drive into town in a desperate search for more coffee and some online action. I had my game plan buzzing through my head. First, I'd cruise my *Passion* site, swipe on a ton of guys, check out Facebook, text guys back, do a website or two (Sheila had rave-texted me about an awesome Celebrity Fashion Faux Pas photo montage that she said was absolutely hysterical), cyber-flirt some more, head back to Facebook, do a dozen or so YouTube videos, and then close the evening off with a swiping and sexting binge. It was going to be heaven.

Unfortunately, none of this happened. I had barely made it out of the driveway when somehow I managed to wrap the car around a damn tree. Other than a nasty cut on my leg (who knows how that happened) requiring a couple of stitches in the emergency room, I was just fine. But the car? That was a different story.

"You were texting, weren't you?" Gramps asked, relieved that my injury wasn't too serious but still pretty pissed about the whole stupid situation.

"Of *course* I was texting," I told him. "The ride to town takes almost thirty minutes. Did you really expect me to wait that long to go online?"

Arghhh! The curse of being an honest granddaughter. George Washington and the cherry tree be damned—what was I thinking, telling the truth?

Hence the ultimatum: Netaholics Anonymous or no more use of the car. No more car meant no more unsupervised trips into town. No more unsupervised trips into town meant no more texting and online play. I'd be a raving lunatic in no time.

"So you're actually . . . *going?*" I could hear Sheila groaning in the background.

"I guess."

"That sucks."

"Tell me about it."

"Really sucks."

"I heard you the first time."

"Really, really, really . . ."

"Sheila! Stop! Seriously. They've left me no choice."

"It's bad enough that you've abandoned me in Boston for two whole months," Sheila said, "but Netaholics Anonymous? That's like pathologically crazy! Your grandfathers, no offense, are fossilized dinosaurs. They're still living in the twentieth century. They think the net is something you hit a ball over. I mean, they're totally clueless as to how to deal with the real world. Yeah, it's too bad you wrecked their car, and I'm sorry about your leg, but shit happens. This whole 'screenager' thing is way too extreme. Even *they* have to know that."

"I know. But I have to go. Just to get Udder and Gramps off my back. They've listened way too much to my parents, and now, with this whole car-crash thing, they've got a stick up their butt too."

"Have I told you how much this sucks?" Sheila asked.

I rolled my eyes. "Believe me, it'll be one and done and then I'll be miraculously cured. It's no big deal. And anyway, think how awesome it will be to make fun of all the morons and losers that show up to this kind of shit show."

"Hmm . . ." Sheila said. "Good point. Text me when you get there."

"Leave your phone at home," Udder told me as I was grabbing the keys to his car. Gramps's car was still in the shop.

"What?" I said. "You gotta be kidding me!"

"Here." Udder patted the living room table. "Put it right here. I promise I won't let it out of my sight."

"I can't be without my phone," I said, my voice getting all whiny and shrill. "That's ridiculous. What if the car broke down? What if something bad happened to me?"

Udder sighed and shook his head. "Darling, remember what happened last time. It's when you have your phone that bad things happen to you. As long as you're not texting and driving we have total confidence in you. And the best way not to text and drive is to leave your phone right here."

I groaned loudly. "I promise to be a good girl and not do anything stupid ever again. Seriously. Pinky swear. I've learned my lesson. But just to be on the safe side . . ."

"No."

"No what?"

"Nomophobia."

"Huh? What are you talking about, Udder?"

"Nomophobia. That's what you have, darling. Face the facts, Meagan. You're a nomophobiac. I'm seriously hoping this meeting will help."

"Making out with a guy one time doesn't exactly make me a sex addict. And anyway, I thought this meeting was about the internet?"

"Nomophobia, not nymphomania. Nomophobia is the fear of being without your phone. That's you all over. It's not just distracted driving that your grandfather and I are worried about—it's distracted *living*."

"Oh my God, here we go again!" I had rolled my eyes so many times that I was dizzy.

"You don't send an alcoholic to an AA meeting with a bottle of booze, do you? Now give me the phone and no one gets hurt."

"This. Is. Ridiculous." I was pissed. Why did adults have to totally overreact to every single thing I did?

Udder patted the table again. "The journey of a thousand miles begins with a single step," he said.

"Really?" I replied. "Silly me. And all this time I thought it was a single text."

I had never driven a car without my cell phone. In fact, I couldn't remember the last time I had been *anywhere* without my phone. Just the thought of leaving it behind was terrifying. I felt like one of those amputees with phantom-limb syndrome. I had the vivid sensation that my phone was still attached to my hand, even though, horror of horrors, it wasn't.

Backing out of the driveway, I kept looking longingly in the rearview mirror, desperate to catch a glimpse of the window of the room where I knew my phone was. I could picture it there without me, sad and all alone. My heart was practically breaking.

I fought the urge to pull a U-turn and head back to Udder and Gramps's. This whole idea of going to a Netaholics Anonymous meeting was absurd. Beyond ridiculous. A step down from stupid.

Nomophobia. *Humph!*

I didn't have a problem *with* technology. I had a problem *without* technology.

And anyway, if anyone was going to this meeting it should have been Sheila. Sheila was in an online league of her own, about as glued to the virtual world as a girl could possibly be. Along with her laptop and iPad, she had two phones—just in case, God forbid, she should lose one.

"Backup," she said. "So I can sleep at night."

Even the opening desktop image on her laptop was a selfie of her and her phone!

And Udder thought *I* was a nomophobiac?

One night, back in the day when Sheila owned only a single iPhone, we were out shopping at the mall and somehow the girl lost her phone.

You would have thought she had been diagnosed with an inoperable brain tumor. She was sobbing, inconsolable.

I had been obsessed with finding this exact brand of drifter-white treaded platform shoes with lug soles and this sweet little buckle in the back, and we had gone to five zillion stores in a fruitless attempt to find a pair, and now Sheila didn't have a clue as to which of the stores she had left her phone at. To make matters even worse, by the time we realized the magnitude of the mistake, the stores were all closing. I kid you not! The security guards had to practically drag Sheila, kicking and screaming, out of the mall! After a painful and sleepless night, we skipped school the next morning in order to be first in line when the stores opened and we went on a tear, racing through the place like our skirts were on fire, flying in and out of stores, terror in our eyes. When, thank God, we finally found it at (duh!) the very last store we had been to, she burst into tears and cradled her phone like a lost baby, stroking it, petting it, cooing to it.

That very same day, she went out and bought a second phone, an awesome silver iPhone X where her face was her password. I felt like a dinosaur with my outdated iPhone 7. I was consumed with jealousy.

The point is, I wasn't nearly as bad as Sheila. Then again, I had never lost my phone for more than fourteen minutes. Actually, fourteen and a half. Fourteen and a half horrible, terrifying minutes. I shuddered to think of that debacle.

But nomophobe? I don't think so.

Still feeling the sensation of the phantom phone in my hand, I drove down from the hills into Northampton and pulled into the parking lot of the Unitarian Church on Main Street, where the meeting was supposed to be. I headed down the back stairs, hoping to get this nomophobe nightmare nonsense over with as quickly as possible.

Chapter 5

"Hello," a guy about my age said. "My name is Derek and I'm a netaholic."

Derek was tall and slim with longish hair and big brown eyes with lashes that went on forever. He nervously wiped his lips with long, slender fingers. Eyelashes, fingers, and lips. I nonchalantly repositioned my body, somewhat annoyed that this guy, most likely a total loser, was giving me that tingly feeling.

"Welcome, Derek," the group creepily replied in unison.

Oh God, I groaned silently to myself, trying not to look at him. *What kind of shit show have I gotten myself into?*

I had posted myself close to the back door, in case I needed to beat a hasty retreat. The place was giving me the heebie-jeebies: butt-busting folding chairs, that dank and dreary church-basement smell, the watery brown coffee that tasted worse than dishwater. Plus, there was a three-hundred-pound lard-ass sitting next to me, as orange as Trump, who looked like he hadn't emerged from his mother's basement in decades. And who had gone shower-less for even longer.

This whole farce was Udder and Gramps's idea, not mine. Pinkie swear or not, if I had to run, I was damn well going to get the hell out of there as quick as possible. Nomophobia? What I had was no-mo-phone-ia. That sacred place in my palm where my phone should have been comfortably resting was now itching like I'd grabbed a fistful of poison ivy.

One by one, all of the people in the circle introduced themselves in the same nauseating way. "Hello. My name is (whoever) and I'm a netaholic." Everyone except me. When it came my turn, I fidgeted with my phoneless hands and stared at my feet, desperate to avoid any eye contact.

"Hello," I finally said. "My name is Meagan and I'm just here to check out this group. You know, see what it's all about. It's not like I have, you know . . ." My voice trailed off awkwardly.

"Welcome, Meagan," the group responded, a tad less enthusiastically, perhaps sniffing the odor of bullshit.

Derek was the designated dude for this meeting. The freak of the week. Front and center, he was the lead-off hitter who got to spill his guts all over us.

He was eighteen, a year older than me, had just graduated from high school, and was a definite piece of work. An online fantasy-baseball addict, he was the owner of five (count 'em, five!) fantasy-baseball teams, his sick obsession with major-league statistics consuming all of his free time. For the last two years, he would rush home from school, jump online, spend the whole afternoon and most of the night in protracted negotiations for a left-handed pitcher and a utility infielder, snag a couple of hours of tortured sleep wracked with fantasy-baseball-filled nightmares, and finally stagger back to school. And then do it all again. Night after night. For two years! Even in the winter, when the real teams weren't even playing, he'd be scouring the net, searching for prospects, looking to bolster his roster.

He had quit his high school baseball team after his sophomore year because it interfered with his online fantasy baseball.

My phoneless thumbs texted Sheila. *Fantasy baseball! OMG! How effed is that?*

To his credit, Derek was actually reasonably amusing in a self-deprecating kind of way. Bemoaning his lack of any offline social life, he divulged that his idea of a wet dream was a rain delay. His fantasy of a *ménage* à *trois* was a home run against the Minnesota Twins.

He'd been "clean" (as they called it) for exactly three months. That's why he was the one who got to strut his stuff. What "clean" actually meant was a bit of mystery to me. Laptops only for schoolwork? Texting only on alternate days? Derek wasn't saying.

But three months doing whatever he was doing, or not doing, was huge. At the end of his rant, he even got a little coin thingie with "Three Months" written on it, and everybody clapped like crazy. A little bling goes a long way. Tears welled up in those big brown eyes of his.

My thumbs twitched another *totally effed* on my phantom phone.

Karen, the second to speak, was celebrating the return of her driver's license after six long, bus-filled months. My unfortunate incident with the tree (why'd it have to be there anyway?) was nothing compared to hers. Her license had been revoked after her third accident in a week had killed a cat and taken out a parked car, two mailboxes, and a fire hydrant. Texting and driving did not work well for Karen. Nor did texting and walking. She had broken her nose smashing into a stop sign.

Karen the Cat Killer had been "clean" for half a year. She got an even bigger and glossier coin thingie.

After another rousing round of applause, the rest of the meeting was taken up with details of the potluck dinner they were planning a couple of Fridays from now on the sixth of July. The group was all over that one, excitedly delegating who was to bring which dish.

A Netaholics potluck? I was seriously ready to throw up.

LOSERS, twitched my fingers.

And then, thank God, the torture session was over.

Just as I was attempting to slip out unnoticed and bolt for the hills, the dude-in-charge who had been running the meeting tapped me on the shoulder.

"Hi," he said, holding out his hand and smiling. "I'm Jonathan. I'm so glad you joined us this evening."

Good lord, I thought to myself. This is how it all begins. One shoulder tap, one smile, one handshake, and then they have you. I had to watch myself like a hawk. A single false move and I'd be sucked into this insidious techno-is-a-no-no black hole, never to emerge again. I'd be bunkered up in some dilapidated, fortified compound in the middle of dipshit nowhere without the net, without a phone, without a computer. Tethered on the shortest of leashes, I'd be working a pottery wheel for sixteen hours a day, selling cheap-ass ceramic cereal bowls at farmers' markets to fund their technology-free cult.

I was onto their shit. I knew what was going down. Jonathan's smile didn't fool me in the least.

There was, however, one slight hitch. One minor problem. Jonathan was hot as hell too. A little bit older than me, probably pushing twenty, but boyish and impish and charming. What was it about these netaholic dudes anyway? Why did they all have to have such awesome lips? Was it a requirement? What was up with that?

Help! my useless thumbs air-texted to Sheila. *OMG. More lips. Get me out of here!*

"Hey," I said to Jonathan, interlocking my fingers to keep them from twitching. "Thanks. Yeah. I enjoyed it. I mean, I didn't really enjoy it, but, you know, it was . . . um . . . interesting."

"It always is," Jonathan said. "Never a dull moment with this crowd."

"I imagine not," I replied. "With losers like that, you've sure got great material to work with, huh?"

Jonathan wrinkled his nose and turned his head sideways to look at me.

"I mean, you're right," I continued, gritting my teeth. "Definitely not dull. It was sharp. Knifelike. Serrated." I made back-and-forth cutting motions with my hand and a bee-like buzzing noise with my lips.

Spontaneous conversation? Definitely not my forte. Like I said: text over talk anytime.

Jonathan managed a laugh. "Can you join us a week from Friday for the potluck?" he asked.

"Uh . . . well . . . you know . . . I'm sort of busy taking care of my grandfathers and all."

"Your grandfathers?" Jonathan lifted his eyebrows.

"Yeah. They're gay. And arthritic. Which means I can't always leave when I want to. Not that I'm saying that I really. . . .want to." Stammer, blush. Blush, stammer.

"Well, if you change your mind, let me give you my number."

"Ha!" I laughed.

"What?" he asked.

"You asked to give me your number? Kind of ironic, don't you think?"

"One occasionally has to make phone calls," Jonathan said, winking at me. "But only for emergencies. Other than that, we're all about removing that technological defect of character. That shortcoming. Steps six and seven of our twelve-step program."

"Good to know," I said, taking a step backwards. "But sorry. Believe it or not, I don't have my phone on me."

"No worries," Jonathan said, hot lips sneaking up into a grin. He scribbled down his number on a napkin and handed it to me.

Damn! There went that tingly feeling again.

I turned and fled.

I had just clicked my car door open when I noticed Derek, the fantasy-baseball dude, standing forlornly in the parking lot, staring into the window of a car.

"Hey," I called out. "You okay?"

"Actually," he said. "I could be better. I don't suppose you have your phone on you?"

Were these guys for real? Anonymous netaholics and all they can do is ask for my cell phone? Seriously?

"Believe it or not, for the first time in forever, I don't. Why? What's wrong?"

"I locked my damn keys in my car. Again. I am such a moron."

"Ugh," I said. "I hate it when I do that." Actually, I had never done that, but for some strange reason, it seemed the right thing to say. "Anything I can do?"

"I was going to. . . No. Never mind. I don't want to inconvenience you."

"What?" I asked. "Can I give you a ride somewhere?"

"Well," he said. "I have an extra set of keys at home, and I don't live that far. You sure you wouldn't mind?"

Chapter 6

"I thought we weren't doing offline guys?" Sheila asked.

I had called Sheila the moment I had gotten back from the NA meeting and given her the blow-by-blow. My grandfathers still had this ridiculously clunky old seventeenth-century rotary-dial phone connected to a receiver with this horribly annoying, curly cord that was forever twisting itself into a tangled knot. I had no idea such contraptions were still in use. I had seen one in an antique store a few years back and didn't have a clue what it even was.

"What are you talking about?" I asked her.

"You know. The pinky swear we made. Never hook up with a guy offline. They're way too much to deal with. Need I remind you of the Caleb catastrophe?"

$$(\diamondsuit)$$

It was sophomore year in high school when Sheila and I had finally come to the stark realization that the boys in our school were completely screwed up. Confronted with the painfully cruel fact that the penised race in our neck of the woods consisted entirely of zombies, stoneheads, dweebs, perverts, nerds, nutcases, and morons, we had pinky sworn to keep it safe, keep it sane, keep it online. That may sound overly harsh and bitchy, but it was God's honest truth. Our high school was a who's who of pathetic losers. There were exactly two guys in the entire student body worth taking a second glance at. Two!

"Why didn't you ask one of them out?" Udder had suggested when I divulged this pitifully sad state of affairs to him.

"I couldn't," I told him. "They were already dating each other."

"Ahhh," Udder said, shaking his head and smiling. "The straight girl's burden. All of the good guys are gay."

"Oh my God," I said to Sheila, continuing the conversation. "I gave Derek a ride home. Chill."

"Ah-*ha!* You even remember his name! He probably had his keys on him the whole time, and this whole ride thing was a devious ploy just to get into your pants. And I can't believe you actually took his phone number. No offense, but is a lunatic asylum really the best place to pick up guys?"

"I wasn't picking up guys!"

"Meagan. You scored two phone numbers in fifteen minutes. You must have been giving off the fuck-me vibe."

"I was not . . . arghhh!" I groaned into the phone. Sometimes there was no reasoning with that girl.

Sheila viewed the world entirely in sexual terms. Every action, every word, every flick of the hair or arch of the eyebrow was some sort of come-on to her. There was nothing that didn't cry out SEX! Things weren't black and white—they were vaginas and penises, or V's and P's as she called them. She made Freud look soft on sex. All of this was sort of weird because, like me, she was still a virgin. All of her relationships had been exclusively online, but, boy oh boy, if there was a gold medal for sexting, she'd be permanently up on the podium. It was Sheila who put the X in *seXt.*

The girl was right about one thing: I had scored two phone numbers. But I wasn't flaunting my girl thing. I really wasn't. Jonathan and Derek were just trying to be helpful.

Jonathan had given me his number as part of his invite to the potluck. Derek had given me his number in case I wanted a "sponsor." Evidently that's what netaholics called someone you could turn to when the urge to binge-surf the net or text till your thumbs fell off became a little too overwhelming.

Sponsors. Seriously? How lame was that?

Of course, why I had gone and given them both *my* cell number was a little on the fuzzy side.

"I don't know what your issues are, Meagan," Derek had told me when I was dropping him off back at his car. (What was it with males thinking I had *issues?*) "But, you know, if something comes up, give me a call. We can talk. Maybe I can help." And then he smiled at me with those gorgeous lips of his, which made me drop *my* car keys.

"'If something comes up'?" Sheila said, groaning. "Seriously? He was *so* coming on to you. If that wasn't a pickup line, then farts don't stink."

"Oh my God, Sheila, it's not always about sex!"

Sheila snorted. Even though she was over a hundred miles away in Boston and I was languishing in the hills of Western Massachusetts tethered to an ancient landline, I could still see her giving me the look.

"Good luck believing that one," she chortled.

Chapter 7

"It's all about sex," Gramps said, drawing deeply off his joint. "Always has been. Always will be. Just look at those two."

Caught up in a sensual daydream involving cell phones, recovering addicts, lips, and slender fingers, I shuddered involuntarily at the interruption. Sometimes it seemed as though Gramps could read my mind. It was a little creepy.

"Who's having sex?" I asked, bolting upright. "Where? What are you talking about?"

"Those two," Gramps said, pointing toward the garden pond. "Just look at them going at it."

Perched on a water lily were two little winged creatures, firmly attached to each other, evidently doing the deed with wild enthusiasm.

"What the heck are they?" I asked, backing away anxiously.

"Dragonflies," Gramps responded. "Golden-winged skimmers, if I'm not mistaken. *Libellula auripennis.*"

I laughed. "Aura penis? You gotta be kidding me!"

"*Auripennis,*" Gramps corrected, pronouncing the word with a short *e* rather than a long one. "That's their Latin species name."

"Do they sting?"

"No, sweetheart, you're perfectly safe. They don't sting."

Udder called me "darling." Gramps called me "sweetheart." Seriously, how cute was that?

"See how he's holding onto her? See how she's reaching around to take his sperm?"

"Gramps," I said. "If my parents knew what went on here, I'd be on the next bus home. No offense, but you really are a total pervert."

"I prefer the word *naturalist*, sweetheart. There *is* a difference."

I got up and stealthily crept toward the pond for a better look. The two dragonflies resembled one of those figure-skating couples in the Olympics where he's twisting her around in all sorts of bizarre contortions before flinging her into the air to do some triple sow-cow or quadruple toe-loop-flip or whatever the hell they call it. It was about as strange an erotic coupling as one could imagine, straight out of the insect *Kama Sutra*. Try that position at home and you'd be needing a chiropractor for the rest of your life.

"And get this," Gramps continued. "He takes his sperm from the end of his abdomen and transfers it to his penis. And, wait for it, it gets even hotter. He's got a hook or barb on the tip of his penis, which he uses to scoop out a rival's sperm which may already be inside her. Then he gives her his."

"No way, Gramps! Are you just making this shit up?" I asked.

"Truth is always stranger than fiction, sweetheart. The male stays on for as long as he can, hoping she'll fertilize her eggs with his sperm before another guy latches on and ditches it. First can be worst. Last one in rules the roost. Is that wild, or what?"

"Oh my God!" I said. "I so wish Sheila was here. I'd love to see the look on her face!"

First, worm sex.

Now it was the dragonflies' turn.

Who knew the natural world could be so hot?

(◇)

Gramps was deeply, passionately in love with nature, particularly those little critters without a backbone. Even the evil, nasty, blood-sucking ones like mosquitoes and black flies and ticks tickled his fancy.

"'If all mankind were to disappear,'" Gramps said, quoting from E. O. Wilson, one of his favorite naturalists, "'the world would regenerate back to the rich state of equilibrium that existed ten thousand years ago. If insects were to vanish, the environment would collapse into chaos.' Now, you tell me, Meagan, which of us are more important?"

I continued to watch the creepy little winged things bumping and grinding and doing the nasty.

Chaos or equilibrium? Humans or insects? That was a tough one.

I had spent my entire life believing that the only point to being outside was to get right back *in*side as soon as humanly possible. Outside had things like weather and pollen and bugs. Wicked, nasty, scary things. Things that could get you.

Inside was definitely where it was at.

For a brief period, I online "dated" a guy who was insane about nature—something I should have known doomed us from the start. One night he convinced me how awesome it would be to sext outdoors, and, due to some temporary lapse in sanity, I wound up in an Audubon sanctuary after dark, going at it with my phone under the stars.

It was the most terrifying experience of my life. As soon as I got my pants down and started playing with myself I could feel things all over me. Horrible things. Icky creepy crawly things.

And creatures. Creatures I couldn't see but I knew were out there. Snakes. Bears. Maybe even wolves. Hungry, ravenous wolves. Getting closer and closer. Coming for me.

And then, with the guy's sexts coming on fast and furious, this lone firefly landed on my boob and lit right up. There it was, nibbling on my nipple, its hideous insect face grinning up at me, its antennas twitching this way and that, its witchy light going on and off and on again.

Pants in hand, I ran screaming to the car. I drove home in a pantless panic, called Sheila immediately, and she came rushing over. Thank God I had her. She checked every single square inch of my body, looking for ticks and beetles and bumps and bites and wolf marks.

Not a good sext. Just not. Goodbye to that guy.

Yet at this moment here I was, outside, on my hands and knees, staring at two dragonflies going at it. What the hell was up with that?

"I got another dating profile for you," I said to Gramps.

"Let's hear it," he said.

"I'm in awe of your aura, baby, and I got the scoop on you. Why don't we figure-eight and penetrate? Ain't no drag'n this fly down."

Another dragonfly flew up from the pond and landed on my shoulder, staring at me with its big buggy eyes. And, wonder of wonders, I just stared right on back. I didn't freak out. Not even a little bit.

"Irresistible," Gramps said. "That's what you are, sweetheart. Irresistible."

Chapter 8

I worked my offline bum off at Udder and Gramps's. With or without arthritis, they were both total slobs, so unlike my parents, who were over-the-top obsessive neat freaks. A little dust here and a little dirt there had never really bothered me, but my grandfathers' place was pretty ridiculous. Room after ramshackle room hadn't been cleaned in what seemed like decades. They were full of dust and cobwebs and crusty dead beasties and piles of useless crap from my grandfathers' long lives together. Total chaos.

Even though their cell service sucked balls, Udder and Gramps were resolute in their fervent desire to remain in their little slice of heaven in the hilltowns for as long as possible. They loved where they lived. But boy, given their age and infirmaries, they sure needed some help in the housecleaning department. So I rolled up my sleeves and tied back my hair and dove on in headfirst.

The first time I'd enter a room, I'd hold my breath, stick out my broom like a sword and my dust pan like a shield, and brace myself for the horrors I might find. I'd kick open the door and let loose my very best version of the Japanese samurai war cry, *Tennōheika banzai!*—a piercing shriek that I desperately hoped would instill fear in the heart of the wolf or grizzly or mountain lion or whatever other girl-eating critter was lurking behind those closed doors. I needed them to know I was a force to be reckoned with.

The first time I did this, Udder and Gramps come rushing up the stairs (as best as they were able to rush anywhere), convinced that I had stabbed myself with my broom or fallen through the floorboards.

The scariest moment came when I discovered a mouse nest under an old mattress in the farthest room at the very end of the back hallway.

There they were: naked, squirmy mini-mice nursing away, their eyes not even open yet, their mom glaring up at me and growling. Not a mousey little squeak of a growl but a serious, incisor-barring, guttural growl.

Mice: not my favorite little critters. Full of pestilence and nastiness. My first inclination was to whack them to death with the broom and then bury their bodies in a shallow unmarked grave out behind the garden and keep my lips sealed for eternity . . . but I knew that Gramps was a mind reader and I figured he would kill me when he found out and my trips to town to online-binge would be forever banned. So, heart racing, I gathered up my courage and scooped the little goobers into the dust pan, mama mouse still nursing and growling away, and raced outside to the woods.

I didn't fling them away at first chance. Instead, I nestled them ever so carefully next to a moss-covered rotten log and artistically arranged dead leaves on top of the nest to shield the little ones from predators.

I was pretty damn proud of myself.

When I told Gramps, he wrapped his arms around me and gave me a huge hug.

"What did I tell you, sweetheart?" he said. "Irresistible. That's you."

I beamed like a little girl.

Every afternoon, following a busy morning of housework and gardening, I'd convince my grandfathers that I absolutely had to head downtown to pick up a few essential items—milk, bread, a pint of Ben and Jerry's Americone Dream Vanilla Ice Cream with Fudge Covered Waffle Cone Pieces and Caramel Swirl. If they balked, I'd play the menstrual card and start whining on and on about a tampon emergency, and they'd have no choice but to acquiesce. It was the first time in my life I had ever felt anything remotely positive about my period.

Udder and Gramps did force me under considerable duress to sign some stupid statement swearing on the statue of Buddha that I would not touch my phone the entire time I was in the car and then, when I was parked safely in town, use it only to check the weather and any relevant news about the Boston Red Sox, whom Gramps was obsessed with. They clearly wanted no repeat performance of my car-smashing-tree incident, and were doing their due diligence in attempting to keep my online activities in check.

So I'd borrow the only working car (the wrecked one was still in the shop) and, while Gramps napped and Udder read, drive myself down to The Roost in Northampton, park myself contentedly in the Main Street café's window, and blissfully lose myself online.

Hard as it was, I'd keep the first half of the bargain I had made, and drive to town phone-free. Hoping Buddha wasn't the vindictive type, I totally blew off the second half. I mean, seriously, what choice did I have? Internet service in Haydenville was ridiculously slow and spotty at best, so the only way to get my techno-fix was to head down from the hills back into the twenty-first century.

My parents had forced me to leave my laptop at home, so all I had was my phone. How people survived in the olden days before smart phones was way beyond my ability to imagine.

As I drove to town, I'd gently place my phone on the car seat next to me, and I'd find myself talking to it as we got closer and closer to connection.

"It won't be long, now, sweetheart," I'd coo, stroking it affectionately. "I'll have you turned on in no time, my darling!"

As I'd park outside the coffee shop, I'd find *myself* pleasantly turned on, my heart beating faster, my breathing more noticeable. One double shot of espresso and an open outlet for recharging, and I was good to go.

Probably onto what I was up to (clueless as they were, even they had to know it didn't take half a day to buy a pint of ice cream and a box of tampons), Udder and Gramps had set a ridiculous limit on my time away. Two and a half hours! A pathetically meager amount of screen time to check texts and Facebook and web-surf, let alone get back on track with my stack of cyber-boyfriend-wannabes.

Even out of the garden, it was a tough row to hoe—twenty-one and a half hours of drudgery and two and a half hours of bliss. If they only knew the pain they caused me.

It was a Tuesday afternoon, almost a week after the first NA meeting. I was sitting in the café window, totally one with my screen, tingling on the inside, completely oblivious to the outside world.

Udder was right about one thing: I felt a definite physical rush when I was online.

"It's yet another reason why it's all so addictive," Udder had told me, shaking his head sadly.

"Oh my God," I replied. "Please. Do we really have to go there again?"

"Endorphins. Dopamine. Serotonin. Certainly sections of your brain light up when you're on the internet, releasing the good stuff."

"Duh," I told him, rolling my eyes. "Tell me something I don't know."

Anyway, there I was, swiping right to like, left to diss, and then right and left again, those brain hormones kicking in big-time, when I felt a tap on my shoulder.

I jumped.

"Hello," a voice said from behind me. "Meagan, right? We met the other night. Jonathan."

Jonathan! The NA dude.

"Oh my God," I stammered, guiltily exiting out of my *Passion* site. "You scared the crap out of me."

"So sorry," he said.

I immediately went on the defensive. "I wasn't online for long. Seriously. I had some, uh, work to do, and, you know, my grandfathers aren't connected. I mean it's not like . . . you know. . ." I put my purse on top of my phone, hoping to hide the evidence.

Jonathan laughed, his mouth open wide.

Caution! Lip alert!

"No worries," he said. "Explanations not required. I'm just here for my caffeine fix. Can I get you anything?"

More coffee? Seriously? That was all I needed.

"Why not?" I said.

Jonathan headed up to order.

I was already feeling the rush of the caffeine from the earlier double. Another shot of espresso would put me right over the edge.

Jonathan returned and slid my cup over to me.

"Can I join you for a minute?" he asked.

Oh God! The very last thing I needed was a real guy jumping the queue ahead of my gaggle of online guys anxiously awaiting their turns. Seriously. How fair was that?

"Sure," I said. "How much do I owe you?"

He smiled and scooted in next to me. "This one's on me," he said. "And hey, any interest in coming to the meeting tomorrow night? Same time, same place. You know the drill. We'd love to have you."

Me? Go to another NA meeting? Was he joking? Other than the fact that he and Derek were way hot, I had absolutely zero interest in ever going back to that freak show.

"Um . . . ," I said. "I don't know. I think I may have told you, I'm taking care of my grandfathers, and I'll have to see how they're doing. They have health issues, and their ups and downs are pretty hard to know in advance."

"I'm sorry to hear that," Jonathan said.

He had this sweet angelic face, long hair, and a neatly trimmed beard. Deep, dark, penetrating brown eyes. And again, the lips. Damn! If only he'd stop smiling at me. One of my hands strayed under my purse and began gently caressing my phone.

"Given their age, they actually do surprisingly well." I clasped my hands tightly together. "They have this huge garden and everything. And they even keep bees. Honeybees! My Udder says the stings help his arthritis."

"Your udder?"

I blushed. "My other grandfather."

"Awesome," Jonathan said. "Bee-sting therapy. Does it cure netaholism?"

"I wouldn't know anything about that." I locked my hands together even tighter.

"I'd love to see them sometime," Jonathan said, standing up and draining his mug.

"My grandfathers?" I asked.

He laughed again. "I was thinking more of the bees. But hey, I gotta run. I hope I see you tomorrow night. And don't forget about the potluck next Friday. Salads. We need salads. Would that work for you? I could pick you up if you'd like."

"Um . . . ," I stammered. "I don't know. . . . See, my grandfathers . . ."

"Call me for directions," Jonathan said. "I'd love it if you showed. You still have my cell?"

"I do."

"Call me," Jonathan said.

"Thanks for the coffee," I replied, totally buzzed.

"Next one's on you!" He winked and walked out.

Not twenty minutes later, I was happily scrolling through *Passion* profiles when, wouldn't you know, Derek, the freak of last week, walked in. I had just deleted a guy's come-on line ("Hello sweet thief! You stole my hearts with yous enchanting smile. I thinked that a fairy was only a legend but you gorgeous eyes prove me the opposite") as well as some random screen shot of another guy's penis! I had had three shots of espresso in less than an hour and I was completely wired. Both thumbs were going a mile a minute.

"Hello," Derek said, glancing over at my screen filled with the image of a fully aroused you-know-what. "Meagan, right? We met the other night. Derek."

Mortified, I once again buried my phone under my purse.

"Hey," I said. "Hi. I'm just . . . you know . . ."

What the hell was it with these fucking netaholics? Were they stalking me, for God's sake? What part of NEEDING TO BE ONLINE didn't they understand?

"No worries," Derek said, unsuccessfully hiding a smile. "I didn't mean to interrupt your . . . whatever it was I was interrupting. Can I get you something? A coffee maybe?"

"Sure," I said, practically throwing my empty cup at him, my hands already shaking with the caffeine jitters. "Why not? Fill it up! Hell, make it a double!"

What was I thinking? My mind was already speed racing, pedal to the metal, going at full caffeinated throttle. By the time one thought was halfway formed, two or three others had elbowed their way in, swooshing around spastically in my caffeine-addled brain.

Derek left to get in line and before I knew what I was doing, I was back online, surfing my site, swiping left and right and left again, frantically deleting yet another up-close dick pic.

"Do you mind if I join you for a minute?" Derek asked, returning with two cups of coffee.

"Yes," I said. "No. Sit down." I drained my double in three quick gulps, scalding the crap out of the back of my throat.

"Jesus!" I said, crashing my cup down on the table like a drunk at a bar. "What time is the meeting tomorrow night? What are you bringing to the potluck? What possibly possesses guys to send me pictures of their penises?"

In my defense, I am not a big girl. My online dating profile describes me as petite, 115 pounds with my clothes on (110 without my freckles), and, unlike probably every other girl online, it was the God's honest truth. Without much body mass to absorb them, the last two shots of espresso had pushed me to the brink. I barely knew what planet I was on.

Derek sat up straight and stared at me.

"Excuse me?" he asked, softly.

"Oh my God!" I said, a little too loudly. "Sorry about that. I'm just totally wired. Too. Much. Caffeine."

I grabbed my phone, glanced at it, and then shoved it into my purse.

Derek had a hard-to-read look on his face. In my befuddled state, I couldn't tell whether he was alarmed or amused.

"You're sorry about the meeting, the potluck, or the penises?" he asked.

"The penises," I yelled, bolting upright, my hands shaking. "For God's sake, the penises!"

Now everyone in the entire café was staring at me. Servers glanced at each other, worried looks on their faces, most likely pegging me for one of those people-with-issues who sought shelter in coffee shops. They looked ready to do the ol' gently-usher-the-nutcase-out-onto-the-street thing, and hope I didn't create an even bigger scene.

Get a grip, I begged myself. *Get a fucking grip. You're losing it.*

Mercifully, Derek laughed.

He was wearing a T-shirt with the words *NO FRACKING* emblazoned in bold on it, like something resurrected from Udder and Gramps's garden ties on their tomato cages.

"I like your shirt," I said, desperate to change the subject. "I don't have a fracking clue what it means, but I like it."

Not knowing what else to do and desperate to end this awkward conversation, I stood up, raised my coffee cup high into the air with one hand and my phone with the other, and yelled way too loudly: "No more fracking!"

Derek stood up next to me, clenched his left fist, and held it in the air alongside mine.

"No more penises!" he yelled.

Then we both hightailed it out of there.

Chapter 9

"I've got to hand it to you," Udder said. "You're a smooth operator. You've been here, what, less than two weeks and you've already got two real guys hot to trot."

"Stop!" I said. "You're sounding like Sheila!"

I had just recounted to Udder and Gramps my afternoon at The Roost. I had made it seem that I had only gone there to get my caffeine fix, not my online fix. I wasn't about to tell them *everything*.

As always, we were out weeding the garden.

The thing about weeds was that they never quite got the "fuck you" memo. You'd yank them out one day, and damn it if they weren't back in the very same place with a vengeance the next. Tenacious sons of bitches. I hated them.

Yet for some unfathomable reason, I was actually beginning to like weeding. Not *like*-like (as in *being-online*-like) but, you know, *sort-of*-like. The mosquitoes and the dirty sweat dripping into my contacts were a royal pain. My thumbs, previously used only for texting, now ached in a new and entirely different but still incredibly painful way from hoeing and digging and yanking up the weedy bastards. But, other than that, I was actually getting into it. After all, with only two and half hours a day surfing downtown, my phone-less hands needed something to occupy them. My evenings under the covers with my fingers doing their thing still weren't enough of a workout.

Udder and Gramps had even stopped having to tell me what needed to be done. I'd just go out to the garden and get right into it. After the unfortunate incident of the first day when I had mistaken baby beets, spinach, and arugula for weeds and pulled out every single last one of them (oh, the shame!), I pretty much had the system down. Yank, yank, and then yank some more. It was all-out war. Us versus them.

Sons of bitches.

Udder and Gramps were converts to the Church of the Heavily Mulched, so plants were nestled into thick beds of decomposing straw, but damn it if the weeds still didn't find a way to poke their annoying little heads right on through regardless. Woe to all weeds!

Plucking them out gave me a powerful feeling. It was nowhere near the rush I felt when I was online, but still I found myself grunting with approval, particularly after ripping out a ginormous one by the roots.

"Take that, asshole!" I'd yell.

"And another one, and another one, and another one bites the dust!" I'd sing, my voice carrying with the wind, my pile of weeds sailing into the compost bin.

As remarkable as it sounds, while I was in the garden time would fly. There were even brief moments, fleeting as they were, when I actually found myself not even thinking about online profiles.

Gramps and Udder loved it.

"So, darling," Udder said, as we were taking a break from the business at hand, "which one are you going to choose?"

"What are you talking about?" I asked. "I thought I was supposed to kill them all?"

"Not weeds," Udder laughed. "Boys. Derek or Jonathan? Didn't they both ask you to the same potluck? You're going to have to choose one. You can't exactly go with both of them."

"Potluck? I'm not going to any stupid potluck!" I was annoyed they'd even think I'd consider doing such a silly thing.

"Why not?" Gramps said. "You never know—it might be fun. If you can't decide between the two of them just go with both. *Ménage* à *trois*. Isn't that 'in' right now?"

I smiled and thought of Derek and the Minnesota Twins.

"Stop it, Curtis," Udder said. "If you can't be helpful, just keep your mouth closed."

"Boys," I said, shaking my head. "They're like weeds. They spring up everywhere you don't want them to be."

After leaving The Roost, Derek and I had walked (actually power-trot-ted—I was so wired on caffeine that I was racing in circles around him) through town until we finally found a bench in Pulaski Park to peo-ple-watch. Derek was on his lunch break from the Food Co-op, where he worked stocking produce.

"You going to the meeting tomorrow night?" he asked, just like Jonathan.

Once again I was pretty noncommittal, recounting my grandparents' situation and my need to be attentive to them. It was hard not to come right out with it and lay the truth on the line. But seriously, how could he not know that meetings were for LOSERS?

"That's so nice of you," he said. "Moving in with them and all."

"Well, it wasn't exactly by choice," I told him, briefly recounting the unfortunate incident at school and my subsequent banishment to Western Massachusetts. I conveniently left out the late-night stalker incident and didn't divulge too many gruesome details about my online proclivities.

"What do you do at your grandfathers'?" Derek asked.

"Weed," I told him. "That's what I do most of the day."

"Really? I've tried that. The problem was I kept getting batting averages all mixed up. In fact, once after getting stoned I actually traded Mookie Betts for Jacoby Ellsbury. I mean seriously, how stupid was that?"

"I meant *do* it, not *smoke* it."

"Do *it*?" Derek looked embarrassed. He kicked at the loose dirt on the ground and shifted his position on the bench. "Wow. I've been sort of off my game when it comes to *that* for the last couple of years." He stood up and sat back down again. "Not that I ever had much of a game on, if you know what I mean."

Oh my God! Boys could be so thick.

"Derek! I was talking about *weeding*, like in my grandparents' garden."

Derek scrunched his eyes and whacked the side of his head. "Oh. Right. Duh! I was thinking you meant. . . Never mind."

What a cutie. Completely clueless, but way cute.

Derek had been fidgeting around awkwardly the whole time we were talking. I could see he was up to something but I wasn't quite sure what.

"Speaking of pot . . . ," he said.

"Which we weren't."

"Right. Sorry. No pot. But I was hoping for a little luck and, you know, wondering what you were doing next Friday night?"

"The potluck!" I clapped my hands and made little oooohing sounds. "Oh my God! How thrilling is that!"

"I'm pretty psyched myself."

The boy was beyond clueless!

"Are you interested in going?" he went on. "I could, you know, pick you up if you wanted. I mean, only if you were into it and everything. Or we could meet at the potluck. You know, whatever works for you." Derek stood up, did a few shoulder rolls, and then sat back down again.

The ask. Second one in less than an hour. When it rained, it poured.

Weeds, I said to myself. *Boys are nothing but weeds. They may be pretty to look at, but they're nothing but trouble.*

"I don't know what my grandfathers are up to Friday night," I finally stammered, realizing I had taken way too long to answer a pretty straightforward question. "I'll get back to you. Is that okay?"

I could tell Derek was bummed. Once more, he scrunched up his eyes and kicked at the ground.

"Of course. No pressure. Sounds good." The hurt came through in his voice. "Hopefully I'll see you tomorrow at the meeting. Hey, I've got to get back to work. This was fun."

"Later," I said.

"Definitely." Derek stood up and walked away.

Two asks in less than an hour.

Seriously. How weird was that?

Chapter 10

"How do I look?" I asked Udder. I had just finished glamorizing for my second Wednesday-night NA meeting.

"Beautiful, darling. As always."

I took Udder's compliment with a grain of salt. He was not exactly the go-to guy for fashion feedback. His idea of dressing up was plaid pants three sizes too big and a way-too-short sweatshirt with a picture of a moose-crossing sign. Somehow he had missed the memo that gay men were supposed to be fit and buff fashion divas. Well, stereotypes be damned. He and Gramps were two of the most poorly dressed human beings on the planet.

I could look like friggin Frankenstein's bride, and Udder would call me beautiful. It didn't matter what I wore, how I did my hair, whether I dressed up or down—I always got the same response:

"Darling," he'd say. "You look beautiful." He pronounced it "bee-YOU-tee-full."

I did love my Udder!

Fortunately, for fashion feedback I had Sheila. She was my go-to gal who could prettify with the most beeYOUteefull of all of them. Sheila knew every single outfit I owned. In fact, she had helped me buy every single outfit I owned. Without her I'd be lost in the styling department. I got her on the phone to walk me through the difficult decision of which outfit to wear to the meeting.

It was hot and humid, so we went with a sunny Samba sleeveless dress, Georgia peach with phoenix red stripes and a built-in shelf bra. I wasn't exactly well endowed up there, a 32 B-cup being overly generous, but the dress made my boobs look perky and upbeat.

"I still think it's weird," Sheila had said.

"What's weird?" I asked. "That my boobs never came in?"

"That you're hitting on guys in an addicts meeting. We both know that offline is the dark side. I just don't get why you insist on going back there."

"For the five zillionth time, Sheila, I'm not hitting on guys. Udder and Gramps are still pissed about me driving their car into the goddamn tree, so I have no choice but to go back to the stupid meeting. Anyway, can't a girl look nice when she goes out?"

"Keep telling yourself that. Just so you know you're dishing out the M & M's fast and furious."

"I am *so* not giving off Mixed Messages!"

"Oh, I see. That explains why you're obsessing about a dress that makes your boobs stand out?"

"I've gotta go," I hissed at her.

"Call me when you get back."

"Duh!"

I hung up the landline and then gave my phone an affectionate kiss, tucking it comfortably under the sheets of my bed.

"You know, this whole meeting thing is a total shit show," I told Gramps as he was walking me to the car. "A worthless piece of crap."

"You've already told me that," he said.

"For morons and losers."

"You've already told me that too."

"Even if I had a problem, which obviously I don't, there's absolutely nothing I could possibly gain by going there. It's a total waste of my time."

"Of course it is," Gramps said. "Incredibly valuable and precious time so much better spent updating your Facebook page and cruising guys on your dating site."

"Exactly," I told him. I bent down to examine myself in the side-view mirror of the car. "How do I look?" I asked him.

"Gorgeous," Gramps said, giving me a peck on the cheek. "Tell your two guys hello from me."

Evidently. Netaholics Anonymous was supposed to be modeled after Alcoholics Anonymous. Overeaters Anonymous seemed a much more realistic model, since technology, like food, was impossible to swear off altogether. With total abstinence not an option, what tech use was acceptable and what wasn't seemed quite the muddle to me.

At this meeting, there was no mention of God. My uncle was in AA and he was all about turning his will and his life over to a Higher Power. Whenever he visited, it was always God this and God that, which got nauseating pretty quickly. There was only so much God I could take before I'd retreat into my bedroom and get back to heaven online.

The Higher Power here must have been upstairs in the sanctuary, because down in the church's basement He was nowhere to be found. But then again, it was a Unitarian church. Maybe it was taboo to talk about Him at all. The only time I had ever heard Unitarians use *Jesus Christ* in a sentence was when they were cursing Trump.

It also wasn't clear to me what the NA steps actually were, and whether they were really steps or just suggestions. The group was all gung-ho about being "powerless over the internet," about how only a "behavioral and emotional awakening would restore them to sanity," about how essential it was to "remove their shortcomings and defects of character," about how they'd "carry this message to other netaholics." It all made me want to barf big-time. Here they were, pledging to go "completely tech-free"—no texting, no computers (what about work and school?), no nothing, and look what had happened: I had been to only one meeting, and already, two of the dudes had given me their numbers.

I mean, seriously? How absurd was that? Jonathan had rationalized it as only for emergencies, but it seemed an awfully big M & M to me. Think about it: if you went to an AA meeting and two of the guys immediately brought you gin and tonics, wouldn't you think twice about the seriousness of the whole thing?

The whole shit show was just too ridiculous for words. But Udder and Gramps were still on my back, so I figured I'd give it one more meeting and then tell them I was cured.

(◇)

"Hello," the guy up in front of the room said. "My name is Peter and I'm a netaholic."

"Welcome Peter," the group replied.

Once again, we all went around lamely introducing ourselves. When it came my turn, I left it as "Hello, my name is Meagan."

Jonathan and Derek had both chatted me up before the meeting, but it was unclear whether they were just coming up to me or coming on to me. So hard to figure out in an offline world.

Tonight's freak of the week was Peter. Even in a room full of doozies he was quite the catch. He was an internet porn addict, an obsessive aficionado of all online kink and taboo, and a complete train wreck. Even in the age of the free online stuff, he was paying big bucks for the premium hard core. With him it was porn 24/7. He couldn't even sleep without the grinding going on.

To top it off, he had lost all interest in actually doing it. Reality just couldn't compete with the excitement of the net. The last time he had tried to get it on, he couldn't even get it up.

How sad was that? I had to lock my fingers together to keep them from phone-lessly texting Sheila.

Pornography. Yuck! I must admit I had taken an occasional spin on the *PornHub* after a particularly interesting sext with a guy, but there sure didn't seem to be a whole lot out there for us girls to enjoy. Internet porn seemed to me all slam-bam without much of a thank-you-ma'am. Guys sledgehammering away, pounding down like there was no tomorrow. Ouch! It did nothing to make real-life sex seem even a little bit attractive.

It was painfully obvious who the target audience was. It was just guys getting off and girls pretending to enjoy it. Or not. And when the guy was done, that was that. It was all about him.

And really—what girls even looked like that? I mean, other than Sheila, no one I knew had that kind of body. Where did they find those folks, anyway? Photoshop?

Peter went on and on, ramping up the debauchery to an obscene level. It was almost as if he was getting off on telling us about it. After about twenty minutes, Jonathan finally stood up to shut him down.

This did not go down well with Peter the Porno. He didn't seem even close to wrapping up his rant.

"Thanks so much for sharing," Jonathan said, putting his arm gently on Peter's back and trying to steer him to his seat.

"Dude!" Peter said, twisting away. "I'm not done. I haven't gotten to the good part yet."

Oh my God, I thought, my curiosity piqued. What part could that be? Let the guy finish, for God's sake! His whole tirade, sick as it was, was riveting. I wouldn't have been texting even if I had had my phone.

"There will be plenty of time for sharing at another meeting," Jonathan said softly, placing his hand once more on Peter's shoulder. "We need to—"

"Hey!" Peter said, flicking Jonathan's hand away, his voice rising a notch. "Quit busting my balls. I need to . . ."

Things were looking up. This whole shit show was getting better and better. Drama like this could totally keep me coming back.

"You need to sit down!" Jonathan said forcibly, his voice no longer soft.

"You need to back off!" Peter yelled back, visibly shaking.

Evidently scenes like these were not all that uncommon during NA meetings. Folks were pretty vulnerable and could go off on a moment's notice. Take away a dude's computer and phone, and the shit could definitely hit the fan. Make techno a no-no and the shortest of fuses was lit.

The group, not flummoxed in the least, automatically launched into crisis-aversion mode. I was pulled along with the others as we all stood up, held hands, formed a tight circle around Peter, and then began to (I kid you not) *ommm* softly.

I could have died for my phone right then. This is why God put video cameras on phones. This is why He invented Snapchat. The things I could have done with a picture like this!

"*Ommm*," we chanted over and over, tightening our noose of a circle around him.

Lo and behold, for whatever warped reason, this seemed to work its wonders on Peter. Suddenly calm and seemingly transfixed, he stopped his ranting and instead began spinning in a tight little circle within our big group circle. He raised his arms and began waving his hands in the air, conducting us in our *oms*.

And then, damn it to hell, it happened.

Welling up inside of me. Growing stronger by the second. Rising up. Ready to erupt.

The dreaded giggles.

Oh my God, I told myself. *Not here. Not now. Act like a mature person for goodness' sake* (albeit a weird *ommm*-chanting circling person in the basement of an atheist church surrounding a twirling porno addict). *Be strong. Get a grip.*

It was all I could do to contain myself. There was the group, holding hands and smiling, and there was Peter spinning and chanting. It was all way too much to bear.

And then, stupid silly me, I made the fatal mistake of glancing over at Derek.

He had his head bowed and his eyes closed. For the briefest of moments, I thought he was praying but then I noticed that his shoulders were shaking. *No!* I thought. *Not you too!*

Ever since I was a little girl, I'd had this problem with inappropriate laughter. At the most inopportune of times I'd lose it. Bad times. Sad times. Times crying out for compassion and sympathy and warmth and understanding and I'd be the one laughing my ass off.

Which was not funny at all.

I air-texted a quick note to self: check and see if there was a twelve-step program for *that* affliction.

To which I would invite Derek who, curse him, continued to quiver in the corner.

Try as I might, I couldn't hold it in any longer. With a spastic twitch of my head, I burst out laughing. Not just a giggle. Not just a tweet here and a twitter there. A wild wolf-like convulsing howl.

Peter stopped spinning and everyone turned to stare at me. Everyone except Derek, who, with his hands on his knees and his head almost between his legs, looked like he was having trouble breathing.

Poor Peter. There he was, making a searching and fearless moral inventory of himself, admitting to all of us the exact nature of his wrongs, desperately trying to remove his defects and shortcomings, making amends to us—and there I was laughing at him. What kind of a horrible person would do that?

"I am so sorry," I managed to snort. "It must have been something I drank. Too. Much. Coffee."

I turned and rushed up the stairs and out of the basement without a backwards glance.

First the café.

Now the church.

Was there anyplace I wasn't running from?

Chapter 11

"Don't sweat it," Sheila said. "I'm sure it happens all the time."

"I don't think so," I groaned. "You should have seen the looks on everyone's faces. Oh my God, you would have thought I had stabbed the poor guy."

"Hey, if he's twirling around in a circle chanting porn or whatever the hell he was doing, then he had it coming. I thought you said that NA was supposed to be some sort of emotional awakening to restore someone to sanity? If that's the case then I'd love to see insanity. This is like the funniest thing I've ever heard."

"No one was laughing but me!"

"You *and* Derek, right? Anyway, I bet the rest were laughing on the inside."

"But *I* was laughing on the outside!"

"If they can't take a joke, then—"

"It wasn't a joke, Sheila! The guy was fucked up."

"We're all fucked up!" Sheila was practically shouting on the phone. "You, me, all of us. I dare you to find someone in the entire world who doesn't have a screw loose. God knows, you have to have a sense of humor about it! Right? Otherwise you're totally screwed."

"But you don't throw it in their face!"

"Chill," Sheila said, calming down just a tad. "If it doesn't kill you, it makes you stronger. Let's move on to more important items. Tell me one more time: on your first date you played Scrabble?" There was total disbelief in Sheila's voice.

"Earth to Sheila. We were hiding out in the park. Drinking coffee. It was so not a date. You and I don't do 'dates.'"

"Right. I remember now. No penises. But Scrabble? The word game?"

"The very one," I said. "Derek's trying to break the online fantasy-sports addiction of his, so now he's totally gotten into board games. That and softball. You know, interacting with real live human beings for a change. Anyway, the game was fun. At least most of it."

"Oh my God!" Sheila snorted like she had a bee up her nose. "Has it seriously come to this? You flee the freak show and end up in some random park playing Scrabble? Please don't tell me it was strip Scrabble. Or sex Scrabble!"

"What are you talking about?"

"Strip Scrabble. You have to take off an item of clothing for any word under ten points. And then there's sex Scrabble where you're only allowed to make dirty words and then you have to do something with them. You know, act them out. Like he would have put down *lick* and then you would have had to—"

"Oh my God, Sheila," I said. "How do you even know this?" As I already said: Sheila had precisely zero experience in the doing-it-with-a-guy department. "Anyway, we were out in the park. In public."

"He's a guy, Meagan. Remember? This is what guys do. Anyway, why was it only 'mostly fun'?"

After bolting from the meeting, I had wound up in Pulaski Park, Northampton's downtown outdoor hangout zone. It was the same place I had gone with Derek after my awkward outburst at The Roost.

I power-walked seventeen laps around the park, one for each year of my so-called life, cursing myself, my immaturity, my thoughtlessness, my total lack of empathy, my complete disregard for other human beings, my inability to get my act together.

In the past, whenever those nasty little brain demons reared their ugly heads, I had a readily available escape route: the net. There was nothing like a little *Passion* play to distract me. Swiping left, swiping right—I could escape all of my troubles by immersing myself in a never-ending online parade of boy toys. A swipe to the right, and it was playtime. A swipe to the left, and that boy was gone forever. I could be a sex goddess one moment and a callous bitch the next, sending off one snarky text after another and not giving a rat's ass if feelings were hurt or egos bruised. There was no one to stop me. No one to stare at me with hurt in their eyes the way that Peter had done at the netaholics meeting.

Without my phone as a crutch I was alone with my thoughts. No security blanket to wrap tightly around me. It was a new experience and a totally terrifying one.

What if it had been me up there? What if my grandfathers and,

God forbid, my parents were even a teensy-weensy bit right? What if I had been the one over-angsting about my netaholism or CRD (Cyber Relationship Disorder) or nomophobia or whatever other pathological diagnoses Udder and Gramps had hurled my way? What if some loser had started to laugh out loud at *me*? How would that have made me feel?

Damn it to hell! This was all Udder and Gramps's fault. They were the ones to blame. None of this would ever have happened if they hadn't forced me to go to the stupid NA meeting in the first place.

This is why I stayed online. Online, if you laughed no one knew if you were laughing *at* someone or *with* them. No one could see you. When there was nobody there, then there was no body language to worry about.

But wait a minute—if nobody was there, then what did that make *me*? Also a nobody? And if there's nobody there and I'm not there, does that mean there is no there at all?

Holy shit! I was on the verge of losing my mind!

Trying to knock some sense into it, I had deliberately banged my head on the historic Calvin Coolidge clock every time I completed a lap, but it wasn't doing the trick. Exhausted, I finally collapsed onto a park bench. Wallowing in self-pity, I put my head in my hands.

"Meagan!" said a voice from behind me. "I was hoping I'd find you here."

I jumped.

It must be Peter! Peter the Porno! Stalking me. Come to exact revenge for my belittling his spiritual awakening and his twirling dance move.

I desperately tried to remember the self-defense tactics we had learned in gym class. Think, Meagan, think! Was it a kick to the groin and then a poke in the eyes, or did you go for the eyes first? Damn it! Why did I have to be texting during that part?

"*Tennōheika Banzai!*" I yelled, hoping the Japanese battle cry would strike fear into my assailant's heart the same as it had done with the wolves in Udder and Gramps's closets. I turned around and whacked him right in the middle of his chest, directly between his eyes and his groin. A compromise blow.

Shit! It wasn't Peter! Peter was probably still spinning away in the church basement. This was Derek!

My blow knocked the coffee cup out of his hands, spilling it all over his pants.

"Oh my God!" I cried out. "I am so sorry!"

"*Banzai!*" he gasped, doubling over in pain.

Once Derek had recovered somewhat from getting the wind knocked out of him and the pain from the first-degree burns on his groin had settled down to a manageable level, he sat down next to me on the park bench.

"I was so embarrassed back there," I told him, after I apologized for the five thousandth time. "I can't believe I did that to poor Peter."

"You and me both. Once you lost it, I fell apart too. But hey, come on. That dude was way over the top."

"No," I said. "He wasn't. He was just laying his shit out there for all of us to see, looking for a little empathy, a little support. Isn't that what the twelve steps are supposed to be all about? *I'm* the one who deserves to be stepped on. I mean, I laughed at the guy. Not *with* him, *at* him. I am such a bad person. I really am. Peter must hate me. This is what I do to guys. I have no heart."

"You and me both," Derek said. "I'm like the Tin Man. Hollow inside. Go ahead, bang on my chest again. Only a little softer this time."

I clenched my fist and lightly punched him.

"Hear the echo?" he said. "Nothing in there. Heartless."

"We're like twinsies," I told him. "In a sad and totally pathetic way."

We fist-bumped each other.

"Check this out," Derek continued. "I was asked to leave my auntie's funeral because of the fantasy baseball draft. Everyone was on their knees praying and there I was, online, frantically searching for a left-handed pitcher. I couldn't even get offline long enough for them to put her in the ground. How heartless is that?"

I still didn't have a clue as to what fantasy baseball actually was, but going online at a family funeral did not seem like the best of choices, even to me.

"Pretty bad," I admitted. "But I can totally relate. I was at my little cousin's bar mitzvah, and the whole time he's reciting from the Torah, I'm, duh, texting away. Somehow my phone slips out of my hand and slides across the floor into the aisle and the rabbi stepped on it. I totally freaked. There was my poor cousin, on the verge of becoming a man, and I practically tackle the rabbi to get his friggin foot off my phone. I am a wicked, wicked human being."

"Ouch," Derek said. "But I'm way worse than wicked. I make the Wicked Witch of the West look like Mahatma Gandhi with a broom. My grandparents planned this once-in-a-lifetime trip to the Caribbean, right? And guess who skipped out? Go on, do it. Guess."

"Um . . . would that be—"

"Me? Damn right it was! I found out that one of the hotels we were staying at wasn't connected. For three days I'd have to be offline. So what did I do? Totally blew the whole thing off. My grandmother still hasn't forgiven me."

"That's sad," I said. "Really sad. But listen to this: last spring I had a contest with myself to see how many guys I could string along on

the net at once. Twenty-seven. I was 'seeing'"—I did the little air quo-
tation marks with my hands—"twenty-seven guys online at the same
time. I told each of them that they were the only one. That I was being
exclusive. I swear that three of them were on the verge of proposing
to me, for God's sake. Do you know how time-consuming that was? I
had to skip school just to keep track of the chaos I had created. I didn't
sleep for a week. Tell me—how effed is that? You want heartless? *That's*
heartless!"

I was going to ask Derek to thump me on my chest but, given that
my boobs were there, it seemed inappropriate. After all, I didn't want
him to get the wrong impression.

We were both on a roll, our words tumbling out fast and furious. I'd
barely finish one sob story before Derek would interrupt with one of
his. We were one-upping each other with our tales of cyber doom and
gloom as if it were a contest to see who was the most screwed-up.

If we'd been two guys, we'd have had our weenies out seeing who
could pee the furthest.

"The last time I had a girlfriend, I was a sophomore in high school,"
Derek said. "A sophomore! She dumped me because I couldn't remem-
ber what grade she was in." He was pacing up and down in front of me.
Thank God he wasn't spinning in circles or *ommming* away like Peter.
That would have completely freaked me out.

"I couldn't remember her age, her birthday. Crap, I kept getting her
name wrong, for crying out loud, calling her Xander, who's the shortstop
for the Sox, rather than Sandra. She was making hints about diamonds
on Valentine's Day and I just assumed she was talking about a baseball
field. But ask me the batting average of any right-handed catcher in the
American League. Go ahead, do it. Ask me."

"Um . . . Big Poppy?" I ventured. He was the only baseball player I
could name. At least I was pretty sure he was a baseball player.

"David Ortiz wasn't a catcher, just the greatest designated hitter OF
ALL TIME! And now, damn it, he's retired. But it was .286."

"Two-eighty-six what? Is that how many hits he had?"

Derek just stared at me.

"Anyway," I told him. "I dare you to top this: a few weeks ago
there was this boy, Caleb, the first and only guy I've ever been with.
'Been' being way too strong a word for it. For some unfathomable reason I actually hooked up with him offline rather than on, clearly a
huge mistake. What could have possibly possessed me to do *that* I'll
never know. I mean a real guy? In the flesh? Seriously? What was I
thinking?"

Derek looked down at the ground and shuffled his feet.

"You want to know what happened?" I asked him. "Do you?"

"Something tells me it wasn't pretty."

"You can say that again. The whole time we're making out and, who knows, maybe even getting ready to do something else I know absolutely nothing about, do you know what I was doing?"

"I can only guess. Were you—"

"Exactly. Cruising other guy's profiles on *Passion*, my dating site. How effed is that, huh? The first time I've ever done *anything* at all with a guy, and I mean anything, I'm online the whole time looking for other guys? What does that say about me? Huh?"

Derek just shuffled in place some more.

"I don't know," he said softly. "Maybe you're just—"

"Totally fucked up? I guess so. No offense, but that makes your whole fantasy baseball thing look like, I don't know, child's play."

"Actually, baseball sort of *is* child's play."

"Shut up, you!" Once again, I playfully punched him in his chest. "Can I finish my story or not?"

"Sorry."

"You should be. Anyway, suddenly I look up from my phone, and I see him staring at me, and I realize—holy shit! There's an actual live human being here. Not some phantom out there in cyberspace that I can swipe left and be done with. Needless to say, I totally freak and go flying out of his apartment like a ping from my phone."

"I thought it was bat out of hell?"

"Whatever. Anyway, end of story."

Derek looked awkwardly away. I realized that my last outburst was perhaps a little TMI. If I had been online, I'd have deleted this pathetic confession way before hitting Send. No such luck here. This was far and away the longest conversation I had ever had with a boy, so it was no wonder I was babbling away like a lunatic. Texts were never this messy.

We both took a deep breath and paused for a moment. It was just getting dark and the summer street life of Northampton was in full swing. College kids hand in hand and couples with strollers and a Rasta on a skateboard and a street person with a shopping cart full of bottles and cans were all parading past our bench. All of them on cell phones.

"Why didn't you laugh at *me* last week when I was doing my thing?" Derek finally asked.

"I was going to. I really was. You just finished a little too quick."

"That was my move, you know. The spin-and-chant thing that Peter was doing? That bastard stole that one straight from me. I'm actually pretty pissed."

"If it's any consolation, I would have laughed even louder if you had done it."

"Thanks. That makes me feel so much better about myself."

We both laughed.

"Do you want to get a cup of coffee?" he asked, reaching down and smoothing out his pants. "Something happened to the last one I had."

"You actually trust me to be around you on caffeine?"

"I like to live on the edge. Walk on the wild side."

"Give me another cup and *I'll* be spinning and chanting."

"I still don't get why it was *just* mostly fun?" Sheila asked again.

"Well," I stammered. "We had one other minor incident."

"Yes!" Sheila said. "Tell me! I live for minor incidents!"

That was true. Sheila loved my awkward screw-ups, just as I loved hers. Starting in middle school, we had made a pact that we would always share our screwtopias with each other, no matter how seemingly inconsequential, online and off. At times it almost seemed as though Sheila did stupid stuff just so she could one-up me, but that was hard to prove.

"Well," I said. "We got coffee and then headed back to our bench at the park."

"*Your* bench?"

"A bench. And then, just like that, Derek pulls a Scrabble board out of his backpack."

"You gotta be kidding me. He actually carries a Scrabble board around with him? That is like ultimate geekdom."

"Tell me about it. So we start playing. You know how I do *Words with Friends* online, so I know my way around the board. Anyway, remember how in Scrabble you sometimes play a word that isn't a word but you'd swear that it *was* a word? You know, it looks right the moment you play it, but it's actually totally wrong?"

"I don't have a clue as to what you're talking about," Sheila said. "But go on."

"Okay. So I played YOINK. It was awesome. The Y was on a double letter score, and the K was on a double word score, and I got, I don't know, thirty-six points or something. I was way behind, in desperate need of a sweet move. Thirty-six points put me in the lead. I was pumped."

"'YOINK'?" Sheila asked. "What the hell is YOINK?"

"That's exactly what Derek said. But when I played it I swear I thought it was the sound a pig makes. YOINK, as in *oink*, only with a Y. Like I said, it looked so right at the time."

"Maybe it was a Yiddish pig," Sheila said.

"Exactly! Anyway, Derek, who has channeled all of his fantasy sports shit into Scrabblemania and is now totally obsessed and super-competitive, got all bent out of shape. I was pretty wired on caffeine and I got way defensive and I'm laying on the bullshit like 'It is *too* the sound a pig makes, only it's slang. In Appalachia.'"

"You told him YOINK is Appalachian for pig snort?" Sheila asked.

"I did."

Sheila laughed.

"So I refuse to back down and Derek is practically foaming at the mouth. Evidently, he's not used to losing. Finally he gets so agitated that he says, 'I know! We'll let Google decide!' and I'm like, 'Whoa! No friggin way, dude. We're not Googling it. You're a netaholic, remember? It's at moments like these that you have to stay strong. Resist the urge. Do what's right!' And he's like, 'But this is an emergency!' And I'm like, 'Boy, that's Satan talking. The Devil's in Google and you know it. You gotta man up!' By this time, Derek is practically screaming. I mean we're going at it like, I don't know . . . like you and I do."

"All over YOINK?" Sheila asked.

"All over friggin YOINK! Suddenly Derek makes a move toward his phone and I give him a push only it's a little too hard and he knocks over the board and me and my cup of coffee which goes, once again—"

"All over his manhood!" Sheila cried out excitedly.

"Exactly!"

"Two for two, not bad." I could hear what sounded like Sheila fist-bumping the phone.

"Yeah, right. Huzzah and hooray for me. So there we are, lying in a heap on the ground with Scrabble letters and coffee all over us."

"That is so awkward!" Sheila said.

"Totally. And then guess what he did?"

"Spun and chanted?"

"Close," I said. "He kissed me."

"He what?"

"Well, sort of kissed me."

"What do you mean 'sort of'? How do you sort of kiss someone?"

"He kissed my hand. And apologized."

"Let me get this straight," Sheila said. "You don't do offline guys, except you've totally got this one by the short hairs. The only experience you've ever had with a weenie is to spill coffee all over his. Twice. You cheat and lie in Scrabble, which he's obsessed with. You push him, knock him over, and upend the game. And then, before the dust has even settled, he kisses your hand and apologizes?"

"Exactly."

"Oh my God," Sheila said. "And just so I'm perfectly clear, he is way cute, right?"

"Way cute."

"Wow." Sheila was silent for a moment. "I've got one thing to say about this. One very important thing."

"What?" I asked, desperate for some enlightened, perceptive pearl of wisdom. Something to help me navigate through these tumultuous, uncharted real-life relationship waters, waters that I had vowed never to swim in in the first place.

"Tell me!" I begged.

"YOINK!" Sheila grunted. "YOINK, YOINK, YOINK!"

Chapter 12

Gramps and I were sitting out in the garden watching day turn to night. It was the Fourth of July. Independence Day. A gorgeous fireball of a sunset to close out one of the longest days of the year.

Udder and Gramps had placed large standing stones in certain spots on their property. If you sat down smack-dab in the middle of the garden with your back to Fat Buddha, the stones marked the locations on the horizon of the rising and the setting of the sun at the celestial high points of the year, the equinoxes and the solstices. I had missed the summer solstice, but the early July days were still blissfully long and the nights short. Learning that the sun rose and set in the very same place at the very same time on the very same day, year after year, century after century, was comforting to me. Whatever random dysfunctional chaos and disorder there was in my own little life, at least there was some sort of predictable order in the universe.

Huzzah and hooray!

We didn't need any sparklers or Roman candles or bottle rockets to celebrate the Fourth. The meadow leading down to Udder and Gramps's orchard was ablaze with fireflies. They were everywhere. Hundreds of them. Nature's very own light show.

I told Gramps my horror story of the firefly flashing-on-my-boob debacle.

He laughed. "Leave it to you to go ballistic over a lightning bug."

"Lay off," I said. "Look at how much better I am. A month ago, if I had witnessed fireflies going off like this, I would have had post-traumatic stress and run screaming back into the house!"

"With or without your pants on?" Gramps asked. "But you're right. By the time you leave us, we'll have you out-mommying Mother Nature. No more screenager. You'll be a *greenager*."

"Yeah, right. As if that's actually going to happen."

Gramps flicked his lighter and took a hit off his joint.

"You know why they light up, don't you?" he asked.

"I know why *you* light up."

"I was talking fireflies, not weed. You know what their lights are for?"

"Um . . . so they don't crash into each other? Like headlights on cars?"

Gramps laughed again.

"Sex," he said.

"I should have seen that one coming," I told him. "It seems like it's always about sex. You must have been a piece of work as a teenager, Gramps. You're bad enough as an oldster."

I settled down contentedly in my garden chair for another delightful segment of *Gramps's Kinky Sex Guide to the Insect World*.

"Please don't tell me those are their little weenies lighting up. That would just be too weird."

"You are a goofball," Gramps said. "One big, gigantic goofball."

"Yeah, but I'm *your* goofball." I snuggled up close to him and held his hand.

"And I am so glad of it."

"So, if it's not their you-know-whats turning on and off, what is?" I asked.

"Their abdomens. The males patrol the meadow, flashing their abdominal lights, hoping to interest a female. Looking for love with bioluminescence lighting the way."

"You gotta be kidding me. The males are flashing the females? Is that even legal?"

"What goes down in the meadow, stays in the meadow. If she's interested, if she digs his flash, she'll flash him right on back."

"Silly me. And I thought flashing was only for pervs."

"Think again. Generally, it's the guys that are doing the flash-and-fly while the females perch in the grass or the trees waiting for Mister Right to get it on with."

"Oh my God. So the flash is their pickup line? *Come on baby light my fire.*"

"Well said. And look carefully. What do you notice about the flashes? Do they all look the same to you?"

I gazed intently down into the meadow. The little buggies were flying everywhere, lighting up the sky. One enormous sex scene. A wild firefly orgy going down right before our eyes. First the sun and then this. It had been quite the day for light shows.

"They don't seem any different to me."

"That's because you're not a firefly," Gramps said.

"That I am not. I am many things, many of them fucked-up, but a firefly? No."

Gramps squeezed my hand again.

"There are all sorts of different types out there, and each flashes a little bit differently, depending on their species. You can't mate with a different type."

"Words to remember," I answered. "Only date within your own species."

"Exactly," Gramps said. "If you're a firefly, you gotta know who's who."

"Makes sense," I said. "For us humans, too. Not to change the subject, but I'm not entirely convinced boys are even my same species. Plus, they give off way too many confusing flashes. But Gramps, how do the fireflies know which one is which?"

"Color, number of flashes, interval of time between flashes, flight pattern, even the time of night when they're active."

"Seriously? You mean, some check out early and others party on till dawn?"

"You got it," Gramps said. "But here's the rub: sex can be deadly. Females of one species—*Photuris*, I believe—will mimic the flight pattern of another species. One much smaller than they are. She lures the guys in with her fake flashes. They fly over, all hot and bothered, thinking they're going to get laid, and then *chomp!* Down come her mandibles. She's so much bigger that she eats him right up."

"Holy shit!" I said. "Makes you think twice about the whole oral sex thing. Maybe walking out on Caleb really was the smartest thing I ever did."

"Beware the impostor," Gramps said.

"Just like *Passion*."

We were silent for a moment.

"Is there a moral to this story, Gramps?" I asked. "Are you trying to tell me something here? Like I'm giving off the wrong friggin flash or something? That my flight pattern is all screwed up?"

Gramps laughed again.

"I hadn't even thought of that," he said. "But now that you mention it . . ."

"Thanks a bunch." I turned away in mock annoyance. "I take back what I said. Evidently I am nothing but a fucked-up firefly."

"Ahhh, but you're *my* firefly." Gramps placed my hand back into his. "My goofball firefly sweetheart."

We sat in silence, relishing our voyeurism, transfixed as the night sky lit up with sex, sex, and more sex. One of nature's many mating miracles.

"If there is a moral," Gramps said, "it's this: It doesn't get any better than this, sweetheart. Watching nature orgasm. This is what matters."

And then, as if on cue, all of the fireflies in the entire meadow seemed to light up at once. A single flash of brilliant light.

Like the grand finale of the Fourth of July fireworks display.

Chapter 13

I was out in the orchard, mowing between the rows of apple trees. It was still the first week in July and the cutest little apples were just beginning to form at the end of the twigs and branches. Jonathan Reds and Cortlands and Macouns. Udder and Gramps had taught me the names of all the different types of apples. The trees were bursting forth with ripening fruit. Gramps said it was going to be a banner year.

Much to my delight I felt my phone vibrate. I was stunned. Who knew that there was a sweet spot at the far end of the orchard where, for some unfathomable reason, you could actually get reception?

I knew I wasn't supposed to have my phone on me, let alone have it on, but it had somehow wormed its way into my pants pocket without me even knowing. Like the One Ring with Frodo the Hobbit. Sneaky little bastard.

I had been having trouble managing the mower. If I hit too big a clump of grass it would sputter loudly and shut off. Starting the finicky thing up again meant yanking so many times on the pull cord that I'd practically dislocated my shoulder. My phone vibrated again, so I left the mower running and scooted behind a tree to answer.

"Hey," a voice said.

"Hey Sheila," I answered. I could hardly hear a thing. What with the mower and the wind and the shit cell service down in the orchard, I could barely tell that the voice was human. I just assumed it was Sheila. Who else would call me?

"I'm not Sheila," a guy's voice said. "This is . . ."

I couldn't quite make out who.

"Hey," I said again, no idea who the hell he was. "What's up?"

"I was wondering again about you going to the pot . . . ," the voice said, trailing off into a dead zone.

"To smoke pot?" I yelled, putting a finger in my ear.

"To . . . uck. With me."

"Fuck?" I said.

"What?"

"Sorry." I yelled even louder. "I'm out in the orchard. The reception is terrible. I can't hear a damn word you're saying!"

"The potluck. On Fri—"

Oh my God, I said to myself. It must be Derek! The boy who could just not stop his firefly flashing. He was asking me out again!

What had possessed me to give him my cell number in the first place? Too much caffeine could make a girl do such stupid things.

I swept the hair out of my eyes, yanked up my shorts, rearranged my boobs, and wiped my brow. Thank God Derek couldn't see me. I was dripping sweat. Grossness personified.

No offline guys, I told myself. *Stick with the plan and tell him no. That's what makes the most sense. Nip this thing in the bud now. Put my foot down before things get out of hand. Just say . . .*

"Yes!" I said. "I mean, I guess."

"How about five-thirty? I'd love to . . . ees."

"Tease?" I asked. "Squeeze?"

"What?" the voice said.

"Say it again!" I yelled.

"Bees. See the bees. I'll . . . ick you up?"

"Dick? Lick?" I was shouting into the phone. Thank God I was down in the orchard with the mower still running and Udder and Gramps MIA. If anyone had heard my end of the conversation, they would have thought I was clinically insane. Either that or a call girl.

"Pick! Five-thirty."

"Sounds like a plan!" My voice was going hoarse.

He said something else totally incomprehensible and then hung up.

Hmmm . . . , I thought to myself. *The best laid plans . . .*

Taking a break from mowing, I poured myself a nice tall cup of coffee, an earthy funky Sumatran blend that was one of Gramps's faves. Then I took a walk down the road where I might possibly get service and a little privacy so I could call Sheila. I still wasn't buying any of the netaholic nonsense, but I had to admit the whole live talk over texting thing had a certain *je ne sais quoi.*

"Derek asked me out again," I told her.

"And you said . . . ?"

"Um . . . well . . . you know . . ."

"You said yes, didn't you? Classic! That's just the way *not* to get involved with a guy. But remember, no YOINKS this time."

"We've moved way beyond Scrabble. He asked me to the potluck on Friday."

"Wow! The addict's potluck?"

"The very one," I said.

"That ought to be interesting," Sheila said. "Is Peter the Porno going to be there?"

"Oh God," I groaned. "I didn't think of that."

"What else did Derek say?" Sheila asked.

"I don't know. I could hardly understand him. At first I thought it was you. The service was shit and the lawn mower was on. He's going to pick me up and come by early to see the bees."

"The bees?"

"Yeah," I said. "You know how Udder and Gramps keep bees?"

"Why would anyone in their right mind keep bees?" Sheila asked. "That is just so weird."

"Everything here is weird," I answered. "And no one is in their right mind. So it all makes perfect sense."

"How does Derek even know about them?" Sheila asked.

"About Udder and Gramps?"

"About the bees."

"Let me call you call back," I told her, as another number flashed across my screen. "Someone else is trying to reach me."

"Hey," Derek said.

This time, with no mower and much better service, I could actually tell it was him.

"It's me. Derek. How are you?"

"Hey," I said, a little confused as to why he was calling again so soon. "I'm great. I took a walk down the road where the service is better and the mower's off, so I can actually hear you."

"Uh . . . that's good," Derek said, also sounding confused. "I was wondering if you changed your mind about tomorrow night? You know, the potluck and all."

"You mean what to bring? I was thinking about a big salad from my grandfathers' garden. It's like veggie paradise up here. The peppers are on friggin steroids. And the tomatoes—oh my God! They're practically the size of watermelons. Plus they've got a shit-ton of garden greens with names I can't even begin to pronounce."

"Wow," Derek said.

"Yeah. Maybe I'll even bring some honey from the bees."

"Bees?" Derek asked.

"Yeah, the ones you wanted to see."

"Your grandfathers have bees?"

"The connection must have been worse than I thought," I said. "I can show them to you when you pick me up. Five-thirty. Right?"

There was yet another awkward pause. "Five-thirty? Tomorrow?"

What was up with this dude? Was he trying to back out? Damn if I was going to allow myself to get asked out and then get dumped immediately. If anyone was going to end this relationship it was going to be me.

Wait a minute . . . relationship? What relationship? What was I even thinking about?

"Five-thirty," I commanded, my voice rising a notch. "Sharp!"

There. That would teach him. There was going to be no messing around with me.

"Um . . . sure," Derek said, not sounding sure at all.

"Thanks for asking me," I said, not at all sure that I was really all that thankful, especially with the way that he was doing the asking.

"Asking you?" Derek asked. "Tell me the truth, Meagan. How much coffee have you had today?"

"I'm sorry," I said. "I gotta go. My friend Sheila is trying to call me. I'll see you tomorrow at five-thirty."

"Tomorrow?" Derek asked. "Five-thirty?"

Oh my God, I thought. He was the one who needed caffeine.

"Who was that?" Sheila asked.

"Derek. Calling me back. I don't have a clue why. I think all of that fantasy baseball crap has wreaked havoc with his short-term memory. Anyway, where were we?"

"Um . . . ," Sheila said. "I think I asked you how Derek knew about the bees."

"The bees," I said. "That's right. I was talking to him at The Roost about Udder's arthritis and . . ."

I took the phone and whacked myself in the head.

"Shit!" I cried.

"What?" Sheila asked. "What just happened?"

I whacked myself again.

"I can't believe what I just did. Oh my God! How could I not have figured out who was who? I am such an idiot."

"Tell me!" Sheila said.

"I just made a huge screw-up. It was *Jonathan* who I told about the bees. Not Derek."

"And . . ."

"And so it must have been Jonathan who I said yes to the first time. Not Derek."

"Jonathan?" Sheila asked. "The other netaholic dude?"

"Yes, Jonathan! No wonder he was acting so brain-dead."

"Who? Jonathan?"

"No! Derek!" I shouted.

"I thought it was Derek you wanted?"

"I don't want either of them! We don't do offline boys, remember?"

"I'm confused. Is it Jonathan or Derek who's brain-dead?"

"*Me!* I'm the brain-dead one!"

"Is that why you said yes to Jonathan?" Sheila asked.

I was practically screaming. "Have you been listening to me at all? I said yes to both of them!"

"Let me get this straight: you said yes to Jonathan who you thought was Derek and then yes again to Derek because you don't want to go out with either of them?"

"Exactly! How could I have gotten this so wrong? Online, I can juggle twenty-seven guys at once. Offline, I screw up at two. What am I going to do?" I was smarting from my head whacks.

"Look, Meagan. You know I'll always love you no matter what choices you make, no matter how screwed-up I think they are. But let me remind you of one thing. None of this would ever have happened if you had just stayed online. God gave us *Passion* for a reason. There is a definite moral here."

"You're not being helpful!" I said.

"I'm being *truthful*. And sometimes the truth can hurt."

I whacked myself with my phone one more time and then hung up.

Ouch! She was right. I had given myself a wicked headache. The truth really did hurt.

Chapter 14

"You've got yourself into a bit of a pickle here, haven't you darling?" Udder said.

We were sitting in the kitchen cutting up cucumbers and cramming them into a jar. A dash of dill and a little bit of vinegar, garlic, salt, and water and, presto-chango, they magically became pickles.

"I don't know what to do," I told him. "Maybe one of them will relapse and not be able to leave his laptop. Maybe the other will get pulled over for texting and driving, and then not show. This whole pickle thing has got me piqued."

"There is a simple solution to this, Meagan," Udder said. "Call them back and tell them you made a mistake."

"What? Are you kidding me? I can't do that!"

"Because . . . ?"

"Because I already said yes!"

"I'm confused," Gramps said. He had just come in from the garden with another basket full of cucumbers. "Are you interested in getting involved with a guy?"

"No! Of course not!"

"Which is why you said yes to both of them?"

"Gramps!" I whined. "You're sounding like Sheila."

Udder sighed. "Meagan. You are a strong and assertive young woman. You are seventeen years old and soon to be a senior in high school. But listen to yourself. You're acting just like you did when you were thirteen."

I groaned. "I feel just like I did when I was thirteen. What am I going to do?"

"*Ménage* à *trois*," Gramps said. "Threesome. Just like I mentioned before."

Udder shot him a killer look.

"Just saying," Gramps grumbled.

"Don't!" Udder shot back.

"It's all your fault!" I said, tearing up. "Both of yours. I should never have gone to that stupid meeting in the first place, and then none of this would ever have happened. Sheila's right. If I had just stayed online everything would be fine. What's wrong with me?"

"Nothing is wrong with you, darling," Udder said soothingly. "You're just . . ."

"Screwed-up," Gramps said. "You don't have Cyber Relationship Disorder. You just have plain old Relationship Disorder."

Leave it to Gramps to call it like it was. At least I could count on him for a straight (ha!) answer.

"Curtis, if I hear one more—"

"Wait!" Gramps said. "I've got another brilliant idea."

"Please," Udder pleaded. "Spare us!"

"We'll get your Udder involved. He could be like a coyote or something. You know, this older gay man who preys on hot younger guys."

"You mean a cougar?" I asked.

"Whatever." Gramps put his arms around Udder and pulled him in close. "When Jonathan and Derek show up he could swoop in and sweep them off their feet. Look at him! Look how hot he is! In no time at all, they'll abandon you and be swooning all over him. Problem solved."

"Thanks, Gramps," I said. "I feel so much better now."

"Curtis!" Udder said. "If you make one more inane comment then I swear I'm going to . . ."

I dropped the cucumber I was holding onto the floor. "Wait just a minute here." Idea lightbulbs were suddenly flashing over my head like fireflies. "Gramps, you could be onto something! What you said just might work."

"*On* something is more like it!" Udder reached over and took the joint out of Gramps's hand. "Meagan, you can't be serious."

"See?" Gramps said. "I do *too* have good ideas."

"No offense, Udder, but, cute as you are, you're not going to cut it. But what about Sheila? What if I got Sheila in on this?"

"Sheila?" Udder said. "From what I know of that girl, I'm not sure she's the one to—"

I interrupted him. "Gramps, you are brilliant. Totally brilliant!" I gave him a kiss on his scruffy cheek.

"I call front-row seat!" Gramps said, grabbing for his joint back.

Chapter 15

Sheila was supposed to have arrived at Udder and Gramps's at four on Friday. That would have given us at least a brief window of opportunity to rehearse our plan of attack before the boys arrived. Unfortunately, she couldn't get off early from work at the convenience store, and the damn summer construction on the Massachusetts Turnpike had slowed traffic down to a nightmarish crawl. She had pulled in just minutes before Derek and Jonathan were set to arrive.

We were going to have to wing it.

We had spent way too much time the evening before discussing what Sheila should wear. How much skin should she show? How much cleavage? Should she wear makeup or not? Everything was open to so much possible misinterpretation.

Clothes! For us girls the whole wardrobe conundrum was always front and center, especially when we were in school. If you dressed like you didn't care, you were labeled a nerd or a slob—and who wanted to take crap for that? If you dressed up, you had to navigate the incredibly fine line between hot and slutty, between looking good in an appropriate way as opposed to looking good in a way that brought out catcalls.

I knew I should be able to dress however the hell I wanted and not ever be harassed for it. Ever. But, try as I might, it was pretty darn difficult not to fall prey to the bullshit, particularly when rules changed overnight following a music-awards wardrobe bombshell.

It was a full-time job just deciding what to put on in the morning.

Even choosing what to wear for your selfie Facebook photo or dating site profile was stressful. Which angle brought out my best look? Was my face too fat? What about my thighs? And, oh my God, what do I do about my hair?

The whole thing was excruciatingly difficult and screwed-up on so many levels. It was yet another thing that made seventeen so damn exhausting.

Not that it would make much difference what Sheila wore. She could wear nothing but a beat-up burlap bag and still be beautiful, that Arab American look of hers absolutely stunning. Long and lean, she had that toned body that made so many other girls just feel bad about themselves, wrong as that was. And her hair. Oh my God. Long, wavy tumbles of jet-black curls that just cascaded around her face like a Rapunzelian waterfall.

Anyway, the more I thought about it, the more I realized that this whole boy thing had to be stopped immediately before it totally got out of hand. I don't know what I had been thinking saying yes to either of them in the first place, let alone both! And to a Netaholics Anonymous potluck? Seriously? Maybe all that second-hand pot smoke from Gramps's perpetually lit joints was making my brain funny.

Online boys I knew I could handle. Offline? I don't think so.

The general gist of our plan was to stick with the KISS approach— Keep It Simple and Stylish. I would act distant and aloof, whatever feminine charms I possessed (if any) blanketed under Gramps's billowing beekeeping outfit. Immersed in my full-body, heavy-duty, polyester bee suit—ventilated helmet, veil, and thick gloves awkwardly pulled up to my elbows—I'd look like a hazardous-waste worker sent out to clean up an oil spill. There wouldn't be a single inch of skin showing. I'd be a walking *Do Not Enter* sign. Totally off-limits.

Sheila, on the other hand, would dress for success in a sexy, red, spaghetti-strap, cut-out, Boho maxi dress, the one she looked *so* sweet in.

The trick was to get each guy to think that Sheila was there for the other one. That we were double-dating or something. Given that we knew absolutely nothing about single-dating, let alone double, that part of the plan was still a little bit fuzzy. But when Sheila cranked up her irresistible sex appeal and started coming on to both of them, before you could even wink, I just knew they'd drop me like a hot sweet potato and swarm all over her like bees to zucchini flowers. I'd be off the hook, Sheila would head back to Boston leaving a couple of shattered hearts behind, and that would be that.

What could possibly go wrong?

"Darling," Udder said when I divulged the bare bones of this brilliant plan to him, "I cannot begin to tell you how ridiculous this whole thing sounds. There is not the remotest chance in the world that it will possibly—"

"You're just jealous because it's Sheila being the temptress, and not you," I told him. "Anyway, it's going to work. It has to work. There is no Plan B."

Jonathan had arrived at exactly five-thirty, followed immediately by Derek. I could sense the boys' confusion as to what the hell the other one was doing there, but fortunately Sheila's nonstop blather allowed zero time for questions.

After brief introductions, Udder had banished Gramps to his bedroom, thinking he'd be less likely to create a scene and compound an already extremely awkward situation. I could still see Gramps peering out of his open window, pot smoke wafting in lazy circles around his head, giving me the thumbs-up sign.

I had promised both boys that I'd show them the bees, so the four of us made our way down to the hives at the southern end of the orchard. It was a warm and muggy evening and the bees were pouring out of the entrance to the hive.

"The queen leaves the hive only once, for a single nuptial flight," I lectured, yanking down on my beekeeping suit, which was already giving me a vicious wedgie.

Helping out Gramps for the last couple of weeks had made me fairly confident that I could pull off a passable insect-tour-guide routine. I was hoping my crash course in all things bees would be sure to please. But then again, why did I even care? The goal was to get the boys off my back, not buzzing all over me.

I opened up the hive and held up a frame full of honey and hundreds of bees. "She mates in midair with a drone, a boy bee who is good for one thing and one thing only."

"Getting down and dirty?" Sheila asked, batting her eyelashes at the boys. "Netflix and chill with a little bit of the horizontal boogie? Taking old one-eye to the optometrist?"

"Sheila!" I shouted through my veil. "Stop! You're scaring the bees."

The boys looked down awkwardly. Sheila wasn't sounding enticing at all. Just perverted.

"Skroggin'?" she nattered on. "Skonkin'? Shaggin'? Shaboinkin'?"

I waved my gloved finger at her. "I'm going to have to wash your mouth out with soap, young lady. May I please continue?"

Sheila batted her lashes at the boys once more.

"The worker bees are the girls. It's the girls who sip the nectar from the apple blossoms and turn it into honey. It's the girls who do the pollinating. It's the girls who care for the queen and feed the larvae and clean out the hive and do everything else that needs to be done. All the boys do is—"

"Hide the salami!" There she went again. Sheila and her wonderful way with words.

"Sounds like quite the life," Derek said, gazing at me instead of Sheila. "Get it on with the queen and slack away the rest of your day."

"How wrong you are!" I banged my fist down on the hive, sending a cloud of bees soaring skyward. "In the end, those little boy-bee bastards get their just rewards. A moment of bliss and then *BAM!* Off with his penis." I made a karate chop motion with my hand.

Still staring at me, Derek took a step backwards.

"Drones ejaculate with so much force," I continued, "that the tip of their penis explodes when they come inside the queen. Then they plunge dead to the ground. Ha! Take that, slacker. He comes. He goes. Sexual suicide."

"You gotta be kidding me!" Sheila was grinning. The boys seemed too shell-shocked to comment. "Next time a guy *drones* on and on about how much he's dying to get inside of me, I'll be sure to hit him up with this one. But seriously? You're telling me the queen only has sex once? In her entire life? And then the guy gets off and dies on her?"

"I don't know about you," I told her, "but I'd be pretty damn traumatized if a guy's penis ripped off inside of me in midair and then I watched as he plummeted to his death. That's not exactly a turn-on."

"Really?" For the third time, Sheila batted her long eyelashes at both boys. "Sounds kind of kinky to me."

"I'd be willing to bet," Jonathan offered, "that if it were the king running the show, things would go down a little different."

Sheila raised her fist high into the air, shouting, "Down with all kings except King Ludd!"

"King Ludd?" Both Jonathan and Derek spoke at the same time. They had looks of astonishment on their faces.

"You know King Ludd?" Jonathan asked.

King Ludd.

Where to begin?

When we were sophomores in high school, Sheila got it into her head that she was destined to be an actress. It turned out to be one of those short-lived adolescent identity disasters that brought out the gag reflex in both of us whenever the horrid memory of it reared its ugly head.

Sheila had managed to score a spot in our high school musical-theater production of *The Hero of Nottinghamshire*, a dreadful dramatic disaster about the Luddites in England in the 1800s. It was written and directed by a theater student, a pompous and arrogant playwright-wannabe who had neither musical talent nor any degree of playwriting ability. In exchange for the part of Linsey Lou Ludd, the philandering wife of the hero, Sheila did the guy's math homework for a whole month.

The intent of the play was to dramatize the first-ever organized rebellion against the Industrial Revolution. For all its faults (which were many), the play did contain some elements of historical accuracy. The words to the songs were actual poems or tunes from the time.

The setting was England in the eighteen-teens. Before that time, weavers and combers and dressers of wool—all of those people who made the cloth that the rest of Great Britain relied on—had worked out of their own homes. Life wasn't easy but at least workers had some degree of control over their own profession.

Enter the wealthy industrialists with their huge factories and their massive industrial looms. Home spinners couldn't compete. The onset of the Industrial Revolution meant an onslaught against these rural workers. It marked the beginning of the end for the homespun industry and the way of life and community that went with it.

For a few fateful months, the common folk fought back, raging against the machine. They waged a ferocious war of economic sabotage, smashing the industrial looms, burning down factories, threatening the new class of industrialists. Rebels against the future, protesting so-called progress, they called themselves Luddites, taking their name from a mythical king, Ned Ludd.

Not surprisingly, the British Empire and the moneyed classes did not take kindly to this threat to their industrial domination. With armed force and way too many trips to the gallows, the rebellion was brutally crushed.

The Hero of Nottinghamshire, with its adulterous, conspiratorial, excessively violent script, was perhaps the worst theater production ever. Sheila's total inability to sing even remotely on key was shocking. Unlike a Comedy Central or *Saturday Night Live* satire on bad musical theater, this show wasn't even remotely funny.

The play did nothing to convince the suffering audience that technology was the root of all evil. In fact, it had had just the opposite effect. Halfway through the first act, the vast majority of the crowd was on their cell phones, their downturned faces softly lit by the tiny screens.

It was a total flop. Sheila never acted again.

But the songs, the godawful songs, lived on. And now Sheila had the audacity to burst into one:

Chant no more your old rhymes about bold Robin Hood
His feats I but little admire
I will sing the achievements of General Ludd
Now the Hero of Nottinghamshire

"I can't believe you know about King Ludd," Jonathan said to Sheila again, yanking on his ears and wincing. "He's one of my heroes. The founding father of NA."

"Know about him?" Sheila said. "I worship the dude. I'm the one who put the Ludd in Luddite, for God's sake. Back in Boston they call me Queen Ludd. I've never seen a machine I didn't want to destroy!"

Sheila tipped her head back and once more began to sing.

And night by night when all is still
And the moon is hid behind the hill,
We forward march to do our will
With hatchet, pike and gun!
Oh, the cropper lads for me,
The gallant lads for me,
Who with lusty stroke,
The shear frames broke,
The cropper lads for me.

"For the love of God!" I begged Sheila, cringing. "Stop! Please stop!"

Sheila still remembered every friggin verse of every friggin song from that accursed musical. For the past two years, she had sung them incessantly whenever she wished to torment me. She'd get me to do her bidding just by threatening to sing a verse. And now, here she was, doing the same damn thing, torturing the three of us down in the bee yard.

What was she thinking?

This was definitely not the plan! She was supposed to be turning the two guys *on*, not *off*. Driving them to a state of desire, not sending them fleeing over the state line! Alien as I looked in my bee zoot suit, they'd both be leaping into my arms if she kept this shit up.

Even the bees amped up the volume of their buzzing, hoping beyond hope to drown out the torturous sounds emitting from that girl's mouth. How anyone so beautiful could sing so horribly was one of God's great mysteries.

"Is she just making this shit up?" Derek whispered to me.

"No! These are, like, two-hundred-year-old songs!"

"Is she all right?" Jonathan asked.

"No! Just listen to her! Of course she's not all right!"

Come all ye croppers stout and bold
Let your faith grow stronger still
Oh, the cropper lads in the county of York
Broke the shears at Foster's mill.
The wind it blew,
The sparks they flew,
Which alarmed the town full soon,
And out of bed poor people did creep
And ran by the light of the moon.

There wasn't any light of the moon to run by, but the three of us were more than ready to head for the hills.

The beehives were enclosed by an electric fence that Gramps had erected to keep bears out. Years ago, his first foray into beekeeping had been met with disaster. Mama and her cubs, honey dripping off their fur, were as happy as could be. Gramps and the bees were not. Hence the electric fence.

Sheila was still singing (if you could call it that) another Luddite lullaby at the top of her lungs. Clutching his ears in obvious pain, Derek took a step backwards right into the electric fence. The electric fence that I had somehow forgotten to turn off.

Whoops! My bad.

"Yeowww!" he yelled, mistaking the burst of electricity pulsating through his body for bee stings. "The bees! They're all over me!"

Sheila stopped singing. "Bees!" she yelled, panicking. "Run away! Run!"

She flung off her platform shoes and hightailed it back toward the house, Jonathan a few short steps behind.

Derek's pants had somehow gotten entangled on the electric fence and, unable to move, he was getting the crap zapped out of him. I could have sworn sparks were shooting out of his pants. I gave him a good hard push and he toppled over backwards.

"Holy shit!" he gasped, staggering to his feet and reaching out for me to steady him. "What the hell happened? Did I just have sex with the queen?"

He nervously felt around his crotch.

"Did my thing explode?"

"What did I already tell you?" Grinning through my bee veil I thrust my gloved fist high into the air. "No more penises!"

Chapter 16

Riding in cars with boys! Something I had never been comfortable with.

A car was a confined, claustrophobic space which, at least when moving, provided no safe avenue for escape. As I've mentioned a million times before, spontaneous conversation was just not my thing. I had become so hardwired to communicating on the net that it had almost reached a point where I had to air-type a response before it went verbal. But now, here I was, riding in the back seat with Derek on the way to the potluck, with no cell phone to escape into. Nothing to do but (*gasp!*) talk.

Without my safety net, I was terrified.

Once Derek had recuperated from his near-death experience with the electric fence, and Sheila and Jonathan had apologized profusely for fleeing his electrocution and abandoning him in his hour of need, we had all piled into Jonathan's car. Sheila was still reliving her sophomoric self, back to starring in her play, spouting off Luddite propaganda like crazy. There was no stopping her.

"I don't consider carpooling optional," she'd said, climbing into the front seat with Jonathan solving the awkward puzzle of seating arrangements, much to my relief. "I'm of the firm belief that Karl Friedrich Benz, that son of a bitch, should be charged and convicted of crimes against humanity. I don't give a shit if he's long dead. I'd be the judge, jury and executioner on that one. I'd happily exhume his body just to off him again!"

I rolled my eyes in the back seat. Sheila was so full of shit you could have powered the engine on her fumes.

But she was no ditz. Not only was her sex appeal off the charts, but so was her brain. She had an almost photographic memory and could dial up the most obscure facts in a heartbeat.

"Karl Friedrich who?" Derek asked.

"Benz. The inventor of the damn automobile. Exhaust, carbon dioxide, climate change, suburban sprawl, death by driving. It's all his fault! I'd spit on his grave if I knew where it was."

"Ladenburg," Jonathan said, going head-to-head with Sheila in the Obscure Facts department. "In Germany."

"Seriously?" Sheila asked. "You know where the bastard is buried? That is so hot!"

I watched as she reached over and gave Jonathan's thigh a squeeze.

"Cars, computers, and cells," Sheila continued. "The Three C's of the Devil. If I had my way they'd all be at the bottom of this river. I hate them. I loathe them."

I did my utmost not to smirk too loudly.

Squeeze or no squeeze, it didn't seem as if Sheila's magic was having the desired effect. Unlike at the second NA meeting, now that I had come to my senses I had done my best to dress for lack of success, hoping for the opposite of the boy-magnet look. I had shed my beekeeping outfit for baggy sweatpants, an old T-shirt with a picture of my high school mascot (a ridiculously lame blue bear) and had done my hair up in uneven pigtails like a deranged tween. But damned if Derek wasn't sidling up closer and closer to me in the back seat while Jonathan continually checked me out in the rearview mirror. Watching the road did not seem to be his top priority.

"Car!" I yelled to Jonathan.

He refocused just in time, swerving the steering wheel hard to the right and narrowly avoiding plunging us off the bridge and into the Connecticut River and certain death.

"Red light!" I yelled. He dragged his eyes away from the mirror, slammed on the brakes, and miraculously stopped inches from the car in front of us. Then, once again, he began staring me down in the rearview mirror.

"Green light!" I yelled. The crescendo of honking horns behind us had become almost unbearable.

All of this while *not* texting and driving.

I looked over at Derek, who, after Jonathan nearly made roadkill out of a bicyclist, had turned an even more vivid shade of green than the traffic light.

I was surprised. I had naturally assumed that all boys equated bad driving with thrill rides and the closer they flirted with death the higher the high fives, yet here was Derek whimpering away like the Cowardly Lion in *The Wizard of Oz*.

"I swear I'd take the electric fence over this," he whispered, scooting even closer to me and reaching out to hold my hand.

Oh my God. Once again, the boy-free game plan was clearly not going as planned. Here I was, holding hands with the boy in the back, while the boy in the front couldn't keep his eyes off of me.

What the hell was happening? After all, Sheila was . . . Sheila.

She was cute *and* beautiful. A tsunami of sensuality. So what if she couldn't sing worth shit, because *boy* could she talk. None of that SCDD (Spontaneous Conversation Deficit Disorder) that I suffered from. Smart as hell, when Sheila got on a roll you'd even lose sight of her hair for the captivating way of her words. She could string sentences together that made your nose bleed. Of course, not all of them made sense, but hey, you couldn't have everything.

Those two boys should have been panting at her feet by now, smitten with lust and desire, wanting nothing to do with me and everything with her. But for some reason that just wasn't happening.

How strange was that?

Sheila was still blathering nonstop as we pulled up to the potluck house. Her semi-lucid Ludditisms had continued unabated for the entire hellish drive, which we had miraculously managed to survive.

"Don't you worry, girlfriend," she whispered to me, closing the car door. "I'll have you out of this mess, at least half of it, in no time."

Sheila had taken Jonathan's arm in hers and forcibly led him into the house. He turned to gaze back at me as they disappeared through the doorway.

I was stunned. Sheila had no more real-life experience with offline boys than I did, yet here she was appearing so calm and debonair, acting just like she owned the show. How did she do it? How did she know how to behave around a boy? Maybe, given that this was all just an act, that brief bout of theater experience in *The Hero of Nottinghamshire* really had done some good.

Most of the zucchini green had faded from Derek's face and he was just beginning to look human again. He had finally stopped holding my hand after Jonathan's car had come to a complete stop in the driveway, the front bumper nestled snugly into another car's rear.

"You okay?" I asked him.

"I don't know!" he said. "Feel my pulse. It's like two hundred. I swear, that car ride took ten years off my life. Please, can we just plead the Luddite way and walk home?"

I laughed.

"Whose house is this again?"

"Peter's," Derek replied. "The guy we made fun of in the group."

"Oh my God! You gotta be kidding me! Peter? This is Peter the Porno's potluck?"

"The one and only."

I reached out, grabbed Derek's hand, and held it tightly.

Chapter 17

It was New England in July, and the weather was truly spectacular: mid-eighties, bone-dry, a little breeze flirting with the trees. Peter the Porno lived with his parents, and their house had a lovely back patio overlooking the rolling valley farmland with an awesome view of the Seven Sisters, the hills of the Mount Holyoke range.

Peter had the grill going, and the two big picnic tables were already crowded with potluck extravaganzas. I got plenty of high fives and fist-bumps when I unveiled my prize of a salad.

Social ineptitude aside, I figured I'd best get apologies out of the way immediately, so I shuffled up awkwardly next to Peter.

"I am so sorry," I told him, timidly taking his hand and shaking it. "About the other night. At the meeting. I acted like such an idiot."

"Me too," Derek said, standing next to me.

"No worries," Peter replied. "I probably got a little carried away there, didn't I?"

"Dude," said a guy to Peter. He was someone I also recognized from the NA meeting. "You were awesome. Straight from the heart." He turned to me and reached around to pick a pepper from the salad. "I'm Jeremy," he said. "Nice to see you again. I dig the veggies. Totally yummilicous. Orgo?"

"'Orgo'?"

"Organic," he said. "I don't do conventional."

"Conventional?" I asked.

"You know, pesticides, herbicides, synthetic fertilizers, that kind of crap. I'm not down with that."

"Um . . ." I stammered. "I think they're okay. I mean, everything in the salad is from my grandfathers' garden and they're pretty careful about what they put into it."

"Right on!" he said, pulling out a handful of greens and munching away. "Goat shit?"

"Excuse me?" I asked.

"Goat shit. Are your grandfathers into that? It's the bomb."

"My Gramps smokes a lot of weed, but I've never heard him mention goat shit before."

Derek, who (curse him!) had left me all alone to fend for myself, mercifully came back with drinks and handed one to me.

"Hey Jeremy," he said. "How's it going?"

"Dude!" Jeremy said. "Your woman is right on. We're talking goats here."

"Um . . .," I stammered again. "I'm not his—"

"Milk, cheese, butter, yogurt," Jeremy continued. "And you know what else? They're fossil-free mowers. Let 'em loose in a field, and *boom*—the job is done. They're like hoofed locusts. And to top it off their shit is to die for. Nothing tastes better than greens grown in goat shit." He reached over and grabbed another handful of my salad.

"Don't get him going, Meagan," Derek said. "Jeremy's gone from netaholic to goataholic. Traded in one addiction for another. Get him preaching the gospel of the goat and we'll be here forever."

"I don't believe in raising animals for food," a petite brunette said, joining in on the conversation. It was Karen. Karen the Cat Killer. "I think it's cruel penning goats in like that. Making them do our work. It's like slavery. Inhumane. Immoral. How can you possibly justify raising an animal and then eating it? It seems so wrong."

I couldn't help but wonder if Karen's conversion to animal rights proponent had come before or after her unfortunate encounter with the feline.

"I'm not eating the goat!" Jeremy said.

"Yeah, but you're milking it."

"That's totally different."

"Said like a true guy," Karen huffed, shaking her head in disgust. "So totally oblivious to the trauma you're putting the she-goat through. Manipulating her body so her nipples are constantly producing? Turning the poor thing into a milk machine? You don't think that's traumatic for her? You don't think that's abuse?"

I took a deep breath. This was all so very new to me. People at the few parties I had ever been to talked a lot about boobs. Just not goat boobs.

"You and your rampant misogyny drive me nuts," Karen continued. "This is the reason why this planet is imploding! This is the reason why we're all going down!"

"Because he's milking the goat?" I asked timidly.

Karen shot me the evil eye. Derek just smiled.

"Toto," I whispered to him. "I have a feeling we're not in Kansas anymore."

I really did feel like Dorothy in Oz. A stranger in a strange land. Here I was at a potluck party and no one had their cell phone out. No one. Party at home? It was a drink in one hand and a phone in the other. Unless they were talking boobs, they'd hardly be talking at all. Just texting away.

But here? There wasn't a cell in sight.

I immediately noticed one huge difference: at a phone-free party, you could say anything, anything at all, and not have it immediately be questioned by a gaggle of Googlers. A definite upside to cell phone abstinence. Back in Boston, in the rare times there was a conversation going on, whenever *anyone* said *anything*, there was an immediate on-slaught of cell-phone fact-checkers rabidly disputing all of the ins and outs of the allegation. "Actually," someone was bound to say, glancing briefly up from their phone having just googled the nutrient values of animal manure, "llama shit has a much higher nitrogen content than goat shit." That would be all it took and folks would be off to the Google races. It would be phosphorus this and potassium that, and before you knew it, the data deluge, like an avalanche, was bound to engulf you. In no time flat, the entire thread of the conversation would be lost. You'd be totally overwhelmed with a mind-boggling amount of shit on goat shit that, truth be told, no one really gave a shit about anyway.

"Let's go find Sheila," I said to Derek, leaving Jeremy and Karen to have at it over animal rights and the political correctness of free-range organic goat yogurt.

I found Sheila by the food table. She was holding court next to my salad, surrounded by a gaggle of guys, her arm still firmly entwined with Jonathan's.

"Here she is," Sheila said. "Just the girl I was telling you about!"

A number of the guys looked down awkwardly.

Oh no, I thought, a sinking feeling rising in my stomach. I could see that mischievous glint in Sheila's eyes. Someone had brought beer (an obvious difference between NA and AA), and a half hour into the party, lightweight that she was, Sheila was already half in the bag. From past experiences, most of them unpleasant, I knew that once Sheila started pounding down the brews anything could happen. When beer got the best of her, her mouth became the loosest of cannons. Wasted, Sheila put the *pro* in *inappropriate*.

"Um . . . ," I stammered, slipping into my usual social speech-impediment mode. "Hello?"

"I was telling everyone about how you're the queen of celibacy." Sheila took another sip of her beer.

Oh my God! I desperately made the *Zip it!* motion, moving my thumb and finger quickly over my snarling lips, but Sheila was launched into a beer-fueled roll. Trouble with a capital T.

She took another big sip, draining her bottle. "Purity through abstinence. Self-cleansing. Not just from the text but also from the sex. But totally on board with self-pleasure. Right, Meg?"

Sheila never called me Meg unless under the influence.

I got what she was going for. Promoting my sexual unavailability. Reinforcing that wall around my guy-free zone. But this? Seriously? This was *not* what I had in mind.

"But she does it the right way, don't you girl? She's a Luddite of self-love. No battery-operated toys for her. No sirree, thank you, mama. Even rechargeable ones are a pleasuring no-no. My goodness, Meg won't even use a dildo. Not even a Fair Trade, sustainably harvested, rainforest rubber one. It's a techno-free zone down there. No unnaturals need apply. For my girl, it's fingers or garden veggies only."

Sheila had once again kicked off her platform shoes and was now standing on her tippity-toes, her back arched and her hands fluttering in the air. I was half expecting the group of guys to circle her and begin *ommming* away, just the way they did when Peter the Porno created his shit show of a scene at the NA meeting. But instead they just continued to stare at her. Everyone except Jonathan and Derek, who just stared at me.

"Which did you say you liked better, Meg? I can't remember. Was it cucumbers or zucchinis?"

Enough! Even for Sheila this was way, way, *way* over the top. I was pissed. What was she thinking? That guys wouldn't be turned on hearing this? Seriously? This was the stuff dudes' fantasies were made of.

"Wait a minute," Sheila continued, almost toppling over backwards. "What about those weird winter-squash thingies. The ones that resemble giant testicles and a huge . . ."

My blush was redder than the Valley Girl Beefsteak Tomatoes that Gramps grew in his garden. A full facial flush.

Once more I grabbed Derek's hand and fled.

"Wow," Derek said. "Your friend is . . . something else. I'm not sure I've ever met anyone . . ."

"Quite like Sheila? Nor will you ever again."

My face had turned more of a pansy pink, but I was still seeing red. *Just wait till I get my hands on that girl*, I thought. The sparks were going to fly! Maybe I'd march her down to the beehive fence and force *her* to sit on it. Maybe that would zap some sense into her.

Derek and I were sitting on a stone wall at the edge of Peter's garden, watching the sun beginning to set on the mountain range in the distance. Little wisps of ephemeral clouds were slowly marching toward the distant hills and then fading away to nothingness. Here for a moment and then gone forever. The impermanence of everything.

Not to be outdone by the sun, the fireflies were just beginning to do their thing and light up the sky, just like at Udder and Gramps's.

I had no words. None. I was totally mortified by Sheila's outburst. I didn't want to so much as think about what Derek was thinking.

So we just sat and stared.

Derek finally broke the silence. "I wonder why they flash?" he asked.

I should have kept my mouth shut, particularly after Sheila's manic monologue on self-pleasure. Launching into another episode of "The Totally Bizarre Sexual Lives of Insects" would do little to enhance the pro-abstinence agenda.

But damn if Gramps's enthusiasm for buggie boinking hadn't rubbed off on me. No matter how awkward the social situation seemed, keeping something as outrageous as firefly sex to myself seemed just plain wrong. And knowing we were in a phone-free zone where I could play fast and loose with the facts and totally get away with it was comforting.

Derek listened in rapt attention as I spewed out my fun firefly fuck facts.

"First bees. Now fireflies!" he said. "Sheila's right. You really are an insexologist!"

Halfway through my soliloquy, just as I was getting to the juicy part about the big bad female chowing down on the poor little wooer, I realized we were holding hands again.

Me. Sitting on a stone wall, fireflies flashing away, holding hands with a boy. What was up with that?

I really did feel like I was thirteen. The squeeze of his fingers was sending earthquake-like tremors up and down my spine. An 8.7 on the Richter scale. Maybe even a 9.1. I felt like the female firefly sitting in the grass, watching my guy (same species this time) flash me. Who knew how turned-on you could get just by holding hands?

What was going on with me? The brain was pleading, *Drop it, stick with the plan, girl*—but the hand was like, *Yo, sis, just try and stop me.* It was as if it were disconnected from the rest of my body. A mutiny. A five-fingered rebellion.

"You okay?" Derek asked.

"Depends on who you ask," I told him.

"Finally!" Jonathan said. "I've been looking for you everywhere!"

I had left Derek to go pee and had just come out of the bathroom, and there he was: Jonathan. Without Sheila. Ambushing me in the kitchen.

"I'm dying to show you something!" he said, taking my hand.

No! Not another hand-hold!

Jonathan guided me through the living room and across the hall into Peter's bedroom. He sat down on the side of the bed.

Oh my God, I thought. *Here we go, here's where the weirdness begins.*

I couldn't *believe* that he actually had the balls to take me into Peter the Porno's bedroom! Yuck! Yuck with a capital Y! I lifted up my shoes to see if they were sticking to the floor.

"Check this out!" Jonathan said, shifting positions on the bed.

Oh my God! Check what out? Please don't tell me this would be the time when the pants came unzipped.

"Jonathan!" I said, readying myself for another *Tennōheika Banzai!* "We need to talk."

"Wait," he said. "Let me show you this first."

Before I could stop him, Jonathan reached behind Peter's bed and opened up what looked like a miniature little door halfway up the wall.

I opened my mouth in surprise.

"What the hell is that?" I asked.

"Straw!" Jonathan said. "This house is insulated with straw bales. That sweet little door in the wall is so you can see inside. Is this awesome or what?"

"Straw? Like the Three Little Pigs' house?"

"Well, like the first one, anyway. It's totally renewable. Totally sustainable. Do you have any idea what the R-value of straw is?"

"Do I have any idea what an R-value *is*?" I asked.

"R-value. Resistance to heat flow. You know, how well a house keeps the heat in. The better the insulation, the greater the R-value, which means less fossil fuel to heat the house. Straw bales are like an R-30."

"Unbelievable!" I said, not having a clue as to whether that was unbelievably good or just unbelievable, but so unbelievably relieved that his weenie was still in his pants that I came across as unbelievably enthusiastic. "Is that like, berry high?"

"What?"

"Straw. Berry. Get it? Never mind. Stupid joke."

"If it was blueberry, my favorite, there'd be nothing left. I would have eaten it all. Anyway, it gets even better. Do you know what the attic is?"

"Of course I know what an attic is."

"I mean do you know what the R-value of Peter's attic is?"

"Not a clue."

"70! An R-value of 70!"

"You gotta be kidding me!"

"And there's more!" Jonathan said.

"No!" I gasped, my voice rising a notch. "More?"

"Check it out! Window quilts!" Evidently Jonathan was totally oblivious to my sarcasm. He leaned over and pulled down an insulating shade over the bedroom window. "They add an additional R-5 to the window!"

"Un-fucking-believable!" I yelled even louder, this time with a voice usually reserved for faking orgasms during those very few times I had dropped the sext for the phone sex.

"If you want a real treat we could go upstairs and check out the mini-split heat pump." Jonathan attempted to stand up but somehow his jeans had gotten caught up in the quilt of the bed. I reached out and grabbed his hands to help him to his feet.

Right then, as luck would have it, Derek walked in.

"Oh!" he said softly, his face falling. "Am I interrupting?"

"No!" I said.

"Yes!" Jonathan said.

"Hey!" Sheila said, walking in right behind Derek, yet another beer in hand. "What did I miss?"

Somehow I had managed to extract myself from the extreme awkwardness of the bedroom fiasco, once more pawned Jonathan off on Sheila, and was now back at the stone wall with Derek and the fireflies.

"I wasn't holding hands with Jonathan," I blurted out. "I really wasn't. I was just helping him up. We were looking at the straw bales in the walls in Peter's bedroom. They have an R-value of, like, three hundred or something. Maybe more. Pretty awesome, huh?"

Remember: no phones, no fact-checking.

Why was I being so defensive? I didn't have to explain any of this to him. What business of it was his, anyway? This was my life. I could check out R-values in a bedroom whenever I chose with whoever the hell I wanted.

"No worries," Derek said, looking very worried.

"Listen," I said, taking his hand in mine. I took a deep breath. It was time to have the talk. DTR. Define The Relationship. Not that there was, mind you, any relationship to define.

"I don't want you to get the wrong impression, Derek. I like you. I really do. It's actually quite weird how much I like you. But that's beside the point. Here's the deal. I'm only in Western Massachusetts for a couple of months. Less than that, actually. Just long enough to help get my Udder and Gramps's house and garden in order. I told you that already, remember? That and I'm trying to get my act together and . . . you know . . ."

"B.U." Derek said.

"What?" I took a quick sniff under my armpits. I distinctly remembered lathering on a liberal dose of my Teen Spirit Pink Crush antiperspirant deodorant ("The harder you play, the harder it works!") before coming to the potluck. Had I gotten so hot and bothered that it was no longer doing the trick? I couldn't smell anything too ripe.

"I don't think it's me," I told him.

Derek laughed.

"Not 'P.U.' *B.U.* Boston University. I got accepted there. That's where I'm going to college in the fall."

"Wow," I said. "Congratulations. That's a great school."

"Thanks. I'm psyched. Scared shitless, but still psyched. Anyway, it's in, you know, Boston."

"Really?" I arched my eyebrows. "Who knew? I just assumed Boston University was in Seattle or Salt Lake City, or maybe somewhere in Africa."

Derek laughed again.

"I'm just saying, come the end of August, I'll be going to school in Boston. And, you know, you'll be going back to school in Boston."

"Please!" I squeezed his hand and groaned. "Don't remind me."

"Are you just getting out of a bad relationship?" Derek asked, his fingers gently massaging mine. "Is that it?"

There went my damn hand again. Massaging his fingers right on back. "Well . . ." I paused and bit my lip. "It depends on how you define a relationship. Other than that one offline debacle I already told you about, I've never been in an ITF. And with that one, I was barely in it long enough to get the hell out. And thank God I did." I wiped my brow theatrically.

"ITF?" Derek asked, looking confused.

"In The Flesh."

"Oh. I get it. So . . . you've never been in a *real* relationship?"

Awkward!

"Like I said, it depends on your definition of relationship." I took a deep breath. "Online, I've had tons of them. And you're absolutely right: mine have all been bad. Serial crash-and-burns. Complete catastrophes."

For some reason I found myself grinning. It was a little odd how overly cheerful I made the whole shit show sound.

"So what is this, then?" Derek asked.

"What is what?"

"This." He gently squeezed my hand.

Somewhat reluctantly, I let go.

"Listen," I told him. "I'm having a pretty hard time here, and you're not exactly making it any easier."

"Is that a good thing or a bad thing?" he asked, staring straight at me.

"It's just that . . . when I'm up at my Udder and Gramps's I can't get connected to do *my* thing. Do you have any idea how incredibly difficult that is for me?"

"Actually," Derek said. "I think I do."

"Oh yeah, right." I rolled my eyes. "Blowing off your grandma and the whole trip to the Caribbean."

"Thanks for reminding me."

"Sorry. But back to me. Do you know how incredibly close I am to one hundred thousand *Passion* points?"

"Passion points?" Derek asked, his eyebrows arching up comically.

"Yeah. On my dating site. The more times I swipe the more points I get. I cash them in for discounts on all sorts of awesome online stuff. I'm, like, *obsessed* with accumulating them. How do you think I got these shoes?" I picked up my feet and wiggled them for him to examine.

"Wow," he said, giving the laces a little tug. "There's a marketing tool for you."

"You better believe it. But seriously, how am I supposed to get another pair if I can't do my thing online? And anyway, I sort of just . . ."

"Just?"

"Am not."

"Am not what? Going online? Getting more points? Buying shoes?"

"Going to do it anymore."

"But I thought you've never done it?" he asked.

Once again I rolled my eyes. "Offline? Yeah. But online? That's a different story. Listen Derek, I don't really know what's going on with me right now. I mean, I've been totally locked into this virtual reality thing for as long as I can remember, even if it's not virtuous or, for that matter, even real." Once more I grabbed his hand, gave it a squeeze, and then quickly let go. "I'm just totally confused about the whole thing."

"You and me both," Derek said.

"Like I've already said, online is my thing. It's who I am. It's what I do. It's just . . ." I gave another theatrical sigh. ". . . So much easier out there. When it comes to relationships, online there are so many fish in the sea. So many guys just swimming in that endless pool of possibilities."

"Yeah, but aren't most of them sharks or stingrays or piranhas?"

"Of course they are. Which is why, whenever I'm online with one guy, I can't help but think that there's bound to be a better one out there just waiting for me to reel on in. I'm like a catch-and-release girl, one online hookup after another. And the good thing about it is that no one ever gets hurt."

"Yeah. Right. Try telling that to the swimmers."

"I don't have to. I'm online, remember?"

"But once again, we're not online *now*, are we? This is a completely different kettle of fish."

"Maybe," I babbled on, once more taking his hand back in mine. "But regardless, I'm just thinking I need to press the pause button on this whole offline thing. Get back to doing what I do best."

"But that doesn't make any sense to me." With his free hand Derek was fiddling with his hair, twisting it one way, and then twisting it another. I couldn't take my eyes off him. "I mean, why go *off* off if you've never even been *on* off to begin with?"

"Derek," I told him. "I didn't understand a single word you just said. But listen to me: what if I really *was* an internet addict? I mean, I totally know I'm not."

"Of course you aren't," Derek said. I could see him trying to hide a smile.

"It's stupid to even speculate about such a ridiculous thing."

"Totally ridiculous."

I punched him in the chest. "Stop being so snarky. But let's just say, hypothetically speaking, what if I was? What if I have APD, Addictive Personality Disorder, to go along with all of my other fucked-up acronyms? And then, get this, what if I suddenly traded one addiction for another? Online relationships for offline? Seriously—how bad would that be?"

"Come on, Meagan. That's being a little extreme, don't you think? How is an offline relationship an addiction?"

"Derek, I came this close to doing it with a guy I had only texted with a few times and couldn't give a shit about. How crazy is that, huh? An online *slut*" (I cringed at the word) "is one thing—but offline? That's something else entirely. And you want to know what makes the whole thing even more complicated?"

"Is that even possible?" Derek asked.

"Unfortunately, yes. I'm good on the net, Derek. Really good. At least when it comes to . . . you know . . . certain things." I squirmed in my seat. "I mean, it's an art and, not to brag, but I'm a master at it. Seriously. I'm like the Vincent van Gogh of the net."

"Van Gogh? Isn't that the dude who went crazy and cut off his own ear?"

I cuffed Derek on his ear. "My point is this: how do I know if I'd be any good off of the net? How scary is that, huh? What if I really suck?"

Ouch! Wrong choice of words.

Derek gave my hand yet another squeeze. "Well," he said, those big brown eyes of his getting even bigger, "there's only one way to find out, isn't there?"

We were silent for a moment, holding hands, once more watching the fireflies do their thing. Turning on and off and on again.

I knew I should let go of Derek's hand. This back-and-forth squeezing thing was sending, to say the very least, a whacked-out-up-the-wazoo M & M. He probably figured I was a *femme fatale*, a predatory female firefly flashing out the teaser decoy signal, just waiting to pounce and devour him for dinner. Not a sensual, erotic, playful pounce but a cannibalistic orgy of blood and guts and gore that would leave him withered and wasted by the wayside.

It was just that holding his hand was so . . . delightful. Even in the midst of such a massively awkward conversation, his hand was so warm and soothing. I just couldn't seem to let go.

"You know," Derek finally said, "for someone who has supposedly lost the art of spontaneous conversation, you're a pretty damn good talker."

This time I took both of his hands in mine. "You know," I told him, looking right into his eyes. "For someone who's been squirreled away in their basement memorizing batting averages for the last two years, you're pretty damn good yourself."

"What are you doing?" I asked Sheila, nervously grabbing for her phone. We were standing on the other side of the stone wall, hidden from the potluck crowd, alone for the first time. Derek had gone off to get us another round of drinks. Non-alcoholic. Unlike Sheila, there was no way I was going to let my judgment be clouded by booze. My thinking was muddled enough as it was. "Put your phone away, for God's sake! What if someone sees us?"

"Chill!" Sheila said, texting away. "I'm a guest, not a member, so who gives a crap? No one can see us, anyway. Plus, they're too way busy droning on and on about their awesome phone-free lives to even care. Just let me get back to this one guy who's hitting on me. He seems sort of hot."

"Sheila! I mean it. Put it away. Now!"

I grabbed her cell and shoved it into her purse.

"Holy shit, Meg! What's wrong with you? Don't tell me these crazies have got you under their evil spell?"

"*Shhh!* Not so loud!"

Sheila laughed. "Oh my God! I can't believe this." She made the sign of the cross and backed away from me. "Stay away from me! What if it's contagious?"

"Stop it, Sheila!"

"No. *You* stop it. I've never seen anything like this, Meg. Netaholics are bad enough, but these people have gone hard-core eco-freak. Here's what I can't wrap my brain around: why would someone swear off text shit and then give a shit about goat shit? I don't get it. Just because tobacco and barley are crops doesn't mean recovering smokers and drinkers go all anti-agriculture on you, for Christ's sake. That's like throwing the goat baby out with the bathwater. But just look at these people. I'm like, what the fuck? Where's the connection?"

"Maybe you should ask Jonathan."

"Believe me, I tried. He went all Earth First weirdo on me. Evidently, they've been inviting these anti-tech radical rabble-rousers to their NA meetings and now they've been totally brainwashed by them. For the love of God, it's 2018 and they're acting as if it's 1811 all over again. The Return of the Luddites. Sounds like one of those gruesomely bad Netflix movies. Silly me—and I thought *The Hero of Nottinghamshire* was sucky enough. But this? This is way beyond ridiculous. I've never heard so much over-the-top politically correct bullshit in my entire life! It's as though these anonymous netaholics had their gray matter wrung through the wringer."

"Netaholics Anonymous. They're pretty out of the closet about it."

"Well, they should get back in, lock the door, and throw away the key. They've elevated the crazy to an insane level. They've swallowed the extremes of netaholism, Ludditism, and environmentalism, and then barfed back up a whole new beast. Enviro-Ludd-nuts or something. Maybe it's a Western Massachusetts thing, because I can't imagine any of this shit going down in Boston."

I looked around anxiously to see if anyone could hear us. "I imagine they call it something a little bit different than 'shit'," I said to her.

"Well, I call it *lunacy*, only that's way too weak a word."

"Okay. I get it. You've made your point. You can stop now." For some bizarre reason I was starting to feel a little defensive about the whole NA/Luddite thing.

"Do you know some of them actually hang out their wash to dry?" Sheila continued. Once she was on a rant, there was no reining her in. "On clotheslines. Can you imagine that? 'Retire the dryer' because it uses too much energy?"

"I'm doing that at Udder and Gramps's!"

"My point exactly. The brain washing and clothes drying has already begun. I'm surprised they even wash their clothes to begin with! And, listen to this. I just got my period, right? And damn if I don't run out of tampons. I can't find you anywhere, so I ask some random girl for one and, oh my God, she goes through the roof! She's like, 'Tampons? Are you for real?' And I'm like, 'Uh, well, in that I'm bleeding all over the place, I guess that I am,' and she goes, 'Girl, you gotta do better than that. Think of the amount of landfill space used tampons take up.' 'Um, I'd rather not,' I tell her. This just gets her into even more of a huff. 'How many tampons do you use in a year?' she asks me. I mean, seriously, here's a girl I've never met and she's asking me how many friggin tampons I use in a year? Can you believe this shit? Anyway, I'm like, 'Uh, I don't exactly count,' and she says, 'I bet you don't. Say you use twenty per cycle. That would be two hundred forty in a year. Two hundred forty! Think of the environmental impact of that. Think of the waste of resources. How can you possible justify tampon use?' Seriously? All I want is a damn tampon and she's making it out to be a crime against humanity. And, wait for it, it gets even more insane. She reaches into her purse and pulls out this menstrual cup thingie."

"This what?"

"Exactly. 'You stick this cup inside you and it catches your flow,' the girl tells me. 'Then you dump it out and reuse it. It won't dry out or disrupt the natural environment of your vagina. And it's so much better for the Earth.'"

Sheila was using this bitchy, sing-songy mocking voice, which was beginning to annoy the crap out of me.

But she wasn't finished. "All I wanted was a goddamn tampon and instead I get a three-hour lecture about menstrual health and saving the planet. I'm telling you, Meg, these people are beyond nutso."

Sheila had worked herself into a frenzy and her voice had gotten way too loud, something that happened whenever she drank. Once again, I glanced nervously over the stone wall to see if anyone was watching.

"*Shhh,*" I hushed again.

Sheila ignored me. "And the shit doesn't end there. One guy was trash-talking this other dude because he brought his tofu burgers to the potluck in a plastic bag. 'Plastic is evil, man!' he starts yelling. 'Ban the bag! Ban the bag!' I thought someone was going to throw a punch, for God's sake. I mean, there's doing it and then there's overdoing it. They're even down on recycling. 'If you can't reuse it, don't use it,' one girl told me. They're like the green Gestapo. It's scary."

Sheila drained the last of the beer in her bottle, burped three times, and continued her rant. "Did you see what one dude was wearing? Epiphytes. They were superglued to his shirt."

"Epi-what?"

"You know, little air plants. His shirt was covered with them. 'I breathe in their oxygen,' he tells me in this super-creepy, New Agey way. 'They breathe in my carbon dioxide. Our relationship is one of love and mutual respect. We are symbionts.' Seriously? Certifiable whack job or what?"

"What'd you do? Suggest that he glue on zucchini and cucumber plants instead?"

"I may have." Sheila put her bottle down and put her hand on my arm. "By the way, I hope you were okay with the whole self-pleasuring riff. I actually thought that was pretty inspired."

"Are you kidding me?" I gruffly pushed her hand away from me. "No, I am not okay. What were you thinking? I've never been so embarrassed in my entire life. I'm pissed at you, Sheila. Really pissed. That was *so* not funny."

"It wasn't meant to be funny. It was meant to drive the drooling dogs away. Which, by the looks of it, *you're* clearly not doing."

"What are you talking about?" I asked.

"Don't play dumb with me, girl. And don't think I didn't see you!"

"Didn't see me what?"

"Holding hands with Derek? And *then* holding hands with Jonathan? What were you thinking?"

"I wasn't holding hands with Jonathan," I said, avoiding her eyes. "And with Derek I was just . . ."

"Meg! We're not thirteen anymore, even though you're certainly acting like it!"

"Okay. So I was holding hands with Derek. It's not like it means anything."

"Yeah, right." Sheila threw her head back and laughed. "Congratulations, Meg!"

"Congratulations?"

"You've just made the great leap forward from Online Relationship Disorder to General Relationship Disorder. A much more inclusive category of fucked-up-ness. You must be very proud."

"Why does everyone keep telling me this? God, Sheila, you sound just like my grandfathers."

Sheila grabbed me by my shoulders and looked straight at me. "Listen to me, Meg. Why am I here? Huh? Tell me. Why?"

"Um . . . you mean, like, in a cosmic sense? Like, what is our purpose in life and that kind of thing?"

"Jesus, Meagan, stop! Did I come all the way from Boston so I could listen to two dudes go at it over compact fluorescent versus LED light-bulbs? So I could sit through an endless rant on the evils of bottled water? Seriously! Was that it?"

I avoided her eyes and instead picked at the purple nail polish on my thumb.

"I don't think so. You know why I'm here. It's to get you out of this offline mess you've somehow managed to get yourself into." Sheila tried to grab my hand but I flicked hers away again.

"So, I'm confused," she said, not letting go of this. "How exactly does holding hands with Derek and Jonathan fit into that picture?"

"I told you!" I could hear the defensive, peevish tone in my voice. "I wasn't holding hands with Jonathan. And with Derek? We're *friends*, for crying out loud!" This whole conversation was approaching a 9.7

on the Stupid scale. Maybe even a 9.8. "Friends hold hands. It's like what these . . . people do around here."

"You mean these clinically insane Ludd-nut green-assed no-text crazy people do?" Sheila snorted. "Not to be redundant, but if *you* were still texting, none of this would ever have happened."

I snorted right back at her.

"Think about it," Sheila said, grabbing both my hands and holding them tightly in hers so I couldn't break free.

What was with this incessant need for people to hold my hands?

She fixed her eyes on mine. "You can't text the way you're supposed to and hold hands at the same time, can you? No. You can't. If you had your phone, you wouldn't be in this mess now, would you? Maybe that's the reason you're holding hands with him in the first place. It's a substitute for your phone. Just something to do with those two things attached to your wrists. It's like a pacifier instead of a nipple. And a pretty piss-poor substitute, if you ask me.

"Look," Sheila continued, "I think I've made excellent headway on Jonathan. Give me a little more time and he'll be wanting excellent head. But not if you keep holding hands with him in some porno addict's bedroom!"

"We weren't holding hands!"

Derek returned, drinks in hand. He froze in place, staring wide-eyed at Sheila and me now holding hands.

"Hey," he said, his eyes darting back and forth between us.

"Hey," we both replied. I dropped Sheila's hands and sat on mine.

Sheila stood up and gave Derek a kiss on his cheek. "I need to go check out the grill. Rumor has it someone brought Madagascar Hissing Cockroaches to eat. Farm-reared insects! Woohoo! Not that I'm into the carnivore scene but, you know, I'll take bugs over beef *any* day!"

I watched Derek as he watched Sheila give a final jiggle, wiggle, and wink, and wove her way back toward the house.

"Have I told you that your friend is . . ."

"You have!" I said, once more reaching for his hand.

The potluck party was in full swing, but I just couldn't seem to leave the stone wall with Derek.

"I've been thinking about what you told me," he said, handing me what looked suspiciously like a barbecued bug in a bun. I placed it down carefully on the wall, solemnly put a napkin over its charred body, and pushed it as far away as possible.

Okay, I thought. *This is it.* The end of the relationship, or whatever the hell this mess was called. Sheila had taken care of Jonathan and now Derek was going to bail on me.

Huzzah and hooray!

But wait a minute. If all of my troubles were soon to be over, why the hell was I suddenly feeling so deflated? Why was I having trouble catching my breath?

I dropped his hand and anxiously gripped mine.

"What did I say to you again?" I asked, trying not to let panic creep into my voice.

"The endless guys swimming in the pool of possibilities," he replied. "Have you ever heard about that study they did with jam samples in the supermarket?"

"Say what?" I was a little unclear as to what jam had to do with swimming.

"I read about it online. Researchers set up a table in a supermarket with a couple of dozen samples of jam on it. Shoppers could stop by and try them out for free and then, if they were into it, buy the one they liked the best. Loads of people stopped and sampled, but hardly anyone bought."

"Strawberry," I said.

"Strawberry?"

"Yeah. That's my favorite. Or blueberry. I really like that one too."

"Good to know. I'll remember that. Anyway, the same folks doing the study went out a few days later and set up another table, this time with only a half dozen samples of jam, a quarter of the previous table's. Way fewer people *stopped*, but way more people *bought*."

Okay . . . so why exactly was Derek telling me this? The story was coming out of left field and seemed to have absolutely no relationship to relationships.

"Am I missing something here?" I asked, perplexed. "I mean, is there like a moral to this story?"

"Too many choices can make for paralysis. More is not always better."

Again, we sat in silence. Not an awkward silence. Not an *oh my God I cannot think of anything to say* silence. Just a pleasant, comforting quiet.

"I'm a little confused," I finally said. "Are you suggesting I should stop sampling and just buy?"

Once again, Derek took my hand in his and gave it yet another squeeze. He let the question go unanswered.

Just let go, I told myself again. *Just do it now. Don't prolong the issue.*

"What about you?" I asked.

"What do you mean?"

"Are you looking to just sample or are you interested in buying?"

Oh my God, I silently yelled at myself. *Shut up!* If that wasn't a come-on line then nothing was.

"Depends on the flavor," Derek answered. He reached over with his free hand and gently brushed away the firefly that had now relocated to my shirt and was flashing like crazy. Just like me.

The tremor inside me ratcheted up a few notches. I was approaching a 9.7.

"Do you have a favorite?" I asked.

"Strawberry," he said, looking right at me and smiling. "Definitely strawberry. I'd walk home with that one in a minute!"

If that was his idea of a bail line then . . .

After the potluck, Jonathan drove the three of us home. I used the excuse of helping a totally trashed Sheila make it back into the house as a way (admittedly, an awkward way) to ditch the two guys.

Avoidance. My *modus operandi*. When confronted with difficulty, run away.

I had just gotten into my pajamas and was getting ready for bed when Sheila staggered over to the bedroom window to close the curtains. "Uh oh," she slurred. "Take a little look-see outside."

I joined her at the window. There was Derek, leaning against the garden fence, gazing out into the orchard.

"Oh my God," I said. "That one is still here. What am I supposed to do now?"

"What do you want to do?" Sheila asked.

I put my sweatpants and T-shirt back on and went outside to join him by the fence.

We didn't say a word. A full moon was just rising from the east end of the apple orchard, and the night sky was once again lit up by countless fireflies. We just stood by the fence and stared.

"You're still here," I finally said. I was desperately trying to be annoyed with him. He was such a persistent son-of-a-gun, and he was totally messing with the plan.

"The fireflies," Derek said. "I was just wondering about the fireflies."

"Wondering what?" I asked.

"Wondering how sad it must be if you were one of the males flashing away and you saw the wrong female flashing you back, only you didn't know it. You'd be like, yeah! I am going to knock this one out of the park! It's home run time! And then, before you knew what hit you, *BAM!* You're dinner. Striking out I could handle. I've done that plenty of times. But dinner? Ouch."

Who knew that this whole firefly thing would take on such a life of its own? I thought about my conversation with Gramps about the lightning bugs. About me giving off the wrong flash. About my screwed-up flight pattern.

Poor Derek. I could see him wordlessly flashing away, his whole body practically lighting up—I had to turn my head away, it was so blindingly bright.

I tried to put myself in his shoes, or rather his wings. He was probably perplexed as hell, wondering whether or not he was even interacting with his own species.

"What do the bees do at night?" he asked, looking, as I was, to move on to safer subjects.

"Hang out," I told him. "Just like us. Wanna go see?"

Hand in hand, we walked back down to the beehives. The hot, humid night had sent the bees pouring out of the entrance. In the moonlight we could see thousands of them spilling over the wooden sides, hanging on to each other, furiously fanning away, methodically trying to cool off their hive by beating their wings and moving the air.

"Mind the electric fence," I said. "Twice would not be nice."

"Believe me, I'm still in shock," he replied.

We sat and watched the bees.

"Boy, they just don't stop working, do they?" Derek said.

"You mean the *girls* don't stop working. Remember that the *boys*—"

"I know, I know. They're a bunch of lazy, good-for-nothing bums. I got the message loud and clear."

I laughed.

"Can I ask you something personal?" Derek turned and looked at me. We were still holding hands. "You don't have to answer if you don't want to."

"Does it have to do with female fireflies going down on guys? Or drone-bee penises that explode in midair?"

When Derek laughed, he did a little shake-rattle-and-roll with his whole body. He just sort of quivered in place for a moment. A quaint, cute little quiver. And the whole time he laughed, he continued to flash away. Laugh and flash. Flash and laugh. Over and over and over again.

"I though you said those things were off-limits?" he asked.

"You're right, I did. So, as long as it doesn't have to do with that, or, for that matter, cucumbers and zucchinis, go for it. Flash, I mean ask away."

"Let's just say, hypothetically speaking, you were out shopping at a market."

"Okay."

"You've got your basket slung over your arm and you've already picked out your whole-wheat bread and your organic peanut butter and now the only thing left for you to buy for that perfect picnic lunch is—"

"Madagascar Hissing Cockroaches?"

"Close. But let's go with jam instead. So off you go to the jam aisle—"

"Is there such a thing?"

"In this market, yes. But, wait a minute. Oh no! Yikes and double yikes! For some strange, unfathomable reason there are only two kinds of flavors."

"Tragedy!"

"Exactly. Only two. Strawberry and blueberry."

I clapped my hands together. "Oooh la la! Lucky me! My two faves."

"But wait a minute. There's a catch."

"Oh no!" I made my best frowny, pouty face. "Why does there always have to be a catch?"

"'Cause then my hypothetical dilemma thingie makes absolutely no sense at all. Which it may not anyway, so just humor me and go with it. Okay?"

"Got it," I said, taking his hand back in mine.

"You're going on a picnic with two friends and you only have enough money to buy—"

"Let me guess . . . one jar of jam."

"Bingo. And one of the friends likes strawberry while the other guy, I mean 'friend,' likes blueberry."

"Hmmm. . . And just who might this other guy, I mean 'friend,' possibly be?" It suddenly seemed pretty damn clear to me where Derek was going with all this. How did he possibly know what Jonathan's favorite flavor of jam was? Was that something you shared in a netaholics meeting, like a hidden handshake or secret sign or something?

"Answer the question," Derek said.

"I didn't know there was one."

"Strawberry or blueberry. Your choice."

I was no longer swimming in an endless pool of possibilities. Instead I was standing next to one. It was time to fish. Or cut bait. Or . . .

"Honey," I said, my brain buzzing with bewilderment, "I've really got to get back to the house and check on Sheila."

Hand in hand, we walked back up the hill.

Chapter 18

"Hey!" I said.

"Hey!" Jonathan replied.

Jonathan? Oh my God! What was *he* doing here?

It was Saturday morning after the potluck, and he had just pulled into Udder and Gramps's driveway. Now he was leaning up against the garden fence watching me do my morning ritual—harvesting vegetables, weeding the garden, and squeezing the guts out of bean beetles.

Harvest, weed, and squeeze. Harvest, weed, and squeeze. It was quite the gig.

Flustered to see him, I stood up, stamped my feet, clapped my hands, and turned around.

"What are you doing?" Jonathan asked, looking quite confused. That seemed to be the usual effect I had on boys: sending them into a state of profound confusion.

I burst into the gardening song that Udder and Gramps had taught me a few days before:

Oats and beans and barley grow,
Oats and beans and barley grow,
Do you or I or anyone know how oats and beans and barley grow?

Even though I was making a complete fool of myself, I had to admit: my voice was much better than Sheila's.

First the farmer plants the seeds,
Stands up tall and takes her ease,
Stamps her feet and claps her hands,
And turns around to view her lands.

Once more, I stamped my feet, clapped my hands, and twirled around.

Jonathan looked bemused.

"Don't you know the old kid's song?" I asked him. "My grandfathers still sing it. Not that they grow oats and barley, but there's a shit-ton of beans here! Anyway . . . what the hell are *you* doing here?"

I had thrown on my usual gardening outfit—a ridiculously oversized *DUMP TRUMP* T-shirt, courtesy of Gramps, and my blue, low-waist short-shorts, courtesy of the Urban Outfitters half-off department. No shoes. No bra. It was still morning, but the July sun had risen early and my T-shirt was already drenched in sweat, my knees and thighs streaked with dirt.

"Um . . . ," Jonathan said. "I wanted to apologize for last night. I mean, I don't feel like we connected in the way I was hoping. You know, I really like your friend Sheila. I really do. But she was sort of . . . I don't know . . . getting in the way. It was all a bit awkward."

Oh God. Here we go again. Flash, flash, flash.

"No worries," I said. "I'm pretty used to it. She does this to me all the time. I've never met a guy she hasn't stolen."

"Seriously?"

"Actually, I'm not serious at all. In fact, I deliberately invited her last night just so she could sweep you off your feet and steal you away from me. Save you from the trauma of unrequited love."

"Seriously?" Jonathan asked again, looking even more confused than before. Just like Derek, the poor guy didn't know which way was up.

My newfound ability to converse spontaneously was having unforeseen consequences. Being so new at it, my mouth would fully engage before my brain had time to process the incoming information. Textless talking meant no editing before hitting the Send button.

"Cucumbers?" I offered him, pointing to my basket full of them. "Zucchini? I've got way more than even *I* can handle."

The intent here was not to make Jonathan squirm. It really wasn't. But squirm he did. He was looking in every possible direction other than mine.

"A hike," he finally managed to say.

"A what?"

"A hike. I was going to go on a hike this morning. I tried calling you but . . ."

"Phone-free zone." I pointed to the crude sign Gramps had made hanging in the garden next to Gandhi. An image of a cell phone with a slash through it.

"Cute!" Jonathan said. "Anyway, I was sort of wondering if . . ."

"A hike?" I interrupted. "As in walking up a mountain or something?"

"Exactly!" Jonathan said, a hopeful look on his face.

"Oh my God! Sheila would just love that. She is so into hiking. I think she backpacked the whole Appalachian Trail in one week last summer."

"Isn't the Appalachian Trial, like, over two thousand miles long?"

"Okay. So it may have taken her two weeks. I can't remember. Let me go get her."

"Um . . . actually . . . I was thinking more about . . ."

"No worries. I'm fine with you going with her. I really am. And anyway, there's no way I can possibly leave this garden. I mean, look at it. You close your eyes and the damn zucchini grows another inch. If I didn't pick 'em now, they'd engulf the whole house. They're like Jack's beanstalk, for God's sake, only minus the Jack and squash for the magic beans. And fortunately, as of yet no giants. And here's the good news: we didn't even have to trade in a cow for the seeds."

I reached under the squash leaves, gave a quick twist and pull, and held up a seven-inch zucchini for him to look at.

"Perfect size," I said. "I like them young and tender."

Jonathan opened his mouth to speak but nothing came out.

"Don't get too close. They may be carnivorous, for all I know. Anyway, let me go get Sheila for you. She's been sleeping off last night but I'm pretty sure she's risen from the crypt by now. She'll be thrilled."

"Leave me alone!" Sheila groaned, pushing me away. She grabbed back her pillow and once again secured it firmly over her head.

"You gotta get up!" I yelled, wrestling the pillow away from her and flinging it across the room. "Now! You're going on a hike!"

"Go away! I'm hung over! Come back tomorrow!"

"Up! For God's sake, Jonathan is here and he's taking you on a hike." I pushed her into a sitting position.

"No. Hike. Just. Sleep." Sheila lay back down and curled into the fetal position.

"No rest for the wicked. Come on. Upsy-daisy!" I sat her up again.

"A hike?" she said groggily, her voice still raspy from the party the night before. "You've got to be kidding me!"

"Nope. Jonathan is down there waiting." I felt sort of mean pushing Sheila so forcibly onto Jonathan, but that was the plan, right? And Sheila had totally bought into it.

"He asked me on a hike?"

"No! He asked me. But you're the one going. Come on. Please. You've got to get dressed. Now!"

Once more Sheila lay back down in bed but I pinched her hard and made her sit up again.

"No! No! And no again! I am *not* going on a damn hike. I'm too hungover to even sit up."

"You have to. Please. For me. Best friends forever, right? How many times have you said you'd take a bullet for me? Well, the gun's been fired. Are you going to jump in front of me or not?"

Sheila groaned. "I cannot believe that after what I told those guys, they are still so into you!"

"Told them what?"

"Well . . . you know."

"That I'm a celibate, masturbating Luddite?"

"Yeah. That. And the other thing."

"Oh God," I said, rummaging around in her duffle bag looking for something for her to wear. "There's more?"

"Kind of."

"Kind of what?"

"Kind of yeah."

"Why do I think I don't want to hear this?"

"It's not that it's bad or anything."

"Out with it then!"

"I think I may have told them you were a lesbian," Sheila said, grimacing.

I threw a pair of shorts at her.

"A lesbian? Seriously?"

"Maybe I said you were bi. Or gender-fluid. It was at the end of the party and I can't exactly remember where I was going with that one." Sheila lay back down and I had to pinch her, this time even harder, to get her up again.

"Oh God! And you told this to . . . ?"

"Um . . . as I recall there was quite a crowd at the time. So maybe . . . everybody?"

"Derek was there?"

"Derek. Jonathan. Peter the Porno. That girl Karen. The goat dude. Practically the whole party. You must have been in the bathroom at the time."

"Sheila!"

"What? We love lesbians. And wasn't that what I was supposed to be doing? Making you distant and unavailable to the guys? And anyway, nothing else seemed to be working—now, did it?"

"Earth to Sheila! Spouting off that I'm a celibate, masturbating, Luddite lesbian is not exactly a turn-off! These are *guys*, Sheila! *Guys!* This is what their friggin fantasies are made of! They think with their penises, remember?"

"Oh, I see. And are you telling me that holding hands with the entire party was not a turn-*on*?"

"Derek is not the whole party!"

"Derek, Jonathan, me . . ."

"I was not holding hands with Jonathan. And I only held your hand because you were too loaded to make it to the car without me." I ignored the whole hand-holding scene with her down by the stone wall.

I heard a noise, went to the window and looked out, just as another car was pulling into the driveway.

"Holy shit!" I said. "Derek is here too? For God's sake, Sheila! What have you done?"

I had finally gotten Sheila halfway presentable and hurried her out of the house so we could face the two boys. Fortunately, even in her hungover, bedraggled state Sheila still looked incredibly hot.

"Hey," Sheila said, scrunching up her eyes in the morning light and rubbing her forehead.

"Hey," Jonathan said.

"Hey," Derek said.

"Hey," I said.

This was ridiculous. Once again, guys were popping up like weeds. I wouldn't have been surprised to see Peter the Porno and Jeremy the Goatherd pulling in next. And, given what Sheila had blabbed, who knows, maybe Karen the Cat Killer was only a car length behind.

"What's going on?" Derek asked. He and Jonathan were anxiously eyeing each other.

"Cukes and zukes," I said, holding out the basket of garden goodies. Oh my God, where was the duct tape for my stupid mouth when I needed it?

"Jonathan and I are going on a hike," Sheila said, forcing a smile.

"A hike?" Derek asked, looking relieved.

"A hike!" Sheila chirped, once more shooting me her patented killer look. "Joy of joys! Thrills, chills, and daffodils! I am totally psyched. Thanks so much for asking me." She turned toward Jonathan, and put her hand on his arm.

"Well . . . ," Jonathan stammered. "No offense. But I actually sort of—"

Sheila interrupted him. "I hope you don't mind stopping on the way for about sixteen cups of coffee." She had already drained the mug that I had brought down to the garden for myself. "A few more pick-me-ups, and I may just be able to pick up my legs to move."

"You think *I* get wired on caffeine?" I said, winking at the boys. "Just wait till you see Sheila!"

"Actually . . . ," Jonathan said, "I was hoping that . . ."

"Have a wonderful time!" I quickly ushered the two of them into Jonathan's car. There was no way I was going to let him finish even half a sentence. "Sheila, remember who you are. Don't do anything I wouldn't do!"

From inside the car Sheila glared at me. Jonathan glared at Derek. Derek stared at me. And I just wondered what kind of a monster mess I had created.

"Bye," Sheila said.

"Bye," Derek said.

"Bye," I said.

Jonathan was still trying desperately to get a word in edgewise, "This isn't exactly what I—"

"Bye!" I yelled again, slamming his door shut, running around the car like I was in some sort of manic Chinese fire drill, and then slamming Sheila's door. I slapped the hood twice, gave the bumper a kick, and sent them on their merry way.

Guys are so predictable. You dangle a pair of braless breasts out there and, even with the veil of a grimy T-shirt on, it's as though you'd swung a sledgehammer at their heads. I'm not for a moment saying mine rate a 10, or even close to it. Compared to Sheila's, they're not even in the same ballpark. But I could see Derek staring at where my tan line, bordering on a burn from working in the garden, ended, and where the whiteness of my boobs began. His neck was doing this swiveling contortion. He looked like one of the owls that Gramps and I had seen in the woods behind the orchard.

"*Who's awake?*" I sang. "*Me too. Who's awake? Me too!*" It was turning out to be quite the singing morning.

"Huh?" Derek said. "What?" Once more: total confusion.

"A Great Horny Owl. That's the call they make. Gramps taught me. We've actually had real conversations with them. Seriously. They sit in that dead branch in the tree over there and we *whooo* back and forth. It's so sweet!"

"You're like the wildlife whisperer," Derek said. "Bees. Fireflies. And now owls. *Whoooo knewwww.*"

I laughed.

"Anyway," he asked. "This owl thing is relevant . . . how?"

"It isn't," I said, pointing a zucchini accusingly at him. "The question is, are you? Why are you back here again?"

After our beehive chat the previous evening, I had once again panicked, bailed, and fled indoors, leaving him all alone still flashing away, with only the circling fireflies to keep him company. I had stood next to the window, watching him as he leaned on the garden fence for the longest time, staring off into space.

Derek glanced around awkwardly and kicked a pebble with his foot. "Actually, I was wondering if you were left-handed."

Now *I* was the one who was confused. Left-handed? Please don't tell me he was inquiring about my self-pleasuring technique! I silently cursed Sheila. Was I never going to live down the fingers-versus-vegeta-bles thing?

"You're joking, right?" I asked.

"No, no. Not at all. I'm the coach of a left-handed softball team. Actually, we fudge a little. My center fielder and second baseman throw right but bat left. And, if you really want to know the truth, most of the other players are totally right-handed, but," Derek's voice went into a whisper, "you have to promise to keep that to yourself." He resumed talking normally, albeit a little nervously. "Anyway, we're down a player for this afternoon's game and I'm in desperate need of a left-handed shortstop. Or a right-handed one. Whichever you are would totally work."

"I thought you were off the fantasy baseball thing?"

"I am. This game is for real."

"Wait a minute: you came all the way out here to ask me if I wanted to play baseball?"

"Softball. I tried calling but . . ."

I pointed to the phone-free garden sign.

"Awesome," he said. "Anyway, why else did you think I came here? I can't exactly, you know, ask you out or anything."

Now it was my turn to kick at the dirt on the ground. "You can't exactly ask me out . . . um . . . why again?" I was having a momentary lapse of memory.

"Because you're a celibate, relationship-adverse . . . you know . . ."

"Masturbating lesbian. Oh, right. Sorry. I forgot."

Derek looked at me quizzically.

"Anyway, it's just softball. Slow-pitch. It's really fun."

I tightly gripped the zucchini in my hand and considered my options.

What made the most sense was to put the kibosh on this whole Derek thing right now. Tell him assertively, in no uncertain terms that, once and for all, thanks but no thanks, this awkward little game we were playing was over. No more last ups. No more extra innings. We. Were. Done.

But shortstop? For a softball game?

Why did that suddenly sound so appealing?

I wasn't bad at sports. High school gym classes had their share of total klutzes and girlie-girls scared to death they'd break a nail, but I certainly wasn't one of them. Gym teachers would watch me hit a ball or score a goal or make a basket and they'd be all over me.

"You're a natural," they'd say. "You've got a good arm. You should try out for the team!"

"What team?" I'd ask.

"THE team!" they'd unfailingly answer.

But I just didn't care.

I had better things to do with my time.

Like, duh, go online!

When we did play softball in gym class I was actually pretty good at it. After all, there really wasn't that much to it. When it was your team's ups, you sat on the bench texting and then you got up and hit the ball and ran the bases. When it was their team's ups, you stood in the field texting until you caught the ball or scooped it up and threw them out.

Rocket science? I don't think so.

I looked down at the zucchini still in my hand.

To play or not to play. That was the question.

"Xander's got nothing on me!" I took the zucchini in my left hand, went into an exaggerated windup, and flung the squash hard at Derek.

A little too hard. Caught totally by surprise, the poor guy couldn't get his hands down fast enough. He took my fastball, or rather fastsquash, right between his legs.

"Oh my God!" I said, grabbing his hands and helping him to his feet. "I am so sorry. Error, shortstop. My bad!"

Derek let out a groan. "I thought we had a pact here? I thought we had a deal!"

"A deal?" I asked, not letting go of his hands.

"No penises!" he shouted in a high-pitched, castrato-like squeal.

This much was becoming crystal clear: no matter what the circumstances, repeatedly saying it, even shouting it, was just *not* going to make it so.

Chapter 19

So I said yes. I mean, after all, what choice did I really have? I knew enough about the sport to know you *had* to have a shortstop, and it wasn't like he was asking me out on a date or anything. I was doing him a favor. That was it. At the potluck I had made my position on offline boys crystal clear.

"You look nice this morning," Gramps said, kissing me on the forehead and repositioning a wayward strand of hair that was sticking to my eyelash. "As always."

After hitting Derek in the you-know-whats, I had gone back into the house to put on a bra, socks, and sneakers, and I was heading back outside.

"No wonder the dogs can't stop sniffing around here," Gramps added with a grin.

"Curtis!" Udder said. "Stop it! That's degrading and insulting. Meagan does not need that from you."

"I didn't call her a dog. She's just the opposite. I called her *guy* that."

"He's not 'my guy,' remember?" I poked Gramps gently in the side.

"You could have fooled me. Just look at him."

All three of us glanced out of the kitchen window and there was Derek, once again propped up on the garden fence, his head pitched backwards, his eyes closed, and his nose tipped comically up into the air, sniffing away.

We all laughed.

"All right, you know the drill: Udder, don't you dare do the laundry. Gramps, watch the weed and stay out of the garden weeds while I'm gone. And I'm telling you right now: if anyone dares to touch that vacuum cleaner, there will be hell to pay. That's my job and both of you know it. Do you understand me?"

"Aye aye, captain," they said, saluting me.

"Ready to go?" Derek asked, seemingly recovered from yet another groin-grimacing incident.

"Let's do this," I said, scrambling into the passenger seat of his car.

Once again, I had left my phone at Udder and Gramps's, just as I'd done when I went to the NA meetings. Not that this was one of them, but at a softball game with Derek and God only knows what other NA'ers it just seemed the appropriate thing to do.

But it wasn't easy. Far from it. Going into town without my phone, knowing I could be online in an instant and doing my thing, was incredibly painful. Without my phone I felt as though there was a hole in my soul. Anxious as I was to find myself once more in a car with a boy, I desperately longed for that soothing sound of the *ping*, that spine-tingling thrill of an incoming text. My FOMO—Fear of Missing Out—was freaking me out. How could I possibly know what was happening online if I was off? I knew that something incredibly important was going on out there in Cyberland, something much more important than a silly softball game, and it seemed tragic not to be in on the action. The whole phone-free thing was like donning the Cloak of Invisibility. It made me uneasy and jumpy.

The last time I had been downtown online binging, I had not only managed to swipe away one hundred twenty-five boys (which meant one hundred twenty-five more *Passion* points—huzzah and hooray for me!) but also get my celebrity fix with the lowdown on such need-to-know, must-see essentials including:

> *19 of the Most Cringe-Worthy Celebrity Near-Naked Photos*
> *12 Body Parts Celebrities Have Shockingly Insured*
> *8 Tragic Facts about Celebrity Child Movie Stars Gone Bad*
> *14 of the Creepiest Celebrity Photobombs You've Ever Seen*
> *10 of the Worst Celebrity Wedding Cakes Ever*
> *13 Reasons Celebrities Are Just Like Us (Spoiler Alert: Some Do Their Own Laundry!)*
> *15 of the Most Embarrassing Celebrity Haircuts*
> *20 Outrageously Funny Photos of Celebrities Being Scared S**tless in Haunted Houses*
> *9 Celebrity Pets Caught Hilariously Doing Things They Shouldn't Have*

One link after another had finally led to a what-the-fuck link which had led to a how-the-hell-did-I-get-here link and before I knew it my bladder had practically exploded and hours had passed and I had missed cooking dinner for Udder and Gramps, and by the time I got home they were super-pissed-off and accused me of violating the only-go-down-town-for-two-and-a-half-hours agreement we had made and blah blah blah, and before I could stop myself, I had made a bunch of snarky comments I really shouldn't have and then gone storming off upstairs to my bedroom, slamming every door I could find only to come down a half hour later to grovel and apologize and beg for forgiveness.

Whew! The downtown part had been great. The other part? Not so much.

But now, will wonders never cease, here I was: sitting next to Derek on the way to a softball game . . . and we were both totally phone-less.

In the past, whenever I was in a car I'd be texting on my phone. If I was driving I'd text. If I was a passenger I'd text. And whoever I was with—a parent, Sheila, another kid—they'd be doing the exact same thing. On the extremely rare occasions (I could probably count them on one hand) when I had actually been in a car with someone who wasn't on their phone, I'd just phub away—phone snub whoever I was with without ever thinking twice about it.

But now, with Derek, no phone meant no phub—hence the rub. Once again, I actually had to talk, not text.

"Jonathan's not on your team?" I asked him. After making a quick pit stop at The Freckled Fox in Florence to refill my mug with coffee, we were on our way to Florence Fields in Northampton for the softball game.

Derek looked at me anxiously, as if the hand-holding-that-wasn't-really-hand-holding incident in Peter the Porno's bedroom was still bugging him. "I know Jonathan's good at a lot of things," he replied. "But fortunately, softball isn't one of them."

"Fortunately?"

"Well, you know . . . I mean . . . it's sort of nice not to . . ."

Amused at his fumbling for words, I tried to hide my smile.

"Got it," I said. "But what I don't quite get is the left-handed softball thing. Is that like a weird league rule or something? Does everyone have to do it?"

"No, not at all," Derek said. "Just our team. And, like I said, we don't really do it either."

"And the reason is . . ."

"Well, we decided to mix it up a little. You know, get a little creative, combine politics with sports. Be a team with a message."

"And that message is . . . ?"

"Anything from the left."

"What sort of 'left' are we talking about?" I asked.

"The political left. Progressive politics. The Lefty Luddites. That's us."

Derek turned to me and proudly pointed to his T-shirt with the team name boldly displayed in electric yellow letters on the bright blue front.

"Awesome," I said.

Derek smiled.

"So is your Trump shirt," he said. "I love it."

I was wearing a T that Gramps had bought me with a picture of President Trump's face photoshopped to look like Hitler's, toothbrush moustache and all. Very frightening.

"I'm not even allowed to say Trump's name out loud in front of Udder and Gramps," I said to Derek. "They refer to him as 'evil incarnate,' 'the spawn of the devil,' 'he-who-shall-not-be-named.' At first I thought they were talking about my phone, but now I know they mean the president."

"I'm liking your grandfathers more and more," Derek said.

"His crazy late-night tweets have done nothing to raise their opinion of cells, that's for sure."

"Nor mine. The man is a lunatic. If you want to wear that T-shirt, it's fine. Totally fits in with the message. But if you want to change into one of ours for the game, I've got an extra shirt for you." He reached into the back seat and pulled one out of his bag. "I figured you for a small, but I brought a couple of sizes."

"You think I'm small?" I asked.

"No, of course they aren't, I mean, *you* aren't. It's just that . . ."

"Eyes on the road," I ordered, slipping "Trump/Hitler" off and the small-sized "Lefty Luddites" on.

"Whoa!" Derek pulled a Jonathan (or was it a Karen?) and swerved into the breakdown lane, narrowly missing a parked car, two mailboxes, and a fire hydrant.

Yet another reason why fully autonomous cars are the wave of the future.

Chapter 20

"I want to be perfectly clear about this," I said to Derek as we pulled into the playing field and parked right behind the backstop. We got out of the car and started walking toward the bench. "No M & M's. No mixed messages. This is not a date."

"Definitely," Derek said. "Not a date. I wouldn't dream of mixing sports with pleasure."

"Good. To recap last night's conversation. I don't do offline guys. Understood?"

"Got it. No date. No guys."

"No nothing. Not even hands." I crossed my arms, furrowed my brow, and tried to look as stern as possible.

"And, just so I know where you're coming from, is it no . . . you know . . . that too?"

"What?" I was confused.

"I mean, no guys. That much is clear. But . . . Sheila said you batted for the other side."

"What are you talking about?"

"You know . . . the girl-and-girl kind of thing."

"Oh my God, I totally forgot about that."

"You totally forgot that you're a lesbian?"

I let out a long sigh.

Here we go again, I thought. Off on yet another rambling, painfully awkward, offline, real-world conversation. I tried to remember that factoid I had learned in history class—was it Patrick Henry who said "Give me my cell phone, or give me death?" or was it some other dude?

"Look, Derek," I began. To tell the truth or not, that was always the dilemma. I recalled another one of those Revolutionary War heroes, George Washington, who had famously replied "I cannot tell a lie" when busted by his father. But one's sexual orientation seemed way bigger a deal than cutting down a stupid cherry tree. "Sheila had a few too many last night and got a little carried away. I mean, I had asked her to come to the potluck to . . ."

I stopped walking, my heart pounding away, panic engulfing me. I was not in my element. Instead of a comforting screen staring back at me, here were Derek's big brown eyes staring right through me. With those damn pouty lips and his longish hair with that one wayward, kinky curl that he kept having to flick off his left eyebrow that I was finding so difficult not to reach over and give a playful yank.

Here in the now of the non-virtual, face-to-face world, everything was so much more . . . real.

Arghhh!!!

"You asked her to come to . . . ," he persisted.

"Okay," I said. "Can you handle the truth?"

"I'll do my best."

I leaned over to him and whispered in his ear. "I am not a lesbian. I'm not bi or gender-fluid or anything like that. Of course I watch queer movies on Netflix, but I'm totally straight. But don't you dare tell anyone or I'll have to kill you! Do you understand me? And I swear I'll do it in a slow and painful way! I'll be worse than Trump. Way worse. I'll be like Vlad the Impaler. I'll decapitate, disembowel, and dismember you. Then I'll bury what's left of you in a shallow grave in the garden, and leave your remains to be consumed by the goddamn bean beetles! Do I make myself clear?"

Derek looked confused.

"All of this because you're not a lesbian?"

"Believe me, I wish I was. Girls are so much less confusing than guys."

Derek's eyebrows edged upward in the most ridiculous of ways, his kinky curl fluttering back and forth. By this time, we were sitting on the bench, and his hands, clasped tightly in his lap, began to twitch. I locked my arms up even tighter.

"You could have fooled me," he said.

I did my best to scowl. "Like I said, Sheila got carried away. She's just trying to look out for me and do the right thing."

"So Sheila's a lesbian?"

"No! No one's a lesbian, for crying out loud!" I couldn't believe we were still having this is-you-is-or-is-you-ain't-a-lesbian conversation. "Why is this so confusing to you?"

It was Derek's turn to sigh. "Sorry," he said. "But just so I'm perfectly clear, no . . ."

"No penises. No vaginas. No nothing." I unfolded my arms, reached out and took his hand firmly in mine. "Come on. Let's play ball."

The Lefty Luddites were clearly not your ordinary run-of-the-mill-co-ed-rec-league softball team, the kind where everybody's just out to have fun on a beautiful summer day and nobody really gives a shit about the score. No way. This was a team that took softball seriously, that ratcheted the game up to a whole new level.

Not only were they over-the-top dedicated to kicking ass on the playing field, but they were also dead serious about proselytizing their left-wing political propaganda to the max.

Rather than a twelve-step recovery program like NA, they had synthesized their shtick down to three steps. As best as I could figure it out, it went down something like this:

Lefty Luddites Step Number 1: Win. Games were not to be taken lightly. The Luddites were out to have a good time, but damn if they weren't going to do whatever it took to pound out the runs.

Testosterone was practically oozing out of Derek's orifices as we sat on the bench. I could almost see it: a wispy hormonal fog rising above him. He even smelled different.

"Show me a good loser and I'll show you a loser," he growled, having abandoned his Mister Nice Guy persona.

I had noticed a similar characteristic in Gramps. He was the epitome of a left-wing progressive ideologue—all about peace and love and co-operation and respect and compassion and blah blah blah. But put him in front of a TV with the Red Sox on and he went nutso.

"Kill the bastards!" he'd yell. "Annihilate the sons of bitches!"

Just the other morning I had come down to breakfast, and found him grumbling at his cereal. I had just assumed it was his arthritis acting up and he was down on the whole getting-old-is-a-total-drag thing.

"I am so sorry," I said, putting my arms around him and giving him a huge hug.

"How did you know?" he asked, still scowling away.

"How did I know . . . ?"

"That the Sox lost, for Christ's sake! In eleven innings! Again! They have no relief pitching! How can you possibly win games when you have no goddamn relief pitching? Tell me! How?"

I did not even attempt an answer to that most profound of questions.

Lefty Luddites Step Number 2: Educate and Agitate. Whenever the opportunity presented itself, the Luddites espoused the "technology is evil" paradigm, promoted rebellion against the satanic worship of all handheld electronic devices, and called out opponents on their heinous addiction to everything online.

The game hadn't even started yet, and the Luddites were all clustered around the bench, chatting it up, fist-bumping each other, getting psyched.

Across the infield? The mirror opposite. Sitting on their bench, each and every member of the Willy Wonkas, this week's opposing team, was sheltered in their own online cocoon, mindlessly texting away, unaware of even their own teammates' existence. One big group phub.

Karen the Cat Killer, today to be less harshly referred to as Karen the Pitcher, led the team in a chant:

One, two, three, wow!
Put away your cell phones now!
Four, five, six, hey!
We've got a softball game to play!

The Wonkas didn't even glance up from their phones, completely oblivious to our verbal haranguing.

I empathized with the Wonkas. I really did. If that were *me* sitting on *their* bench, I'd be doing the exact same thing. This whole Lefty Luddites, Big Brother shaming approach to texting didn't sit well with me. If the Luddites wanted to give each other crap for their own texting antics, that was fine. But the "disgrace and debase" tactic toward the other team seemed a little harsh. Yelling at people to stop texting when everyone else sitting next to them was doing the same thing was just not going to work. If it were me sitting on their bench listening to some crazies ranting and raving from across the field, I'd just get pissed off and text even more. There had to be a better way to change behavior.

I kept my mouth shut while the chanting continued.

Lefty Luddites Step Number 3: Educate and agitate some more. But here the Luddites broadened the political agenda beyond the typical anti-technology Ludditisms.

Every game, one of the Lefty Luddites was given the task of promoting their very own "lefty issue of the day." They could bring signs, lyrics to songs, chants, inspirational verse, performance art, whatever floated their boat. Throughout the game they were affectionately called King or Queen Ludd. His or Her Royal Highness would give the rest of the Luddites a short sermon on their hot-button topic and then, as long as it conformed to the rigid criteria of left-wing political propaganda, they were ready to play ball.

So far the season had gone like this:

- *Stop the Occupation—Support Palestinian Rights!* Lefty Luddites 12, Gone Fishing 8.
- *System Change, Not Climate Change!* Willy Wonkas 11, Lefty Luddites 10.
- *Black Lives Matter!* Lefty Luddites 17, Bubba's Balloons 14.
- *Abortion Rights Now! Keep Your Laws Off Our Bodies!* Lefty Luddites 8, Hot Dogs 7.
- *Transgender Equality in the Workplace!* Lefty Luddites 23, Dashes and Dots 0. Game called due to mercy rule. Evidently the poor Dashes and Dots really, really sucked.
- *Immigrate, Don't Discriminate!* Lefty Luddites 4, Whodunits 2. Low-scoring because all of the Luddite girls wore burkas in solidarity with their Muslim sisters. This totally messed with their ability to see the ball, let alone hit it. Fortunately, the Whodunits were blind as zucchinis, even without burkas.

"Wait a minute," I asked Derek. "The only game you've lost is the climate-change game?"

"Depressing, isn't it? Our tying run—me!—was tagged out at home to end the game. Believe me, I didn't sleep for a week afterwards. That's why this rematch is the most important game *ever!*"

Politics had definitely never been my thing. My parents and I were always way too busy texting to have any sort of discussion about it. I didn't read about it. I didn't talk about it. I didn't even go online about it. I totally failed to see how anything political was relevant to my life in any way, shape, or form. In my view, politicians, no matter their political party, were all the same—full of bullshit and bluster and bravado and blah blah blah. From what I could tell, all they really seemed to care about was getting themselves elected and reelected.

Udder and Gramps were a different story. They were politically hyperactive to an insane degree. They'd go on and on about this issue and that, peace and economic justice and gay rights and climate change and power to the people. Every morning they'd start their day by listening to Democracy Now on Valley Free Radio and launching into a tirade against Trump and his shenanigans. All of this would just go in one of my ears and straight out the other without once even tweaking so much as a single solitary neuron in between.

It wasn't that I didn't care. I did. I mean, seriously, who's against peace, for Christ's sake? And I couldn't quite figure out why anyone would give a shit about who slept with whom. It was all good. And I knew Trump was evil. I mean, everyone knew that, right?

I just had better things to pay attention to. I was a busy girl. I mean, just managing the incoming on *Passion* took a huge amount of my energy. I took my obligation to promptly message back pretty damn seriously. I even gave the creeps and losers a decent brush-off as long as they kept their penis pictures to themselves. Keeping up with my gaggle of guys online was practically a full-time job.

Politics just seemed so distant and foreign. Meaningless. I couldn't see the point of getting all bent out of shape over it. I had enough on my plate as it was.

The only issue I had ever paid any real attention to was climate change. The idea of no electricity completely freaked me out. With all of these weird weather events and increasingly frequent power outages we were having, the likelihood of literally being offline seemed to be increasing exponentially and then, how the hell would I charge my phone?

CA: Charge Anxiety. Another acronym to add to my repertoire.

Anyway, sitting there on the dugout bench with a bunch of political zealots my very own age was quite the trip. An eye-opening experience.

Today was Derek's turn to be King Ludd.

The pet issue he had chosen was fracking, the same thing I had yelled about that first time we had coffee together at the café.

"And fracking is . . . what again?" I asked. I had sort of thought that maybe it was some new slang for fucking. But it wasn't as though the Luddites were prudes or anything, so I couldn't quite figure out why they'd be so down on that.

"Hydraulic fracturing," Derek said, pulling his cap down and squinting at me in the sunlight. Even when he went all weird-eyed on me he was way cute. "It's a sick way to get oil and gas out of the ground."

"Sick as in *good*? Or sick as in *bad*?" The trouble with slang was that it could be so confusing at times.

"Wicked bad. They drill down deep into the earth and then inject a shit-ton of water and secret toxic chemicals under pressure in order to fracture the rock. It releases oil and gas, which they pump back up out of the well so we can use it."

"And . . . why do we hate it?"

Derek abruptly stopped squinting at the word *we* and looked at me with eyes wide open.

We. I had meant it to mean the softball team, not Derek and me. *We* was way too relationship-heavy a word to use. Whenever Udder used it to describe something that he and Gramps liked or didn't like, I found it super-annoying. It was as if their identities were so intertwined that they were the same person. Not *I* but *we*. Obviously I didn't mean for Derek to interpret it that way. Obviously.

"Why do '*we*' hate it?" he repeated softly, lingering over the *we,* and staring at me even more intensely. "Rather than *tell* it to you, let me *yell* it to you."

Derek leapt up on top of the bench, cupped his hands, and, in a booming voice loud enough to startle even the phone-obsessed Willy Wonkas, let loose his "frack facts."

"Filthy, unsafe drinking water," he yelled. "A contaminated blend of crazy chemicals that are making people sick. Is this what we want?"

"No!" the Lefty Luddites yelled back.

"Is this what we need?"

"No!"

To be honest, I was still pretty confused as to what fracking actually was, but it did sound sort of scary.

"Land disruption. Air pollution. Noise pollution. Earthquakes."

Earthquakes? Seriously? I had always secretly wanted to experience an earthquake. I mean, not a big one where people died and whole cities went down and you lost power and couldn't charge your phone or any sort of shit show like that. But a manageable little tremor here and a cute little jolt there and maybe a crack in the wall or a falling bookcase? I could see being part of that. Plus, the whole tingly feeling I had gotten from holding hands had raised my opinion of quaking earth considerably.

But Derek was probably right. A little hand holding or Mother Earth rocking and rolling on her own was one thing, but us crazy-ass humans bringing on the tremors ourselves was a whole different story.

"Is this what we want?" Derek yelled.

"No!" we yelled back, my voice for the first time joining the others.

"Is this what we need?"

"No!" I yelled even louder.

"Drilling next to homes, schools, even in the middle of cemeteries. Is this what we want?"

For some unfathomable reason I was getting into this. Who knew yelling political affirmations at the top of your lungs could be so titillating? Yelling at texters was one thing, but yelling at *frackers*? I could get into that. Plus, Derek was working himself up into quite the full-body frenzy, which, try as I might to ignore it, was turning me on.

"Leaks and spills and methane and carbon emissions that will make climate change even worse. Is this what we want?"

Oh my God! Fracking contributed to climate change? Now I was totally against it.

"No!" This time my voice was louder than anybody else.

"Is this what we need?"

"What we need," the umpire interrupted, tapping Derek on the shoulder, "is to play ball."

In the Lefty Luddite tradition, we all bowed low to the guy. All hail the umpire! Then we grabbed our gloves and swarmed onto the field.

I hadn't been on a softball field in what seemed like forever, but it didn't take long to get back into the zone. It was kind of like learning to text: once you know how to do it, you never forget.

First up for the Willy Wonkas hit a sharp ground ball to my right. I scooped it up and threw deftly to first. The Luddites cheered. I glowed.

"Take that, frackhead!" I yelled. The thrill of the first out, combined with caffeine from my fourth cup of coffee, had me feeling fabulous.

Next batter up: a screeching liner that I snagged to my left.

"Natural gas my ass!" I yelled.

The team cheered again.

Another grounder to me, another triumphant yell, and just like that, three up, three down, and the top of the inning was over.

"You were awesome!" Derek said, high-fiving me. "And I've never heard anyone yell so loud!"

"Udder and Gramps's froggies got nothing on me," I told him.

"Froggies?" Derek asked, looking as confused as always.

Udder and Gramps's pond was full of frogs. Some so small they were the size of your thumbnail.

But boy, could they croak. The first few nights I spent at the farm-house I cursed the little rascals for the racket they made. Seriously, how the hell was I supposed to get my beauty sleep with all of that damn croaking going on?

Gramps explained how frogs and toads have this remarkable ability to inflate their vocal sacs and amplify their croaks so they can be heard up to a mile away. Pretty impressive for such little dweebs.

Of course, as always seemed to be the case, it had everything to do with sex. The boys serenading the girls. Calling them in for a good time. The age-old *please-won't-you-do-me* croak.

Sort of like the firefly flash. Only louder and without the pyrotechnics.

For someone as small as I was, I could inflate my vocal pouch with the best of them. My yells could probably be heard in the next town over.

It was our turn at bat. Karen the Cat Killer, aka Karen the Pitcher, led off with a hard-hit single to center. Derek followed with a bloop single to left. Peter the Porno (yeah, he was there too) got an infield hit. Two quick pop-fly outs followed with the runners holding.

Bases loaded and I was up. I took a few practice swings and strolled to the plate.

Holy shit! I thought to myself. *This is intense.* I mean, I knew it was a game. It was co-ed rec-league softball, for God's sake. But with caffeine coursing through my veins and my knees knocking together, it felt as though the fate of the entire free world was at stake. I hadn't felt this way since hitting fifty thousand points on *Passion*.

On the first pitch, I let the caffeine get the best of me and swung before the ball even left the pitcher's grip. On the second pitch, I held off way too long. The ball was in the catcher's mitt before I weakly waved my bat.

"Patience!" Derek yelled from second. "Wait for your pitch!"

Patience? Was he kidding me? Patience was definitely not something in my playbook.

Wait for it, I told myself. *You can do this.* I tried to visualize the ball as an evil bean beetle zooming towards my bat.

BAM! I took a vicious rip and sent a solid line drive over the leaping shortstop's head. Two runs scored.

"Frack yeah!" I yelled. "I mean, fuck yeah!" I was hopping up and down on first, pumping my fist in the air, basking in my glorious new role as softball diva. The team went nuts. Derek was spinning around in tight circles, Peter-the-Porno-at-the-meeting like, after scoring from second.

"Right on!" Jeremy the Goat Guy yelled, fist-bumping me after our side was finally retired.

"How about *left* on?" I suggested.

"Brilliant!" Jeremy said, laughing. "'Left on' it is!"

"Hey." Karen the Cat Killing Pitcher sidled up next to me on the bench as Derek flied out deep to center field to lead off the fifth inning. The side of her left hand was lightly touching mine. "That was fun at the potluck last night."

PING PING PING! It wasn't my phone going off but my gaydar, picking up on her pick-me-up vibes. For crying out loud, now I had lesbians all over me as well? Karen had most likely missed the Meagan-is-celibate message at the potluck party and only caught the Meagan-is-gay announcement. *Thanks, Sheila,* I thought to myself. *Thanks a bunch.* This was exactly what I *didn't* need.

"So," Karen continued. "You're single?"

"Which one?" I asked. "Not to brag, but I've hit three of them."

Karen laughed. "No. I meant are you seeing anyone?"

Karen was way cute. She had that short sticky-outy hairdo, which totally worked for her. She was willowy but muscular, with intense blue-blue eyes and pouty lips, and boy, could she pitch! If I were a lesbian I could definitely see being all over her. As long as I could drive that unfortunate running-over-the-cat-while-texting incident out of my head.

"Oh!" I said. "*That* kind of single. Me? Yes. But you know, no."

"Yes.... but no?" she asked. It seemed as though no matter what their sexual orientation was, I could confuse the hell out of everyone.

Karen scooted even closer to me.

"And that means . . ."

"Single no more!" I picked up my bat, strode to home plate, and crushed a double down the left-field line.

It was the last of the seventh and we were up by a run. Final at-bats for the Willy Wonkas. They had runners on first and second, with nobody out.

Derek, playing first, was beside himself. You would have thought it was game seven of the World Series, for God's sake. He was doing his player/coach thing—shouting out orders, positioning players, pulling his hair.

"Meagan!" he yelled. "Two steps toward second. Jeremy, five steps back. Karen, give 'em hell!"

I had reached the pinnacle of my caffeine-fueled high and was jumping up and down, yelling encouragement to Karen, my vocal sac inflated almost to bursting.

Their best hitter was up. She was a big bruiser of a woman with thick eyeliner and even thicker arms. She had already been on base three times. She scowled at me. She scowled at Karen the Cat Killer. I imagined that she scowled at the entire universe.

"Come on Karen!" I screamed. "You can do it!" What I wanted to yell was "If you can kill a fucking cat, then you can strike out this bitch!" Somehow, mercifully, I managed to hold my tongue.

Who knew there could be this much phone-free fun?

"Two steps toward second!" Derek screamed again. Even without yanking on his hair, it was sticking straight up.

Bruiser fouled off her first two pitches and then, *boom*, hit a sharp line drive headed toward trouble. My feet left the ground in what seemed like slow motion and, Wonder Woman–like, I snagged that liner out of thin air. The runner on second, thinking the ball was going to drop in for a hit, had headed to third so I tagged him out and, from my knees, threw to Derek at first, doubling up the girl there. Game over! A fracking triple play!

"Holy shit!" Derek yelled, racing over, picking me up and swinging me around.

"Oh my God!" Karen cried, putting her arms all over me as well.

"Left on!" Jeremy shouted, running in from right field and joining in the melee.

I did a little victory shake, rattle, and roll and raised my fists high in the air.

"I am Queen Ludd!" I yelled.

Chapter 21

Whooping and hollering, we raucously celebrated our stunning victory. Derek had hugged me so hard I though my ribs would break. Jeremy had told me I was the most "left-on" woman he had ever had the pleasure of playing with. Peter the Porno had done a reprise of his spin-and-chant move, just for me. Even the big ol' bruiser from the Willy Wonkas had shaken my hand.

And if that wasn't strange enough, Karen had given me her cell number and, whispering, made me promise to text her if my situation changed.

Text her? Seriously? Wasn't she the one on the road to recovery? Hadn't I heard her go all eloquent at the NA meeting, espousing her intent to remove her defects of character (Step Six) and shortcomings (Step Seven)? Hadn't she just led us in a chant of *one, two, three, wow— put away your cell phone now*?

And now here she was asking me to text her? That seemed a pretty casual bargain with addiction, if addiction it really was. It certainly didn't square well with the whole Netaholics Anonymous twelve-step thing. Even I could see that.

Like everything else in my life, it was all a bit on the confusing side.

Derek and I were sitting alone on the bench. Our teammates had left and it was just the two of us. I had my glove on my head to shield away the late-afternoon sun.

"You were awesome!" Derek said for the five zillionth time.

"I don't know," I croaked. I was exhausted. My throat was vocal-sacked out, painfully swollen from overuse. The rush of victory had come and gone, and now, with the caffeine wearing off and my team-mates history, I was coming down hard.

"Angsty is a little more like it," I muttered.

Yet another one of the super-annoying habits that I had: whenever any-thing good happened in my life I managed to make the least of it. Not that I ever really had expectations that anything good was going to hap-pen, mind you—but on those super-rare occasions that it did, I'd come crashing down pretty damn quick.

I desperately longed for my phone. Whenever those expectation demons leaped out at me, my escape route had always been online. It worked wonders. I was seventeen, for God's sake, and one of the very few kids I knew that wasn't on antidepressants. My phone was my Prozac.

Parents ignoring me? Go online. Offline guys making me anxious? Go online. School way too sucky? Go online. Online, I was always on my game. Online, I wasn't Queen of the Party or even Queen Ludd—I was Queen of the Fucking Universe, my thumbs serving as obedient minions conquering everything in their path.

Expectation is the root of all heartache, my parents had told me. Online I had no expectations of even having expectations so the pres-sure was totally off.

But offline?

Yikes!

"Angsty?" Derek asked. "Are you kidding me? You just made a triple play! Plus, you had three RBIs. I've never seen anyone have a better game! You sure you're not just feeling guilty about showing the rest of us up?"

"No way. That part was totally sweet."

"Then what are you angsting about?" Derek had scooted up next to me on the bench, about as close as he could be without actually touching me.

"It's nothing," I replied, sighing melodramatically. "Really. I don't want to be a downer." I reached into my back pocket for my phone, but it was nowhere to be found. Old habits are hard to break.

"Tell me," Derek said, his voice soothing and kind. "I want to hear."

"I don't know," I said. "Just the usual. What am I doing with my life? Why am I here? What is my purpose on this planet? Why does the enormous zit on my cheek refuse to go away? So much angst. So little time. And to top it off, for whatever reason, I've got a healthy dose of the ol' TSS thing going down today."

"TSS? I'm so sorry. That's, like, the thing you get from tampons, right?"

I gave him the look. "Derek! Not Toxic Shock Syndrome. Taylor Swift Syndrome."

"You gotta be kidding me. Taylor Swift actually bleeds just like you mortals?"

Once more, the look.

"Wait a minute," he said, excitedly. "Don't tell me you're talking about the Taylor Swift baseball curse?"

"The what?"

"The curse. Haven't you heard about it? Taylor Swift plays these gigs at baseball stadiums and after each show the home team implodes. Houston. Washington. San Diego. Those clubs were all doing great until she showed up and cursed the stadium with her presence. She plays, suspiciously terrible games follow. Coincidence? I don't think so!"

"How would you possibly know this?" I asked.

Derek looked around to make sure nobody was near and then whispered conspiratorially into my ear.

"The net. But please, for the love of God, don't tell anyone."

"Aha!" I shouted. "Not so pure now after all, are we?"

"Darling! Please! I only use it for emergencies."

"Excuse me?" I asked. WTF? Who did he think he was using the D word?

Derek took his hand out of his glove and then put it back in. "My bad," he said. "Too many old-time movies on Netflix. Anyway, why TSS?"

"Here's the cold, hard truth, Derek. I'm seventeen years old. Seventeen. Do you know what Taylor Swift had done by the time she was my age? Had a number-one album. Toured with all of the greatest country music stars. Already dated and broken up with every hot guy out there. Present company excluded."

"Actually, I dated Taylor. She made a lousy shortstop so I dumped her."

"I should have known. But here's the point: what have I done with my life? Let's see now . . . hmm . . . spent more time cruising profiles of loser guys on dating sites than any other human being alive. Had unfulfilling sext with half of them."

"Which half?" Derek asked.

"What?"

"Which half did you sext with? The half with the penis or the half without?"

"Don't be a dick," I told him. "Do you see where I'm going with this? I mean, seriously, I look at Taylor Swift and then I look at myself and I think, *Blah!* What am I doing with my life?"

Derek laughed.

"It's not funny," I told him.

"I'm not saying it is," he said. "But aren't you being a little hard on yourself? Don't let the down take you. I mean, seriously, if we're all going to compare ourselves to Taylor Swift then we're TS'ed."

"Toxic shocked?" I asked. "Taylor Swifted?"

"Totally screwed. Anyway, look at what you *are* doing. I bet Taylor Swift never moved to the country to take care of her grandfathers."

"Earth to Derek. Correct me if I'm wrong but that's just a little different from being the GREATEST POP STAR EVER! Plus, I'm going back home in a little over a month, remember?"

"I'm trying not to. Anyway, I bet Taylor Swift doesn't grow the sweetest zukes and cukes on the planet."

"This is true. But Taylor Swift also has more boys than she could possibly know what to do with. That and you can't write a number-one song about breaking up with a squash."

"Knowing Taylor the way that I do, she probably could. But there's no possible way she could have turned a triple play the way you did to win the biggest softball game *ever!*"

He fist-bumped me.

"You do have a point about that one," I told him.

"And I bet Taylor Swift doesn't know a tenth as much about insect sex as you do."

"Keep it up. I'm actually starting to feel a little bit better about myself." It was true. He had me smiling now.

"And," Derek continued. "You may not believe this, but I'd rather listen to you sing than her any day."

"You're right. I don't believe it."

"Plus, you're way cuter."

Whoa, whoa, whoa. Enough of this. Things were starting to get a little out of hand here.

I turned and stared at Derek. I stared long and hard and unblinkingly until he looked away awkwardly. I continued to stare as his eyes wandered from his shoelaces to the crack in the bench and then to a tiny spider edging its way up the side of the backstop fence. He took his glove off his hand and put it on his head, too.

"What are you doing?" I finally asked him.

"Shading out the sun, just like you."

"I don't mean with your glove. Why are you saying all of this shit about me?"

"Shit? I wouldn't exactly refer to it as 'shit.'"

"You know exactly what I'm talking about, Derek. Why are you doing this?"

"I'm sorry, Meagan, but I'm a little confused here. I was telling you—"

"Quiet," I said. "Stop talking."

We sat staring into the outfield grass for a minute, maybe even more. Finally I turned to him.

"How many times do I have to tell you that I'm not here to get into a relationship? What part of that don't you get? Huh? What part of that don't you understand? I sound like a damn music loop, playing the same annoying bit over and over. Or, to be totally retro about it, a broken re-cord. Okay: so maybe you don't scare me nearly as much as most offline guys do. And maybe I like you a heck of a lot more than I thought I possibly could. Maybe when I'm talking to you I'm not even thinking about texting. But for the last time: I'm not getting involved with a guy. Any guy. Not even you."

"I get that," Derek said. "I really do."

"No," I said. "You really don't. If you got that you wouldn't be acting so damn adorable."

"Meagan, I'm not really sure what you want from me."

"I don't know what I want from you, Derek. Don't you see? That's the problem. All I know is that you're totally screwing up the whole offline, boy-free thing. You really are." I reached out and put his hand in mine and squeezed it tight. "Thanks a lot. Seriously. Are you happy now? Satisfied? Huh? Are you?"

"I think that—"

I took my free hand and placed it over his mouth.

Finally, when the silence had grown unbearable and I couldn't take it any longer, I dropped my hand from his mouth and leaned in close to kiss him.

Chapter 22

"You are never going to believe what I did!" Sheila said, reaching out and taking my hand. It was getting late on Saturday afternoon and Sheila had just returned from her hike with Jonathan. I had been hiding behind the zucchinis while he dropped her off. Anything to avoid yet another awkward moment with a boy.

"Please don't tell me you lost your phone!" I said.

"No, thank God! Something new. Something totally crazy. Something having nothing to do with my phone."

"That's not fair," I whined. "How am I possibly supposed to guess it now?"

"You're not. Never in a million years."

"Tell me." I demanded. "I'm dying here."

"I had lunch in the top of a tree!" Sheila was grinning from ear to ear.

"You what?"

"Lunch! In the top of a tree. With Jonathan and a porcupine."

"A porcupine? You mean the animal thingie with quills?"

"The exact same! It was the cutest little goober I've ever seen."

"Jonathan or the porcupine?" I asked.

"Both," Sheila said. "Actually all three. The tree was also totally adorable. I even kissed its bark."

"You've got to be kidding me. Did Jonathan drug you or something?" I stared into Sheila's eyes and noticed a shimmering glazed look. "Oh my God, he did, didn't he? What was I thinking, Sheila? How could I possibly have let you go out offline unsupervised like that? Do we need to call a crisis hotline? An ambulance? The police?"

"Chillax, girl. I think I'm in love."

"What? With Jonathan?"

"No! Not with Jonathan!"

"With the porcupine?"

"Stop!" Sheila cried, looking annoyed with me. She reached down and pulled a cucumber off of its vine and took a bite out of it.

"With who then?" I asked.

"With nature! With Mother Earth!"

I dropped the hoe I was holding onto my big toe and winced in pain.

Sheila? *My* Sheila? In love with nature? Having lunch in a tree with a porcupine? I dug around deep in my ears, searching for balls of wax. There had to be a clog in there somewhere. I couldn't possibly be hearing things correctly.

"You're joking, right?" I asked, coming up empty-fingered.

"Never been more serious in my life," Sheila said.

Hiking? Tree climbing? Porcupine watching? Bark kissing? And all of this with a boy offline? Sheila was rewriting the rules faster than that triple play I had turned.

"Who knew?" she continued. "We hiked for like five miles or something, and I only took my phone out a few times to take pictures. We must have gone up and down ten mountains. It was awesome! And the trees. I mean, I always thought that trees were, you know, just trees. But Jonathan knew the names of all of them. Every single one. And they're all so different. Did you know that? Some like the shade, some like the sun. Some grow in wet places, some in dry. Some lose their leaves in the winter, some don't. Some are total paradise for porcupines. Some they couldn't care less about. My God, Meagan, you should have seen him. He was way up in the canopy munching on hemlock needles."

"Who? Jonathan?"

"No, you idiot. The porcupine. He didn't seem to mind that Jonathan and I were eating lunch only a few limbs below him. It was so awesome."

"Oh my God," I said. "How was Jonathan?"

"Cute! Maybe even cuter than the porcupine! And gorgeous lips! An eleven."

"Out of ten?"

"Maybe an eleven and a half."

"Trees and lips," I said.

"Trees and lips and the world's sweetest porcupine. Who knew?"

Who knew was right. Remember: all this was coming from a girl who a few short hours earlier had thought that anything involving unnecessary exposure to the great outdoors was an absolute no-no.

"Just out of curiosity," I asked, "did Jonathan tell you why he's so active in NA?"

"Highmountain Tauren," Sheila said, rolling her eyes.

"What?"

"It was his character in *World of Warcraft*. Descended from Huln, brave hero of the War of the Ancients."

"You gotta be kidding me? Jonathan was an online game addict?"

"Crazy, huh? For almost three years, that's basically all he did. Believe me, I heard all about it and it wasn't pretty. But he's totally stoked with himself now. He's made the change from Highmountain Tauren to getting high off of real mountains. It's made a world of difference."

"Wow," I said.

"*Wow* is right. One potluck, one hike, one lunch in a tree, and I think I might be falling for the guy."

"The one with or without the quills?" I asked.

Sheila laughed.

"You seriously like him?" I asked, incredulous at this radical turn of events.

"I do," she said. "I really do. But enough about me. How'd it go with Derek?"

"Oh my God!" I said, dropping the hoe once more on my toe again and grimacing in pain. "Do you really have to ask?"

Chapter 23

Sheila, Udder, Gramps, and I were sitting out in the garden. Saturday afternoon had turned into early evening, and the summer sun was still high in the sky. We were watching the bees methodically work the squash flowers, darting in and out, sucking up the nectar, their hind legs covered with enormous bright orange balls of pollen.

Gramps was getting high. He had carved an elaborate pipe from one of the smaller zucchinis, hollowed out the inside and put in a screen on top. He was really quite pleased with himself. Who knew you could do so much with that most versatile of vegetables?

I was leaning forward in my garden chair, snipping the tops off newly dug misshapen carrots. One looked like a mermaid. One like a unicorn. One like a dude with a fully erect penis. I snapped the hard end of that one off and, dirty though it was, chewed on it with a vengeance.

"Speaking of boys," Gramps said, watching me chew away. "Let me get this straight."

"Good luck with that," Udder snorted.

"Sheila," Gramps continued, "you like Jonathan, but he doesn't like you. Is that right?"

"I like him," Sheila answered. "And he likes me. He even said he did. He just doesn't seem all that interested in me."

"Because he's interested in Meagan."

"Exactly," Sheila sighed.

"Who doesn't like him."

"I like him," I said. "Even though I've hardly talked to him at all. I'm just not interested in him."

"Because you're interested in Derek."

"Exactly," I said.

"Even though you're not supposed to be interested in anyone."

"Bingo."

"And then there's Karen the Cat Killer," Udder said. "Let's not forget about her."

I had, as (almost) always, told my grandfathers everything.

"Please," I said, groaning. "Can we just leave Karen out of this?"

"By the way," Sheila said. "I hate to bring this up, but remember that guy Caleb? The one you walked out on when he was . . . you know . . . whatever? He keeps texting me, wondering why you won't get back to him. He says he's sorry for whatever he did. He wants a do-over."

"How in hell's name did Caleb get *your* number?"

"Remember how you accidently hit Send All that time when you were sexting him? Somehow he must have figured out that you and I were besties."

"Somebody hit me with a hoe!" I said, groaning again.

"Not to belabor the point," Gramps said, "but can you retell the part where you kissed Derek one more time?"

"Oh my God. Please! What do you want from me? Do I really have to humiliate myself and repeat that shit show of a story again?"

"Yes!" all three enthusiastically answered.

When I kissed Derek on the bench after the softball game, he did not kiss me back.

I repeat. He did not kiss me back.

There I was with my tongue in his mouth, flicking this way and that, and I got nothing in return. Absolutely positively nothing. His mouth was like a vast empty black hole. Lipless, tongueless, terrifying.

My first kiss that actually meant something to me, my first kiss with a boy I actually liked, and that was what I got? Seriously? What was wrong with me?

"No," he had told me, pushing me away. "Stop."

"Stop?" I was incredulous. Not that I knew a damn thing about boys, but when, in the entire history of the universe, had a straight guy *ever* refused to kiss a girl back? I wasn't even aware that *stop* was in a boy's vocabulary.

"You want *me* to stop?" I asked.

"I can't do this, Meagan. I really can't. I'm sorry, but I really need to go."

Derek had stood up, turned his back on me, and walked away to his car without saying a word. We drove back to Udder and Gramps's in complete silence, the most awkward car ride of my life. The whole time I felt sick to my stomach.

And now, huzzah and hooray for me, I got to relive, once again, the whole humiliating episode for the entertainment of Sheila, Udder, and Gramps.

"You know, darling . . . ," Udder said.

"'Darling!'" I wiped my tearing eyes with the back of my sleeve. "Derek called me 'darling.' And then when I kissed him he didn't kiss me back!"

"Darling," Udder continued, reaching out and holding my hand. "As I recall, you told him that you weren't dating. That you weren't interested in guys, that you were celibate, that you were a lesbian. Is all of that not true?"

"Well, yes, everything but the last bit. I'm out of the closet as a non-lesbian."

"Put yourself in his shoes," Sheila said. "You say you're totally off-limits and then you slip him the tongue? I mean, seriously, girlfriend. He's a sensitive, sweet guy. I can't exactly blame him for being so confused. You're dishing out more M & M's than that candy store on Main Street."

"Sheila! Whose side are you on?" This time I really did start to cry.

"Yours, of course! I'm just saying . . ."

"Don't! I know you're mad at me about Jonathan, but you don't have to—"

"Jeez, Meagan, don't be ridiculous! I'm not mad at you about Jonathan. I'm just thinking about Derek. The poor guy probably thinks you're just totally messing with him. He probably thinks—"

Just then a car turned into the driveway, followed quickly by a second one. Sheila and I took one glance and then, hand in hand, ran like crazy into the house.

Chapter 24

"What are they doing now?" Sheila asked. She was frantically putting on deodorant while brushing back her hair and searching for a different top.

"Talking to Udder and Gramps," I said, peeking out my bedroom window while I hid behind the curtains. "God only knows what Gramps is telling them. But I don't get it: I can see why Jonathan is here but why is Derek back? What the heck is going on?"

Sheila gave me a quick once-over. "You might want to put your bra back on. Then again, maybe you don't. Depends on what you're looking for."

"Looking for?" I asked. "More like running from!" I peeked out the window again. "What do you think they're saying?"

"Don't ask me. I'm still high from the all that secondhand weed smoke. I'm not even sure if I can get it together to go back down there."

"What?" I grabbed her by the shoulders and shook her. "You have to, Sheila. I can't possibly face those two boys alone!"

"If I had known there would be this much drama . . ."

"You would have come that much sooner."

"Exactly." Sheila gave me a big hug. "Ready?"

"Hey," I said, super-awkwardly, picking up the hoe and scraping at the ground in front of my shoes.

"Hey," both boys said, even more awkwardly than me.

"Hey," Sheila said, looking at Jonathan with a look I had never seen from her before.

Gramps still had his zucchini pipe in his hand and was now pointing it at the boys while lecturing away. "If, after rubbing noses, the female porc is still interested, the male stands on his hind legs and sprays her with his urine."

Oh my God! What was Gramps doing? Couldn't that man, just for once, keep his animal sexcapades to himself?

"Gramps!" I scolded. The whole scene was so embarrassing. "I don't think Jonathan and Derek are interested in how perverted porcupines are."

"Yes we are," both boys said simultaneously, apparently relieved to have someone taking the lead in the conversation.

Gramps looked at me and grinned. "And he doesn't just spray it. That's not nearly good enough for our porc. No way. He shoots it. Under high pressure. It's like a Super Soaker, which, not to change the subject, just made its way into the Toy Hall of Fame."

"There's really a Toy Hall of Fame?" Jonathan asked.

"There really is," Gramps said.

"Did Barbie get voted in?" Sheila asked.

"Barbie, G.I. Joe, Raggedy Ann and Andy . . ."

"How about Mister Potato Head?" Derek asked.

"Front and center. In fact, they just announced this year's finalists. The Magic 8 Ball, Matchbox Cars, My Little Pony, Transformers, Wiffle Ball— "

"Wiffle Ball?" Derek exclaimed. "That is so awesome!"

"Please," Jonathan begged, "please tell me Twister made it."

"Holy shit!" Sheila shouted. "I love that game!"

I snorted, knowing for a fact that Sheila had never played Twister in her entire life.

"You do?" Jonathan asked. "It's like my favorite!"

"For Christ's sake!" I yelled. "Can we please just finish with the damn porcupine sex already?"

Gramps grinned again. "I'd be delighted," he said. "So, after doing the deed—which, I might add, is done very carefully—and he's too exhausted to continue, the guy is gone. Hits the road. Seven months later, she not only has to give birth to the quilled little devils, also done very carefully, but she'll have to raise those sweet little porcupettes all on her own."

"That kind of sucks," Derek said. "Gives us guys a bad name."

"As if you need another reason," I muttered, not knowing whether I wanted Derek to hear or not. Part of me was totally amped that he had returned. But most of me, per usual, was scared to death and confused as hell as to what was to happen next.

Sheila had corralled Jonathan over in the garden and, wanting to leave them alone, I had headed down to the beehives. Derek followed tentatively.

"Mind the electric fence!" I told him tersely. "One shocker's quite enough for the day."

We sat in silence for a while watching the frenzied flight of the bees.

"Why are you here again?" I finally asked.

Derek wrinkled his nose and rubbed hard at the space between his eyes. He had the tiniest bit of dandelion fluff stuck in his eyebrow. I reached over and roughly flicked it away.

He turned toward me and let out a big sigh.

"You have my glove. You took it by accident. I'm here to get my baseball glove."

"Softball."

"Whatever."

"Is that the only reason?"

"Look, Meagan." Derek sighed again. "I'm sorry about this afternoon. I really am. I hope I didn't hurt your feelings. This whole . . . thing is new to me. It's like some sort of Netflix romcom binge-fest gone totally tragic. What was I supposed to do back there on the bench? Huh?"

"Well . . . let me think . . . hmm . . . for starters, how about kissing me back?"

"I know this sounds crazy, Meagan, but I'm not into the hookup thing. I'm just not."

"Oh. So you're going to go all sensitive-guy on me and expect me to buy that?"

Derek stood up, did a few shoulder rolls, and then sat back down next to me. After a few moments he said quietly, "You've told me repeatedly you're not into me."

"Did that kiss seem like I wasn't into you?"

"No! That's the problem! Don't you see? That kiss seemed like the exact opposite. How can I say this: Look, thanks to you we just beat our number-one rival in softball. Sad and pathetic as it may be, I live for this shit, Meagan. I really do. Particularly now that I'm offline. I count down the minutes between games. And this afternoon, rather than celebrating the greatest victory EVER, do you know what I've been doing? Do you? I've just spent the last two hours at home banging my glove against my head."

"I thought you said I had your glove?"

"Then I was banging *your* glove against my head, which makes it even worse. Look at me! Look at the bruises between my eyes!"

I reached over and pulled out more dandelion fluff from his eyebrow. This time a little more gently. Derek jerked his head away and grabbed my arm.

"Stop it, Meagan! Just stop it. You keep throwing me curveball after curveball. Just like in baseball."

"Softball."

"What*ever*! I have absolutely no idea what position I'm playing here. I could be in left field. I could be behind the plate. I don't have a clue. And, at the risk of overdoing the baseball metaphor . . ."

"Softball."

"Just when I think I've struck out, you go and do something like that!"

"Like what?" I asked. "Pull dandelion fluff out of your eyebrow?"

"No! Kiss me!" Derek's dander was clearly up.

"Now you want me to kiss you?"

"No! Yes! I don't know! I'm saying that's what *you* did! Back at the bench! You kissed me!"

"Yeah, I did. And I didn't get a whole lot back now, did I." A lengthy pause ensued as I did my best not to cry.

"Meagan, how long have I known you? Huh? How long?"

"I don't know. Two weeks?"

"Actually, thirteen days and sixteen hours, but who the fuck is counting."

"Please watch your goddamn language. The word is *frack*, not *fuck*. And it's creeping me out that you're counting."

Derek stood up, sat back down, and stood up again.

"Where are you going with this, Derek?" I asked, striving for calm.

"For the five millionth time, I don't have a clue! I don't know if I'm coming or going. I don't know if I'm up or down. All I know is one thing, Meagan. There is just one thing that I am completely sure of!"

"And that is . . . ?"

"Hey!" Sheila tapped me on the shoulder. Caught up in the awkwardness of the conversation, I hadn't seen her coming. "Jonathan and I are heading into town. Do you guys want to come along?" Sheila took another look at me.

"Is everything all right?" she asked.

"Everything is fine!" I yelled, standing up and stamping my feet. "Just fine!"

I got up and fled back up the hill and into the house.

Chapter 25

The whole what-the-hell-is-going-on-with-my-totally-pathetic-personal-life quandary had thrown me into a major tizzy.

Boldly resisting the overwhelming urge to head into town for an online binge, I instead threw myself into total cleaning overdrive, vowing to make up for the years of neglect shown to Udder and Gramps's house. There was not a single room that I didn't sweep, vacuum, polish, rinse, shine, scrape, scrub, dust, mop, and wipe. I was a housecleaning tornado, a washing whirlwind, a girl possessed. I had this manic need to rid every corner of dust, dirt, and grime. Nothing was beyond my grasp. For the next few days I barely stopped cleaning to sleep or eat, subsisting entirely on caffeine and raw zucchini and cucumbers from the garden. I had deep, dark circles under my sunken eyes. I was seeing double, which only increased the intensity of my cleaning. Before, there had been only one bed in each room to sweep and vacuum under. Now there were two.

I was driving Udder and Gramps totally bonkers. They'd try to nap and I'd be vacuuming under their bed. They'd try to shower and I'd be inside the tub cleaning the grout with a toothbrush. They'd try to read and I'd have carted away the couch for a deep cleansing.

If cleanliness was next to godliness, then within the week I had become a saint seven times over.

Once the whole house was finished, I went right back in and started over again.

And the garden. Oh my God! The weeds would see me coming and they'd practically yank themselves out of the ground, suicide preferable to the torture I inflicted upon them. Even weeds that were nowhere near the garden got wind of me coming and were pulling up their roots and heading for the hills. I had holes in my gardening gloves and the head of the hoe was mangled and bent from the endless, crushing blows to all things not vegetables. I was polishing the cucumbers and the zucchinis while they were still on the vine. I forced Udder and Gramps to take off their shoes before opening the garden gate so they wouldn't get the plants dirty.

By Tuesday morning, my grandfathers couldn't take it anymore.

Even Udder, usually calm and cool as a cucumber from the garden, was visibly agitated.

"Darling!" he said, loudly and gruffly as I was frantically searching for an extension cord long enough to reach the garden so I could vacuum the dirt out of it.

"Stop!" I cried. "Please don't call me that anymore!"

"Hand me the vacuum," he continued, walking slowly toward me. "Hand me the vacuum and no one gets hurt."

"No!" I said, backing away, holding the hose and nozzle out in front of me like a weapon. "Dirt is evil. Dust is the devil. Just let me . . ."

"Hand him the goddamn vacuum cleaner!" Gramps thundered. He and Udder grabbed one end while I held tightly to the other. It was a tug-of-war. We were pulling from both sides when the hose popped off, sending me tumbling over backwards and engulfing the three of us in a cloud of dust and dirt.

"Meagan!" Gramps roared, wiping his eyes and coughing. He didn't even try to help me up. "You're acting crazy. This bullshit has got to stop!"

"Calm down, Curtis, dear—let me handle this."

"Then handle it! I swear to God, if that vacuum goes on one more time I'm going to take the garden hoe to it!" He gave the machine a vicious kick.

"Meagan," Udder started again. "Darling. We know you're under a lot of stress. We know you have a lot of anxiety, but cleaning your way out of it is just not going to work."

"Goddamn right it's not," Gramps grumbled.

"It's all your fault!" I cried out. "If you weren't so pissy about me being online I'd be out of your hair in a minute." I shook my hair, trying to fling the vacuum debris from it. "First you take away my phone. Now you want to take away my vacuum? Is nothing sacred?"

When push came to shove it always seemed best to blame others.

"Any form of obsessive–compulsive disorder thrives on stress and anxiety," Udder continued.

"I am not obsessive–compulsive!" I cried, reaching out to caress the vacuum, desperately wanting to cradle it in my arms. Nomophobia be damned. Now I had novacuumphobia.

And OCD? Seriously? That was all I needed: yet another dysfunctional acronym to add to my increasingly long list of psychiatric disorders.

"You're right!" Gramps said, pushing the vacuum out of the way with his foot. "You're not OCD. You're just crazy!"

"Curtis! You're being really offensive! Leave! Now!" Gramps picked up the vacuum and then, still scowling at me, stormed out of the room.

"Isn't this why you wanted me here?" I cried out. "To get the house in order? To help out in the garden? To get you through the next few months? Am I not doing that? Huh? Am I screwing that up, too? Can't I do anything right?" I burst into tears and sat down hard on the living room floor.

Udder scooted over next to me and, joints creaking, sat down and enveloped me in his arms. I could hear Gramps dragging the vacuum, thumping and bumping up the attic stairs, most likely on his way to some secret place where he could hide it away from me.

"I know it's not easy being seventeen," Udder said, sighing right along with me as I dried my eyes on his shirt. "And I'm sure it's not that easy for Derek either. Or Sheila or Jonathan or anybody else. No matter how old we are, things can be confusing. That's life."

"But why does no one seem nearly as confused as me? I've got that one totally nailed down, don't I? Look at me. I came here a wreck, and now I'm even more of one. I just keep screwing things up again and again. I can't even vacuum right!" I started to cry again.

"You're a wonderful vacuumer, darling. The best ever. But you could probably ease up on that just a teensy bit. And anyway, the way you've gone at it I'm not sure there's a speck of dust within a mile of this house."

"So what should I do?"

"Other than painting the upstairs bathroom I think you've done it all." He smiled and squeezed me tighter.

"No! I mean about my personal life. About Derek."

"Boys can be challenging."

We were quiet for a moment. Udder held me, rocking me back and forth like I was a little girl again.

"Do you like him?" Udder asked.

"Of course I like him! Why do you think I'm such a miserable wreck?"

"Does he like you?"

"Yes. No. I don't know. He says he does and then he doesn't. I go to kiss him and he doesn't kiss me back. Then he shows up and just confuses things even more. This is why real life sucks, Udder. I'm not cut out for this stuff. I'm just not."

"Darling, don't confuse being confused with suckiness."

"What are you talking about?"

"Confusion is not necessarily a bad thing. In fact, it's what gives life its meaning. It's what makes things interesting, challenging, exciting. Think about what a drag it would be if you always knew how everything would turn out."

"I do know how everything will turn out. It'll be a total disaster. As always."

"I would not call your life a 'disaster.' Seriously, look at the rest of the world. Most girls would trade lives with you in a heartbeat. Seems to me you've got it pretty darn good."

"*I* wouldn't call it 'pretty darn good,'" I grumbled. "My life isn't exactly a piece of cake."

"Tell that to the girls your age in Syria. Or Niger. Or Afghanistan. Or a holy host of other struggling countries out there. Anyway, cake is way overrated, darling. It's hard to make, it's fattening, and after the sugar high dies you're even more down in the dumps than you were before."

"I'd still like to try a piece now and then. Is that too much to ask? Just a few crumbs thrown my way would be nice."

"I'd call Derek more than a crumb. From what I've seen of him, he's way sweeter than that."

I put my arms around my Udder and hugged him.

"Why can't I just be old, arthritic, and gay like you?" I asked.

"Not all of us can be so blessed," Udder answered, hugging me even tighter.

Chapter 26

As totally confused as I was about my own life, what I really couldn't wrap what was left of my brain around was the new Sheila. My best friend had made the leap from indoor nomophobe to outdoor nature goddess in a single solitary afternoon, as radical a transformation as you're ever going to get from a girl. It was a stunning turn of events. Nature had taken Sheila by storm, the way heroin had taken that senior in our high school. One hike, one lunch in a hemlock tree with a porcupine and a cute guy, and that girl was hooked.

This from a girl who, just like me, had previously gone to incredible lengths to limit her interactions with Mother Nature to the absolute bare minimum. Sheila hadn't just disliked nature: she abhorred it. Nature was the dung of the devil. Satan with the runs. Something to fear more than fear itself. The sight of a city squirrel would send her over the edge. She refused to watch nature programs on her laptop because she was afraid of poison ivy. Even a trip to the beach was met with resistance, sand and surf being way too natural for her.

"Sunshine is so *passé*," Sheila had told me. "Why do you think the Goddess gave us tanning salons to fake and bake in?"

And then, wonder of wonders, this happens: she eats lunch in a tree with a porcupine and, presto change-o, she pulls a one-eighty.

Who knew something like this was even a possibility?

I had it figured that by the time you were a junior in high school, your personality was pretty much etched in stone. Who you were by then, whether you liked it or not, was who you were going to be. I mean, you could teach a dog a few new tricks (not that Sheila was a dog—Derek maybe, but Sheila? No way!), but it was still the same old dog. But now this had happened. Sheila had gone and done the unthinkable.

I assumed it would be just a phase. A brief fleeting affair with the offline world and then back to reality online. Something she'd chortle about later in life. "I remember when I ate lunch in a tree with a porcupine!" she'd say, and no one would believe her. Not even for a second.

Sheila as Nature Girl? That made about as much sense as me as Luddite. Which means it made no sense at all.

Or did it?

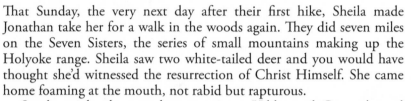

That Sunday, the very next day after their first hike, Sheila made Jonathan take her for a walk in the woods again. They did seven miles on the Seven Sisters, the series of small mountains making up the Holyoke range. Sheila saw two white-tailed deer and you would have thought she'd witnessed the resurrection of Christ Himself. She came home foaming at the mouth, not rabid but rapturous.

Sunday night she stayed over again at Udder and Gramps's, and called in sick to work at the convenience store on Monday, demanding that Jonathan do the same with his job at the copy shop. They hiked the Metacomet-Monadnock Trail on the Mount Tom Range, spotting four red-tailed hawks, nine turkey vultures, and a skunk.

"A skunk?" I asked.

"It was the sweetest thing I've ever seen. I just wanted to pick it up and snuggle it." It was Monday night and she was packing her bag to head back to Boston.

"Please tell me you didn't!"

"I would have. But Jonathan, that party pooper, held me back."

"At least guys are good for something." I reached into her bag and took back one of my favorite pairs of socks that she had stolen. "Speaking of which, you've gone hiking with Jonathan for three straight days and I've barely seen you touch your phone since you've been here. Are you sure you're not sick or something?"

Sheila stopped packing and sat down on the end of her bed. She looked perplexed.

"Isn't this what you asked me to do? Get Jonathan off your back?"

"Yeah, of course it was. And, you know, thanks. I really mean it. But I hadn't quite figured you'd want him all over yours."

"Has it really been three days?" Sheila asked, looking a little dreamy-eyed. "Wow! It seems as though it's only been three minutes. Either that or three years. God, Meagan. I sure didn't see this one coming. Nature. Jonathan. And now this."

"Now what?"

"Jonathan wants to build a cabin way out in the woods somewhere. He wants to take another gap year before he goes to college. Do the back-to-the-land thing. Grow his own food. Raise his own goats."

"Seriously? With Jeremy the Goat-Roper?"

"No. Not with Jeremy."

"All by himself?"

"I don't know. I was thinking . . ." Sheila paused for a long time. "Maybe with me."

I laughed.

"I'm being serious," she said, looking annoyed.

"You've got to be kidding me!" I sat down hard on the bed next to her.

"All I know is I'm crushing on him. And I'm thinking, at least I'm hoping, he may be starting to feel the same way. No offense, but he didn't mention you at all today. Not even once. And that's a good thing, right?"

"Huzzah and hooray! And now he wants to build a cabin with you?"

"Well . . . no . . . he didn't exactly say with me. But . . . you know . . ."

"No! I don't know. Tell me!"

"Well, I was thinking . . . you know . . . maybe *I'd* want to build a cabin with *him*."

I shook my head vigorously. That damn earwax *must* be clogging things up. I could see Sheila's mouth moving, but her words just didn't seem to make any sense.

"You? Live out in the woods? In a cabin? Sheila, three days ago I had to drag you kicking and screaming out the door to go on a hike. And now you've gone all *Little House on the Prairie* on me?"

I went to the window and opened it wide. "Help!" I yelled, only partly in jest. "Who stole my Sheila? Somebody give me back my Sheila!"

"Stop!" Sheila said. "This is all your fault. You're the one who made me come here. You're the one to blame."

"A cabin? In the woods? Just you and Jonathan?"

"Forget about it. I don't know what I was thinking. The whole thing is just stupid."

We were quiet for a couple of minutes as Sheila finished packing.

"But you know," Sheila finally said. "Here's something I've never confessed to anyone. Not even to you. Secretly I always thought *Little House on the Prairie* was kind of sweet. Think about it: Jonathan could be Pa. I could be Ma. You could be—"

"Laura Ingalls Wilder? Frontier girl extraordinaire?"

"I was thinking more of Jack the Brindle Bulldog."

"*Grrrrr!*" I growled, gently biting her on the arm.

Chapter 28

"Don't you miss your parents?" Udder asked. "It's been almost a month since you've seen them."

"My parents? Are you serious? How could I possibly miss my parents when I have my Udder and Gramps?" I got up from the kitchen table and gave them both hugs.

As I said before, when it came to my parents there was not much to miss. I had sent a couple of snarky postcards to each of them since I had arrived here, touting my spectacular recovery, but it wasn't like I was exactly close to my mom and dad the way some girls are. And when it came to the issues that were driving me completely insane, they'd be about as helpful as a porcupine in a hot-air balloon.

Asking my parents for advice on relationships? I don't think so.

But Udder and Gramps? Wow! Now they were a different prickle of porcupines. They had been together now for thirty-seven years. Not months. *Years.* As soon as marriage equality had come to Massachusetts in 2004, they had tied the knot and made it official.

"How do you do it?" I asked.

"Do what?" Gramps replied. "Miss your parents? Truth be told, we don't miss them all that much either." We were sitting in the living room at the end of the day. Gramps and Udder were snuggled on the couch. I was kicking back in the easy chair, taking a break, for once, from my obsessive cleaning and weeding. Gramps was stroking Udder's thigh while his head rested on his shoulder, their thinning white hair mixing together. Seriously—how cute was that?

"No," I said. "I'm talking about love. As in: stay in love. After all these years, how the heck do you still do it?"

"Who says we're in love?" Udder said, snuggling even closer to Gramps. "Your grandfather is one royal pain in the butt. If you knew a tenth of all of the things I've had to put up with over the years!"

Gramps snorted.

"Me? My God, man. There have been times when I've wanted to—"

"Stop!" I said. "I'm being serious. I really want to know. When you two got together how were you so sure it would all work out?"

"We weren't," Udder said. "We didn't have a clue."

"I did!" Gramps said.

"Oh, Curtis, stop. You did not. I was the one who had to beg you to move in with me. And even after we got married you refused to wear a ring for the first five years."

"You didn't wear a wedding ring?" I asked. "For five years? Why?"

Udder groaned. "He had this thing about how it wasn't the government's or the church's or anyone else's right to sanctify our relationship and he wasn't going to buy into the whole establishment bullshit of wearing a piece of extracted metal mined by exploited workers from a dictatorial country around his finger to legitimize our love." Udder smiled and reached out to hold Gramps's hand, and then sang out the first lines of "Isn't It Romantic?" in his deep baritone.

"He had to stick it to the man even on our wedding day," Udder continued.

"But you were in love."

"That we were."

"That's my question. How did you know? And how do you still do it?"

"We have a little blue pill marked with the letter V to thank for that." Gramps switched his hand from one of Udder's thighs to the other.

"*Ewww!*" I yelled, covering my ears and shutting my eyes. "That's not what I'm talking about!"

"Actually," Gramps continued. "Sex has a lot to do with it. Sex is, I don't know . . . sex. The pleasure of the flesh, even for those of us who are, let's just say, past our prime, is not to be underestimated. Let me tell you something, Meagan. I feel damn lucky, after all of these years, to still be so in lust with the man I am so in love with." He turned toward Udder and kissed him.

I was stuck between a YUCK and a WOW! It was hard to imagine (not that I wanted to) these two white-haired, wrinkly, gnarled, arthritic, seventy-somethings going at it in the bedroom. There was something about them doing the deed that was really quite unimaginable. Parents having sex was weird enough. But my grandfathers? The fact that Gramps and Udder could still get it up, even with the help of Viagra, was something I had never dared to contemplate. I shook the image out of my head.

"Forget the sex. Even though I've never done it, that part at least I kind of get. What I really want to know about is *love*. I don't have a clue about that."

"Who does?" Gramps replied. "It's like what the Supreme Court justice said about pornography."

"Which was?"

"'I know it when I see it.'"

"Thanks, Gramps," I said. "A terrific analogy. Really helpful. Really comforting."

"*Love is a smoke raised with the fume of sighs,*" Udder intoned. "*Being purged, a fire sparkling in lovers' eyes; being vex'd a sea nourish'd with lovers' tears: what is it else? A madness most discreet, a choking gall and a preserving sweet.*"

"I didn't understand a word of what you just said," I told him.

"Love, darling. Shakespeare. *Romeo and Juliet.*"

"Ahhh. Those two lovebirds." I rolled my eyes. "As I recall, that relationship had a super-happy ending, didn't it?"

"*When Love speaks, the voice of all the gods make heaven drowsy with the harmony.*"

"Oh my God, Udder! You're creeping me out here."

"Why all these questions, Meagan?" Gramps asked. "Is there something we should know about? What's going on?"

I squirmed awkwardly in the chair and let out a long, drawn-out Shakespearean sigh, channeling Juliet, mistress of angst.

"Derek," I said.

"You're in love with Derek?"

"No . . ." I hesitated, trying to make my tongue do that *tsk*ing sound. "Of course not."

"Is he in love with you?"

"How could anyone possibly be in love with me? But . . . we were talking down by the beehives the other night and he was like . . . I don't know. This was after I kissed him and got nothing back. And then he goes off and says . . ."

"Says what?"

"Nothing."

"Wow," Udder said, reaching out again to hold Gramps's hand. "He must have it bad."

"How could he possibly say he loved me?"

"I thought he didn't."

"Of course he didn't! We've known each other for barely two weeks. What was he thinking? Why would he do that?"

"Do what?"

"Not kiss me back!"

"*Who ever loved that loved not at first sight?*"

"What?"

"*Hear my soul speak,*" Udder continued. "*The very instant that I saw you, did my heart fly to your service.*"

"Please, Udder! Stop before I call an exorcist! What am I supposed to do? I knew I should never go out with an offline guy. What was I thinking?"

"I thought you weren't going out?"

"I'm not. I thought you were just old and arthritic, not deaf. Have you been listening to a word I've been telling you?"

"*Love is the answer,*" Gramps said, "*but while you're waiting for the answer, sex raises some pretty interesting questions.*"

"Gramps! Please! I told you—no more Shakespeare!"

"Actually, that was Woody Allen."

"This is seriously not helping!" I put my face in my hands and pushed down hard on my eyeballs, firefly-like flashes of light bursting everywhere.

"Do you love him?" Udder asked me.

"What?" I asked, my voice all shrill and whiney. "How many times have you asked me that? I barely even know the guy!"

"Yes, darling, but, given time, could you love him?"

"We shouldn't be harassing her," Gramps said. "We should be congratulating her."

"Congratulating me? For what?"

"For curing yourself of your Online Relationship Disorder. Like we already told you, now you've just got plain old Relationship Disorder. Also known as love. Out of the frying pan and into the fire, sweetheart. Excellent job! We are both so proud of you."

I got up, sighed a sigh that would have made Juliet rise from the dead, kissed them both on their foreheads, and dragged my sorry ass upstairs to angst away even more in the privacy of my room.

Chapter 29

It was Wednesday night.

To go or not to go to the NA meeting, that was the question. Common sense strongly dictated that I just drop the whole netaholics thing, Derek and all, like a rotten zucchini. File it away in the dark recesses of what was left of my brain as just another awkward mistake.

Udder suggested it might be helpful if I made a list of the pros and cons as a way to get to a decision.

"We're fine with you not going," he said supportively. "You've given it a good shot and now it's your call. If you think it's time to move on, then do it."

"But why won't you just tell me what do to?" I asked. More like begged. "Please?"

"Darling, '*Life is like a game of cards; the way you play it is free will.*'"

"Shakespeare?" I asked.

"Nehru."

"I wish it was more like softball. At least I'm reasonably good at that."

I took Udder up on his suggestion and made a list. On the "Reasons to Go to NA" side:

1) Have a legitimate excuse to get out of the house. (I loved my Udder and Gramps dearly, but being around them 24/7 was making even me smell like an old fart.)

2) Eyewitness another techno shit show. (Listening to the freak of the week spill their guts out was actually becoming pretty hard to resist. My FOMO, in the past confined solely to the net, was now spilling itself out into real life.)

3) Drink good stuff for free. (Karen the Cat Killer had promised to bring in some Kick Ass Arabica whole-bean dark roast, organic, shade-grown, fair-trade coffee, deliciously simmering with notes of chocolate malt, molasses, and licorice. Guaranteed to make my spoon stand up straight. Yum! Definitely hard to resist.)

4) Derek. (Oh my God. No matter how hard I tried, I just couldn't seem to get that damn boy off my brain. Seeing him would be . . . well . . . seeing him.)

On the "Reasons Not to Go to NA" side:

1) Guilt by association. (Showing up to yet another Netaholics Anonymous meeting might make the tongues wag—not that I really knew any tongues to wag. But still, continuing to surround myself with offline lunatics could give folks the impression that I was one of them. That I actually had a problem, when, as I've made abundantly clear, I certainly did not.)

2) *Passion.* (Why would I even contemplate driving all the way into town and not spending the entire time online? I had already cut back on cruising my dating site to such an extent that system texts were now popping up, accompanied by heartbreaking emojis all sobbing and sad-faced, wondering where the heck I was, begging me to return. "We've missed you!" one said. "We're worried about you!" "Come back, come back!" I had always prided myself on my high *Passion* rating score, but almost overnight it had plummeted from a 9.7 to a 7.4, which was completely humiliating. My flagrant disregard for incoming texts had demoted me from that pinnacle of being an almost perfect *Passion* player, the one thing (other than softball) that I was doing reasonably well with in my life. To top it off, losing those *Passion* points meant those sweet discounts from online advertisers were starting to dry up. Totally unacceptable.)

3) Derek. (Given our non-relationship, showing up at the meeting—with Derek there—would be beyond awkward. After what he did to me—or was it what he didn't do?—why would I ever want to see him again?)

To go or not to go. To go or not to go. To go or—

"What are you wearing to the meeting tonight?" Gramps asked, plopping himself down on the sofa and lighting a joint.

"I don't know," I told him. "What do you think of this white skirt and cream-colored top? I also thought I might throw on this scarf I found—I think it's Udder's." I did a little whirl and twirl, modeling my outfit for him.

"You look—"

"Bee-YOU-tee-full," Udder interrupted, coming in from the kitchen.

Like I said before, common sense dictated I should bail. But then again I had four items on the to-go side and only three on the not-to-go side. Plus, common sense, as everyone knew, was grossly overrated.

The meeting took place at the height of the *Pokémon Go* craze, a new cell phone time-suck and online brain-fuck guaranteed to make you lose your mind. Heroin be damned—one poke at *Pokémon Go* and you were an addict's addict.

Gullible lunatics traveled around their cities and towns using their phones to search frantically for mythical monsters that *were not real*— but damn if the players didn't think they were. The point was to use their onscreen Poké Ball to capture "wild" Pokémon (Pokémons? Pokémen? Who the hell knew?) and, duh, get Poké Points.

This was the madness that had taken the world by storm.

"I was on the news last Saturday," Claire, this meeting's freak of the week, told us. "And not the way I always dreamed I'd be. Not as some fashion diva or YouTube pop phenom or research chemist who just discovered a cure for every disease known to humankind. No way. I was on the news and it wasn't pretty."

Oh God, I thought, my thumbs once again automatically air-texting away. *Here we go again.*

"I had my head buried in my phone playing *Pokémon Go*, desperately trying to snatch up Squirtle, the cutest little blue-green turtle you've ever seen, and I got, you know, distracted."

I couldn't help but feel bad for Claire. Yet another certifiable NA loser. Another poor, hopelessly lost soul. You dream big, with fabulous visions of doing good in the world, and then something comes along as insidious, as cunning, and as deadly as *Pokémon Go*, and in less time than it takes to play a word like SQUIRTLE in Scrabble, you're totally screwed. One moment everything is good in the world and the next you've thrown it all away to catch a make-believe turtle! Go figure.

"Squirtle?" I whispered to Derek. "Squirtle the Turtle?"

Derek said nothing.

I had planned on sitting as far away from Derek as possible. He had adopted the if-you-don't-acknowledge-it-then-it-doesn't-exist strategy, which was fine when *I* did it but really annoying when someone else did. However, the room was packed and seating was limited, so I was sort of forced to sit next to him.

To talk or not to talk. I didn't have a clue as to where I was at with that boy, but, now that he was right next to me, the urge to bug him was impossible to resist.

"Next time I'm using that word in Scrabble," I whispered. "YOINK and SQUIRTLE. What do you think of that, huh?"

Derek gave me a confused look.

Claire continued, futzing with her hair the whole time she was talking. "I had almost caught up with the little guy and had him totally in my sights when, *crap*, wouldn't you know it, I walk off a bridge and fall into a river."

"How the hell do you just walk off a bridge?" I whispered, fighting back another round of inappropriate laughter.

Derek turned away from me.

"For a moment I thought I was still in the game," she yammered on, "and that it was, you know, even more realistic than usual. But then I inhaled a mouthful of water and it all got a little too real." Claire had twisted her hair so tightly around her finger that it seemed stuck there.

"Talk about 'in over your head'!" I whispered. I was on a roll!

This time Derek pinched me. I slapped his hand.

"Someone saw me and called 911 and, before I could even make it to the riverbank, the police, the fire department, an ambulance, and the local television news team had arrived. They hauled me out of the water, sputtering and dripping like a half-drowned rat."

"More like a half-drowned turtle," I whispered.

"It was quite the scene. 'Another *Pokémon Go* survivor,' the newscaster said, cameras rolling. I mean, she was totally unable to hide her glee at my misfortune. It was like she was getting off on it. 'Fortunately, this one didn't bite the dust, but she sure did take quite the dive. If this craze goes on much longer, they'll have to dedicate a whole new wing of the hospital to its victims. Now with her phone on the bottom of the river, will it be *Pokémon Go* or *Pokémon No-Go* next time for Claire? Stay tuned!'"

I was biting my fist to keep from giggling.

"I was like a celebrity," Claire continued. "My thirty seconds of fame. I got called by the *Boston Globe*, for God's sake. The *Globe*! They wanted to interview me about the dangers of Pokémon addiction. Needless to say, this was not the fame I had in mind. Not exactly how I wanted it all to go down.

"Anyway, to cut it short, here I am."

"Welcome, Claire," we called out in unison.

I turned toward Derek and slapped him hard on his thigh.

"What are you doing?" he hissed, turning to me with wrinkled brow and a scowl on his face.

"Sorry," I said. "I thought I saw Squirtle climbing up your leg."

What did I tell you? Another night in paradise.

Chapter 30

"How was your hike?" I asked Sheila.

Sheila, back again for yet another weekend stay with me, had spent all day Saturday out in the woods with Jonathan.

"*Arghhh!*" she cried.

"What? What happened?"

"Asshole. Son of a bitch!" she spat out.

"Jonathan?" I asked, alarmed at the tone of her voice. "Oh my God! What did that boy do to you now?"

"No, no. Not Jonathan. Jonathan's awesome. It's the bastard I battled on top of Mount Tom that I can't stand."

"What? Don't tell me the porcupine turned mean on you!"

"No! Of course not!" she said. "Just let me catch my breath. I'm still hyperventilating."

Sheila had collapsed in the shade of one of the mutant zucchini plants and was furiously fanning herself with one of its ginormous leaves. It was the usual melodramatic way for Sheila to begin a story. One thing about Sheila: she was quite the drama llama.

"So, we hike up to the top of the mountain, right? It's overlooking the Connecticut River, beautiful views into the Berkshires, totally awesome. There we are, perched on the top watching hawks, when all of a sudden we get buzzed by a drone."

"A drone? One of those flying aircraft thingies?"

"Exactly," Sheila said. "Can you believe it? We're out in the middle of nowhere, conversing with the nymphs of nature, communing with the wonders of the world—and a drone whizzes by."

"Anyway, it really pissed me off. I mean, maybe there are places for those things, but the top of Mount Tom is definitely not one of them.

So, I climb on over to the next ledge and there's this yahoo at the controls, pounding down the brews.

"'What the fuck are you doing?' I ask him. 'You're scaring away the birds *and* videoing my boyfriend feeling me up.'"

"Wait a minute!" I said. "Jonathan is your boyfriend? Jonathan was feeling you up?"

"Well, the boyfriend part isn't quite official yet and I still had my shirt on, but yeah."

"I thought you were birdwatching?"

"We were. I can multitask, you know. Can I please get back to my story?"

"We have a lot to talk about," I said, raising my eyebrows.

"So the guy opens up another beer and starts going off on me. 'Go back to Baghdad, bitch!' he says."

Sheila's Middle Eastern features—creamy complexion, large hazel eyes, jet black hair, and lavishly long eyelashes—made her stand out in a crowd. She was proud of her heritage and did not take lightly to ethnic slurs of any kind.

"Can you believe it? This pervert is drinking and droning, on top of a mountain in a state reservation, for God's sake, getting off videoing Jonathan and me fooling around. And then he starts slamming me? Seriously? The creepy voyeur video stuff, I couldn't give a shit about. Video away. See if I care. But you know what really pissed me off?"

"I can't imagine."

"The asshole is totally spooking the birds. The poor red-tailed hawks were going nutso with the drone zipping through their air space. Totally freaking out, flapping like crazy, not knowing which way was up. What a jerk! The guy was asking for trouble."

"And something tells me you gave it to him."

"Damn right I did. I walk on over and give the son of a bitch a kick."

"Seriously, Sheila? You *kicked* the dude?"

"No! I kicked the *drone*. By this time he had landed the thing and it was just lying there, staring up at me with those big freaky robot eyes. I didn't mean to do it any serious damage. I just wanted to, you know, make my point. But I guess I kicked the thing just a little too hard."

"Oh no."

"Oh yeah. It starts rolling down the ledge, and before I could grab it the damn drone had tumbled over the edge of the cliff. Air time over! Fly no more, beyotch!"

"Oh my God! Where was Jonathan?" By now I was almost as breathless as Sheila.

"Jonathan was still back at our ledge getting his pants on and searching for his shoes."

"His pants on?"

"Yeah, I forgot to tell you that part. Anyway, the drone dude is practically bursting blood vessels, screaming bloody murder. He leaps up to go after me, trips on his six-pack, and falls flat on his face. I hightail it out of there, grab Jonathan, and we head for the hills. God, Meagan, we had to hide out in the woods for over an hour until the dust had settled enough so we could sneak back to the car and make our getaway."

"Jesus, Sheila!"

"I know. Pretty awesome, huh?"

"For a felony, yeah. Don't you think you may have possibly overreacted? Just a little bit?"

"Hell no!" Sheila exclaimed. "Those things are evil. It got what it deserved."

"You can't just go around destroying people's stuff, Sheila!"

"Can and will," she said. "And I'll do it again in a heartbeat. Let me tell you, Meagan, it was quite the afternoon. Hawk watching. Drone destroying. Boob play. Hand job. Doesn't get much better than that. Anyway, I've got to go shower and change. Do you think Gramps would mind if I borrowed a little bit of his weed? Jonathan and I are headed out to a documentary on climate change, and, you know, getting high might take a little of the edge off of that. By the way, I hope you don't mind me abandoning you like this."

"No, no. Of course not. Go right ahead. Leave me stranded on Saturday night, sad and lonely, with only my grandfathers for company. Huzzah and hooray! We'll probably play Scrabble again."

"Scrabble? I thought that was Derek's game?"

"It is. I'm just. . . you know . . . boning up and all. Just in case." I turned away from her and picked at the zit on my chin.

"You sure you're not jealous?" she asked.

"Sheila! That was the whole point of you coming out here in the first place. Now, if you can just pull the same stunt with Derek like you've clearly done with Jonathan, then I'll be good to go."

"You're on your own with that one, bestie. I'm a one-boy girl. And please, no referring to what I've got going with Jonathan as a *stunt*."

"Then what is it?" I asked.

"Haven't a clue," she said, purring happily to herself as she got undressed. "You sure you're not mad at me?"

"Mad at you? No. Worried about your sanity? Oh yeah. You better believe it."

"Never been saner," Sheila said. "And don't wait up for me. Who knows, I might just get lucky and not be back tonight."

"I'm not sure luck has anything to do with it," I told her, and we both laughed.

Chapter 31

Derek.

What to do about Derek.

I had slipped away quickly after the last Wednesday Netaholics Anonymous meeting because, whispering aside, I honestly couldn't deal. But absence from Derek was certainly not making the heart grow any less fond.

Try as I might, I could not get that boy out of my head. He was like a brainworm, insidiously boring his way deep into my skull, twisting this way and that. I kept picking at my ears, worried that it wasn't wax but gray matter oozing out.

Udder and Gramps had headed into town for dinner and abandoned me. There I was, all alone, with no car to flee in. Desperate for Derek relief, I walked endlessly up and down the road in a futile search for the end of the dead zone so I could escape online.

No such luck. Goddamn hilltowns. It was like living in the twentieth century, for Christ's sake. Still no service.

Fuck the phone, I told myself. If I couldn't get online, I had other options. I was a big girl. I could think of something else to escape from that boy.

Meditation! That could work! I had been learning a little bit about that, thanks to the mindfulness-based stress-reduction cassettes (how twentieth century was that?) that Udder and Gramps occasionally listened to. They said it helped them with their arthritis. Derek withdrawal seemed to be almost as painful, so I figured I'd give it a go.

They had one feminist tape (go figure) that went on and on about wrapping your breath around your fallopian tubes, opening up your ovaries and making your uterus smile, but that just didn't float my boat, so instead I went with being one with a lake. No matter what storms or ill winds or crashing waves ruffled my surface, deep down my inner waters would be calm, tranquil, and peaceful. Believe it or not, it wasn't nearly as lame as it sounded.

So I meditated. Dressed in my loosest shorts and Gramps's Dump Trump T-shirt, I sat by myself, legs crossed yogi style, in the early evening shade of the orchard, and chanted my mantra (*honeybee, honeybee, honeybee*) over and over. Doing my best to be a lake.

I focused all of my attention on my third eye, that sacred place behind my eyebrows, that seat of my soul, and concentrated on my breath. But damn if my third eye refused to cooperate. It wandered at will, sometimes cross-eyed, this way and that, but always wondering about, you guessed it—Derek. Curse that boy!

Giving my mind a little R & R, freeing it from chaos, going to that place of peace and serenity was sure a lot easier said than done.

To get all basebally (or was it softbally?) about it: my brain, for all of its faults, was a wicked good pitcher. It kept firing boy thought after boy thought right smack down the middle of the plate, high heat, strike after strike. Fouling these off was out of the question. After a while I couldn't even swing, for God's sake. I'd just stand there looking, bat on my shoulder, paralyzed. Thought after thought, all with Derek front and center, hurling down from the mound, threatening in no uncertain terms to retire the side in nine pitches if they weren't heard and recognized IMMEDIATELY!

Why are offline guys so scary?

Why does just the thought of love put me over the edge?

What is it about a relationship that makes me grab my bat and my glove, turn my back, and run (not walk) out of the ballpark?

Why does Derek have to do the things that he does? Why couldn't he have just left me alone? Why is he even alive?

Why? Why? Why?

Lake or no lake, Derek-induced thoughts, sneaky bastards that they were, had co-opted the whole ballgame and used meditation to flood my brain and strike at the heart of the amygdala. It was a losing cause. Meditation only seemed to make it that much clearer just how confused I really was.

I was practically drowning in the damn lake, my third eye just weighing me down.

All right then, if I couldn't meditate, I could sure as hell masturbate. At least I knew I was good at that. A little self-pleasure, a bit with the clit (next to my phone, my guaranteed go-to gal) would definitely propel me into that blissful zone of forgetfulness. It was healthy and safe and so much calorie-free fun.

So I hid myself away in the furthest reaches of the orchard where no grandfathers returning early from dinner might accidently wander, and I stretched out in the summer sun. Fearing the wrath of King Ludd, I resisted the urge to use the MyVibe app on my phone and, instead of having my cell vibrate my cares away, let my fingers do the walking. *Arghhh!* What was I thinking? Masturbate and not fantasize about Derek? Hello! Earth to Meagan! Had that secondhand pot smoke warped all of my brain cells?

No matter how hard I tried to substitute other players into my erotic dream team, it was always Derek pitching, Derek catching. It was Derek (*ooh la la!*) in every position. I'd bring up to bat the image of every hot guy I had ever sexted with but, just as I was rounding third and heading toward home, there he'd be. Good ol' Derek. Blocking the damn plate.

This whole thing was beginning to piss me off. And seriously, how many baseball (softball?) metaphors could I possibly entertain before driving myself completely crazy?

Okay. If I couldn't meditate and I couldn't masturbate, then at the very least, I could caffeinate. Self-medication through major-league caffeination. That would definitely do the trick.

Meditation, eliminating thought, had been a complete disaster. Masturbation, sexualizing thought, while considerably more fun, had brought Derek into even sharper focus. But coffee. Coffee! If I could abuse enough caffeine, then the damn thoughts would be flying by so fast and furious they wouldn't have a chance in hell of even being recognized. I'd be too busy dodging neuron fastballs to make sense of any of them.

Huzzah and hooray!

What could possibly go wrong with that?

(◇)

I was a little fuzzy as to exactly how many cups of coffee I had consumed before the lightning bolt struck and out-sizzled the most brilliant idea ever!

Some thoughts are like a fine wine, taking their own sweet time to come to fruition. The longer they ferment, the better they are.

Not this one! This thought burst forth like hooch out of a backyard still. *BAM!* I was almost blind from the moonshine.

Regaining my sight and having recognized the impossibility of solving the boy issue on my own, I had the epiphany that I was in desperate need of a compatriot to ride to my rescue. Some dazzlingly heroic third party to resurrect this whole relationship fiasco of mine. Sheila was way too strung out on Jonathan and Mother Nature, plus I was having serious concerns about her mental stability. Udder and Gramps were way too old to be of any use. That left . . .

King Ludd! His Royal Highness! I'd use King Ludd to act as an intermediary between Derek and me.

Brilliant or what?

Here's what I'd do: I'd handwrite a letter to Derek from Ned Ludd himself, the mythical king, the fearless leader of the Luddites, the anti-tech titan, the *Man*, asking for a do-over. A do-over with Derek! That would solve all of my problems.

Okay. So maybe this didn't really fit into the boy-free game plan. Maybe I really was so socially inept that I'd never be able to navigate the offline world of real life, so why even try? Maybe it was a little unclear what writing to Derek in a King Ludd persona could possibly hope to accomplish? Maybe requesting a do-over when the whole Derek thing already seemed *done over* made about as much sense as a squirtle yoinking, particularly after that pathetic, ill-timed, poorly prepared crash-and-burn pass I had made. Maybe I should just stick with the plan and beat back any thoughts of real offline romance until I figured out what the hell I was doing with my fake online romances. Maybe too much coffee was not necessarily a good thing.

But still, it was painfully clear to me how desperate I was for a do-over. It was all I could think about. And if I didn't do something about doing it over now, I wasn't sure I'd ever muster up the courage to try to do it over ever again.

When lightning strikes you just gotta go with it.

As soon as Udder and Gramps came home, I borrowed the car and, leaving my phone behind even without being asked to (can you believe it?), I drove like a maniac downtown, found a corner table in the basement of the Haymarket Café, and began my handwritten manifesto to Derek.

As was the case with everything, writing a letter by hand wasn't nearly as easy as it seemed. It had been ages since I had ventured back in time and gone keyboardless. Even though I had sent out those few sparse postcards to my parents, I could still barely even remember how to hold a pen, so writing legibly was proving incredibly difficult. But a typed letter from the anti-technology king of kings? That was just wrong.

Some of the letters I loved to make. Take a *y* for instance. They were the cutest little things ever. I just wanted to take one home, snuggle with it, and squeeze it to death. I was practically yoinking out loud over them.

But *x*'s? I was cursing the cursive out of those sneaky little bastards. They gave me the heebie jeebies.

Not only was writing a problem—but spelling? Oh my God! The computer goddess gave us spellcheck for a reason. I couldn't recall any of the rules, screwing up the most basic of words. Was it *I* before *E* except after *T*? After *P*? Who the hell knew?

Sitting in the café, doing my thing the cavegirl way with good ol' pen and ink, brought into super-sharp focus just how wired-up the rest of the world was. Everybody else's head was buried in their laptop or hunched over their iPhone. Not a voice to be heard. Mine was the only piece of paper in sight.

I was beginning to attract stares. I could see little thought bubbles (in cursive even) forming over people's heads, just like in the comic strips.

"W'sup with that girl? Is that a pen in her hand? Is that shit even legal anymore?"

This, of course, only fueled my newfound, caffeine-induced sense of superiority.

"Look at me!" I wanted to shout. "I can fucking write, bitch!"

I ordered a double cappuccino and furiously began my manifesto. Thank goodness, Udder and Gramps were generous with the spending money, because I was breaking the bank with my high-end coffee addiction.

Damn these addictions! I seemed to be accumulating them quicker than I changed socks.

Chapter 32

Sir Derek,

The following guide has come into my possession from a certain young woman who has a particular affinity for your company and wishes to extend the fondest of thoughts to you. Thanks to you, her eyes have been opened to the appalling epidemic of technological addiction so widely evident in the world today. In an attempt to help bring light to the darkness, she has written the following manifesto and asked that it be posted prominently and promptly in public places around town.

The Luddite's Guide to the Top Ten Things to Do with Your Thumbs (and Fingers) Offline

1) Read a book. Caress those sensual pages between your fingers. Relish the feel of actual paper. Ignore the odd stares from prying eyes in the café. "What's that thing she's got in her hands?" they will whisper. "Someone help me out here. I can't quite remember the word for it. Not a Nook but a . . . ?"

2) Doodle. Grab a pencil and go to work. Let the mind wander and the fingers create. Fantastical figures, shifting shapes, psychedelic images—just make sure to keep your creations out of the hands of your therapist. We don't want to get involuntarily committed, now, do we?

3) Play the piano. You don't have to know how. You don't even have to own one. Air piano is a beautiful thing (much more soothing than air-texting), and when you practice, it won't drive your family and friends crazy. Just close your eyes, listen to the music in your head, and play. (Note: so as not to appear insane, perhaps doing this in private makes the most sense. Reread item number two above about involuntarily commitments.)

4) Whittle. All you need is a knife, a random piece of wood, and a couple of hundred band-aids in case you cut the shit out of your finger.

5) Pet something. A cat. A dog. Even a turtle (a real one—not some Pokémon rip-off). Anything that moves. They'll love you forever for it, unless, of course, they don't. In that case, the band-aids left over from whittling will come in handy again.

6) Bite your nails. Okay—I know it's disgusting and unsightly and unsanitary. The list of negatives goes on and on. But let's face it, there are few things more satisfying in life than picking off a long thick one. (Remember, we're talking nails here and not boogers. Granted, picking your nose is also sweet, maybe even more so, but public picking is beyond gross and will never receive the Good Luddites' Sanitary Seal of Approval. So, for the love of God, stick with your nails, please.)

7) Knit or crochet. Yeah, yeah, yeah. It's weird. It's retro. And everybody will dread opening up gifts from you. But still, as far as addictions go, it's a pretty healthy one. Plus, with all of those lame, half-finished, sorry excuses for scarves wrapped tightly around your neck, you'll never be cold again. Added benefit: if you're a straight guy, this can be an awesome conversation starter with random knitting-obsessed women.

8) Floss. Not only is it good for your teeth but you can take the string and make mobiles with seashells or unused utensils or pieces from your smashed cell phone. (But, unlike with your knitted creations—don't even think about giving this shit away.)

9) Rub a worry stone. It may make you look neurotic and insane, but we're on number nine here, and, gimme a break, the caffeine is starting to wear off and I'm running out of ideas.

10) Masturbate. Enough said. The ultimate safe sex. Double important to keep in mind the privacy rule for this one.

While the writer has expressed a willingness to consider constructive criticism regarding this list, she has also emphatically indicated her firm belief that the above is perhaps the most brilliant thing EVER WRITTEN, and any suggestions for changes, no matter how tiny or inconsequential, will be RIDICULED and SPAT UPON. She eagerly awaits your whole-hearted approval.

May news of your conquests spread far and near,
May your enemies take the alarm.
May your courage, your fortitude, strike them with fear,
May they dread your Omnipotent Arm!

Respectfully,

Ned (King) Ludd

P.S. Following additional reflection and a great deal of angst and soul-searching on her part, the writer respectfully requests a conversation do-over. Her last attempt at a face-to-face ended in a bizarrely awkward and uncomfortable way for all involved. She remains cautiously optimistic that, at your convenience, you will acquiesce to this request. It was far from easy for her to make it. At the time of this writing, she was on perhaps her nineteenth espresso/cappuccino and her hands were shaking and she couldn't believe she was actually putting this down on paper and maybe, just maybe, getting up enough courage to actually send you the damn thing.

P.P.S. In an acknowledged moment of weakness, the author went off the wagon, fired up her phone, and spent hours wasting her precious time YouTubing softball triple plays. She wishes to reiterate that HER triple play was, hands down, the BEST EVER!!!! She is also desperately hoping to be invited back to play shortstop again, given that YOU WILL NEVER EVER FIND ANYONE EVEN CLOSE TO AS AWESOME AS SHE IS!

P.P.P.S. Knowing that texting is evil and a phone call way too awkward, the writer had every intention of hand-delivering this letter to your humble abode. However, clear-thinking girl that she is, she has since thought better of it. What if you weren't home? What if, à la Tess of the d'Urbervilles, the letter was slid under your door and wound up hidden under a rug and you never saw it and everything spiraled downhill from there and our fearless heroine ended up strung up by her neck and swinging on the gallows? Therefore, she plans on hiding in the bushes near your house, giving this letter to some random neighborhood kid and paying them a quarter to hand deliver it to you in person, and then skedaddling away once you receive it.

P.P.P.P.S. The writer had contemplated going all van Gogh on you, cutting off her ear, and mailing it to you as a token of her undying affection, but then, thankfully, she thought better of it because it just might impact her ability to hear the ball coming when she's busy, once again, being the BEST SHORTSTOP EVER!!!!!!!!!!

Okay. I know this sounds like the strangest letter ever written, that it made little (if any) sense, and that it in no way came even remotely close to solving the Derek dilemma. But difficult times called for extreme actions—even if they were clinically insane.

I downed one more cup, closed my eyes, clicked my heels together three times while holding my breath, and, with thoughts of King Ludd dancing through my head, drove to Derek's. I had been to his house once before after the first NA meeting when he had locked his keys in the car, but still, without my phone, finding the damn place was no walk in the woods. Forty wrong turns and sixteen random-strangers-giving-me-conflicting-directions later ("go right at the third traffic light . . . on second thought, the second light . . . or maybe it's a left?") I finally got lucky and somehow stumbled onto his street.

As fortune would have it, his neighborhood was crawling with kids. After significant negotiation, I talked one into a dollar delivery (so much for a quarter—kids these days!), watched from behind a bush, secret-agent-like, as she hand-delivered my letter to Derek, and then snuck back to my car without being seen. This time it only took thirty wrong turns (see—who needs Google Maps?) until I finally made it back to Udder and Gramps's.

"I'm confused," Udder said, scratching his head as I summarized the day's escapades to him. "What exactly is the endgame here? What do you hope to accomplish with this? What are your expectations?"

"I have none. Expectations are the root of all heartache—remember?"

"Buddha?"

"Shakespeare."

"*Touché*," he replied, smiling. "But isn't the point to—"

"Quiet."

"I thought your intent was—"

"Shhhh." I put my finger over his lips, kissed him on his forehead, and then went happily back out to the garden.

Having dispatched a few more of those pesky bean beetles, I then walked down the road and miraculously found that sweet spot so I could text Sheila (I know—hypocrisy with a capital H, but after all of that handwriting, my thumbs needed to feel normal again) and gave her the play-by-play of my brilliant coping strategies.

Meditate.

Masturbate.

Caffeinate.

Pontificate.

"Wouldn't it have been easier if you just ate instead?" she texted back. "Boston cream donuts are the solution to so many of the world's problems."

Chapter 33

I was out in the garden doing my death-to-all-bean-beetles thing when Derek drove up. He got out of his car, dressed ridiculously in a poufy silk tutu and a rhinestone-studded royal tiara. As I was wont to do in these times of grave emotional turmoil, I hid behind the zucchini.

Derek knocked at the door, handed a letter to Gramps, and with a furtive look in my direction leapt back into his car and sped away.

I raced to the house.

"Damn!" Gramps cursed. "First it's arthritis. Now it's dementia. I swear, I just imagined some cross-dressing lunatic standing at my door who looked suspiciously like—"

"What did he give you?" I asked.

"Refresh my memory," Gramps said. "Are you thirteen or seventeen?"

"Who the hell knows anymore? And why, in God's name, was Derek dressed like that?"

Gramps shook his head. "Teenagers do the strangest things. Particularly adolescent boys in heat. He said he was King Ludd. Here to deliver a message to his ladyshit."

"His ladyshit?"

"Maybe he said 'ladyship.' I don't know. He was speaking in this faux British accent and it was awfully garbled."

I grabbed the letter from Gramps and sprinted upstairs to my room. Locking the door behind me, I grabbed a flashlight, climbed into my bed, pulled the covers over my head, and, trembling under the sheets, read the following:

Dearest Madam,

The gentleman who received your recent correspondence wholeheartedly agrees that your Luddite's Guide to the Top Ten Things to Do with Your Thumbs (and Fingers) Offline *is, as you so aptly stated, the most brilliant broadside EVER WRITTEN! The gentleman would not dare to suggest any changes, even if he were to be spat upon, ridiculed, and then hung by his neck on the gallows à la Tess of the d'Urbervilles. Your profound dexterity with the written word (handwritten, no less—impressive!) combined with your wit and wisdom, shines through like the sun on the smoldering ruins of the cursed Yorkshire woolen mills. The gentleman lifts his eyes to heaven and then bows low with each and every thought of you as he promises to post your broadside in the most public of places.*

Shake off the hateful yoke of the silly old men! Their roguish ministers, nobles, and tyrants must be brought down!

Let your faith grow stronger still.

With undying respect,

Ned (King) Ludd

P.S. The gentleman wishes to further inform you that he has lain awake night after sleepless night, tortured with turmoil, replaying that poorly mis-handled shit show of the infamous kiss-that-wasn't-a-kiss over and over. He spends every moment of each and every day wondering what the hell he was thinking. In the gentleman's defense, that kiss came out of fucking NOWHERE and our poor, socially inept hero was grossly ill-prepared and, to put it mildly (to say nothing of literally), totally gobsmacked. Nonetheless, upon witnessing his countenance upon reading your suggestion of a do-over, orgasmic is way too lame a word to describe his feelings, though I am quite certain that he would blush with shame if you were to misinterpret his ela-tion as being in any shape or fashion sexual in nature or having anything to do with the male organ. He is well aware that PENISES have no place in polite conversation and only receive the Good Luddites' Sanitary Seal of Approval under tightly controlled circumstances.

P.P.S. While the gentleman understands from previous experiences the ef-fect that caffeine can have on your Ladyship, he sincerely hopes that the vast quantity of said jitter juice in no way clouded your judgment in your recent correspondence. He offers profound prayers that you harbor no regrets at any of your wonderfully written words. He does, however, respectfully suggest that perhaps nineteen espressos/cappuccinos may be a tad too many and ARE YOU FUCKING CRAZY? NINETEEN? JESUS CHRIST, WOMAN! I'M SURPRISED YOU'RE STILL ALIVE!

P.P.P.S. With all due respect to the ability of those little bastards (children! yuck!) conniving to squeeze a hard-earned dollar out of you for a few seconds' worth of mindless work, I shall actually hand deliver this letter into the hands (not under the rug—poor Tess!) of your esteemed patriarchs (aka Udder and Gramps) in the confidence that you will receive it in a timely manner.

P.P.P.P.S. The gentleman wishes to convey thanks for not sending him your ear. He would prefer to see it attached to your spectacularly beautiful face as you make yet another TRIPLE FUCKING PLAY, the last of which was the MOST AWESOME SOFTBALL MOMENT EVER!

P.P. . . . S.(I can't remember how many P's.) Speaking of softball, the gentleman begs the honor of your company as shortstop this Sunday, July 22nd, at 4:00 pm in Florence Fields, where the Lefty Luddites will kick ass on the playing field. Perhaps at the conclusion of their much-anticipated resounding victory, your Ladyship could join said gentleman at the restaurant of her choice (Miss Flo's Diner—please? Please?!) for conversation, a bite to eat, and perhaps a discussion of do-over logistics. If a caffeine infusion is necessary, I am quite sure that the aforementioned eatery is well equipped to handle your Ladyship's needs. God knows, they might even give you free refills, which could save you from having to mortgage your grandfathers' farm just to get your damn fix.

P.P.P. . . oh forget it S. I'll just count the seconds until I see your Ladyship again on Sunday.

Chapter 34

"You're what?" I asked.

"I'm on the run, sister." Sheila was panting furiously. "The cops could be here in no time."

Sheila was crouched behind the go-to hiding place: the zucchini plants, growing like giant sequoias in the corner of the garden. Straight out of the *Little Shop of Horrors*, they were girl-eating mutant monstrosities. Gramps had asked me to prune the plants back, but to do so, I'd need to borrow a chainsaw from the neighbors. I had planned to pick the smallest zucchini to use as my bat for the Sunday-afternoon softball game, but I was terrified that the mother squash would hunt me down and do me some serious damage.

"Oh my God, Sheila! Don't tell me you took out another drone? I didn't think the Amish even allowed those things."

"Of course they don't, sister. That would totally fuck with their *Gelassenheit*."

Sheila had come in from Boston on Thursday afternoon and then driven with Jonathan down to Lancaster County, Pennsylvania, to be one with the Amish. A pilgrimage to a sacred site. A classic road trip to witness the Way. If anyone was pulling off the Luddite thing with any degree of success, it was the brothers and sisters of the Amish persuasion. Their enclave in the Keystone State was a required stop in any hipster Luddite-wannabe's travel itinerary.

Sheila had spent two nights camping with Jonathan, tent and all, down in Pennsylvania. I was sworn to secrecy, because if Sheila's parents ever discovered she had gone camping overnight with a boy rather than staying over at Udder and Gramps's with me, they'd have shit the bed.

By now it was abundantly clear that she had worked her magic on that boy. They were celebrating their one-month anniversary *and* Sheila's eighteenth birthday on this road trip. One whole month!

It was hard to fathom Sheila spending the night with a guy. Having sex and not just sext. I hadn't seen this coming at all! My best friend had gone on the pill and was now engaged in a full four-bagger while I had struck out at the plate and hadn't even made it to first base. It wasn't that I was jealous. Or even envious. It was just that I was . . . okay . . . a teeny bit jealous and incredibly envious. That and feeling totally left behind.

"Their *Gelassen*-what?" I asked. "And stop calling me 'sister.' You're creeping me out."

"It's what the Amish call each other."

"They call each other '*Gelassenheit*'? Isn't that what you say when someone sneezes?"

"No, fool-face, they call each other 'brother' and 'sister.' It's revolutionary. Unifying. *Gelassenheit* is self-surrender, submission, contentment, a calm spirit. It's like the core values of the chosen ones."

"Don't tell me you've gone all Amish on me, Sheila. Nature girl I can handle. But from Muslim to Amish in twenty-four hours seems a little extreme, even for you."

"Ahhh, but what a sweet twenty-four hours they were, sister!"

Once more, Sheila furtively peered out over the top of the squash, scanning the horizon for the heat.

"So what'd you do this time?" I asked. Sheila's transformation from apolitical urbanite to political neo-Luddite had happened so quickly that I was finding it exhausting just trying to keep up.

"Gas station TV," she whispered, parting zucchini leaves to look down the driveway.

"The Amish watch TV?" I asked.

"No. Of course not. Don't be disrespectful. No cars. No radios. No internet. No television. It's sick. I'm totally thinking of converting. I mean, seriously, how awesome would it be to trade in my shit car for a horse and buggy! Promise you'll visit me when I move down there?"

"But I thought you were moving into some cabin with Jonathan?"

"Maybe it will be an Amish cabin."

"Wherever it is, I'll be sure to visit," I said graciously. "But what happened with the television?"

"Pinky swear to secrecy?"

"Duh!"

We wrapped pinkies, clicked our foreheads together twice, and whistled the opening notes to Taylor Swift's "Love Story," our ritual of secrecy since seventh grade.

"Okay," Sheila said. "Check this out. There we were, driving back from Pennsylvania on the Mass Pike and we pull into a service area.

Jonathan asks me to get gas while he goes to pee, and while I'm filling up the tank there it is. Front and center. Screaming in my face. The son of a bitch is perched right on top of the pump."

"What is?"

"A television!" Sheila whispered. "Gas station TV!"

"Uh oh."

"'Uh oh' is right. Here I am, still feeling the *Demut* and the *Gelassenheit*, my head immersed in the Amish live-simply-so-that-others-may-simply-live vibe. And there it is, this fucking monstrosity blasting right in my face. Shouting out its ads for shit, shit, and more shit. Capitalist claptrap crap. I've just spent a weekend with the good folk and here I am being brutally assaulted by the boob tube! The evil predator. The opiate of the masses!"

"Not good," I said.

"Not good at all. I try to turn it off, or at least turn the damn volume down, but I can't. I yell at it but I swear it just gets louder. It's mocking me. Hurling insults my way. Smiling like Satan. Trying to pull me into the devil's workshop."

"What about the *Gelassenheit*? The calm spirit?"

"Screw the calm spirit. It's something you have to work up to. Meanwhile gasoline is spurting out everywhere because there's something wrong with the damn nozzle, and I totally lost it."

"How can you lose a gas nozzle?"

"More like beat the shit out of it."

"The nozzle?"

"No! The television. I took the windshield cleaner thingie out from the bucket next to the pump and started wailing at it. Before I could stop myself the screen had cracked and that beyotch was history."

A car pulled into the driveway and Sheila dove back into the zucchini. It was only the mailman.

"Did anyone see you?" I asked her when she came crawling back out.

"I don't think so. Jonathan came back from peeing and then we sped the hell out of there."

"He must be getting used to that sort of thing. First the drone. Now the gas station TV. Is nothing safe?"

"Don't make fun, Meagan. I'm a fugitive. On the run. I'm going to have to forge a new identity. Get a new hairstyle. Change my name and everything."

"I thought you already did that," I told her.

"I did?" she asked.

"Yeah. Queen Ludd. Remember?"

Sheila laughed, a porcupine screech that sounded like an Ewok playing a kazoo. It echoed through the garden and made the leaves on the zucchini plant quiver. She thrust her clenched left fist high up into the air.

"Queen Ludd it is!" she shouted. "Just try and get me, you sons of bitches! You'll never take me alive!"

Chapter 35

Sheila and I had spent the morning in the garden weeding and killing beetles (it gave me some small degree of satisfaction to know I could at least do *that* better than her) and now we were on our way to the Lefty Luddites Sunday softball game. It was the day after Sheila had gotten home from her Amish road trip, and she was still pretty anxious and jumpy. Such is the life of a fugitive on the run. You reap what you sow.

"I'm thinking of rethinking my whole life plan," Sheila told me as we pulled out of the driveway.

"You have a plan?" I asked her.

"No. Not really. Actually, not at all. But the whole time Jonathan and I were down in Pennsylvania with the brethren I was practically drowning in epiphanies. They were flooding through my brain, dripping out of my ears. I could barely breathe. It got me thinking about rethinking everything."

I had begged Sheila to come to the game with me. The whole do-over with Derek thing was freaking me out and I desperately needed her moral support, just in case things went weird again. Ever since I had exchanged letters with Derek via King Ludd, I had been thinking of nothing else. I was so nervous that I'd bitten my nails down to the quick, enough to make them bleed. Onychophagia: chronic nail biting. What was I thinking, doing that? Now one of my pathological impulse control disorders was going to make it hard to put on my softball glove. I desperately wanted to impress Derek and turn another triple play, or at least a double play, and now it was going to be hard to play at all.

Anyway, softball was definitely not Sheila's thing but, with Jonathan at work, Sheila had nothing better to do.

"Epiphanies about what?" I asked her.

"About everything. Who am I? Why am I here? What is my purpose on this planet? Do I really need to shave my legs? Try combining those brainworms with no sleep."

"Oh my God, Sheila. I've been thinking about the same things. It's like we're conjoined twins. Seriously. I start one sentence and—"

"I finish it. Creepy, isn't it?"

"Totally. Why didn't you sleep?"

"Sex," Sheila said. "Jonathan was awesome. And, believe it or not, I think I sort of knew what to do. I mean, he sure seemed to like it."

"How?" I asked, dying for information. I still could hardly believe that Sheila was no longer a virgin.

"How did we have sex?" Sheila's eyebrows went up. "Do I really have to tell you that?"

"Of course you do! But what I really want to know is how did you know what to do at all? I mean, we've been giggling about this for, like, forever."

It was true. Ever since the seventh grade, Sheila and I had spent innumerable hours trying to wrap our brains around the whole sex thing. I mean, how did the penis even get where it was supposed to go?

"And now," I went on, "you've actually gone and done it. I mean, Earth to Sheila—this is earth-shattering! I can't believe you're being so blasé about the whole thing. You're finally no longer a virgin but you're acting like it's no big deal."

"Meagan," Sheila said grinning, holding her hands out a few inches apart. "Believe me. It was a huge deal!"

I almost drove off the road.

"Oh my God! Did it hurt?"

"Yeah. A little. But he was really gentle."

"Did you like it?" I asked, still blown away by what I was hearing.

"Yeah! A lot! A real, real lot!"

"Are you going to do it again?"

"You better believe it!" Sheila's grin took up the entire car.

"The first time must have been so . . . weird," I said. "I still don't get how you knew what to do?"

Sheila grinned conspiratorially. "Promise me you won't tell Jonathan?" she whispered.

"These lips are glued shut."

"I googled it."

"What?" I asked.

"Googled it. How to have sex for the first time. I took an online tutorial. It was actually pretty helpful."

"Weren't you scared to death?"

"Of going online? No. Why should I be? Unlike you I haven't totally sworn off the hard stuff."

"Not going online, you idiot. Scared of having sex."

"Duh! I was petrified."

Coming to grips with Sheila losing her virginity with Jonathan in a tent of all places way out there in the middle of Amish Country with only an online tutorial for preparation was quite the challenge.

"But you actually did it," I said.

"I did."

I took my hand off of the steering wheel to wipe my brow. "Well, thank goodness Jonathan's all over me."

"He better not be all over you. If he's playing both of us then I'll totally lose it."

"Sheila! I meant *gotten* over me."

"Fat chance, girl! Whose name do you think he was calling out the whole time he was coming?" There she was, grinning again.

"*What?*" Once more I almost drove off the road.

"Chillax! I'm kidding." Sheila did an encore of her Ewok kazoo laugh. "You've got to get over yourself, girl. I'm not letting that boy go, that's for damn sure." Her hair was blowing this way and that from the open car window. She looked radiant.

"So that's the take-home message? Jonathan's a keeper?"

"It sure is one of them. That and sex, totally weird as it is, is pretty amazing. But, believe it or not, there's way more to it than that."

"More to it than sex? Tell me!"

Sheila rubbed her forehead and gazed intensely ahead. "Okay. How about this: what the hell are you and I going to do with the rest of our lives, Meagan? I mean, I know we're only in high school and all, but the whole trajectory of what comes after seems so meaningless. So pointless. Go to college. Get a shit job. Live a boring life. Have unfulfilling affairs. Raise whiny kids and even whinier grandkids and then die. Seriously? Is that all there is to it?"

"Oh my God, Sheila—you have sex for the first time, and *that* was your epiphany? Holy crap! You've just given me yet another reason to run away from an offline relationship." I put on the blinker and turned down the road heading to the playing field. As fascinating as this conversation was, I was starting to get super-anxious about the conversation that I was going to have with Derek.

"Look at the adults we know," Sheila continued. "No offense, but look at your mother. Look at her job. She does advertisements for shit cereals. Dancing cavemen in drag and dinosaurs on roller skates selling processed sugar? There's more nutrition in a Dove bar dipped in soda than in the crap that she sells. And her love life? It's been a disaster. A train wreck. By far the best thing she's done in her entire life was to have you." Sheila reached over from the passenger seat and put her hand reassuringly on my arm.

"Oh my God," I said. "And look at little old whiny train wreck me!"

"Exactly. And *my* mother? Even worse. Personal investment counselor who kisses the asses of filthy rich folks all day long, most of them white men way past the age of getting it up. Her clients are busy raping the planet and bringing the earth to its knees and all she does is stuff money down their pants. If we were in Germany in the 1930s, she'd be the one investing in gas chambers."

"Sheila! I brought you along for moral support, not to make me want to cut myself."

"Let me tell you something, Meagan. When Jonathan and I were down in Amish country, it was a different story. That communal spirit. That sense of belonging to something bigger than yourself. That's what I want, Meagan. That's what I need."

"To become Amish?"

"No. Not Amish. But something that's not me, either. At least not the old me. I need a total Sheila do-over!"

We pulled into the ballpark lot and parked behind the backstop. There was Derek, waiting for me, leaning on his bat and chewing on his glove.

Sheila turned and gave me a big hug. "Speaking of do-overs, may the force be with you. On and off the playing field. Remember," she said, kissing me on the top of my head. "Queen Ludd is watching."

Chapter 36

"What do we yell?" Karen the Cat-Killing Pitcher shouted.

"To hell with the cell!" the Lefty Luddites responded enthusiastically.

"What do we do best?"

"Detest the text!"

"Why won't we be beat?"

"We'll defeat the tweet!"

Hearing myself holler this made me shake my head in wonder. What a long, strange trip this was turning out to be.

The Lefty Luddites stood up on our bench and turned solemnly towards Bubba's Balloons, our opponents for the game. As always, their heads were scrunched down, faces buried in their phones, not listening to a single word the Luddites were chanting.

Gently swaying back and forth with our arms locked around each other, we sang to the tune of the old John Lennon song "Give Peace a Chance":

All we are saying

Is give offline a chance . . .

All we are saying

Is give offline a chance . . .

Derek had substituted his large Lefty Luddite jersey for one a tad too small, so a little bit of skin showed between his tee and his pants. His hair swept up in little wings on the side and his eyes were twinkling with that pregame excitement. Sitting back down on the bench next to him with the thought of the imminent do-over wreaking havoc with my brain, I kept crossing and recrossing my legs.

"Hey," he said to me awkwardly.

"Hey," I replied even more awkwardly.

I started to lean in closer to him but he scooted aside, leapt onto the bench, and launched into his pregame pep talk.

Rumor had it that Derek was the only co-ed slow-pitch rec-league coach in the history of the game who would actually scout other team's practices. Karen whispered to me that she had even seen him film other team's games so he could analyze opposing players' strengths and weaknesses and chart their pitches.

Man, did that boy have issues.

"They've got someone new on the mound," he solemnly announced. "Be patient at the plate and don't let her intimidate you. She can bark all she wants. But we'll be the ones doing the biting." Derek scrunched up his face, bared his teeth, wiggled his fingers tiger-claw-like, and made guttural growling sounds. I recrossed my legs again and growled right back at him.

Today's lefty political rant of the game was the evil of income inequality. Peter the Porno, today's King Ludd, was working himself into quite the frenzy. Thankfully, he was managing to keep his hands out of his pants and not spin around in too many circles.

"The richest forty-two people on this planet have more wealth than the poorest half of the planet's population," he shouted. "Is this fair?"

"NO!" we yelled.

"Is this right?"

"NO!"

"And the richest one percent have more wealth than the rest of the world combined. Is this fair?"

"NO!" we yelled.

"Is this right?"

"NO!"

The umpire tapped Peter on the shoulder.

"It *is* fair to say that I'm 99 percent sure we have a game to play today."

"Let's kick ass!" Peter yelled as we rushed the field and took our positions.

Kick ass we definitely did not. Karen the Cat Killer's pitches had a dreamy, ethereal, slow-motion feel to them, as if they were simply floating in midair. Batter after batter was walloping the crap out of the ball. Their shortstop, ninety pounds soaking wet (if that), knocked the stitches off with a three-run triple. After half an inning, we were down six to nothing.

"Focus!" Derek shouted to us. "Let's get right back into this."

For all his hard work, Derek's scouting report was totally bogus. Their pitcher was all bark *and* bite. She was a beefy Amazon with spiked hair, an evil eye, and a foul mouth. Her arms were the size of my thighs. We were three up and three down with the ball never leaving the infield, one weakly-hit little squib grounder after another.

The second inning was no better. Nine to nothing.

"We! Are! The One Percent!" Bubba's Balloons taunted as they continued to kick our asses.

By the fourth inning, the rout was on and the game was pretty much history. It was 16 to 2. Pathetic. Our only big hit of the game, thank you very much, was my two-run single hugging the left field line in the bottom of the third.

To add salt in our already festering wounds, the Balloons, now losing interest given the lopsided nature of the score, had once again begun texting when sitting on the bench. Even the umpire, who was about my age, was standing on the plate texting in between innings.

And then there was Sheila. Poor girl. Watching softball was just not her thing. She had been bored to tears throughout the entire game, particularly during the Balloons' ups when we were out in the field and she had no one to gab with. Her mood was deteriorating rapidly. It didn't help matters that a foul ball had ricocheted sharply off her thigh.

"What do we want?" she yelled from the bleachers.

Crickets. We were too demoralized to yell anything back. Plus, it was hot and humid as hell and it was hard to breathe, let alone yell.

"No texting!" I heard her grumble.

It was the bottom of the fifth and I was up. I got a solid piece of the ball and sent it screeching down the right field line. Hoping to stretch a single into a double, I slid hard into the bag at second well before the tag.

"Out!" the umpire called.

"*Out?*" Sheila screamed from the bleachers. "Are you crazy?" She scampered down from her seat and stood behind the backstop, glaring at the umpire. "She was safe by a mile."

"She was out!" the umpire repeated.

"Dude! You didn't even see it. You were sneaking a peek at your phone and you know it. I was watching you. Everybody knows she was safe."

"I saw the whole thing. She was out."

"I'm serious. You got a game to ump, ump. Put the damn phone away and do your job."

"I'm serious," the ump responded, phone still twitching in his hand. "Go back to the bleachers where you belong."

This was not the correct thing to say to Sheila. Particularly a bored, sweaty, grumpy Sheila who was just learning to flex her Luddite muscles.

She emerged from behind the backstop and held out her hand to the ump.

"Give me your damn phone," she ordered.

The umpire looked up and nervously took a step backwards. "What are you? Nuts? Go away."

"Seriously," Sheila continued, a little louder this time. Even the Balloons had stopped texting to watch. "You know the studies they did with rats and cocaine? The rats would give up food, water, even sex for a line of coke. Can you imagine that? Well, dig this, dude: phones are the new cocaine. Don't be a rat. Just give me your phone. Now."

"I'm not giving you my phone!" The umpire licked his lips apprehensively. "I told you. Go away!"

In a flash, Sheila reached out and snatched the phone out of his hands.

"Snapchat this, loser!" She waved the phone over her head.

"Hey!" he yelled. "Give that back to me!"

"Abuse it? You lose it."

"Come on!" The umpire stomped his foot like a little kid. He was royally pissed off. "Give me my phone back!"

Amazon woman came strolling to the plate.

"What's up with you, girl?" she barked, puffing up her enormous chest. I swear to God, I could have easily fit a dozen of my boobs into one of her bra cups. "Give him back his phone."

"Not a chance!" Sheila was pissed off too.

Amazon made a grab for the phone, but Sheila leapt deftly out of the way. She turned and raced toward first, followed closely by the scary Amazon woman and the umpire, who was still steaming. Sheila rounded first and sped toward second, lustily cheered on by the Lefty Luddites, who miraculously had rediscovered their lost voices. Other than my hit, it was the most action we had seen all game long. Rounding second she streaked toward third, still in hot pursuit by Amazon and the ump. Rather than making a break for home she veered off into foul territory and then, deploying her newly acquired porcupine-like climbing skills, scampered up the nearest tree.

"White oak!" she yelled down. "*Quercus alba*. If I see anyone google it, this phone is history."

Amazon circled the trunk, growling tiger-like just like Derek had done. The ump was standing off to the side, wringing his hands and making gurgling noises in the back of his throat.

"Does anyone know this girl?" he asked. His hands were shaking. "Can somebody please talk some sense into her? Seriously. That's my phone she's got. My whole life is in that thing!"

The Lefty Luddites all looked at me.

"Dude," I told him. "What you do on your own time is none of my business. But when there's a game on, your phone is off. Got it?"

The umpire begrudgingly nodded.

"No more texting!" I demanded.

"No more texting," he said softly.

"I can't hear you!" Sheila yelled from high up in the oak tree. She had the ump by the shorthairs and he knew it. She wasn't about to show him any mercy.

"No more texting!" he said, a little louder this time.

"Pinky swear?" I asked.

"What?"

"Forget it."

I shouted up to the treetop.

"Sheila! Drop the phone and no one gets hurt."

Sheila was way, way up in the tree. It was windy and the branches were swaying this way and that, back and forth, but there was Sheila, almost at the top, swaying right along with them, grinning from ear to ear, casually tossing the phone back and forth from one hand to the other.

Certifiably insane or not, that girl had nerves of steel! Nonetheless, someone had to be the adult here.

"Come on, Sheila," I called up to her. "You've made your point."

"Make him say it one more time!" she yelled down.

Once more I glared at the ump.

"No more texting!" This time he yelled it.

Sheila let go of the phone. I watched it fall, ricocheting off branch after branch. Using my newly honed shortstop skills, I made a leaping lunge to my left and caught it before it hit the ground. I flipped it over to the ump, who grabbed it and cradled it like a baby.

"Big Brother ain't nothing," Sheila yelled down. "It's Queen Ludd you need to fear!" Using two fingers, she pointed at her eyes, and then pointed down at the umpire. "I'm watching you, dude. I'm watching all of you!"

Chapter 37

"Sheila," I said. "This shit has got to stop."

The three of us—Sheila the Cell Phone Stealer (aka Drone Kicker and TV Smasher), Derek, and me—were sitting on the bench following the softball shellacking. Twenty-five to four. Ouch.

Following an inspirational postgame pep talk by Coach Derek ("Remember the pain we feel right now. Embrace it. Channel it. Let it motivate us to kick ass next game!"), the rest of the team had headed home. The one-on-one do-over with Derek was looming and I was anxious as hell, but Sheila's on-field antics required immediate intervention.

"I'm not kidding," I told her. "You're acting crazy. First the drone strike. Then the gas station TV debacle. And now this? You're going off the deep end here, Sheila. This is not good."

Derek, ignoring my attempt to discipline Sheila, gave her the sha-ka-shake—loose fist, extended pinky and thumb.

"Don't you dare reinforce her poor decision-making," I interrupted, punching Derek in the arm.

"I'm not," he said. "I'm just saying—"

"Don't. If you can't agree with me, then don't talk at all." I was sounding suspiciously like Udder scolding Gramps, or my mother harassing me, but Derek needed to be put in his place.

"Particularly if you want her tongue in your mouth," Sheila chimed in.

"Oh my God, Sheila. Will you please stop! We need to focus on your behavior!"

"What is this, Meagan? Seventh grade? You sound like my mother."

Great! So now I sounded like her mother, my mother, *and* Udder.

"You can't keep going off like this. You can't smash drones. You can't destroy televisions. You can't steal umpire's phones."

"What are you talking about? I not only *can,* but I *did.* And I'd do it again in a heartbeat. Did you see the look on the dude's face when I climbed that tree? Was that awesome or what? He'll think twice before texting while umping again."

Sheila stood on the bench and raised her left fist high in the air. "I am Queen Ludd! Fear me!"

Derek started up with the shaka-shake thing again, but I slapped his hand.

"Look," I said, "the two of you might think this is funny, but I don't. You're going to get into trouble, Sheila. Serious trouble. This stuff is pretty extreme."

"Was Jesus not an extremist for love? Was Martin Luther King Junior not an extremist for civil rights? Was Gandhi not a—"

"Come on, Sheila. Stealing a phone is not exactly doing the King thing."

"It is too. The King Ludd thing! Look, Meagan, I'm speaking truth to power. Naming and shaming. Raging against the machine."

"Also known as vandalism and thievery and just being a royal pain in the ass."

"What do you think, Derek?" Sheila asked. "Should I have done a sit-down strike on home plate instead?"

"Well," Derek said. "I mean . . . you know . . ."

"Do that damn shaka thing and you can kiss the do-over goodbye," I threatened.

This time Sheila punched me in the arm.

"Stop being such a scaredy-cat," she said. "Remember what the man said. '*Our lives begin to end when we become silent about things that matter.*'"

"Yogi Berra?" Derek asked.

"Shakespeare?" I inquired. "Woody Allen? Buddha?"

"MLK," Sheila replied. "Look, I'll leave the two of you to go at it. I gotta head back to Boston. If I call in sick one more day at the store, they're going to fire me. But I'll be back Friday night. Jonathan and I are going out to listen to music at the Parlor Room. It would be fun to have the two of you come."

Sheila gave me a hug and kissed me on the forehead.

"I love you," she said, "even if you are acting like a grumpy old man about all of this. Just remember, '*if the world were perfect, it wouldn't be.*'"

"MLK?" I asked her.

"Jesus? Buddha?" Derek added.

"Yogi Berra," she replied.

"Wow," Derek said. "I am deeply moved. I really am." He raised his hand to do the shaka-shake, thought better of it, and quickly put it back in his glove.

"I love you too," I told her. "But I'd much rather love you out of jail than in."

"Derek," Sheila said, ignoring me but giving him the same killer look she had given the umpire. "You now know what I am capable of doing. You treat her badly and you'll never play softball again. Ever. That *or* procreate. Do you understand me?"

Sheila reached into her purse and tossed me a three pack of condoms. "If you're rounding third and heading toward home, these could come in handy."

"Sheila!" I cried, throwing them right back at her, blushing my brains out.

Sheila stashed them back in her purse and walked away, singing "We Shall Overcome" very loudly and not at all on key.

Chapter 38

We were sitting in the booth at the farthest end of Miss Flo's diner. I had put a quarter in the old-fashioned jukebox on the table and we were blasting classic rock—Chicago's "25 or 6 to 4," so appropriate for the occasion. Derek was shaking way too much salt onto his three-cheese garlic omelet, stirring it around, and then moving it from one corner of his plate to another. He had barely eaten a thing.

There was more salt on his omelet than cheese. He seemed to have the same issues with salt that I had with coffee—not quite knowing when to quit.

"You know," Derek said. "It's just occurred to me how stupid I think this whole baseball thing is."

"What?" I asked. I was incredulous. "Are you kidding me? I thought you lived for that? I thought it was like your whole life? Don't tell me you're saying this just because we got crushed today."

"No, no. I didn't mean *baseball*. I meant the baseball *thing*. Bases and fooling around. What Sheila was talking about."

"What was Sheila talking about?" I asked.

"First base, second base, third. A home run—a four-bagger. The whole making sex out to be a competitive game thing. It's just plain stupid." I took a napkin out of the box on the table and wiped a blob of the omelet off his shirt.

"I never did understand the whole baseball sex thing," I told him. "You're the coach. Explain it to me."

Actually, I totally understood the whole baseball sex thing. I just wanted to watch Derek squirm. And damn if he wasn't the cutest squirmer EVER, particularly when *he* blushed.

Which, luckily for me, he now proceeded to do. In spades.

Or was it hearts?

"Well . . . you know . . . I mean . . ."

"No. I don't know. You have to tell me."

Derek took a deep breath. "Guys. I mean, it's probably mostly guys, but I guess some girls do it, too, look at sex as a contest. A sporting event. First base is kissing. Second base is . . ." Derek put his hands out over his chest and did this awkward little shaking motion, sort of like the shaka thing, only not. "You know what I mean. Breasts."

"Please, when you're around polite company, I would respectfully ask that you refer to them by their anatomically correct and proper name: *boobs*. What's third base?"

Poor Derek. All he could do for that one was to point to his lap, his face making the bottle of ketchup look positively Anglo.

"Ah ha! Now I'm getting it. And I assume a home run is . . ."

Derek nodded his head and didn't say anything. There was no way I was going to let him off that easy.

"Getting some motion in the ocean? Doing the horizontal bop? A little bit of the ole jig-jig-jiffy-stiffie jelly roll?" I could sling the fucking slang as well as Sheila.

"Actually," Derek said, "I was thinking more along the lines of making love."

"What?" I asked. "I've never heard it called *that* before."

Still blushing, Derek laughed.

"So why's it all so stupid?" I was finishing up my blueberry pancakes and was longingly eyeing his barely touched omelet. Playing the role of the only adult at the ballfield had done wonders for my appetite.

"Because it's not a game. Making love, I mean. The point is not to hit a home run. The point is to show someone how much you care for them."

I sort of had it figured out that Derek was a super-sensitive guy and all, but equating sex with caring for someone? Wow! I had no idea that there were boys out there who actually thought this way.

"I mean," he said, still fumbling with his words and his omelet, "when you're around guys, they're always like *How far did you get with her.* And if someone says, you know, *second base* or whatever, they'd be like *Ehhh, better luck next time,* or some crap like that. It's like if you don't hit a home run, then nothing else matters."

"Not even a triple?" I asked, smiling. This was getting interesting.

"Well, maybe a triple. But the point is, sex is not baseball."

"Of course not. It's softball. Until you're really into it. Then it's hard-ball." I laughed at my own joke. "Anyway, how many home runs have *you* hit?" I couldn't believe I was actually asking him this question.

"Me?" There was Derek, squirming in his seat again. "None. Zero. Full disclosure: I've never really been up to the plate. I don't even know what a batter's box looks like."

"Seriously?" I asked.

"Seriously." Derek had stopped blushing and was looking quite serious. "But back to this whole sex thing."

"Silly me. I thought we had never left it."

"I don't want to keep dissing guys or anything. I must sound like a traitor."

"Go ahead. Be my guest. Diss away."

"They, *we*, really are so fucked up. I mean, guys think of sex as this linear thing. A beginning with a definite end. And if you don't 'score,' then it's as if it doesn't even count. That it never even happened. And it's so not like that, or at least it shouldn't be. I mean, think about this." He reached over and took my hand in his and gently massaged my fingers. "Not counting that disaster of the kiss-that-wasn't-a-kiss-and-shall-never-be-mentioned-again, we're not even close to first base. I'm not even sure we've stepped up to the plate. But for me, right now, this is pretty damn awesome."

"There you go!" I told him, squeezing back. "Being a typical guy. Not practicing what you preach. First base. Home plate. I thought you said this wasn't a baseball game?"

"Thank goodness it isn't. Particularly after the walloping we got today."

"Actually," I told him. "I'm pretty surprised that you're still smiling. Twenty-five, or was it -six, to four? Ouch. I thought you'd be weeping into your plate. No need for salt on your omelet. Just seasoning it with your very own tears."

I had figured he'd be totally bummed about the final score. You knew it had not been a good game when the highlight of the afternoon was watching Sheila get chased around the bases by an Amazon and an umpire.

"*How many salty tear-drops did you waste, salting a love you never tasted?*" Derek asked.

"Yogi Berra?" I asked him. "Woody Allen? Martin Luther King Junior? Jesus?"

"Close. Shakespeare. *Romeo and Juliet.*"

"Oh my God," I said. "Them again?" Now it was Derek sounding like Udder.

"Listen, Meagan," Derek said. "How could I possibly be bummed when I'm sitting here holding hands with you?"

My turn to look like the ketchup bottle.

"Thanks," I told him. "But first let me get one thing straight. The other day. When you delivered the note to Gramps, wearing the tutu and tiara. Is there something you're not telling me?"

Derek laughed.

"I don't have a clue as to what you're talking about," he said. "That was King Ludd."

"I see. So King Ludd is a transvestite?"

"*Shhh!*" Derek said, looking around furtively. "Not so loud. I don't want anyone else to hear. Spies could be everywhere!"

"Whoa, whoa, wait a minute," I said. "I am totally confused here. Are you actually telling me that *you're* King Ludd? The great one himself?"

I stood up from the table, put my right foot behind my left, bent my knees, and lowered myself down into a deep curtsy.

Derek tapped me once on each shoulder with his butter knife.

"You may rise," he said, solemnly.

"All hail the king!" I shouted. Other diners looked up from their phones in curiosity. I figured it was important for me to show Derek that I was quite capable of making a total and complete fool of myself in virtually any location, just so he was quite clear what he was getting himself into.

Derek put the knife down and then reached out as if to touch my face. He stopped abruptly.

I did my best to scowl at him. "Don't you dare tell me you were about to shaka again!"

"No way," he said. "I just thought there was a piece of a pancake on your cheek. I was going to wipe it off but I realized it was a—"

"A what? A zit?" I picked up my napkin and frantically tried to hide my face behind it.

"No. A freckle."

"Wait!" I put the napkin down. "You thought one of my freckles was a piece of a pancake?"

"No. Not at all. I mean, maybe."

"That's great. Really great. Just what every self-conscious girl is dying to hear. My entire face looks exactly like a pancake."

"Your face is awesome!" Derek said. "I love freckles. I worship them. I can multitask *too*, you know. I'm a netaholic *and* a freckleholic."

"A freakaholic, more likely."

"Seriously. I can't get enough of your freckles. I'm totally addicted. Look at you. Your face. Your neck. Your shoulders. You're just dripping with freckles. They're flowing off of you like a freaking freckle fountain. You're a freckle-fest."

"Derek!" I stood up and put my hand on his shoulder. "Thank you so much. That's like the nicest thing anyone has ever said to me. Seriously.

You make me feel so much better about myself. I've spent years trying to sandblast the little bastards off of my skin and now, with one single word, you've totally transformed how I feel."

"Meagan! I totally meant that as a compliment."

"The freck you did." I could tell he was being totally sincere but I still couldn't help messing with him.

"I'm serious! I told you, I'm a certified frecklemaniac. Why else do you think I'm even hanging around with you?"

"Damn! And all this time I thought it was for my wit, my charm, and my incredible intellect. That and my amazing ability to turn a triple play."

"No! Not at all. Well, maybe the triple play . . . but mainly it's your freckles. Did you know they're the latest hot fashion accessory? Fake freckle products."

"You gotta be kidding me!"

"I'm totally serious. People pay big bucks to get temporary freckle tattoos on their faces."

"People are also clinically insane."

"Freck yeah they are. And you're not helping. Think how many people look at you and are consumed with freckle envy. It must drive them crazy."

Derek stood up and raised his cup of coffee high in the air.

"To freckles!" he shouted.

"Sit down and eat your omelet, for God's sake. It's getting cold." Once again it was hard to tell whether it was me, Mom, or Udder speaking.

Derek licked his lips and then leaned across the table. "I can't," he whispered.

I leaned towards him as well.

"Why not?" I whispered back.

"Garlic." He mouthed the word.

"Garlic?" I brought my voice back to normal. "I thought you were King Ludd? What are you now, a vampire or something? Vlad the Impaler, also known as Count Dracula? *Ahhhh! Garlic! Run away!*"

"No such luck. Just the thought of blood makes me woozie."

"Then what is it?"

"What do you think, Meagan? Eating garlic gives you . . . you know . . ." Derek blew in my direction. "Garlic breath. The kiss of death."

I reached over and speared a big chunk of his over-salted, garlicky omelet onto my fork and popped it into my mouth.

"There," I said, smiling. "Satisfied? Now we're even."

We had finally finished eating. Derek, garlic breath and all, was leaning in towards me, waiting.

Damn if he wasn't going to make me be the one to initiate.

As I was prone to do around all things Derek, I began to panic.

Technically, this would not be my first kiss. If you were a stickler for details, I supposed you'd have to count those couple of extremely awkward snog-fests at Sweet Sixteen birthday parties in darkened basements with God only knows whose tongue in my mouth. And one couldn't forget that disaster of a hookup-that-really-wasn't with that boy Caleb, which involved quite a few tumultuous minutes of heavy-duty kissy face.

But none of those kisses meant a damn thing. Which, one could argue, meant they hadn't really happened at all.

And my first disastrous attempt at kissing Derek on the ballfield bench? That shouldn't count as a kiss either. Nine out of ten of the world's most highly respected authorities on making out would wholeheartedly agree that if you put your tongue in someone's mouth and there was nobody there, absolutely no one at home, then that didn't even come close to being a real kiss.

So if I—if *we*—went ahead with this, it really should be considered my first *real* kiss.

If only I had my cell to take a selfie.

But no, seriously, wait just a minute here: I was clearly overthinking this. Who cared if it was my first kiss or not? Kissing was just . . . kissing. No big deal, right? I mean, you could kiss all afternoon and just leave it at that. It wasn't like I was hooking up or anything. I wasn't exactly hitting a home run or whatever the hell you wanted to call it. A girl could have a little fun and done and leave it at that, right? I was making out like making out was a way bigger deal than it actually was.

Sure, I was offline rather than on. Yeah, I was violating my number-one rule of relationships (as in: Never Have One Offline). But God knows, a single kiss *certainly* didn't make for a relationship! That was just plain ridiculous.

But wait just another minute! Damn and double damn! If all of that were really true, then why had that first diss of a kiss with Derek made such a mess of me? Why had I spent days agonizing over that catastrophe? Why had I sent the whole manifesto to Sir Derek, begging for a do-over? And why was I on the verge of freaking out right now when all Derek was doing was blowing garlic breath all over me?

Steady your nerves, I told myself. *Brace yourself. It's now or never. You're seventeen, Meagan. You're a big girl. You can do this.*

There Derek was, frozen in space, his lips slightly parted, eyes almost closed, still leaning towards me. The last bite of three-cheese and garlic omelet hardening on the end of his fork.

How long had he been in that position? Minutes? Hours?

I began slowly to lean in towards him.

"Hey!" It was a voice from behind me. "What the hell are you doing here?"

I practically jumped out of my seat.

Lord help me! It was Caleb! Caleb from *Passion*! Caleb who I had walked out on after completely freaking out a couple months earlier. Caleb—my one and only offline online crash and burn.

He scooted into the booth next to me. "I can't believe this, Stephanie," he said, calling me by my *Passion* name and putting his hand on my arm. "What are the chances of me running into you here? What are you, like stalking me or something?"

"What? Me? No! Of course not!" Once again—complete freak-out.

"Classic," he said, moving even closer to me. "You don't mind if I join you for a minute, do you?"

Of *course* I minded if he joined me! What was he thinking? This was perhaps the most important moment in my life and now *he* shows up? How could I possibly not mind!

"Uh . . . sure," I stammered, all logic and common sense vacating my brain.

Derek had slumped back into his chair. His eyebrows were wrinkled. His face had fallen.

"Uh, Caleb this is, um . . .um . . ." My mind went blank. The connection between the brain and the tongue was suddenly severed. I sat there, paralyzed, staring dumbly at Derek with my mouth wide open. Try as I might, I could not get that boy's name out of my mouth.

"Derek," Derek said, after an incredibly long and awkward pause. He gave me the classic WTF look, which sent the heebie-jeebies racing down my spine. "My name is Derek."

"Yes!" I shouted. "He's right! That boy's name is Derek. That's his name."

Somebody shoot me.

"I'm over here visiting a friend at UMass," Caleb said. "How weird that you'd be here."

"My grandfathers," I said. "I'm here helping them out. But he's not one of them." I pointed at Derek with a trembling finger. "He is not my grandfather."

Oh my God! What had come over me? I was acting like a moron. An idiot. An imbecile. A brain-dead dumb-ass.

"Could have fooled me!" Caleb snickered and gave Derek a light punch on the arm. "Just kidding, bro. Just kidding."

Derek looked desperately to me for help, but mentally I was nowhere to be found.

Confronted face-to-face with my in-the-flesh *Passion* nightmare, my monkey brain was reeling into total sensory overload. *Passion* PTSD. Images of that offline fiasco were flooding my synapses, sending my neurons into chaotic overdrive, totally overwhelming my ability to form even a single rational thought.

"Coffee!" I stammered. "I need more coffee!"

Both boys just looked at me. Did either one have any idea how close I was to a complete breakdown?

"Did Sheila tell you I was trying to get in touch with you?" Caleb asked. "I felt bummed about what happened the last time we got together. I was thinking maybe we could . . . you know . . . try for a do-over?"

A do-over?! What kind of karmic screw up was this? Here I was, finally set to start something (God only knows what) real with Derek, and now Caleb comes waltzing in and totally ruins the whole thing. How could this be happening?

Derek. Poor darling Derek. He was now a thousand miles away, or probably wishing he was, all the while wondering what the hell planet I was on.

My head did a weird spastic shaka-shake kind of motion that could be interpreted as a yes or a no or anything else Caleb wanted.

Caleb pulled out his phone and fired off a quick text. "Hey, I'm really sorry, but I gotta run. My ride is waiting. But it was awesome to see you. You still have my number, right?"

"Uh . . . well . . . I don't know."

"Let me give it to you," he said.

"I don't have my phone on me." Now my voice was barely above a whisper.

"Seriously? What's up with that?" He scribbled his number on a napkin and handed it to me. "Text me when you get back to Boston. Seriously. We got to get together. Something tells me things will go down a little bit smoother next time." He then turned to Derek. "Dude, nice to meet you." Caleb went to fist-bump Derek, but Derek's arms remained limp by his sides. He seemed almost as paralyzed as I was.

Then Caleb went to fist-bump me but somehow I miraculously managed to back away. He gave me a wink instead, turned, and walked away.

"I gotta go, too," Derek said, abruptly standing up.

"What? Why?"

"Why do you think, Meagan?"

"Because of what just happened? I am so sorry Caleb sat down. I really am."

"You couldn't even remember my name!"

"Of course I could. I was just flustered. I didn't know that he would . . . it was just that . . ."

"You couldn't remember my name!"

"Caleb! I mean *Derek*. That guy means nothing to me! Absolutely nothing! He never did and he never will. Oh my God, he didn't even know what *my* name was. You saw how he called me Stephanie—right?"

"Yeah, but you knew *his* name, didn't you? And you didn't know mine."

"Stop. Please. Once again, I am so sorry. It was just an Online Relationship Disorder flashback. Not that there was any relationship to flash back *to*. I don't know what came over me. It was like temporary insanity."

"Could have fooled me. At least about the temporary part."

"You have no idea how bad this makes me feel! It won't happen again. I promise! Look at me. Look what I'm doing!" I grabbed the piece of napkin that Caleb had written his number on and, hands shaking, swished it around in my coffee until it turned into mush.

"See? Gone forever! Vanished. Please sit down. Please!" I reached out to grab his hand but he backed away. I grabbed my coffee mug instead. Maybe if I spilled it all over him, that would make him sit back down.

"I gotta be at work, Meagan."

"What about King Ludd? What about our do-over?" I was practically begging. Tears were in my eyes.

"I think it's done over."

"Can I text you later? I mean call you. Or you can come over so we can do something? *Anything?* Please?"

Derek had that hurt-puppydog look and his lower lip was quivering.

He plopped a few dollars down on the table, his share of the bill, and, without as much as a wink, turned and walked away.

Chapter 39

"No offense, Gramps, but you really are totally full of shit."

It was Sunday night. Having cried my eyes out following the debacle of the do-over, I had somehow made it downstairs to join Udder and Gramps in the living room. I was keeping the highlights (or were they lowlights?) of this latest shit show to myself, figuring I'd already burdened the oldsters more than enough with my relationship disasters.

"Meagan!" Udder glared at me from under his bushy gray eyebrows. "Remember what I said about being rude."

"I'm not being rude. I'm being rational. There is a big difference."

"I don't mean to scare you, Meagan," Gramps continued, "but even Udder has heard footsteps traipsing up and down the stairs in the dead of night. Rattling pots and pans. How do you explain that, Miss Know-It-All? Huh? How?"

"Um . . . you with the stoned-out munchies making a mess in the kitchen?"

"Rude, rude, rude!" Udder wagged his finger at me.

"This house is not haunted," I scoffed. "Let me break it down for you: there are no such things as ghosts."

Udder and Gramps had spent the last half hour trying to convince me that their house was haunted. Next to Sheila becoming Queen Ludd and Mother Nature, it was the craziest thing I had ever heard.

"Well then," Gramps said. "Why do you think the cassette player never works? Tell me that. Why do you think I can never get the volume to go up on the television? Why do you think the microwave goes on and off with a mind of its own? Why do you think the dishwasher is always on the fritz? Why do you think we never get cell service?"

"Don't tell me!" I did my very best version of a snarky stage gasp. "Let me guess. Not a gremlin. Not a fairy. Could it be . . . ?"

"Exactly," Gramps said. "A ghost. Probably a Luddite. Ghosts hate all of this newfangled technology crap."

"A Luddite ghost? Are you for real?"

"Yes indeedily."

"I hate to clue you in, Gramps, but cassette players aren't exactly newfangled. Particularly yours. That piece of crap was around before God."

"Better watch it, girl. She's probably listening to this conversation right now. If I were you, I'd refrain from pissing her off."

"Who? God?"

"No! The ghost."

"Oh, so now the ghost is a she?"

"Why not?" Gramps grinned mischievously. "Luddite that she is, she's probably watching your every move. Every time you reach for that cell phone, every time you—"

"Wait. Are you trying to freak me out here? Because if you are, it ain't happening. This whole ghost thing is just lame and stupid."

"Oh! So that's it. You don't believe ghosts can be girls or Luddites?"

"No. I don't believe ghosts can be *ghosts*. This is just one more silly ploy of yours to keep me offline, and it's *so* not working."

"Humph!" Gramps sat back in his chair, folded his arms, and scowled at me. He picked up his newspaper, shook it open, and hid himself behind it.

After a few minutes of silence he suddenly flung the paper onto the floor and glared up at me again. "Answer me this, you-who-knows-everything: Have you ever seen a ghost on a computer? Or a ghost with a cell phone? Huh? Have you?"

"Um . . . no," I said. "But I've never seen a ghost without a phone either!"

Gramps got up, stormed into the kitchen, and began noisily rattling pots and pans.

It was late on a Tuesday night, and Udder and Gramps were still not home. They had gone off to a friend's house to play Settlers of Catan, some board game they were obsessed with, and I was left in the big old house all by my lonesome. I had watered the garden, repotted the jade plant, swept the front porch, put away all of the dishes, hung the laundry out to dry, and tackled five zillion other household chores that desperately needed doing. Not that I was complaining. The routine of domestic drudgery had a certain mindless appeal and took my mind, at least briefly, off the fact that I was the world's biggest loser.

At my mother's house, whenever Mom would get all bent out of shape about a towel on the floor or my unmade bed, it was always super-annoying. The more she nagged, the less I did. But here at Udder and Gramps's, I didn't even have to be asked. As a matter of fact, in a bizarrely twisted role reversal, it was starting to be *me* doing the nagging.

"Is it too much for me to ask that when you're done with your ice cream, you could at least put your dirty bowl in the sink?" I'd scold Gramps, hands on my hips, shooting him the evil eye.

Or: "Oh my God, if I find one more sock on the living room couch, I'm going to burn it. Do I make myself clear?"

Scary. Very scary.

Anyway, chores finally done, I was sprawled on Udder's easy chair doing absolutely nothing. I had called Derek at least five zillion times from the landline and had gotten no response. Nothing. I was a complete basket case. I could now only wallow in my idiocy.

Why did I go and let Caleb sit next to me? Why did I go all brain-dead at that crucial moment of my so-called life? Why did I ruin the one and only opportunity I was probably ever going to have to actually kiss a guy I really liked? Why was I such a loser?

Why? Why? Why?

Scratch. Scratch. Scratch.

What was that? I distinctly heard a clawing sound at the front door.

"Udder?" I called out. "Gramps?"

I hadn't heard their car pull up. They usually made quite the racket as they huffed and puffed their way into the house. You could hear their joints creaking a mile away.

The scratching sound started up again.

"Gramps?" I called out again. "Udder?"

Scratch. Scratch. Scratch.

Maybe it was Derek. Maybe he had parked his car on the main road and snuck down the driveway and was hell-bent on trying to scare the crap out of me, seeking revenge for the frack-up at the diner, my moo-doo of the re-do. Maybe he thought I'd go all girly-girl on him and fall swooning into his arms—which was entirely possible.

"Derek?" I called out. "Is that you?"

Scratch. Scratch. Scratch.

The noise at the door was getting louder.

This was not good. This was not good at all.

Here I was, out in the middle of nowhere, heartbroken and all alone, with a ghost clawing at the door.

Wait a minute! *Ghost?* Who said anything about ghosts? That was just plain ridiculous. I was not going to let Gramps's stupid ghost idea float itself into my head. I was going insane enough as it was.

"I don't believe in ghosts," I said out loud. "I don't believe in ghosts. I don't I don't I don't I don't I DON'T believe in ghosts." Now I was shouting.

Scratch. Scratch. Scratch.

Okay. Maybe Gramps was right. Maybe there were such things as ghosts. Maybe everything I knew about everything was TOTALLY and COMPLETELY WRONG and the world really was full of ghouls and demons and LUDDITE GHOSTS who were OUT TO GET ME!

Maybe this one really had come back from the dead and was scratching out a warning sign! *Abandon technology before all is lost! Free yourself from the net while there's still time! Do something (anything!) with Derek, just don't screw it up this time!*

Scratch. Scratch. Scratch.

Oh my God! What was a girl to do in a situation like this?

Option #1: Run upstairs and hide under the bed.

Option #2: Grab the poker from the fireplace and run madly through the house smashing to smithereens anything that ran on electricity in the hopes that the Luddite ghost would finally be appeased and could now rest in peace and leave me the hell alone.

Option #3: Girl up and go strong to the front door to see what the frack was up.

Scratch. Scratch. Scratch.

"Get a grip, girl!" I told myself. "Enough of this nonsense!" I was going way overboard in the mind-race department. I was not going to fall for this paranormal paranoia.

Legs shaking, fighting back fear, I got up and willed myself, one faltering step at a time, fireplace poker waving menacingly above my head, toward the front of the house. It was all I could do not to crap my pants.

The front door had a big glass window in the middle of it. Fingers twitching, I turned on the outside light, looked out, and saw . . . nothing.

I called out one last time, my voice rising three notches and barely registering above a whimper. "Udder? Gramps? Derek?"

Scratch. Scratch. Scratch.

Oh my God! From out of nowhere a ghostly face suddenly appeared in the door window. A ghostly face with a hideous death grin. A ghostly brown face with a black bandit's mask covering its eyes.

It was the ghost! The Luddite Ghost! Returning from the dead to seek revenge for all the technology that was ruining the world! Lashing back at that sordid symbol of netaholism—pathetic little old me! Come back to give me comeuppance for all the pain I had caused Derek. Come back to put the hurt on me!

I screamed, staggered backwards, tripped over the umbrella stand, and fell flat on my ass, whacking myself in the head with the poker.

SCRATCH! SCRATCH! SCRATCH!

SCREAM! SCREAM! SCREAM!

A car pulled into the driveway. I could hear Udder yelling something out the window.

"Hurry!" I managed to yell through the flowing tears and the trickling blood. "For God's sake, hurry!"

"I thought you didn't believe in ghosts?" Gramps asked, wiping away the blood from my freckly forehead with a washcloth.

"I didn't. I mean I don't."

"Could have fooled me. When I opened that door, you were blubbering like a baby."

"Can you blame her?" Udder put a large dab of antiseptic cream on my head wound. "You poor darling!"

"Ouch!" I jerked my head backwards. "Not so hard!"

I was sitting on the couch, wedged between them, still shaking.

"We should have warned you," Gramps said. "That's not the first time that scoundrel has pulled a trick like that."

"No worries," I said. "It only took twenty-five years off my life. That and permanent brain damage. Not a big deal. Really."

"You poor darling!" Udder repeated, putting three band-aids on my forehead and sealing them with a giant kiss. "We will never leave you home alone again! Ever! There's no knowing when that bandit will return."

"A raccoon!" I shook my head in disbelief. "I can't believe I went into cardiac arrest over a freaking raccoon!"

The scratching noise and the face at the front-door window had not been the Luddite Girl Ghost back from the dead to haunt the hell out of me. It had been a damn raccoon! A raccoon clawing its way up the front door to raid the decorative morning glories that had climbed up the trellis next to the entrance.

"That little devil's a mischief maker, that's for sure," Gramps said, adding his wet kiss to my forehead. "Son of a gun!"

"To think I thought it was a ghost!" I was embarrassed at having even entertained such a ridiculous notion.

"It's totally understandable. Ghost. Raccoon. They do look exactly alike." Gramps smirked.

"You're making fun of me, aren't you? Here I am on my deathbed and you're mocking me. Seriously?"

"Sweetheart! I would never dream of doing such a thing. Anyway, do you know why he's got those big ol' black circles around his eyes?"

"I thought you said the ghost was a girl." I was still trying to get my breath back to normal.

"No, silly. I'm talking about the raccoon."

"Tell me then. I have no idea."

"It's because of our ghost! She's obviously been keeping him up all night, haunting the hell out of *him*. Poor thing. It probably hasn't slept in weeks!"

I picked up the poker, threatening to give Gramps his very own big ol' black eye, but figured one head-whack was more than enough for the evening.

Once more, I called Derek. I am not a praying girl, but desperate times called for desperate actions. I beseeched Aphrodite and Eros and Venus and Cupid, the gods and goddesses of desire and sex and the L-word, hoping beyond hope that they'd intervene on my behalf and force that boy to pick up the damn phone.

Huzzah and hooray! For once somebody up there was listening.

"Hey," Derek answered. He was alive! Alive and answering his phone! His *Hey* was soft and somewhat joyless, but I was rejoicing.

"Caleb?" I asked. "Is that you?"

Silence.

"Too soon to joke?" I asked.

"So not funny."

"Sorry. And about the other afternoon? Really sorry. Like, really, really, *really* sorry. Sorry to the gazillionth power. Definitely not my finest moment."

Derek snorted.

"Any chance of a do-over of the do-over?" I asked, trying to keep my voice a notch above a groveling whimper. "I mean, seriously—how many more times are we going to have to break up before we can make up and then . . . you know . . . make out? You've got to forgive me. You just have to. I'm dying here."

"Meagan, you are a piece of work. Are you aware of that?"

I smiled. Now the boy was actually stringing sentences together!

"Nothing worth having comes easy," I replied, quoting from the magnet on Udder and Gramps's refrigerator.

Derek snorted again.

"You better give me another chance," I told him. "It may be the last one you'll ever get. I'm not long for this world you know. Given the extensive nature of my vicious head wound I'll most likely be dead by tomorrow morning. Maybe sooner. Then you'll be sorry. Then you'll wish you had made up with me."

I recounted in vivid detail my near-death experience with the evil ghost raccoon, taking artistic license and adding a few fictional touches here and there, just to spice it up and make things a bit edgier.

It was great to hear Derek laugh. Even if it was *at* me and not *with* me.

"Part of me is going *It serves you right to suffer, girl,*" he said. "But most of me is going *Holy Crap! What a badass raccoon.*"

"You wouldn't be saying that if you were the one mauled half to death."

"Silly me. And I always thought ghosts were nonviolent."

"So *you* believe in ghosts?"

"Not until you told me your *Home Alone* horror show. Now all bets are off."

It was my turn to snort.

"I'm being totally serious," Derek said. "Do you actually think for a second that the face at the front door was really a raccoon's? No way! It was definitely that dead girl your Gramps was telling you about. She must be a shapeshifter, come back to haunt the shit out of you. She probably died in some tragic technological fuck-up at the farmhouse. Maybe when they put electricity in she got electrocuted. Maybe when they installed phone service she strangled to death on the cord."

"And maybe you're insane! Are you even listening to yourself?" One more snort, from me this time. This phone call was turning into quite the snort-fest.

"Look, all I'm saying is that Bertha has probably come back from the grave to warn you not to fall into the same trap as she did."

"Bertha?"

"Yeah, Bertha. I bet that's the dead girl's name. Sort of ghostly and old-fashioned, don't you think? It fits her." His voice got all low and spooky. "Bertha . . . Bertha!"

"Oh my God! You're even more full of crap than my grandfather. And anyway, Derek, don't be ridiculous. Everyone knows that ghosts can't shapeshift. Demons can. But not ghosts."

"So Bertha is a demon? Is that what you're telling me?"

"No, you idiot! The raccoon is a demon. Bertha is a ghost!"

"Aha! So there you have it!" he replied triumphantly. "You *do* believe in ghosts! I just knew it!"

We were quiet for a moment. I crossed and uncrossed my legs.

"Does this mean you forgive me?" I finally asked.

"For believing in ghosts?"

"For that. And the other thing."

"You mean for forgetting my name?"

"I know it's not Caleb," I said. Derek couldn't see my smile, but it was a big one. "And I'm pretty sure it's not Bertha. Wait, wait . . . don't tell me . . . it's right on the tip of my tongue."

Chapter 40

"I gotta tell you, Meagan, I'm totally crushing on these phytoncides. I can feel them coursing through my veins like wonder medicine. Soothing for the soul. *Shinrin-yoku!*"

Sheila and I were taking a walk through the woods across the road from Udder and Gramps's. The birds were singing and the wind was whistling and the clouds and trees were dancing away. Sheila was back for the weekend and waiting for Jonathan to get off work so they could go for a late-afternoon hike.

"*Shinrin* who?" I asked.

"*Yoku*. It's Japanese for forest bathing. Stop walking for a moment."

We made a little nest of fallen leaves and sat down together in it.

"Breathe it in, girl. Feel it envelop you. *Shinrin-yoku*. Tree aromatherapy."

Remember: this was coming from a girl who a month ago ranked nature right up there with a quadruple root canal.

I did as she said. I breathed in deep and I opened my eyes to take in the wonders of the natural world but instead, everywhere I looked reminded me of . . . my phone.

Stop it! I told myself sternly. *Don't do that!*

But I couldn't help it. The shape of the cloud in the sky looked exactly like my phone. The pattern in the bark of the tree trunk strikingly resembled the keypad. The mushroom sprouting from the clump of leaves was the same vibrant yellow color as my iPhone 7. The trees in the distance could easily have been disguised cell phone towers.

Seriously. How sad was that?

There I was, out in the lovely woods on a gorgeous day with my very best friend in the whole wide world breathing in the tree aroma, and all I could think about was my phone?

What the hell was wrong with me?

There was Sheila, passionately in love with trees, while I was still in love with . . . what exactly? The digital ten-foot pole? The e-foreplay? Online guys who were not really real at all?

If it couldn't be Mother Nature then, at the very least, it should have been Derek. Derek's face out there in the clouds, in the bark, in the mushrooms, in the trees. But no. I finally go and actually meet a boy who really seems to want to be with *me* and I'm out here fantasizing about my phone?

Was I seriously that pathetic?

"*Shinrin-yoku*," Sheila repeated.

"Sheila," I said, desperately trying to shake off my netaholic nightmare. "I don't have a clue as to what you're talking about."

"Phytoncides. Ask your Gramps. I bet he knows all about them. They're like these aromatic compound thingies that trees give off to protect themselves from pests. It's doing wonders for me."

"Protecting you from pests? But I thought you liked Jonathan?"

"I'm totally into Jonathan. You know that. But all of the other bugs up my butt—parents, work, college, the internet, crap like that? Gone. These phytoncides are like miracle drugs. Breathe them in. Go on! Do it!"

I took a deep breath.

"Don't you just feel it?" Sheila asks. "It's almost as good as sex. My mood skyrockets. I swear to God, my blood pressure is plummeting as we speak. And cancer? You can kiss that sucker goodbye. I am so not worried about that shit anymore."

"You were worried about getting cancer?"

"Well, no, not really. But if I was before, now I wouldn't be, thanks to these babies. Speaking of cancer, did you know cell phones give off radio-frequency waves?" Sheila could change topics with the flutter of her eyelashes better than anyone. "Talking can increase your chances of getting brain cancer."

"Just talking?

"Talking on cell phones."

"Brain cancer?"

"Will you stop repeating everything I say? God, Meagan, you're acting brain-dead. Stop talking and just breathe. The more phytoncides, the merrier. They help with memory as well."

"What are we talking about again?"

"Cell phones," Sheila said, oblivious to my wit. "They did some study on rats, and the little buggers who were exposed to way too much cell phone use had a higher occurrence of certain kinds of cancer."

"Seriously? Rats talk on cell phones?"

"Evidently the ones in the study did."

"Were they scurrying through the forest at the time? If so, wouldn't the tree's phyto-thingies work their magic, and then the good would cancel out the bad and everything would be all hunky-dory?"

"I think they were in a lab, poor things. Studies on animals. How cruel is that?"

"Were they texting or talking?"

"Who?"

"The rats."

"Don't make fun, Meagan. This stuff is serious science."

"And you know this, how exactly?"

"How do you think? I googled it. On my phone. Just this morning."

I let the irony of this one slip right on by. TIDSI: Think It, Don't Say It.

"I mean, how awesome is it that you take a walk in the woods and you're cured of all that ails you." Sheila stood up, raced ahead and swung herself up onto the lower branch of one of the more massive trees. She wrapped her arms around the branch and gave it a loud kiss. Then she arched her shoulders, tipped her head back, and shouted to the top of the tree: "*I love you, man!*"

"You've gone really weird on me, Sheila."

"Get up here!" Sheila commanded. "Now! Give him a kiss. No need to be frightened. This guy really is all bark and no bite."

"How do you know it's a he?" I asked.

"JUST DO IT!"

I swung up onto the branch and plopped myself down next to Sheila. Not to be outdone by her, I leaned over and gave his branch an open-mouthed wet one, squirrelly tongue and all. After all, what did I have to lose? The way things were going with my sorry personal life, even with Derek somewhat forgiving me, this might be all I was going to get in the fooling-around department for who knows how long. Probably the rest of my life.

"And you want to know the coolest thing?" Sheila continued.

"There's more?" I asked.

"My ADHD. Thanks to the trees it is so much better. Don't you think?"

"Oh my . . ." I hesitated. "Wait a minute. Is this a trick question?"

"The science is in. Nature relaxes the brain. I'm much less anxious. Much less depressed."

"Sheila! Since when have you ever been depressed? And I hate to burst your bubble, but I'm not quite sure that drone bashing, gas station TV smashing, and cell phone stealing is actually consistent with reduced anxiety."

"You're just jealous. More nature means more awe. Awe is good. Awe is healthy. Awe makes me think of things larger than myself."

"Like destroying technology?"

"Exactly."

"Phytoncides?" I asked.

"Phytoncides!"

I stopped, stood stock still, and took a series of deep breaths.

Hey, I thought to myself. *If I could only make it happen.*

Shinrin-yoku. Forest bathing.

At this point I was ready to try anything.

Chapter 41

I had picked a ton of vegetables and displayed them beautifully in the garden basket, placing it right in the lap of the fat Buddha. Zucchini and summer squash. Beefsteak and Big Boy tomatoes surrounded by adorable little Sun Gold cherry toms. Tendergreen bush beans, crunchy cucumbers, and milky white cauliflower. My basket looked like the glossy cover of *Better Homes and Gardens*, a magazine I used to make fun of in the waiting room at the dentist's.

I sat down smack-dab in the middle of the garden and looked around me, fascinated by things I had never dreamed of being interested in before. The delicate intricacy of the squash flowers. The twisted shapes of the green beans. The way the side shoots of broccoli stuck out at such peculiar angles.

Okay. So maybe it wasn't *shinrin-yoku*. But garden bathing was still totally awesome.

Best of all, the whole time I sat there I hadn't thought once about my phone. Just about gardening. How real it was. How grounding. After all, what could be more beautiful than a basket of freshly picked vegetables you grew yourself?

Well, maybe Derek. Derek with his big brown eyes. Derek with his pouty lips. Derek with his—

"Hey," a voice said, startling me out of my daydream.

Oh my God! It was Jonathan.

"Hey," I heyed back.

"How's it going?" Jonathan asked.

Lost in my daydream starring a certain boy with garlic on his breath and omelet on his shirt, I had been caught totally unawares by Jonathan's arrival. I didn't even have time to think about diving for cover behind the zucchini.

I stood up abruptly. "You know Sheila's not here, right?"

"It's not Sheila I came to see," he said, staring straight at my boobs.

My heart sank.

Oh no! I thought. *Here it comes.* I had figured all along that at some point, I'd probably have to deal with the Jonathan thing but, yuck, I was so not ready for it.

Where was *Star Trek* when you needed it? Beam me up, Scotty! Anywhere but here and now.

Poor Sheila. How could Jonathan do this to her? The two of them had spent that wild, wonderful weekend together *Gelassenheit*ing (or whatever-you-called-it) with their Amish brothers and sisters, having crazy, passionate sex and then fleeing like fugitives after the gas station TV incident, and now here was Judas, drooling away, staring at my boobs, totally giving me the look.

Shame on him! Shame, shame, shame!

It totally sucked. This is why guys were such a royal pain in the ass. This is why I had resisted offline boys in the first place.

Okay. So maybe I was being a little too hard on those poor hominids unfortunate enough to have a penis stuck between their legs. After all, we girls pulled the same crap, right? And God only knows, sometimes we could be just as manipulative. Maybe it was just the curse of being human.

Jonathan continued to stare.

"Flatworms," I finally managed to say. For whatever bizarre reason, that was the first thing to pop into my head and then come blurting out of my mouth. So much for TIDSI.

"What?" Jonathan asked.

"You think humans are weird? Try flatworms. They make Sheila seem almost normal."

"I'm sorry, Meagan, but am I missing something here?"

"God only knows how screwed up we are, but flatworms have taken it to a totally new level. Did you know they're hermaphroditic?"

Jonathan sat down on a bale of mulch hay and continued to stare at my boobs. The more he stared the more anxious I became. The more anxious I became the more I babbled.

"Hermaphrodites," I continued, words tumbling out quicker than bean beetles hatching. "They got their little boy thingies, just like we, I mean you, do. But they don't have any little girl thingies. So when two flatworms get together you know what happens?"

Jonathan scratched his beard and looked perplexed.

"I can't imagine."

"Don't even try, my friend, don't even try. Ready for it?"

"Do I have a choice?" Jonathan asked.

"Traumatic insemination!" I pounded my hoe on the ground for dramatic affect.

If it were at all possible, Jonathan looked even more confused. "Traumatic . . ."

"Insemination. That's what they do when they want to get it on. Flatworms take their penis and, *ZAP*, pierce their partner's abdomen with it. Just like that. Slam, bam, thank you ma'am."

"'Partner' seems way too kind a word for it." Jonathan scratched his beard again.

"Unless they're into S and M. And get this, they shoot their sperm right into the wound."

"What?" He cringed.

I felt for the guy. I really did. He didn't have a clue as to where this conversation was going and, frankly, neither did I. But now I at least had his eyes off my boobs and onto my face.

"The little spermies just float around through the pierced flatworm's body until they find eggs to fertilize. And that's not even the weirdest part."

Jonathan shook his head in disbelief. "It gets weirder? Is that even possible?" He shifted position on the hay bale, his eyes straying south again.

If I really wanted him to stop staring at my boobs, then my waxing eloquent about penises (even the nonhuman variety) was probably not the wisest of strategies. But, as always, once I got going, I just couldn't stop.

"Before they do the nasty they fence with their penises."

Jonathan stood up, made a motion as if to reach toward me, seemed to think better of it, and sat back down.

"Fence?" he asked.

"Yeah. As in sword-fight."

"With their penises?"

"Exactly. They're seriously that big. For a flatworm anyway. It's like a tournament. Penis fencing. The prize to the winner? They get to be the boy. The loser? The girl. The girl gets her body penis-pierced. If that's not traumatic, then I don't know what is. Can you believe it? I mean, even with flatworms the girl gets the short end of the stick."

"Or in this case the long end!" Jonathan said, wrinkling his nose.

"But wait, there's more. You want to know the really, *really* weird part?"

"What? But you've totally overshot the weirdness scale already!"

"Not even close, *hombre*. Check this out. Let's just say one horny little flatworm is floating around in a pond all by himself, or herself, or whatever politically correct thing you're supposed to call a hermaphrodite, sad and forlorn and looking for love, and he, or she, can't find someone else to get it on with. Tragic huh? But do you know what the resourceful little munchkins do then?"

"Something tells me this is going to be traumatic as well."

"You better believe it, buddy. They fuck themselves. Right in the head. *BAM!* In goes their needle-like penis right through their very own flatworm head. Hypodermic insemination."

"They fuck themselves in the head?"

"I am seriously not making this shit up."

"And they get pregnant?"

"Yeah they do. It's like the ultimate selfie!"

Out of breath, I put my hoe down and sat on the hay bale facing Jonathan.

"How do you know all of this?" Jonathan finally asked. He was scratching his beard even harder.

"My Gramps, who else? Remember his porcupine lecture? He's a veritable encyclopedia of weird animal sex." During one of his *Truth Is Stranger than Fiction—Sex Lives of the Small and Boneless* talks, Gramps had given me the skinny on these craziest of creatures.

"Meagan, I'm trying to wrap my brain around this whole flatworm thing and why you're going off like this. And I'm thinking there must be a moral to the story. I'm guessing it's not a positive one."

"Look, Jonathan, if you think that I'm telling you to go fuck yourself, in the head or otherwise, I'm not."

"Whew! That's a relief!"

"But while we're on the subject, I think it's really wrong what you're doing to Sheila. She's my best friend, for crying out loud!"

"What? Did Sheila tell you that sex with me was traumatic?" Jonathan looked alarmed.

"No! She said sex with you was awesome!"

"Oh my God!" Jonathan leapt to his feet. "Did the pill not work? Did I knock her up? Is she pregnant?"

"No! Of course not!"

"Then what are you telling me?"

"Come on, Jonathan, don't play stupid here. Sheila likes you. She really likes you. And then you go and do *this* to her?"

Jonathan was scratching his beard so hard I was afraid his face was going to fall off.

"Do what?" he asked. "Flatworm?"

"No! Don't be an idiot. It has nothing to do with flatworms!" I was practically screaming.

"Then what am I doing exactly?"

"Staring at my boobs. Coming on to me. Using *her* to get into *my* pants. It is so not cool! And you gotta know that Derek and I have a . . ."

I hesitated. How to put into words exactly what Derek and I "had" was more than a tad confusing. "You know . . ." I stammered. "He and I . . . It's a . . ."

Jonathan sat back down on the bale of hay and raked his beard one more time.

"Meagan," he said calmly. "Don't get me wrong. I liked you from the moment I met you. And believe it or not, even after this weird flatworm rant, I still like you. But I hate to burst your bubble here: it's Sheila that I really like. I did not come here to see you. I came here to see your grandfathers about their land. Sheila and I are working on this plan and we wanted to run it by them. And, for your information, I have not been staring at your boobs, attractive though they are. There's a beetle that's been crawling up and down your shirt the whole time and it's been freaking me out."

I looked down. He was right. One of those little bean beetle bastards was crawling around down there. I had been too worked up to even notice. I reached down and squished it between my fingers then flung it over the garden fence.

"So you're not here to hit on me?" I asked softly, staring at the goopy remains on my fingers and feeling like a traumatized flatworm.

"No offense, but no! Of course not!"

"And you really do like Sheila?"

"You better believe it. Anyway, *like* might be too weak a word for it."

"Which makes me a complete and total—"

"No! Not at all. Seriously. No worries."

Awkward as it was, I was practically shaking with relief.

"You have a plan?" I finally managed to ask. "With Sheila? About my grandfathers' land?"

Chapter 42

"You've got to be kidding me!" I shook the cord of the landline to make sure the words were coming out right.

"Pinky swear. Never been more serious in my life."

"You're going to drop out of high school, build a replica of Thoreau's cabin on Udder and Gramps's land, and homestead? Seriously?" I had called Sheila right after Jonathan had left Udder and Gramps's.

"I'm not dropping out of high school, Meagan. I'll just, I don't know, do my last year in your grandfathers' town instead."

"Oh my God, Sheila. This is absurd. Beyond absurd!"

"Thanks for the support, bestie."

"Have you even talked to your parents yet?"

"Well, no . . . but . . ."

"They're going to say the same thing that I'm about to say now. Except they'll scream it! This idea of yours sounds like some crazy-ass, low-budget, reality-TV bullshit show that you'd turn on just to watch nature girl and her fling crash and burn."

"Don't be insulting, Meagan. He's not a fling. He's the real thing."

"Whatever. Your parents will freak. Even more about the sex part than the nature part!"

"I'm eighteen years old, Meagan." Even though we were on the phone I could see Sheila scowl. "Eighteen. They can go ahead and freak all they want for all I care. Anyway, '*Some people get an education without going to school. The rest get it after they get out.*'"

"What?"

"Samuel Clements, more or less. Aka, Mark Twain."

"I know who Samuel Clements is, damn it! I can't believe you're serious about this?"

"I was going to tell you, Meagan, I really was. I wanted to surprise you. But first we wanted to run it by your grandfathers and then . . ."

"Poor Udder and Other Udder! How could you possibly drag them into this ridiculous fantasy of yours?"

"Well, they don't know all the details yet, but I'm sure they'll love to help us out."

"Oh my God. I must be getting punked! Either that or I'm still asleep." I pinched myself hard. "For the love of God, somebody please wake me up from this nightmare!"

"Will you chillax! Even Derek thinks it's a good idea."

"Derek? *My* Derek? You've got to be kidding me. He knows about this?"

"Yeah. Jonathan told him. He's totally on board."

"I can't believe this. Am I the very last person on earth to know?"

"Like I said, I still haven't broken it to my parents."

"*Arghhh!*"

"Look, Meagan, I told you Jonathan was thinking about this whole cabin-building thing."

"But you never told me you were serious!"

"Please don't be mad at me. I just wanted to, you know, see how it all played out first."

"You're going to build a replica of Thoreau's cabin? On Udder and Gramps's land? And live there?"

"Yeah, behind the orchard. Sort of near the bees. Maybe we can talk your Gramps into getting more hives. And expand the garden. You know, grow our own. Live simply so that others may simply live."

"Sheila, are you listening to yourself? You don't know the first thing about bees! Or gardening! Or anything! Why are you doing this? Why? Has Jonathan brainwashed you? Is this like some sort of cult thing?"

"'*I went to the woods because I wished to live deliberately, to front only the essential facts of life, and see if I could not learn what it had to teach, and not, when I came to die, discover that I had not lived.*'"

"Fuck Mark Twain!"

"That's Henry David Thoreau."

"Fuck him too!"

"I thought it was 'fuck technology,' Meagan! I figured you'd be all over this, now that you're the techno no-no girl poster child."

"Shut up! I am so not!"

"Why are you so angry with me? I mean, here I am trying to live the good life, trying to do the right thing, trying to live off the land, and you're biting my head off? Jeez, you're the one who got me into this. You're the one who went all netaholic on me! If it wasn't for you, none of this would have happened. It's all your fault."

"Look. I get the whole embrace-Mother-Earth thing. I really do. But there's embracing and then there's strangling. I mean, seriously, a replica of Thoreau's cabin?" I tilted my head back and let loose a snarky little laugh.

"That's the plan. It's not like we're building a mansion or anything. I mean, it's fifteen by twenty feet. Not much bigger than a shed."

"And you're going to live there? With Jonathan?"

"The one and only."

"And Udder and Gramps are good with this?"

"Well . . . you know . . . like I said, we haven't exactly told them everything yet." I could hear the evasiveness in her voice.

"What about a bathroom?"

"We're going to build an outhouse."

"An outhouse? You're going to shit in an outhouse in the middle of the night?"

"Look, Meagan. If I'm going to do this thing, I'm going to do it right, okay? Where has technology gotten us? Huh? Where? Pollution and climate change and addiction and unhappiness." Oh my God. Here she went again. I was growing a little weary of Sheila on the pulpit, proselytizing her newfound religion.

"Where's your revolutionary spirit, girl?" Sheila continued. "We've got to take back power. Take back control!"

"By shitting in an outhouse?"

"'*The journey of a thousand miles begins with a single step.*'"

Where had I heard that before?

"A single crap is more like it. And try telling yourself that when you've got the runs at three in the morning. And I swear to God, Sheila, if you quote Thoreau one more time, I'm going to—"

"Lao Tzu."

"Gesundheit."

Sheila laughed. "That last quote was from an ancient Chinese philosopher. He's totally lit."

"I don't care. Twain. Thoreau. Tzu. I DON'T GIVE A SHIT!"

"There's an open mind for you."

Sheila's cabin-building plan and back-to-the-land transformation was getting me totally bent out of shape. The more we spoke, the more agitated I became. And the more agitated I became, the more resentful and angry I got. That rational voice inside my head telling me to back off was being bitch-slapped by the louder, stupider me.

"What about electricity? Huh? What about seeing at night so you can read your back to-the-land manuals and your foraging-through-the-woods books and *Beekeeping for Idiots*?"

"Beeswax candles. Plus, Jonathan knows a guy who does solar. We'll be able to run a few things off a battery charged by the sun. I mean, seriously, how sweet is that?"

"A few things? Sheila, your bedroom needs its own power plant to fire up all of the crap that you have."

"That was then, this is now. '*A girl is rich in proportion to the number of things which she can afford to let alone.*'"

"Stop it, Sheila. Stop quoting crazy dead people. You're freaking me out. You're not Laura Ingalls Wilder in the little house on the damn prairie! As pissed off as I am at you right now, I still love you—and I'm having a really hard time picturing how you're going to stay safe? How you're going to stay warm?"

"Snuggling. Jonathan and I are getting pretty good at that. Simplicity. Harmony with nature. Anything but a *life of quiet desperation.*"

"This seems like an act of noisy desperation. And what about me? Are you seriously going to abandon me in Boston?"

"You can live with us!"

"With you and Jonathan?"

"Sure! Why not?"

"And Derek too? We can be a snuggly little foursome. Please? Pretty please with a pinkie swear."

"Don't be a bitch, Meagan."

"A bitch? Seriously? Don't confuse *my* sanity with *your* bitchiness."

"Look, when I first came here to bail you out over your boy troubles, I thought this whole Luddite thing was a piece of crap. Just like that stupid sophomore play I was in. But I've changed, Meagan. I've totally changed. Being around nature, being offline so much more, going down to Amish land. That's the real deal. That's what it's all about. I've never felt better in my life."

"Sheila, there's living the good life and there's going off the deep end. You really need to—"

"Sorry. Gotta go. Jonathan's on the other line."

Chapter 43

Following the shit show of Sheila's phone call, I was out in the garden, desperately trying to make sense of what had just gone down, when, wouldn't you know it, Derek pulled into the driveway. Perfect timing or what?

We had made an ambitious plan to attempt to do over the do-over one more time, but the whole Thoreau's cabin thing had me totally freaked. There was being a Luddite and there was being ridiculous. Sheila was doubling down on the latter.

"So," I said to Derek, hands on my hips and a scowl on my face. I had a flashback to my mother standing at the front door, hands on *her* hips, a scowl on *her* face. "I believe you have something to tell me?" I spat my words out.

"Uh . . . I do?"

"You better believe it, buddy! I am so pissed. I can't believe you didn't let on about Sheila and Jonathan and this crazy-ass plan to build Thoreau's cabin."

"I swear to God, Meagan, I just found out. A few hours ago. Jonathan texted me."

"He texted you?"

"I know, right?" He wrinkled his nose and shook his head.

Derek, unlike Sheila, at least seemed to appreciate the absurd irony of the whole backsliding netaholics thing. Once again, I was struck by how lightly these NA'ers took their anti-tech vows. It seemed more like a thirteen-step program, with the thirteenth being: "I will feel free to disregard all of the previous twelve steps at my convenience."

Derek leaned in towards me with the intent to do something. Hold my hand? Hug me? Kiss me?

Seriously? Was he kidding? Now was certainly not the moment for any of that crap.

Fists clenched, I pushed him away.

"Back off, boy. I'm in a foul mood. We definitely have some things to talk about."

"I know we do, Meagan, but right now is not the time." Derek's face turned serious. "We have an emergency on our hands. You up for an intervention?"

The Roost was doing its usual brisk business on the most beautiful of all late July Saturday afternoons. Outside the sun was shining and the birds were singing and the flowers were blooming and the clouds were dancing. Inside it was dark and musty and no one was talking. No one was looking at anybody else. Everyone was lost in their online world, huddled over their phones or laptops, tap-tap-tapping away, oblivious to the fact that the natural world even existed.

Attention!
You are required to keep your eyes on your phone or your laptop at all times. Absolutely no offline communication will be tolerated.
Violators will be forced to go outdoors!

"Look at them," Derek whispered. "They're like the Ringwraiths, the Nazgûl, the Dark Riders from *The Lord of the Rings*."

Oh my God. First Sheila had gone all Thoreau on me. Now Derek was going all Hobbit.

"*Unseen by all eyes in this world beneath the sun,*'" he continued. "Sub in cell phone for ring and technology for Sauron and this is what you get. Can you hear them? The voices of death."

There was Derek, once again being the anti-cell phone purist. Foreswearing any and all digital technology.

Geeky Tolkien weirdness aside, he did have a point. Along with the *ping ping ping* of incomings, there was a strange rasping sound coming from the future NA'ers. It was as if the cell phone phantoms and laptop delusions were sucking out their life force, plunging them into the realm of shadows.

Searching the café, we finally spotted her in the darkness of a corner seat. She was scrunched over her laptop, phone in hand, eyes glazed over and thumbs hard at work, rocking back and forth, rhythmically rasping away with the rest of them.

Derek took my hand in his. "Let's do this!" he said.

"Hey," Derek said, sitting down next to the texting Nazgûl, scaring the crap out of her.

It was Karen. Karen the Cat Killer. Karen the Pitcher. Now Karen the Relapser.

"Whoa!" Karen bolted upright, knocking her phone to the floor and fumbling to pick it up. "What are you two doing here?"

"Peter texted me," Derek began. "He said he saw you here yesterday. That you'd been sitting here all afternoon. And now you're back again."

Wait a minute—Peter texting Derek to rat out Karen for texting? Seriously?

"Wow," she said. "Spies are everywhere. Look, maybe I can catch the two of you later, okay? Not to be rude or anything, but right now I have some serious shit to do."

"Really?" Derek asked. "Like what?"

Karen shot him the evil eye. Not exactly the Eye of Sauron but pretty damn close. The phantoms and delusions of the evil one burned in those eyes. Derek reached out and placed his hand lightly on her shoulder.

"Do you want to come outside with us?" he asked softly. "It's a beautiful day. We could, I don't know . . ." He looked to me for inspiration. "Go to the park and play Scrabble or something."

Karen let out a snarky laugh. "Scrabble?" she asked, her voice incredulous.

"Yeah. It sounds totally lame but it's actually pretty fun—isn't it, Meagan?" Derek once more glanced toward me for support. "Meagan? Are you okay?"

Frozen in place, I let out a tortured rasp.

There it was. Right in front of me on the café table. In plain view on her phone. Beckoning to me. Drawing me in.

Passion. My dating site! Karen was on my dating site!

My preciousssssss! Mine!

"Are you kidding me?" Karen's voice grew louder. "Scrabble? I told you! I've got some serious shit going down here."

"Serious shit?" Derek asked. "Or just shit?"

Karen stood up and stared Derek down.

"Don't you dare judge me! It's none of your damn business what I'm doing here. If I want to be on the net, then I'll be on the damn net!"

"We're not judging anyone," Derek continued calmly. "We're just here to help—right, Meagan? Meagan?"

At that very moment help was the absolute last thing I was able to offer.

The Dark Riders, the Nazgûl, had settled in The Roost. *Come to me,* they were calling. *Come back to your precious!*

I could barely breathe. My whole body was jerking involuntarily.

Seeing her relapsing on the net was one thing, but seeing her on *Passion*, my *Passion*, was entirely something else.

"Help?" Karen was practically yelling by now. "I'll tell you how to help. How about getting the hell out of here and leaving me alone?"

Derek stood up. "We'll be in Pulaski Park if you'd like to join us." He was exuding kindness and calmness and sanity, seemingly oblivious to the altered chaotic state that both Karen and I had descended into. "I'll be the one kicking her ass in Scrabble."

He reached out, took my hand, and led (more like dragged) me out of the café.

Chapter 44

"That went well, don't you think?" Derek had just played the word CRAP for 24 points.

I shuddered in the warmth of the late-afternoon sun, shielding my eyes from the brightness. Shadows were creeping down my spine. I was both freezing and sweating at the same time, my breath shallow and rapid. All of that plus Derek was walloping me 134 to 53.

"Having had the spiritual awakening that we have, it's our obligation to help Karen," Derek continued. "But still, you can lead a horse to water but you can't make her drink. It takes darkness to see the light, you know. Sometimes you have to hit rock bottom before you—"

"Derek!" I rasped. "If you say one more idiotic twelve-step cliché, I'm seriously going to have to strangle you. Keep the mouth closed."

"Excuse me for breathing."

"Breathe all you want," I said, desperately trying to breathe myself. "Just don't talk."

"Look, Meagan, I know you're getting crushed in this game but you could be a better sport about it." He reached over once more to try and comfort me.

Good luck with that.

Darkness had enveloped me. Trouble was brewing. I caught a quick glimpse into the future and knew that the next few minutes were not going to go down well.

I stood up, stomped my feet, and threw the letter J at him. J for Jerk.

"I don't give a *crap* about this game, Derek. What we just did to Karen back there in The Roost was wrong. We should never have gone in there in the first place. Why did we have to go? Why did you make me go? Why?"

Derek looked rather alarmed at my outburst. "I thought we were being helpful," he said softly. "Supporting each other."

"Helpful? Supportive? Seriously? We go in there and embarrass the crap out of her, humiliate her in public, create a spectacle of ourselves, and then run away? Do you actually think that's being helpful?"

"No. I mean, yeah. We showed her that we care about her. That we were there for her. You know—the twelfth step of NA. Carrying this message of—"

"Carry what message? Jeez, Derek, how naïve can you possibly be."

"Meagan. What's wrong? Why are you being so bitchy?"

Oh my God! Talk about the wrong word at the wrong time. Sheila calling me a bitch was one thing. Derek? I don't think so.

"You want bitchy? I'll show you bitchy!"

I grabbed the board and dumped the jumble of Scrabble letters onto his lap. My signature go-to move. When times got tough, dumping something into Derek's lap was all I seemed capable of doing.

"What the hell? What's gotten into you? Seriously?"

I knew what had gotten into me. *Passion.* A single glance at *my* site had once again sent me hurtling over the edge. Back to the dark side. One little look was all it took. My pent-up netaholism had come roaring back to life.

"This whole netaholics thing is bullshit. Stupid crap bullshit!" The words hadn't even left my mouth before I knew how utterly ridiculous they sounded.

"What are you talking about?" Derek was picking up the Scrabble letters and putting them back in the bag, which made me even madder.

"Is it something I said?" he asked. "Something I did?"

"Why can't Karen be on her phone? Huh? Tell me! What is so wrong with that?"

"Sorry! We were just trying to help. God, Meagan, if I didn't like you so much—"

"Like me? Tell me, Derek—what exactly do you like? Enlighten me. Please. I'm dying to know."

"What do you mean, 'what do I like?'"

"What do *you* mean, 'what do I mean?' Jeez, Derek! It's a simple question. You can't answer it, can you?"

"Of course I can answer it!"

"No you can't. And let me tell you why. It's because you don't know me. You don't have a clue as to who I really am." I was working myself up into quite the frenzy. I was practically foaming at the mouth. "Who you like is not me. Who you like is who you *want* me to be. You've built up this elaborate fantasy fairy-tale image of your ideal girlfriend and pasted it on me. It's so painfully clear: who you like is this Luddite, left-wing, offline, Scrabble-playing, garden-girl, beekeeping shortstop. And now this whole Thoreau's cabin thing? Seriously?"

"What are you talking about?"

"This whole farce you and Jonathan drummed up just to get Sheila and me to stay. Thoreau's cabin. Back to the land. If you had just asked to get in my pants it would have been one thing. But this? Seriously?"

"Meagan! I told you! I just heard about it."

"Yeah. Right."

"It's true! I'm just trying to connect the dots here."

"I haven't given you enough dots to connect, Derek! I come out here for a few short weeks to help out my grandfathers and I try on this new techno-free outfit just for fun. It's like I'm rummaging around in the Filene's Basement of life. Putting on this, trying on that, just to see how it looks on me. So what if it did seem sweet for a few brief moments? Good for a few quick laughs? But open up my closet, Derek. Rummage around. Take a look at the real me that really does fit. I live in Boston, not some crazy backwoods farm. I don't keep bees, I text. I don't do nature, I do online dating! Without my phone what am I? Huh? Nothing!"

"Look," Derek said, his voice also rising a notch. Up until now he had been pretty calm, which had only made me more agitated. "I'm sorry you didn't think the intervention with Karen went well. And I'm sorry that you didn't know about the Thoreau cabin thing. And I'm sorry if you feel abandoned by Sheila."

"I do not feel abandoned by Sheila!" I yelled. How dare he know exactly how I felt!

"I can see how you'd be confused."

"Confused? That's the first thing you've gotten right all day! But let me tell you the one thing that I'm not confused about: this netaholics crap. I *love* being connected. I absolutely adore it. The girl in the café in the corner with her phone and her laptop? That's me! That's my thing!"

Derek humphed. "And you call that a real connection?"

"Oh. So now you're telling me what's real or not? You're starting to really piss me off."

By this time my voice was getting way too loud. If we were still at The Roost we would have been asked to leave. Here in the park, the nosy rubberneckers were edging closer and closer, the better to hear while pretending not to. I was having one of those out-of-body experiences: floating high up above the park, looking down on a ridiculous girl making a ridiculous spectacle of her ridiculous self.

"I'm pissing you off?" Derek's voice was almost as loud as mine. "You're the one telling me all I'm good for is a few laughs!"

"That's not what I said, Derek. Don't twist my words."

"Actually, Meagan, it really *is* what you said."

"All right, then maybe it is. But don't you get it? I'm bad news, Derek. I'm poison. If you have any sense at all you'll get up right now and walk away! Actually *run*. Head for the hills and never look back."

"What are you trying to tell me?"

"Just this: boy meets girl at costume party. Boy falls for girl. Girl changes back to real self and boy is blown away."

"Oh. Now I get it." Derek stood up and kicked at the Scrabble letters on the ground. Other than at the softball game, I had never seen him so riled up. And to kick Scrabble letters? I must have really struck a nerve. "How silly of me. I guess everything you've said and done since I met you is total and complete bullshit. You were in costume the whole time. It's all been one big lie."

"Bingo. You nailed it."

"You are so full of crap, Meagan."

"Oh my God, please spare me the melodrama. If you start up with the 'I know the real you' bullshit, then I'm going to barf. Seriously. All over your crotch. Something to add to the coffee stains and stupid Scrabble letters."

"So what about me?" Derek asked. "Huh? What am I to you? Nothing? This whole back-and-forth thing between us has been you just trying on outfits? All of this holding hands and do-overs of do-overs and King Ludd manifestos and Scrabble get-togethers has been one big joke?"

"Oh! So now it's all about *you*, huh? Way to go, Derek! Just like a guy to turn it right back to himself. So fucking typical!"

I could see the anguish in Derek's eyes. I could feel it in his voice. But the whole Caleb debacle and the Thoreau-cabin thing and now the lure of *Passion* had worked its twisted, evil magic on me. I was raving like a lunatic, doing my damnedest to alienate the one boy who had ever actually understood me.

"Maybe I am Neterella!" I shrieked, an evil off-key howl. "Cinderella updated for the digital age. And you're the Prince of Political Correctness. Only this time, Derek, the slipper doesn't fit. It's not even close."

"Look, Meagan. I like you. In fact, as annoying as you can be, I am totally in like with you."

"How can you say that? For the five zillionth time, you don't even know me!"

"I do too! I know the—"

"Stop!" I put my hands over my ears. "I don't want to hear it."

"Why? Why don't you want to hear it?"

"Because it's bullshit!"

"No, it's not! And you know what else? I don't think you're a neta-holic at all. I just think you're scared of boys. Scared of me. And you're using the whole addict thing to somehow justify it."

It was all I could do not to slap his face. "Don't you dare go all Udder on me with the psychobabble!"

"Why? Because it's just another thing you don't want to hear?"

Oh my God! Why was I being so awful to him? Why couldn't I just stop talking? The more I yammered the stupider I sounded. The reality of my fucked-up way of dealing with Derek—with dealing with boys, with dealing with relationships—was smacking me hard in the face. I was falling fast, and hitting rock bottom was going to hurt like hell.

"Derek, listen to me carefully." I tried to make myself sound all calm and reasonable, but my voice was trembling. "I'm moving back to Boston soon. Like I told you from the very beginning, this is not going to work. You know the best thing we can do right now? Cut this off. Stop it right here before anyone gets hurt."

Stupider words had never been spoken.

"Before anyone gets hurt?" Derek looked at me with mouth wide open. "Are you really that clueless? Do you have any idea how I'm feeling right now?" I could see tears welling up in his eyes. "Look at me! Look at me, Meagan."

It seemed as though the whole crowd in Pulaski Park was looking at us, engrossed in the soap opera drama of our fight scene. Everyone was hushed, waiting expectantly to see how this shit show would end.

I couldn't bear to look at him.

"You know I'm going to school in Boston in the fall," he said. "That means our relationship—"

"What relationship! A few weeks does not make a relationship. What do you think I've been trying to tell you?"

"Do you honestly believe that?"

"Believe in fairy tales all you want, Derek. I'm going back to real life."

"Real life? Neterella in Cyberland is real life? Can't you see you're making absolutely no sense?"

"Don't *you* see, Derek? That's the problem. Nothing makes sense. Absolutely nothing!"

"Maybe it's not supposed to make sense, Meagan. Maybe we're just supposed to go with it."

"'Go with it'? Go with *what*?"

"You know perfectly well what. This is like the third time we've almost broken up and I gotta tell you, it's getting pretty—"

"Third time? What are you talking about, Derek? What planet are you even from? You have to make something before you can break it. Everyone knows that. The only thing that you and I have made is one big mess!"

I burst into blubbering tears and, nearly zombie-like, lurched away, leaving Derek alone, slumped over on the park bench.

Chapter 45

It was a dreary Sunday morning and the rain was falling in sheets. Good for the garden but terrible for my mood.

I had borrowed the car and driven like a maniac down to Northampton to meet the devil face-to-face. Not just falling, but leaping off the wagon for a torrid online binge-fest.

One careless glance at Karen's online antics, one tiny peek at my precious dating site, and I was swept back into the waiting and willing arms of the net.

Frodo had the one Ring to rule them all. Big fucking deal. Let him have it! I had *Passion*. Take that, Sauron!

Hiding out at The Roost was out of the question. What if Derek, or some other nosy NA'er, found me there? The very last thing I needed was some netaholic nutcase trying to pull an intervention on me!

I walked up and down Main Street before settling in at the basement of the Haymarket Café, another cyber addict's crack house, with a scarf around my hair and neon green sunglasses pressed into my face—a feeble attempt at disguise.

Screw this celibacy thing, I said to myself. *Why not just go for it with a quick* Passion *hookup?* Hot anonymous sex! Hell, everybody else was doing it, so why shouldn't I? And this time I'd go all in, not chicken-shit my way out of it like I'd done with Caleb. I had even made an extremely awkward stop at CVS and picked up a six-pack of condoms, just to cover my bases. Or rather his.

Why was losing your virginity such a big deal anyway? Sheila had done it. Why couldn't I? It would be a huge weight off my shoulders. Something I wouldn't have to worry about ever again. A sure-fire way to regain my lost *feng shui*, make me feel better, get me back on track. What could possibly go wrong with that?

I crazily cruised guys' profiles, swiping right on everyone that looked remotely hot, and texted come-ons till my thumbs were swollen. My *Passion* points were rolling on in. *Ping! Ping! Ping!* There must have been a thousand guys in the Valley clearly chomping at the bit for a Sunday-morning hookup.

I drank my weight in coffee, and then drank some more. So what if my left eye had developed a nervous twitch? Who cared if I had chewed a hole through the top of my scarf?

Maybe if I'd been back in Boston, I would have screwed up enough courage to text a come-on to Caleb, but there was no time for that now. I'd have to settle for a local.

Ahhh! The beauty of *Passion*! I hadn't even had time to order another cup of coffee and there he was, my pick-me-up from the pick-up site, smiling at me from across the table.

Scared of boys! *Humph!* Derek would be eating his words while I'd be chomping down on someone else. I'd show *him* who was scared of boys.

"You look really nice," this boy said softly to me. "And thanks so much for inviting me here."

This was definitely not what I was expecting. I didn't want to do nice. I wanted to do *it*. But hey, I could still make it work. Maybe the guy wasn't as hot as Derek (who was?), but he was pretty damn close. Tall and twinkly-eyed. Great hair. Broad shoulders. Awesome lips.

I shuddered, pulling my scarf in more tightly around my neck and readjusting my sunglasses.

"Can I buy you another cup of coffee?" he asked. "I take mine with cream and sugar. I'm sort of a lightweight when it comes to caffeine. How do you like yours?"

Silence on my end. I just couldn't seem to speak.

I was more than a little flustered. I had been fully prepared for some snaggletoothed loser with greasy hair and a face full of tattoos, a pool of drool cascading down his chin onto his fully erect shorts. Some horndog who was messing with me and had put up a fake profile picture on *Passion*, the oldest trick in the book. But no such luck. This guy looked better in real life than he did on the net.

"I'm a sociology major at Amherst College," he said, either oblivious to my awkward silence or desperately trying to ease the awkwardness by continuing to jabber away. "I'm really interested in immigrant rights. This whole notion of Trump closing our doors to folks from other countries is really disturbing. We need to be welcoming and embrace diversity, not isolate ourselves from the rest of the world. But really, enough about me. What are you studying, Stephanie?"

Oh my God! What was up with this guy? He was hot, he seemed smart, he was being super-sensitive and sweet.

Thank God I was in a public place with the door just a few quick steps away. If I didn't have a clear escape route, I would have had a heart attack on the spot.

Still getting no response from me, the boy continued talking.

"What kinds of activities do you enjoy doing?" he asked. "Me? I'm like a gardening nut. I love to get my hands dirty growing vegetables. That and play softball. But on a rainy morning like today, you'll more than likely find me indoors with a board game."

That did it. Enough was enough! How many karmic screw-ups could a girl have in one summer? Relying on my superpower of flight, it took me less than five seconds to hightail it back to my car. Shuddering and shaking with my sunglasses on upside down and my scarf practically strangling me, obsessively checking my rearview mirror every few seconds to make sure I wasn't being followed, I somehow managed to make it back to Udder and Gramps's in one piece.

Chapter 46

"Boy trouble?" Gramps asked. He was sitting at the kitchen table watching the rain continue to fall.

"I'm not talking to you," I said.

"Why? What did I do now?"

"You know exactly what you did!" I wagged my finger at him. "This whole Thoreau's cabin thing? Seriously? What were you thinking? I can't believe you'd let Sheila and Jonathan move in on you like this. It's totally crazy!"

"What are you talking about?" Gramps asked. "Nobody's moving in anywhere. If your friends want to build a shack out back and do the occasional weekend love-fest Luddite thing, then that's fine with me. But no one said a word about *living* there."

"They're not my friends," I said. "At least not anymore. But according to Sheila, she and Jonathan will be setting up house in your backyard in no time."

"Meagan! Sweetheart!" Gramps reached over and put his hand soothingly on my arm. "Do you actually think your grandfather and I would allow Sheila, or anyone else for that matter, including you, to drop out of high school and move into a shack out back with their boyfriend? We might be crazy but we're not insane."

"That's not what Sheila said."

"Sheila called us insane?"

"No. Of course not. But like I just told you, she said she's moving in with Jonathan."

"Meagan. No one is moving anywhere. Look, I get what Sheila and Jonathan are trying to do. The back-to-the-land thing and all. More power to them. '*The mass of men lead lives of . . .*'"

"*Quiet desperation*! Please no more Orwellian-speak!"

"Thoreaulian."

"Whatever. It's enough to make me puke. Anyway, Sheila and Jonathan are far from desperate. And no one in their right mind would dare to describe Sheila as quiet!"

"By the way, speaking of desperate, Derek called. Again. The phone has not stopped ringing. He sounded beyond desperate."

"I'm not talking to him either."

"Oh my. How about Sheila? Are you still talking to her?"

"Are you kidding? No! Of course not. She's the one I'm most pissed at."

"I don't quite grasp why you're so upset over this," Gramps continued, pouring himself a bowl of cereal and relighting his joint. "Aren't you the one working on weaning yourself off technology? Embracing the natural world? Now that Sheila is onboard, why are you so angry at her?"

"There's *on*board and then there's *over*board. You can't just drop out of school and build a cabin in the woods."

"Meagan. Look at me." Gramps held up his cereal spoon and swung it side to side like a hypnotist's pendulum. "Listen carefully to my words. I hope this is the last time I have to tell you this: no one is dropping out of anything. Get that idea out of your head. I'm not saying Sheila doesn't have a point. *Some people get an education without going to school. And the rest get it—*"

"Oh my God! Will you stop already!"

"Stop making sense?"

"Stop with the Thoreau or Mark Twain or Talking Heads or whoever! Have you and Sheila been programmed by the same brainwasher?" I stood up and stomped my feet on the ground. "For the trillionth time, how is it that I am the only one being the adult around here? Why is it that everyone else is acting like they're thirteen?"

"We're just embracing our inner children," Udder said.

Gramps took another bite of his cereal. "Listen, sweetheart. If Sheila and Jonathan and you and Derek want to spend part of your summers here in the years ahead, then we'd be honored to have you. Flattered. We adore having you around. Even with all the angst and heartache and drama, maybe even because of it, you are a wonderful girl to be with. We're thrilled that you're learning what it's like to garden and keep bees, and don't tell us for a minute you don't like it. We've seen the change it's made in you. It's all been good. And now if Sheila wants to embrace it, what could possibly be wrong with that?"

"You just don't get it, do you?"

"What's not to get, Meagan?" Gramps said. "More farms, more farm girls."

"This is not a farm. This is a lunatic asylum." I was on a roll. First pissing off Sheila, then Derek, and now my grandfathers. Huzzah and hooray for me! I had now managed to alienate everyone!

"Meagan!" Udder wagged his finger at me.

"I'm puzzled as to why you're so angry and frustrated," Gramps said, scratching his head. "Are you jealous? Is it that Sheila's zooming past you as a born-again, tree-hugging Luddite? Is it that Sheila thought of the whole Thoreaulian-shack-out-back idea first? Is it that Sheila has an actual offline boyfriend who she's smitten with? Is that what's got your goat?"

"Stop it, Gramps!" I was spitting out words. "Don't you dare bring Jeremy into this! I don't have a goat to get. I am *so* not jealous of Sheila."

But I *was* stung by his criticism. My face felt flushed and I could hardly breathe. What gave Gramps the right to say things like that to me? To insinuate that all this time I had just been playing at love and romance and sex with my *Passion* passion? That I had just been playing at being a Luddite with the NA group? That I had just been playing at life, not *living* it!

What gave Gramps the right to know so much more about me than I knew about myself?

"I'm going to weed the garden," I said, not looking either of them in the eyes. "I'm not talking to the both of you. EVER AGAIN!" I got up, stamped my feet again, and stormed away.

"Watch out for the ghost," Gramps called out after me. "She's been hiding in the zucchini lately."

Bertha?

That I could handle.

The truth?

I was far less sure about that.

Chapter 47

"Working on your issues?" Gramps asked.

Oh my God! What part of *I'm not talking to you* did that old fart not understand? Turn the channel, please!

I was out in the garden killing bean beetles, totally riding my wave of self-pity, secure in the knowledge that at that very moment, no one in the whole wide world was even remotely close to experiencing the degree of angst that I was.

When you realize how perfect everything is, you will tilt your head back and laugh at the sky.

That was the quote inscribed at the base of the smiling Buddha sitting serenely on the rock in the center of the garden.

If we could see the miracle of a single flower clearly, our whole life would change.

That pearl of Buddhist wisdom was taped to an upside-down whiskey bottle, one of the many set in the garden to trap the evil spirits.

Increasingly, the garden seemed the only place left to find some degree of solace, some refuge, from all of those evil spirits so intent on dragging me down. With *Passion's* latest spectacular failure to deliver, the garden was my last remaining safety blanket, so much more predictable and comforting than the rest of my life.

In a garden, when you planted beans, you got beans. You fertilized, you mulched, you watered, you weeded, you picked off the bugs, and, with a little bit of luck, a few prayers to the Buddha on the rock, and some encouraging words down those rusty pipes set to communicate with the underground, amazing things happened.

In the rest of my life, when I planted something, who knew what the hell was going to come up?

The miracle of a single bean in the garden: it would poke its shiny new leaves up through the soil and greet the world, and my whole life would change. What could be better than that?

Peace. Serenity. Tilting my head back and laughing at the sky.

But all of that, *if* it was ever going to happen, was for another day.

Today I turned my back on Buddha. Today was a day for death.

Terrible as it sounds, without the beetles to bear the brunt of my angst, God only knows what I would have done with myself.

I wasn't just killing beetles. I was taking sadistic pleasure in devising new and innovative ways to torture them before finally putting them out of their misery—and me out of mine. Vlad the Impaler himself would have been so proud of me. I could hear the beetles begging to be squished, pleading to have me end it right then and there. But no, that was way too quick and easy a way for those bastards to die. I know this did nothing to raise my sympathy factor, but in that place, at that moment, realizing how very imperfect my world actually was, it seemed that it was all that I had to work with.

I sacrificed three beetles on a makeshift rock alter. I impaled six on a stick. I drowned a dozen in the watering can. I even went so far as to bite one in half. It tasted like chicken, or maybe even Madagascar Hissing Cockroach, only crunchy and still squirming. I gagged and spit it out.

My thumbs, still swollen and crampy from my disastrous texting relapse, were now smeared with bug guts, my nails encrusted with their gooey remains. I tilted my head back at the sky and laughed a maniacal, vampirish "HE HE HE HAH HAH HAH!" Probably not exactly what the Buddha had in mind.

Gramps sat back in his garden chair, fired up a joint, and watched me intently.

"I'm glad I'm not a bean beetle," he said. "Torture is way too kind a word to describe what you're doing to the poor things."

"Throw me your lighter, will ya?" I called out, forgetting I wasn't talking to him. "I'm going to burn this one at the stake. What do you think: is fire the most painful way to die?"

"I don't know. Chomping that little guy in two was pretty impressive."

"Thanks. That was one of the most disgusting things I've ever done in my life. And, as you well know, I've got loads to choose from."

"With a little more practice I'm sure you could get used to it. Maybe you could even become an insectivore. Great protein. Low carbon footprint. Wonderful way to impress your Luddite friends."

"You mean my Luddite *ex*-friends."

We lapsed back into silence, watching a honeybee zoom into the blossom of a zucchini flower and start crazily pollinating away.

"No eating bees, though," Gramps said. "I insist you draw the line at that one."

"Gramps! Please! Who do you think I am? I promise I'll stick with the Madagascar cockroaches even if they hiss at me. Who knows, maybe I'll become the world's first roachivore."

The bee buzzed its way out of one blossom and headed right into another.

"You know," I said. "Maybe being the queen bee *is* the way to go. You have sex once and then the guy dies. No emotional connection whatsoever. Seriously, how awesome would that be?"

"Well, speaking from the drone's point of view, not very."

"But it's so much simpler than being in a relationship. You don't have to worry about feelings or commitment or getting hurt or anything. You just do it and it's done."

"Spoken like a true queen."

"Do you see what I'm getting at here, Gramps? Do you? I'm seventeen. I'm way too old for all of this relationship drama. Seriously. I'm done."

Gramps took another hit and blew the weed smoke toward the zucchini blossoms. With every puff in their direction they seemed to double in size.

"You're absolutely right, Meagan. It's a brilliant idea. Totally inspired. You should definitely go right back to doing your *Passion* thing. Just picture every guy as a drone and you'll be good to go. Do him once and he's done. No possible way to ever see him again because he's dead, dead, *dead*. He'll be out of your life forever. *Poof!* Goodbye, guy! So simple. So easy."

"You're messing with me, aren't you, Gramps?" I squinted at him.

"Messing with you? *Moi?* How dare you! I'm in complete support of this back-to-the-internet thing. I'm in total awe of the technology that has made being human so much simpler! Sex without love. Relations without relationships. Intercourse without discourse. What could possibly be better than that? To quote my wonderful granddaughter: *huzzah and hooray!*"

I had to hand it to him: Gramps could snark it up with the best of them.

"If only it were that easy," I muttered.

"Easy? Look at me, Meagan. Look right at me."

I stared up at that old, gray, wrinkled face of his and saw the fire burning in his eyes.

"You're my granddaughter," he said sternly. "Easy is for cowards. Easy is for losers. You and I both know you're better than that. Way better."

Gramps stood up, un-crinkled his back, did a couple of shoulder rolls, let loose a long-winded fart, and hobbled his way back to the house, leaving me, once again, all alone in the garden.

I had killed all of the beetles I could find in the bean patch. With no more death to be had, I lay down with my head on a zucchini and, as yucky as they were, chewed hard on my thumbnails. Number six in *The Luddite's Guide to the Top Ten Things to Do with Your Thumbs (and Fingers) Offline*.

So much for easy.

As if there ever really were such a thing.

Chapter 48

"I'm going to Mom's," I told Udder and Gramps. Annoying as they could be, it was awfully hard to stay mad at the two of them for long. Plus, now that I was estranged from everyone else that I cared about, who else did I have to talk to?

"What?" Gramps asked. "Where the hell is this coming from? You've hardly mentioned your mom the whole time you've been here. I was beginning to think that maybe you were the only teenage fuck-up in the entire world not preoccupied with their mother."

"Thanks, Gramps. I'll take that as a compliment."

"Why go visit her now?"

"It's Mom's birthday on Tuesday, and I'm thinking I should probably be there. You know she's turning fifty, right? It must be like the end of the world for her. I can see why. *Fifty!* Oh my God! Talk about old!"

Gramps looked at Udder. They both sighed and shook their heads.

"It's probably not a bad idea if I make an appearance," I continued.

Gramps had never gotten along particularly well with my mother. Mom was his daughter-in-law, or rather his ex-daughter-in-law now that my parents were divorced. She and Gramps had tangled from the beginning over just about everything—politics, values, money—you name it. I guess Gramps never thought of her as the right choice for my dad, and he was probably right. But given how screwed-up my father was, it was hard to imagine who would have been the right choice for him.

Given Mom's tenuous relationship with Gramps, it was surprising that she had been so gung-ho about shipping me out here for the summer. She must have really thought I was super-messed-up to think that Gramps's influence would actually improve my character.

"Tuesday?" Gramps asked. "As in tomorrow? You won't be gone for long, I hope."

"I don't know." I gave another theatrical sigh. "Maybe I've overstayed my welcome here."

"What are you talking about, darling?" Udder seemed alarmed. "You could never do something like that."

"Was it something I said?" Gramps asked, suddenly looking much older. "If so, whatever it is, I take it back."

"No, no, no," I insisted, reaching out and lightly touching his arm. "It's not that. I mean, I gotta get out of here. At least for a day or two. This whole scene has turned way too weird. I mean, what with Derek and Sheila and the whole Thoreau cabin shit show. It's just not working for me."

"What do you mean, 'It's not working'?" Udder stood up, tightened his belt, and sat back down again, the way he did when he was agitated. "Just like we've been saying, being here has done wonders for you! Look at all of the personal growth you've experienced in the past weeks!"

"Personal growth? All I can see is shrinkage. Even my boobs have gotten smaller."

"That's because you've been working your butt off out here," Gramps said. "What with mowing the lawn and pruning the orchard and weeding the garden and cleaning the house and being at our beck and call day and night, you must be exhausted, you poor thing. We've been working you way too hard. You need to relax. Kick back. Smoke a doobie with me and take a little time off for yourself."

"That's not it, Gramps. I gotta go. I really do."

"Have you told Derek that you're leaving us?"

"What does Derek have to do with this? What does Derek have to do with anything? It's not like he's my boyfriend."

"Could have fooled us," Udder said.

"Stop. Please. Don't give me crap about this or make me change my mind. Can you give me a ride to the bus station tomorrow?"

"Bus station? Are you kidding? There's no way you're taking a bus. We'll drive you to Boston. I haven't seen your mother in a coon's age."

"Do you remember the time she caught me smoking weed at your elementary school graduation?" Gramps asked. We had turned onto the Massachusetts Turnpike and were headed east toward Boston.

"That was not your finest moment," I grimaced, clutching tightly to my seat belt. Gramps drove like people did in the movies—never looking at the road, always staring at the person he was talking to, hands constantly straying from the steering wheel. It was way worse than even

Jonathan's driving. I already felt nauseous and we still had over an hour to go.

"And when her highfalutin Boston Brahmin friends caught me and Udder fooling around on the playroom pool table?" he continued.

"Udder and *me*," I said.

"What? Don't tell me you were there, too?"

"Don't be disgusting, Gramps. I was correcting your grammar."

"Well, excuse me, Ms. Fussybritches. What are you now, the grammar police?"

"She's right, Curtis," Udder chimed in from the back seat. "You should know better. *'Ill-fitting grammar is like ill-fitting shoes. You can get used to it for a bit, but then one day your toes fall off and you can't walk to the bathroom.'*"

"Thoreau?" I asked. "Yogi Berra? Martin Luther King Jr.?"

"Jasper Fforde," Udder answered.

"I should have known." I rolled my eyes. This summer I had heard quotations from just about every person on the planet who had ever philosophized.

"This is why we need to be on our best behavior," Udder continued. "No shenanigans, Curtis. That means no marijuana, keep your hands off my rear end, and speak in grammatically correct sentences. Do I make myself perfectly clear?"

Gramps took his hands off the wheel and saluted. I gripped my seat belt even tighter.

"She does know we're coming, right?" Udder asked.

I squirmed uncomfortably in the front seat.

"You didn't tell her?" Gramps was grinning.

"Oh God," Udder groaned.

I turned around and saw him crossing himself, his eyes raised toward the heavens, performing one of those bizarre rituals left over from his Catholic-school days.

"This will surely be interesting," he said, knitting his brow and shaking his head.

I had no idea that my mom's birthday party was going to be such an elaborate affair. Her newest fling, a lawyer by the name of Edwin Whipple, had gone all out and turned her Fiftieth into an extravaganza extraordinaire. The house was party central, with a caterer and servers and an open bar. With the awkward exception of Gramps, Udder, and me, it was formal attire all around.

As always, my grandfathers looked like fish out of water. Udder had on Bermuda shorts and a T-shirt with "Love Trumps Hate" lettered in red, white, and blue. Gramps's trousers were made for a man twice his size, and he had on rainbow suspenders that made him look like some hick from Oklahoma. A gay hippie hayseed, true, but a hayseed nonetheless. Of course, I was not exactly the height of fashion myself, not with my Lefty Luddites jersey, which for some unfathomable reason I was still continuing to wear, and my dirt-stained gardening shorts, which I had neglected to wash, and a pair of mismatched flip-flops.

"We are a sorry, sorry sight," Udder whispered.

Gramps hitched up his suspenders, laughed, and handed him a drink.

"*Darling!* How *delightful* to see you!"

One of mom's friends had cornered me outside the bathroom. It was creepy that she called me *darling*. When Udder used the word, it came across as sincere and affectionate. With her, it just sounded pretentions and super-annoying.

The woman reeked of Coco Chanel *Mademoiselle Eau de Parfum*, which she was still spraying quite liberally into her ample cleavage as she emerged from the toilet. No wonder. The *Eau de Merde* scent she had left behind took my breath away. Of course, who was I to complain? My entire body stank of *Eau de Bean Beetle Guts*.

"How *are* you?" she asked.

"I'm great," I answered. "How's Sasha?"

Sasha was her beyotch of a daughter who had gone to some stuck-up private boarding school on the North Shore. I had hated her ever since the seventh grade, when she still went to the same public school I did. One afternoon in the girl's locker room right before gym class, she had taken off her top and bragged to everyone how her boobs were coming in and then, looking disdainfully at me, voiced her opinion that mine probably never would. It was one of those sordid episodes that had scarred me for life.

"*Maah*velous!" said Sasha's mom, letting her Boston Brahmin accent play out for all that it was worth. "She's interning for a tech company in town this summer. One that develops apps and all that. It's really quite complex. Way over my head. She's a huge sensation there. Absolutely huge. They can't believe she's still in high school. They're absolutely *dying* to keep her on."

"I'm sure they are," I said, absolutely dying to escape the nauseating combination of the Chanel perfume and the toxic fumes still emerging from her back door.

"And what are *you* up to this summer, darling?" she asked, reading my T-shirt. "'Lefty Luddites'? Is that the firm you're interning with?"

"Uh, kind of." I had asked about Sasha only for the sake of being polite. The very last thing I wanted to do was have a conversation with the beyotch's mother.

"And what sort of work do you *do* there?"

"Oh, you know, the usual sort of thing. Playing the field. Scoring runs. Or at least trying to."

"Oh, you young people with all of your *technology* lingo. My goodness! I am *so* in awe of your expertise in navigating this high-tech world. I can't *imagine* how you do it."

"You and me both," I told her. I turned to flee, but she grabbed me by my arm.

"Can I ask you one *tiny* favor here? If you could just help me out with this silly little thing, I'd be *forever* in your debt." She reached into her purse and pulled out her cell phone. "I can't figure out for the *life* of me how to make the darn thing ring when someone calls. It is *so* frustrating. Could you work your post-millennial magic?"

Oh my God! Adults! They were so incompetent.

"Sure," I said. "What kind of ring tone do you want?"

"Oh, you know, something soothing. Something *classical*. Perhaps Brahms? Or maybe Mozart? I absolutely *adore* his Piano Sonata Number 11. Do you know it? It's *maah*velous."

"I'm sure it is." I fiddled with her phone, loaded on Nirvana's *Smells Like Teen Spirit* and then, furtively, escaped down the hallway toward another bathroom in hopes of finding one a little less stinkified.

"*Darling!* How *delightful* to see you!"

Curses! It was another one of Mom's evil friends. They were like mischievous clones, coming out of the woodwork to torment me. What was it about four cups of coffee, a two-hour car trip, and desperately needing to pee that they didn't understand?

"Your mother told me you were here. She's absolutely *ecstatic* that you came. Absolutely ecstatic!"

Actually, Mom had said about three words to me the whole time I had been at the party. As always, she was so caught up in her own drama and making a "good impression" on Edwin Whipple and the rest of her friends that she barely acknowledged my existence.

"I just ran into Dorothy, Sasha's mother," said the clone. "She says you're an absolute *prodigy* when it comes to technology."

I smiled. I had been called a heck of a lot of things lately, but *prodigy* had certainly not been one of them. Clearly Sasha's mother had not gotten a phone call yet.

"Can I trouble you with just a quick little question? I'm *quite* sure it won't take but a moment."

She reached into her purse and pulled out her iPad mini.

"I just don't understand *why*, whenever I turn it on, the little disc thingie just keeps spinning round and round. It's enough to make me dizzy. I just *can't* seem to make the darn thing stop."

With one hand pushing down on my crotch, desperately trying to fortify the urethral floodgate against the impending tidal wave of urine, I used the other to quickly fix the spinning-thingie problem. Then I changed her home page from *Yahoo* to *PornHub*.

"That ought to do the trick," I told her, watching in dismay as another of Mom's friends beat me to the bathroom door.

Both bathrooms occupied. Damn! Things were getting desperate.

Just then yet another one of Mom's clonish friends popped into the doorway.

"*Darling!*"

Holy crap! What was this, a conspiracy? If one more person, other than Udder, dared to call me *darling*, then fists were going to fly.

"I was wondering if you could—"

"Turn it off, and then turn it back on again!" I yelled, racing out the screen porch door towards the trees in the backyard.

I was crouched behind two chokeberry bushes with my pants around my knees, enjoying blessed relief, when I smelled smoke and heard a cough directly behind me. Freaking out, I pulled up my pants in mid-stream.

"Holy hell!" I cried.

"I'm so sorry, sweetheart. I didn't look, I promise!"

"What are you doing here?"

It was Gramps, squatting behind a white oak.

"What do you think I'm doing?"

"Taking a piss?"

"No, silly. Smoking a joint."

"Oh my God, Gramps. You made me pee all over myself. And seriously? You're getting high? You heard what Udder said, and you know how Mom feels about marijuana. If she finds out you're stoned, she's going to flip!"

"She already has, sweetheart. She already has."

"Oh no!" I was desperately trying to dry my pants with tufts of grass, but it was only making matters worse, leaving them a wet, slimy, streaked shade of pee green. "What did you do now?"

"Trust me, darling, you do not want to know." The voice was Udder's, joining us in the bushes. "Perhaps it's best if we leave sooner rather than later."

We were heading back home to Udder and Gramps's. I had given Mom her birthday present (three zucchinis and a half-dozen cucumbers), kissed her goodbye, and fled the scene.

I was driving. Gramps was still high and there was no way I would ever think of getting into a car with Udder behind the wheel. He drove forty-five miles per hour in the left-hand lane on the Mass Pike and could never understand why everyone was honking like hell and giving him the finger.

My feelings were hurt. I had been away from home for well over a month, and all my mother seemed to want to know about was how I was doing with my so-called issues. Nothing about me, just my *issues*. I don't know what I had been expecting but it was certainly more than that.

Of course, I had planned on staying at least a little bit longer at the party, which would have given me considerably more time to talk to her. But, given the debacle with the television, Udder, Gramps, and I had had to practically run to the car to get away.

"I still don't get why you had to wreck it?" I asked Gramps. "I mean, seriously. Did you see the look on her face? It was her birthday, for goodness sake! I mean, she's not my favorite person in the world, but still."

"Don't exaggerate," Gramps said. "I did not wreck her television. I was simply fiddling with it."

"You weren't fiddling with it," Udder said grumpily. "You were trying to take it down! What were you thinking, Curtis?"

"I swear to God, you're worse than Sheila," I told Gramps. "Seriously. Here we are on the run from Mom's house after destroying her most prized birthday present. I thought she was going to crap her pants!"

"It's not even damaged." Gramps was grinning and didn't look the least bit bothered. "If you ask me, the damn thing should be. Eighty-eight inches! That's obscene."

For her birthday, Edwin Whipple had bought Mom an eighty-eight-inch Samsung super-high-definition television, which, earlier in the day, she had proceeded to have mounted on the living room wall so she could show it off to all her friends. Eighty-eight inches. That's more than seven feet wide. Mom had taken down all of the old photos of me as a baby, me as a little girl, and me as a super-awkward tweenager and replaced them with the television.

This had annoyed the hell out of Gramps.

"Wait till I tell Sheila," I told him. "She's gonna be pissed. You totally stole that one from her playbook. She's going to sue your ass for plagiarism."

"I thought you weren't talking to Sheila?" Gramps asked.

"You better believe I'm telling her about this. This one is way too big to keep to myself."

"'Way too big'! That's exactly my point! Big is not better. Big is bullshit. That TV your mother got is an obscene metaphor for all that has gone wrong with the world. The consumer culture on steroids. The inability of human beings to exercise any degree of self-control over their obsessive need to go on biggering, biggering, and then bickering about who biggered the most."

"You sound like the Lorax from Dr. Seuss," I told him, pulling into the right-hand lane to let a Hummer shoot past us at what must have been, at the very least, eighty-eight miles an hour.

"You did bad, Curtis," Udder said, wagging his finger in Gramps's face. "You were a very, very bad boy."

"I did not destroy anything," Gramps reiterated. "I was simply looking behind it for my wonderful granddaughter's pictures, which are supposed to have their rightful, respectful place on that very wall, and the damn television came unhinged."

"*You're* the one who's unhinged," Udder said.

"Udder!" I scolded. "Don't be rude to my grandfather."

They both laughed.

"And then, to add insult to injury, you had to tell the entire birthday party about the size of your *penis*?" Udder was still wagging his finger at Gramps.

"Oh no!" I cried. "Please tell me that didn't happen. Please?"

"Look, I was simply hammering home my point." Gramps turned and smiled at Udder in the back seat. "Bigger is not always better. Am I right?"

"Oh my God," I said. "Stop! It's not safe for me to drive with my hands over my ears!"

"And let me tell you something else," Gramps continued, totally ignoring me. "Some of them were interested." He raised his eyebrows and grinned again.

"In the size of your penis?" I asked, incredulously.

"No, of course not. They were all pretty appalled at that. However, Jonah Whatever-his-last-name-is's big boy certainly got their attention."

"I can't believe you brought up Jonah again," Udder said, shaking his head. "That's the third party in a row you've put that man front and center. It's like you're obsessed. It is entirely inappropriate."

"Oh God," I said, hands clenched tightly on the wheel. "I don't think I want to know, but I have to ask . . . who is Jonah whatever?"

"He's the gentleman with the world's largest penis. Thirteen and a half inches. When erect."

I swerved into and then out of the breakdown lane.

"Please. Stop. *Talking!*" I begged, cringing.

"And you felt the need to tell your ex-daughter-in-law's entire shocked birthday party this fascinating factoid . . . why, exactly?" Udder asked.

"Because it reinforces the point I was trying to make! Big is not always beautiful. Big is a problem for Jonah. His longest romantic relationship has only been a year. He got pulled aside for additional screening at an airport, for goodness sake, because of the bulge in his pants. It is not, I repeat, *not*, a good thing. Just like the television."

"Wait a minute," I said. "You were actually comparing the size of Mom's TV to the size of some dude's weenie?" I could not believe I was actually having this conversation.

"No! Of course not! Although, now that you mention it, could you imagine an eighty-eight-inch penis?"

"I can't imagine a thirteen-and-a-half-inch one. Who would want to be poinked by that?"

"'*Poink*'?" Gramps asked. "Is that actually a word?"

"Only in Scrabble," I said. "Just like *yoink.*"

"African elephants," Gramps said.

"No," I replied. "Yiddish Pigs."

"And how big are their yoinkers?" he asked.

"What are we even talking about?" I had totally lost the thread of the conversation. It was hard enough driving on the Mass Pike, let alone driving while talking about penis size and God only knows what else with my grandfathers.

"Penises, sweetheart. What else would we possibly be talking about? Did you know African elephants' penises are about the size of your mom's television?"

"Oh my God!" I was desperately trying to focus on the road and not on the size of elephant penises. (Or on anyone else's penises for that matter!) "Of *course* I don't know that. How would I possibly know that? Why would I possibly want to?"

"They drag them on the ground when they walk," Gramps continued.

"Curtis!" Udder said. "You're torturing your granddaughter. Can't you see the poor dear is trying to drive?"

Gramps seemed oblivious to my pain and agony. "Surprisingly, I don't know a thing about deer dongs," he continued, "but I do know that blue-whale members are even bigger than elephant wankers. They have the largest penises on earth. Ten feet long. And if you think that's bad, some animals have penises even longer than their own bodies. Take barnacles, for example."

"Barnacles!" I was whining now. "I don't want to know about barnacles. Please don't tell me about barnacles. I don't want to know about any of this!"

"Barnacle penises are forty times bigger than their own body! Forty times! That would be like Derek having a penis 240 feet long!"

"Oh my God, Gramps—please, *please*, PLEASE keep Derek's penis out of this conversation!"

I was on the verge of pulling a U-turn on the Pike and heading the wrong way against incoming traffic. Anything to get Gramps's attention. Anything to make him stop talking.

"They let theirs go squiggling around the bottom of the ocean on their own just looking for a female to perform with."

"No more barnacles!" I was practically shrieking. "No more whales, or elephants, or boys! Particularly boys. And how do you know all this stuff anyway?"

"How do you think?" Gramps grinned. "Thank God for the internet. At least it's good for something!"

Chapter 49

I was sitting on the steps of Memorial Hall in Northampton, next to a homeless man with a Mickey Mouse T-shirt. I had a cup of coffee in one hand and a flyswatter in the other. I had liberated the flyswatter that some rando had stuck in the statue of a Civil War soldier standing guard next to the steps. It just seemed wrong for a statue to be holding a gun and a flyswatter, so I took the latter. If I had my druthers, I would have taken the gun instead, broken it in two, and trashed it, but it was part of the sculpture. The flyswatter wasn't.

It was hot as hell and my steaming cup of thick, golden-brown espresso was doing nothing to cool me off. I just wasn't into the iced coffee thing. It seemed wrong. Coffee was meant to be drunk hot, even if it brought on heat stroke.

I used the flyswatter to fan myself, which made absolutely no sense at all but somehow created the illusion of moving air. When I was done with my coffee I put the empty cup down in front of me, and immediately a lady in a black leather jacket and six-inch pumps dropped a couple of quarters in. I gave one to the homeless man and he smiled a toothless smile.

I sat and I fanned and I watched as the people walked by. All kinds of people. College kids with clogs, giggling girls with ponytails, men with coats and ties and briefcases, moms with strollers, and dads with babies on their backs. Big people, little people, fat, thin, tall, short—a who's who of ethnicities and ages. Parading by my steps, one after another, an endless stream of humanity for me to gawk at.

Every person was different. Every person was unique. But every person had one thing in common. One tie that bound them all.

They were all staring at their cell phones.

It was hot outside but it was beautiful. The clouds were billowy white cotton balls forming all sorts of baby animal shapes, from porcupines to whales (not a one looked like a phone). The downtown merchants had painstakingly watered their window boxes throughout the July drought, and the zinnias and cosmos and calendulas were alive with color. Storefronts with cutesy creative displays were beckoning shoppers to please please *please* come in and take a peek.

But damn if there wasn't a single, crucial flaw: you had to look up to notice all of this. And other than the babies, the homeless man, and me, no one was looking up.

Folks continued to walk on by. Automatons. Hooked to the machine. Tethered to their phones. Absent of free will. Unknowing. Uncaring. The walking dead.

"Look at them," I said to the homeless man. "It's kind of scary, isn't it? It's as though the world outside their phone has ceased to exist. Nothing else matters. There could be an earthquake right now and they're so clueless they'd walk right into the crack, still texting away."

"Whose fault would that be?" the man asked.

I laughed.

Another couple, without even looking up (God forbid they'd establish eye contact with us phone-less down-and-outers), dropped more change into my coffee cup. Once again I gave half to my new bestie.

"You and me, bro," I told him. "You and me."

A car horn honked as a pedestrian jaywalked his way through a busy intersection, eyes downcast, phone in hand. I was surprised the driver had even noticed. I could see her, inches from an accident, still texting away.

"Where's yours?" the man asked.

"My what?"

"Your phone?"

"It's a long story," I said to him.

"I got time," he said, stretching out his long legs and arching his back. "That's the one thing I'm not short on."

There are listeners and then there are *listeners*. There are people like Sheila who are good listeners but feel compelled to interrupt you every fifteen seconds to ask clarifying questions or to put their own two cents in and, before you know it, the rambling train of thought has run off the track and you don't have a clue as to where you were or where you were going or even what was the point of your own story. I'm not being critical of Sheila. Like I said, she was a good listener. But the homeless man? He was a *great* listener.

As my life story unfolded, at all the right moments he'd nod his head or grunt or even shout out "Really!" or "No!" At one of the breakup scenes with Derek, he stood up, grabbed the flyswatter out of my hand, and whacked the Civil War soldier on the bum.

By the time I had finished, my coffee cup was almost half full with spare change. With the walking dead's eyes glued to their phones it was surprising we had been noticed at all. I counted out half, close to five bucks, and gave it to the man. We sat in silence for a few minutes.

"How old are you?" he finally asked.

"Seventeen," I answered, avoiding his eyes.

"Seventeen going on seventy," he replied.

"Oh my God! Please don't say that! Is it really that bad?"

"No, no, no. Don't get me wrong, honey. I meant that as a compliment. Most seventeen-year-olds have shit for brains. And not good shit, either. You, on the other hand, are wise beyond your years."

In a past life, if a homeless man had stolen my flyswatter and called me "honey," I would have been so creeped out that I couldn't have run away fast enough. But that was then and this was now.

"Thanks," I said, lightly touching his arm.

"Thank you. For the story and the spare change. You've made my day."

We sat silently for a while longer. Two kids my age walked by laughing and snuggling, arms draped around each other, phones nowhere to be seen, breaking the mold, giving me hope.

"Can I give you one bit of advice?" my homeless confidante asked. "More like food for thought. Something to chew on."

"Please," I said. "I'm famished."

"Derek. He sounds like a pretty nice guy."

"He is," I agreed.

"I'm not so sure I'd let that one slip away. Guys are . . . guys. And that's not always a good thing. Take it from one who knows. But from everything you've told me about Derek, he seems to be one of the good ones."

"I know," I said. "But I'm not here to get into a relationship."

The homeless man arched his eyebrows.

"Why?" he asked. "What else really matters other than relationships?"

I was silent.

"I'm just saying. Think about it. That's all."

"Thanks," I said.

"For the rest of your life, anytime you want to sit with me on the steps of Memorial Hall, panhandle, and swat flies that aren't there, you are more than welcome." He smiled a big toothless smile at me.

"Right back at you," I told him.

"Can I keep your flyswatter?" he asked.

"I'd be honored."

We shook hands. I crossed at the crosswalk, turned around to see him carefully placing the flyswatter back in the arms of the Civil War soldier, and wondered what he was going to do with the rest of *his* life.

Chapter 50

The honeybees were out in full force, buzzing their little wings off. I was down by the hives, mesmerized by the nonstop incoming and outgoing. It was late afternoon, as hot and dry as it comes, prime time for wondering.

And so much to wonder about. Would Derek continue to burrow inside my brain, munching away on the refried remnants of my remaining gray matter, and never leave me in peace? Would Sheila and Jonathan actually follow through on the whole Thoreau cabin thing? Would the imminent eruption of the Mount Vesuvius–sized zit on my forehead leave me scarred for life? Was a second pot of coffee a good idea when my left leg just wouldn't stop shaking?

"Sweetheart." It was Gramps, coming down to sit with me. He had a fresh pot of coffee, a high-end Sumatra Mandheling blend that was one of my faves, and two mugs in his garden basket.

"Excellent," I said, pouring myself yet another cup and sighing a long, drawn-out, painfully angsty sigh. "More caffeine. Just the cure for the old monkey brain. Exactly what the doctor ordered for the mind-race loop-de-loops."

"I'm telling you," Gramps said, lighting his joint. "You really should get stoned once in a while. Takes the edge off. It can really help with anxiety issues. It's a proven medical fact."

"Gramps. I'm seventeen years old. No offense, but I'm not convinced that 'just get high' is really the best advice a grandfather should be giving his teenage granddaughter."

"*Ahhhh. . .*" Gramps exhaled deeply. "Probably not. But then again, I'm not exactly an ordinary grandfather now, am I?"

"Probably not," I answered.

I took a big gulp of coffee, scalding the back of my throat, and sighed again.

"Is that a Derek sigh?" Gramps asked. "Or just your generic, fucked-up teen, what-the-hell-am-I-going-to-do-with-the-rest-of-my-life sigh?"

"Both."

"Don't worry." Gramps lay his hand gently on my arm. "The older you get, the more confusing it all becomes."

"Wow. Thanks. So reassuring."

"Only less hormonally driven. Which, I imagine, probably helps."

"Good to know." I sighed yet again.

We were silent for a while, watching the bees. Chaotic as the entrance to the hive was, they still seemed so focused. So sure of themselves.

Finally I spoke. "You know, I've been thinking."

"Here we go again," Gramps said. "How many times have I told you that thinking can be dangerous?"

"But I'm finding it so hard not to these days."

"The curse of being an intelligent young woman."

"I'm back on the whole to bee-or-not-to-bee thing."

"That'll keep you going for a while. Still fantasizing about being queen for the day?"

"I don't know. I'm getting cold feet. The pressure. The responsibility. Laying egg after egg, hour after hour, day after day? It just seems way too stressful. I mean, don't get me wrong, watching a guy plummet to his death after incredibly hot sex would be sweet, but, other than that, I'm not sure I'm cut out for the whole royalty gig."

"Don't tell me you want to be a drone?"

"Stop! I wouldn't know what to do with a penis, and the thought of it exploding, even at the height of orgasm, does not sound overly attractive."

"I'm with you there. As old as I am, I still treasure the withered little thing." Gramps poured himself another cup of coffee. "So what are you going to do? Give up on bees totally? Become a worm? A dragonfly? A lightning bug?"

"No way. I'm sticking with my girls, hanging with my homebees. But what about a worker bee? Just look at them. They're awesome. One: you get to fly around all day, which would be totally cool. I'd gladly change my legs for wings any day, particularly since I haven't shaved them in weeks."

"You *are* looking a little furry in the appendage department," Gramps said.

"Thanks. Two: you get to drink flower juice. . . ."

"Nectar."

"Whatever. All day long. Flying from flower to flower, lapping up that sugary treat. And then at the end of the day making honey out of it? How sweet is that?"

"And think how many more flowers there'll be when Jonathan and Sheila start growing their own."

I let that comment just slide on by.

"You know honey is bee puke, right?" Gramps asked.

"Quiet, you! I'm on a roll here. Don't gross me out. Three: you've got a job to do and you just do it. No endless angsting over this stupid thing or that. You know your task and off you go."

"*Ahhh*," Gramps sighed. "The absence of free will. A cog in a living machine. On many levels, so appealing."

"You got that right. No more waking up in the morning and thinking to yourself, *Hmmm, what should I be doing today?*"

"Exactly. I hate to burst your bubble here, but have you considered the downside to this whole thing? What about that technology you love so much? Texting while flying? I don't think so. Pollinating while online? Definite honeybee no-nos. It's just you and the flowers, sweetheart. And no *Passion* to help you hook up. How would that sit with you?"

"That's the million-dollar question, Gramps. That's what I'm trying to figure out."

"On the plus side, think of the service you're providing to plants. When they're pollinating, bees are like sex workers, only with flowers as their clients. It's like interspecies prostitution, and it's totally legal."

"Wow! That just makes me want to be a worker bee even more!" I said, sarcasm dripping from my words like honey. "But you know what the absolute best part would be? The thing I envy most about the workers?"

"Tell me," he asked, taking another sip from his steaming coffee.

"No more worry about relationships. I mean, you have the mother queen to worship and your sister workers to hang with, and the lazy, good-for-nothing drones to bitch about, but no serious one-on-ones. No dating. And unlike the queen, no sex. Which means no drama. For the working girls, it's pretty much wake up and slurp the flowers. All day every day. Think how much easier life would be?" I reached down and yanked out one particularly long strand of hair twirling its way out of my calf.

"Hmm . . . ," Gramps said. "I have an idea that just might help. You know that upstairs hall closet that you cleaned out the other day? The one with all of the camping gear we haven't used in decades?"

"What does that have to do with anything?" I asked.

"Now that it's clean as a whistle, why don't you just move on in? It's dark, just like the inside of a beehive. You can come out every day, flit around the flowers in the garden, do a little bit of weeding and bug killing, and then head back into your closet. No interacting with anyone. None of those relationships you find so distracting. Like you said, think how much easier life would be."

"That's probably the best idea you've ever had. Leave three meals a day and unlimited coffee outside the door and I'd be good to go."

"Something tells me you wouldn't."

"I just get so . . . I don't know. Tired. It's like I don't know what to do about anything anymore. It's all one confusing mess."

"One glorious, confusing mess. You've got to step back and do the bee thing, honey. Not just smell the flowers, but drink the nectar. Look at yourself. You're young. You're healthy. You're strong. You've got beautiful furry legs. You're smart as hell. You've got just about everything going for you. The mayhem, confusion, self-doubt, and angst are all part of the glorious package, messy as it may be. You have to embrace it. You have to take joy in the struggle."

"I'd call my mayhem more than a little bit messy."

"A first-world problem if there ever was one."

"I know, I know." I got a little teary-eyed. "I'm not fleeing from Syria and trapped in some hellhole of a refugee camp on the Turkish border. I'm a spoiled little bitch. I've got nothing to complain about. I'll shut up."

"That's not what I'm saying, sweetheart." Gramps scooted his chair closer to mine and put his arm around my shoulders. "You're seventeen. You have plenty to complain about, and every right to do so. I know you're having a difficult time making sense of it all. That's what being a teenager is all about. That's your job."

"Well, I want to quit."

"No you don't. And there's no way I'd let you even if you did. You've got to look at the bigger picture. Take a broader perspective. This is what a rich and full life gives you: the good, the bad, and the ugly. Think about how much sweeter the honey tastes after you've eaten shit."

"So the moral of the story is . . ."

"That there is no moral. You're like the bee. You gotta do what you gotta do, you just have a lot more choices."

"Hence the confusion and excruciating angst."

"Exactly."

I bent over and yanked out another leg hair.

"I wish I could do that to all of my faults." I leaned my head against his shoulder. "Just reach over and pluck them out."

"Faults?" Gramps arched his eyebrows. "My granddaughter has faults?"

Chapter 51

"Hi. My name is Meagan . . ." There followed an extremely long and awkward pause. In a summer of so many pauses, this one was by far the most excruciating. If there were a world's record for awkward moments in a single season, I'm totally convinced I would have shattered it at that moment. Then the record would be mine in perpetuity.

All eyes were on me. I was naked and exposed. I cleared my throat, took a deep breath and somehow managed to continue. "My name is Meagan and I'm a netaholic."

"Welcome Meagan," the group responded in unison.

There is terrified and then there's *terrified*. I was *TERRIFIED!*

Once more, there I was: down in the dank and dreary basement of the Unitarian church on Main Street on a muggy Wednesday evening with a bunch of fucked-up netaholics. But this time it was different.

This time the freak of the week was . . . wait for it . . . me!

What had possibly possessed me to do something as crazy as this? I had been snarking at the NA group for weeks, dismissing most of what went on as beyond bullshit. So what if Jonathan had asked me in that sweet way of his to get up and tell my story? Who cared if my grandfathers had suggested it would be a "positive" (*gag!*) learning experience?

Why had I said yes?

Following the Karen the Cat Killer "intervention" debacle, I had replayed the dumpster fire of a disaster with Derek a million times in my head. Over and over ad nauseam. I had dissected and overanalyzed every single word of that conversation until my head was ready to split wide open and spew brains all over the zucchini. I had even written down some of the highlights (or were they lowlights?) so I wouldn't forget. My salty teardrops staining the paper.

What Derek had said that brain-stuck me the most was when he told me he didn't think I was a netaholic at all. *I just think you're scared of boys,* he had said. *Scared of me. And you're using the whole addict thing to somehow justify it.*

Wow! What was a girl to do with a line like that?

How about not sleep at all for the last three nights. Toss. Turn. Think. Repeat. Over and over. Think so much that my ears were clogged, not with wax but with brain goo oozing out.

At four o'clock this morning I'd bolted upright in my bed, with a pounding in my chest.

Derek was right. I *was* scared of boys! *Terrified* being a much more apt description.

But oh my God! The real shocker, the cold hard truth that smacked me upside the head much harder than any hoe ever could, was that Derek was also wrong. Way wrong.

I *was* an addict. A deeply fucked-up addict. An addict by choice. An addict to avoid *real* boys. To avoid *real* relationships. To avoid *real* Dereks.

I really did have a story to tell. As hard as it was, I needed to set the record straight, stand up in front of the group, and spew my brains all over them. And if I didn't do it now, then, who knows, maybe I never would.

And that was an even scarier thought than all of the others combined.

So there I was. Front and Center. The eyes of the world on me. Maybe not *the* world, but *my* world.

Hi, I had told them, registering a 9.8 on the Richter Scale of Terrified. *My name is Meagan.* Followed by the real kicker:

"And I'm a netaholic."

Four more terrifying words had never been spoken.

I nervously twirled the split ends of my hair with my beetle-stained fingers and began.

"When I was a little girl, I had this fuzzy, purply-pink penguin, a stuffed animal that I carried around with me everywhere. I loved that stuffie. I remember once I was at the county fair and I got the end of it caught in the roller coaster car door just as I was getting out. It was horrible. The coaster starting moving again, rolling down the track, but there was absolutely no way I was going to let go of Mister Penguin. I was ready and willing to get dragged to my death still holding onto his floppy wings. Fortunately, someone hit the emergency stop button, and here I am, still alive to tell you about it.

"Anyway, whenever my parents started fighting, which they did all the fucking time, I'd run to my room and hide under my blankets in my bed and hug that penguin half to death. I know it sounds trite and cliché-y: little girl shaking under her covers, thumb in her mouth, clinging tightly to her stuffie. But that was me. Holding onto that penguin made me feel much more secure. Much more safe.

"When my parents stopped screaming at each other, when the dust had settled and the coast was clear, at least for the time being, I'd crawl out, still holding onto Mister P. I honestly don't know how I would have survived growing up without that penguin.

"I still have him under my bed at home. He's tattered and he's torn and he's beat to shit, but he's still pretty and purply-pink. And I still love him.

"Why am I even telling you this? You must think I'm a lunatic!"

I took a deep breath. I wished that I had that penguin in my arms right then and there to hug and squeeze and give me the courage to continue. Except for a few squeaking chairs and suppressed coughs, it was totally quiet. I kept my eyes focused on the wall in front of me.

"When I hit puberty, I traded in Mister Penguin for my cell phone. In a messed-up way, it served the same purpose. I mean, I could hide out on the internet whenever I wanted, and come out whenever I chose. It was like being under the covers with Mister Penguin. Safe. Secure. What could possibly be wrong with that?

"The older I got, the easier it was just to hide. I looked at my parents. I looked at the girls at school. I saw how screwed-up their offline relationships were, so I figured why should I even try? As long as I stayed in my online cocoon, then I wouldn't get hurt the way other people did. It made perfect sense, right? So I didn't go out. I didn't date. I was interested in guys—I mean, I *am* interested in guys. Super-interested."

I couldn't help but notice Derek looking up and staring at me with those big brown eyes of his.

"I just didn't do them offline," I continued, not knowing whether to make eye contact or not. "My one disastrous attempt at a real-life hookup totally crashed and burned and just reinforced my decision that those kind of relationships were just not for me.

"And then this happens. I come all the way over here to Western Massachusetts to help out my grandfathers and all hell breaks loose. Once more, I'm back at the county fair and Mister Penguin is caught in the door of the roller coaster and the damn thing is starting to move and I'm being dragged along, only this time there's no one to press the emergency stop button except for me, and Mister Penguin's wings are wrapped so tightly around me that I can barely breathe and my arms are pinned to my sides and I can't reach the button and . . ." I took a long, dramatic pause and let loose a classic angsty sigh. "You get the picture."

Where was I going with all of this? I didn't have a clue.

"So here's the deal: the world is full of real-life roller coasters. I mean, they're all over the place. Why risk possibly getting dragged away on one?

"But here's what's so totally crazy about the whole thing: there's something really appealing about a roller coaster. I mean, they're still scary as hell, right? But they're also totally awesome. The twists, the turns, the ups—even the downs—they're exhilarating! I'm not always a fan of feeling like I'm on the verge of hurling but . . . without the lows the highs aren't nearly as intense.

"Does anyone see where I'm headed here? Anyone? Because I sure as hell don't."

Now I looked at Derek, hoping for some sort of sign of support from him. Some spark of empathy. Some twinkle in his eye. But his head was bowed and his eyes half closed. Was he even listening? Did he even care?

The me-of-the-past could barely recognize the me-of-the-present up there jabbering away. The me-of-the-past would have died a thousand times rather than make this long-winded, meandering, oh-so-awkward self-disclosure. I no longer felt like I was thirteen years old. Now I felt seventeen going on seventy, having aged a half a decade in a few short weeks.

Somehow I managed to continue. "Again, at the risk of sounding trite and cliché-y, isn't real life just like that roller coaster? Ups and downs and twists and turns. And the internet? When you're on it, when you're totally into it, it's like a roller coaster ride, too. It really is. Don't tell me that those of you who are off don't for a minute miss the thrill of the ride.

"Don't get me wrong: I know there's a lot that's really fucked-up about being online, particularly as much as I've been. I know I can't continue to hide out there forever. But still, to be totally honest, there's so much about being online that I love. I know that's not what I'm supposed to be up here saying, but damn if it isn't the truth. I'm a screenager. I admit it. I can't imagine ever wanting to give up riding that roller coaster.

"But there's a catch, and it's a big one: I want to *be on* the net but not *caught in* the net. Surf the web but not get sucked into its stinky cesspool. I want to be able to get off whenever I want. And then get right back on it whenever I want. Does that make any sense at all? Does it? I want that emergency stop button right in my hot little hand at all times so I can use it whenever I need to. I want to be the one in control.

"And, drum roll please, ready for the epiphany?" I made a *ba-dum ba-dum ba-dum ba-dum tshhhhh* sound. "If I've learned anything this summer, anything at all, it's that there really are ways to get what you want *off*line. I don't need the internet for everything. I'm beginning to think that maybe, just maybe, I can hop off that online roller coaster, without being pushed or dragged away, and then hop right on to an offline one. And have just as awesome a ride. Who knows? Maybe even better. I don't always need the net to catch what I'm really looking for."

While I said this I was *really* looking at Derek. *So* wanting him to know how much of this whole tortuous soliloquy had to do with him. But his head was still bowed and his eyes still barely open.

But then, just for the briefest of moments, he looked up. There it was! Just the tiniest hint of one: a smile on that boy's face.

For the first time since I had started speaking I felt like I could actually breathe.

"Maybe I'm asking way too much here, but this is what I want. I want to have my cake and eat it, too. Ride both roller coasters. Online and off. Is that even possible? Can you even do that and survive? I don't know. I don't have a clue. But damn if I'm not going to give it a try.

"Anyway, thanks. Really and truly. Thanks for listening."

If my life were a movie, then this would be the scene when one person would start softly clapping, and then another one would join in, and then suddenly the whole place would be standing and stomping their feet and screaming and yelling "huzzah" and "hooray" and "brilliant" and then the credits would roll and . . .

Most people clapped. Including Derek and Jonathan. But no shouting out huzzahs and hoorays. No mobbing me with hugs and handshakes. Just polite, albeit confused, applause.

Jonathan gave me a nod and then stood up and introduced another girl, cute as could be, with Rapunzel hair. Her name was Clara. Earlier in the summer she had shattered her personal record by spending twenty-three consecutive days without ever coming up out of her basement, logging in a total of 8,413 random YouTube videos. She actually kept count.

Like it or not, that is one pretty damn impressive roller coaster ride.

Chapter 52

For the five zillionth time that summer, I was kneeling in the garden doing the usual—picking, weeding, and killing—when lo and behold, the Big Three drove up: Sheila, Jonathan, and Derek. In the flesh. Jonathan was driving a truck with a shit-ton of lumber in the back sticking out every which way. Thoreau's cabin in kit form. Just waiting to be put together.

So it wasn't just Sheila and Jonathan raising the roof. Derek was going to be part of the insanity as well.

The three of them stood by the garden fence.

To my great credit, I did not dive into the zucchini or run away and hide.

"Hey," I said softly.

"Hey," Derek said, even softer, looking down at the ground and kicking up dirt with the heel of his shoe.

"Hey," Sheila and Jonathan said. Jonathan gave me a smile but Sheila barely looked at me.

In a summer of so many awkward *heys*, this one was certainly a doozie. I'd not only set the record for awkward pauses, but for awkward *heys* as well.

I had made amends with the oldsters, Udder and Gramps. But with my own peeps? I was still wallowing in self-pity, too busy feeling sorry for myself to reach out to anyone.

I had briefly talked to Sheila, but just long enough to recount Gramps's manic antics at Mom's birthday party. Speaking terms or not, I *had* to tell her about that. But this time, when she had come in from Boston for the weekend, she had gone straight to Jonathan's house without even stopping by to say hello to me.

I missed her. I really did.

And Derek? I missed him too.

Missed was way too weak a word for it. The last few days had been agony. For the first time ever, I truly understood why every decent song out there was about heartbreak and unrequited love and good relationships gone bad. In the past, I had thought those songs were all just sort of schmaltzy and overwrought, silly and melodramatic. Now every word rang true.

Having bared my soul to the NA'ers, I had (duh!) fled the last meeting as quickly as possible. This just after I had told everyone how I was going to ride both roller coasters, online and off. But, once again, the offline one had proven way too hard to hop on to.

The last time Sheila and I had been *shinrin-yokuing* our way through the woods, it had been images of my phone out there in the clouds, in the bark, in the mushrooms, in the trees. But now, after it was probably way too late, it was Derek's face out there instead. On the beehives. In the zucchini. On the smiling face of the Buddha. Here, there, and everywhere.

And now, here they were, here *he* was, standing right in front of me again.

"Thoreau's cabin, huh?" I gestured to the back of the truck.

"The beginning," Jonathan said. "We've got a long way to go."

"Well, good luck with that." I did a half sneer, half grunt. "You'll need it."

What a beyotch I am, I thought to myself. *No wonder no one wants me around. No wonder I have no friends. No wonder everyone hates me.*

I spent the remainder of the morning endlessly analyzing the nuances of Derek's *hey*. Had he *heyed* in a snarky way? In an I-never-want-to-talk-to-your-stupid-ass-face-again way? Or in a please-please-PLEASE-can't-we-just-go-back-to-being-whatever-the-hell-that-it-was-that-we-were way?

There is a rather condescending saying: girls spend way more time thinking about what boys think than boys actually spend thinking.

Which, now that I think about it, is probably true.

"Hey."

The voice in my head sounded so real. It was as if Derek were actually here! As if he were standing right in front of me. As if he were . . .

"Hey," he said again. Oh my God! He *was* here! Leaning against the garden gate, *heying* at me again. Who knows how long he had been watching me viciously grinding bean beetles between my fingers, gritting my teeth, and cursing my fate out loud.

"You're back," I said, wiping the sweat out of my eyes and getting beetle juice (or was it stardust?) into them.

"Yeah, you know, taking a break. *Health requires this relaxation, this aimless life. This life in the present.*"

"Come again?"

"Thoreau," he said. "An early advocator of the chill pill."

I took a deep breath. Here we were, once more out in the garden, speaking again!

Udder had given me a long lecture about self-love and self-forgiveness and finding satisfaction with self in the absence of others, but boy oh boy, once that boy began talking to me, I felt *my* self grow happier than I had been all week.

"And how's that one going down with Sheila?" I asked Derek. "I wasn't aware that *chill* was part of her vocabulary."

"Tell me about it," Derek said. "I'm exhausted just watching her work."

I had to agree. I had spent a good portion of the morning hiding behind a tree in the orchard spying on the three of them as they did their thing, and Sheila, surprise surprise, had been quite the live wire. It was like watching the Keystone Carpenters, or Laurel and Hardy with an even more inept sidekick. At one point Derek hauled a two-by-four out of the truck, accidently whacked Sheila on the side of the head with it, and then a minute or two later Sheila picked up the very same two-by-four, whacked Derek on the side of his head, and hauled it right back into the truck. There's nothing quite like earnest ineptitude!

Gnawing at the throbbing red-turning-blue of blood under his thumbnail, clearly the result of too many missed hammer blows, Derek looked worried. "Something tells me we may have bitten off a little more than we can chew," he continued.

Still kneeling, I fanned myself with a zucchini leaf. The rush of excitement from actually seeing Derek's lips move was making me sweat.

"Just the three of us building a cabin?" he continued. "What were we thinking? I don't have a clue as to what's going on, and Sheila, well, she's just . . ."

"Sheila," I said, laughing out loud. Watching Sheila swing a hammer had been pretty damn funny. I had had to put my fist in my mouth to stop from laughing out loud and revealing my hiding place.

"Exactly. And Jonathan has this vague idea of what to do, but, to be honest . . . it's all a bit confusing. No one quite knows which end is up."

"Where'd you get the building plans?" I asked.

Derek scratched his head and looked down at the ground again. Sawdust was caught in his curly hair, and each time he scratched, flecks drifted to the ground.

"No!" I said, giggling like a girl. (Wait a minute: I *was* a girl!) "You didn't! You naughty, naughty boy. Getting directions *online* for how to build Thoreau's cabin! That just seems so . . ."

"Wrong?"

"I was going to say 'fucked-up.' But fucked-up in a totally understandable way."

"Yeah. Right." He rolled his eyes. "Anyway, I gotta get back to work on the cabin. Wish me luck. The plans sure looked a heck of a lot easier online than they do in real life."

"Tell me about it," I said, doing my best to hold his eyes with mine. "Isn't that the case with everything?"

Oh my God! I was back on the roller coaster.

Chapter 53

It was early evening. The boys were still down by the orchard cleaning up after their day of cabin building, but Sheila had come up to the house to sit with me on the porch. She was bubbling over with enthusiasm and, best yet, total forgiveness for my snarkiness and the harsh words of the past week.

First it was Derek talking to me. Now it was Sheila!

Huzzah and hooray!

Maybe, just maybe, there was hope. Maybe I wasn't such a beyotch after all.

"Do you have any idea how much I love you?" Sheila asked.

"Not nearly as much as I love you," I told her.

"Wrong," she said, scooting over and knocking the wind out of me with a monstrous hug. "Double-triple-quadruple wrong. Without you, none of this would have ever happened. None of it. Without you we'd still be stuck in our online yuck, oblivious to how awesome all of this is." She made a broad sweeping gesture with her arms taking in the garden, the orchard, and the distant trees. "Nature. The cabin. Jonathan. Derek."

"Hmmm . . . ," I muttered. "Derek. What to do about Derek."

"Do you have any idea how much Derek likes you?" Sheila asked.

"Not nearly as much as I like him," I said.

Sheila gave me a punch on my arm. "Wrong, wrong, and wrong again. That boy is crazy about you, Meagan. Crushingly crazy. I swear to God, if you don't make it right with him then it'll be the biggest wrong of your life. Trust me on this one."

We watched as Jonathan and Derek came strolling up the hill, tools in hand, yucking it up.

"Look at them," Sheila said, grinning. "Have you ever seen two bigger hotties in your life? I mean, seriously, how lucky are we? Who would have thought?"

"Who would have thought," I repeated.

"Cool chairs," Derek said. Sheila and Jonathan had left for the evening to go back to Jonathan's. It was actually a relief to see them go. Sheila had hugged me so many times my boobs ached.

Sheila and me. Besties forever. What could be better than that?

Well, to be honest, I could think of something that would be just as good.

Derek and I were sitting on the front porch of the house, drinking coffee and doing our best to rock away the awkwardness of our convoluted relationship.

"Sweet, isn't it?" I said. "We just got them yesterday. They're bona fide Shaker chairs."

"Shaker chairs? I thought those were the massage recliners you try out at the mall. This one is pretty simple."

"Yeah. A real Luddite special. Techno-free. You wanna shake, you gotta do the work."

"Rock on," Derek said, rocking away.

"You know who the Shakers were, right?" I asked him.

"Umm . . . some girl group from the 1980s?"

"Close," I told him. "They were this charismatic pacifist religious sect from the 1800s. Super successful for a while. They all lived together on these communal farms selling seeds and growing medicinal herbs and building furniture and stuff."

So as not to be outdone by Sheila and Jonathan's Quaker road trip, Udder and Gramps and I had traveled the day before to Hancock Shaker Village, a beautifully restored historic village about an hour west of us. It was the former site of one of the largest Shaker communities in the country. That was where we had bought the chairs.

"Why were they called 'Shakers'?" Derek asked.

"Evidently, God would speak to them through music. They'd go into this religious ecstasy and all line up, men on one side and women on the other, and before you knew it they were twisting and jerking and shouting and shaking. The Shaking Quakers."

"So I was right," Derek said, doing a little twist-and-jerk move of his own on the rocking chair seat. "A group from the '80s. The 1880s. Whatever happened to them?"

"Well, as is often the case, there was a fatal flaw."

"Ahhh!" Derek slapped the side of his head. "Damn those fatal flaws. What was theirs?"

"Abstinence."

"Abstinence? From technology? Were they Luddites, too? No innovations in seeds or furniture design, and the whole thing went bust?"

"No. *Abstinence* abstinence. As in: no sex."

How strange was this? Here I was with Derek again, once more talking about sex. I pinched myself to make sure I wasn't dreaming.

"What?" Derek exclaimed. "No sex?"

"Shakers weren't allowed to have sex. *Prohibido.* Everyone had to renounce all 'lustful gratifications' . . . Take up a full cross against all the doleful works of the flesh.' Even married couples."

"No sex?" Derek repeated, his eyebrows raised.

"You heard me," I said. "And no sex meant . . ."

"No fun?"

I shook my head and gave him the look. "More like no babies. And no babies meant no new little Shakers coming down the line. They went all in on adopting kids, but the state got all weird and put the kibosh on that. It wasn't long before the whole sect began to die out. No little Shakers to replace the old folks meant the numbers just didn't add up."

"Wow." Derek shook his head. "You'd have figured someone would have seen that one coming. Anyway, who would have joined a religion like that?"

"I don't know." I scrunched up my nose. "The way I used to feel about boys, I probably would have."

"The way you *used* to feel?"

I gave him a shy smile.

Derek rocked in his chair even faster.

"Today," I continued, "the whole time you guys were down there doing the Thoreau thing, I was up here by myself, feeling sad and lonely and totally left out, with nothing to do but garden and obsess about sex and the Shakers." I left out the part about secretly spying on them.

Derek scooted his chair closer to mine.

"Obsess," I repeated. "Not fantasize." I pushed his chair back to where it had been. "Think about it: no sex meant no babies, right? And no babies meant no new Shakers. It was abstinence that led to their downfall."

"There's a moral for you," Derek said, grinning away.

I ignored him.

"But here's my epiphany."

"Oh my. Another one? That's two in less than a week."

"Aha! So you *were* listening to my NA confessional. Think about it: sex is to Shakers as the net is to . . ."

"Oh my God. I hate these word association things. Umm . . . softball?"

"No, you idiot!" I picked up a zucchini and made as if to throw it at him. He covered up his crotch and I laughed. "Netaholics Anonymous. No texting, no tweeting, no Facebook, no social media—no way to get new converts means the end of NA. Just like the Shakers, abstinence will lead to their downfall."

Derek looked confused. "I'm not sure I'm following you," he said.

"Listen: Netaholics Anonymous wants to recruit new folks, right? Spread the good word about the evils of technology and the joys of life offline. Blah blah blah. How do they do it? Huh? How?"

"I don't know. You'd have to ask Jonathan. He puts up flyers, like at The Roost and all. There's word of mouth. People tell their friends."

"Flyers? You gotta be kidding me? That's like twentieth-century stuff. No one reads flyers. No one reads anything but texts, tweets, or Facebook posts. And friends? The only friends most people have these days are fantasy friends on Facebook. No one has time for *real* friends. They're way too busy texting."

"I'm sorry. Were you just talking to me?" Derek was looking down, thumbs twitching, pretending to text.

"Ha ha!" I fake-laughed. "Very funny. You want to build a replica of Thoreau's cabin, right? I mean, no offense, but . . . seriously? Do you actually think Jonathan and Sheila really have their shit together to pull this off?"

"What about me?" Derek asked. Sawdust was still hanging off his hair and his eyebrows, and now a few flecks had somehow cascaded their way down his face and were stuck on his chin.

I looked at him and laughed for real.

"It was a little on the challenging side," he admitted. "I gotta tell you—I've never used a handsaw before, and I swear I came *this* close to slicing my arm off. Thank God for band-aids. We went through a whole box of them. I'm amazed I still have ten fingers left." He held out his hands and wiggled his fingers at me. The few that weren't bandaged were covered with cuts and scrapes.

"Oh my God," I said, cupping my hands over his and gasping. "You counted wrong. There are only seven left! How are you ever going to play softball again?"

Derek laughed. "Thank goodness we did it the Luddite way. Can you imagine me with a power saw?"

"You? Think about Sheila!"

"She's terrifying enough without one," Derek said, wincing. "She must have hit me with a two-by-four at least a dozen times."

"What? I am so jealous! That's my job!"

Derek grinned. "Seriously. Look at the back of my head."

I brushed aside another layer of sawdust, parted his hair, and found an ugly, purplish bump of a bruise. Nasty as it was, I needed all my self-control not to lean in and kiss it, just like Udder and Gramps had done to my boo-boo following the ghost/raccoon fiasco.

"You poor boy," I sighed. Not a fake sigh but a real sigh. Even with all of the possibilities of bodily bumps and bruises, I was still envious at having left myself out of creating such a glorious ramshackle mess.

"And you know the worst of it?" Derek asked.

"You mean there's more?"

"I sat on a nail. Jonathan had to use a pair of pliers to pull it out. Seriously. I can show you the hole in the back of my pants if you want."

"Thanks. I think I'll pass on that one. But wait a minute—does that make you more of an ass or less of one?"

"Very cute," Derek said, his eyes twinkling. "Thank God I'm up to date on my tetanus shots. Otherwise I'd be in Shitsville. But it did get me thinking: if only we could find someone to help us out who actually knew which end was up."

"That," I said, wagging my finger at him, "is exactly my point. Think how much easier it would be to have more than just the three of you doing the cabin raising, or whatever the heck you call it. Wouldn't it make much more sense to share the cabin fever? Spread the love? Luddites would go totally ga-ga over this whole project. Even if no one is actually going to live there."

"No one could possibly live there. That place is hazardous enough just to look at. The first breath of wind and goodbye cabin."

"But still, with a little bit of work, this Thoreau extravaganza tribute memorial thingie could become an anti-technology rallying spot. A sweet symbolic focal point for Luddite activism. A sacred place for netaholics in recovery. Sort of like when Sheila and Jonathan went down to Amish country. Only dialed down a notch. And not nearly as far a drive."

"I thought you thought the whole Thoreau cabin thing was ridiculous?" Derek asked.

"Ridiculous or not, let's face it," I said, the excitement rising in me. "You need help from fellow brothers and sisters desperate to flee their lives of quiet desperation and start hammering nails. But how are you going to get the word out? How are you going to get people involved? The only way to reach true netaholics is on the net, right? If you're gonna save the fallen from the devil, then you gotta go to hell to do it. No other choice."

"Hell?"

"Hell yeah! But here's the problem: netaholics in recovery aren't supposed to be using the net, right? Not that any of you ever stick to it. But still, it's like a catch-22. Just what we were talking about. If there's no net, then there's no way for netaholics to know about the no-net."

"No way."

"Yes way. Without the internet to point the way to freedom, the lost will not be found and the whole house of cards collapses. Just like the Shakers."

"And probably just like the cabin." Derek was rocking away, practically shaking in his chair. I could tell he was trying to wrap his brain around where I was going with this.

"So, let me get this straight," he said. "Are you telling me the Shakers should have never stopped doing the you-know-what? And that NA members should, too?"

"Not abstain from sex, silly! Let's be reasonable here. But not all NA'ers should abstain from the internet either."

"Wait just a minute here. What about the Netaholics Anonymous steps one and two? That the net has made our lives unmanageable? That only laying off the net entirely will restore us to sanity?"

"Fat chance of that happening. I hate to burst your bubble, bro, but nothing will ever restore you to sanity. So let me break it down for you: if you want new NA members, you'll have no choice but to use the net to bring them in. Otherwise, complete collapse. Goodbye cabin. Goodbye group. Goodbye potluck. Who knows, it could even be goodbye softball team."

Derek stopped rocking and stood up. "Good God!" he exclaimed. "No more softball team?"

"But hold on," I told him. I got out of my chair and began pacing up and down the porch. I put my hands over my ears to stop the rush of ideas flooding through my head from escaping. I took another gulp of coffee from my thermos, a final sizzling jolt of caffeine to propel me to the finish line.

"You ready for the grand finale? You ready for the cure-all-end-all-be-all solution that will solve all of the problems of the netaholic no-no universe in one incredibly brilliant stroke that will rock your world and save the entire planet?"

Derek had sat back down and was now rocking so hard I thought the porch would collapse.

"Don't tell me! Are we back to sex again?"

"Derek! Focus!"

"Then do tell me. The suspense is unbearable!"

"Designated Netter." I shouted out triumphantly.

"What? Like a designated hitter in baseball?"

"More like a designated driver. Think about it: Every Netaholics Anonymous group would have a designated netter. An offline onliner whose job it would be to bring new recruits into the fold. They'd set up websites, tweet, do the Facebook thing, respond to online inquiries, post meetings, text back to potential converts. They'd be the one to stay on top of the latest onslaught of sweet social media shit coming down the pike so they can get the gospel out to the heathen masses. Think of it like a designated sexer for the Shakers."

"Now there's a thought!" Derek scooted his rocking chair closer to mine again. "You might be onto something."

"Of course I am!" This time I did not push his chair away. "Look: in this age of technology run amuck, why the hell aren't there more Luddite groups? Think of all the desperate people out there just itching to throw off their chains, ready to eschew—"

"Gesundheit."

"Thank you. Technology. Yet no one knows about those in the know because they're unknown."

"Say that again?"

"No. Can't you see? It takes technology to oppose technology. You gotta be on the net to get people off it. How are you going to smash the state if no one knows where to go or what time to be there? And you know the biggest obstacle?"

"To not having sex?"

"Oh my God, is that all you can think about?"

"No," Derek said, grinning away. "I think a lot about *having* sex, too."

I ignored him.

"I meant the biggest problem for Luddites building a movement? To recruiting cabin-building buddies?"

"Tell me."

"Finding an anti-technology ally who wants to be the techno-nerd to do the devil's work."

"And the answer is . . . ?"

"ME!" I leapt off my chair high into the air.

"You?"

"Yeah! *Me*. Look at me, Derek." There was no need to tell him that. He had been staring straight at me the whole time. If his eyes had been open any wider, his lashes—sawdust and all—would have fallen right off. "You were there at the last NA meeting. You heard what went down."

"I know. Pretty amazing, huh? Eight thousand YouTube videos in a little over three weeks? That's beyond tubacious."

"No, not Rapunzel, you idiot! *Me*."

"Oh yeah," he said, deadpan. "You."

"In case you were totally clueless," I said, once more picking up a zucchini and holding it menacingly in my hand, "I spelled it all out for you, plain as the sawdusty nose on your face. When it comes to the net, I'm a lost soul, Derek. The chances of me coming totally clean from the damn thing are absolute zero. Maybe less. I—*we*—have just gotta face the facts. But here's what I'm getting at: netaholic that I still am, for some crazy reason I'm still chill with this whole Luddite thing. So you know what that means? *I'll* be the designated netter! I'll take one for the team. I'll go to the dark side to bring light to the masses, certify my insanity, keep my defects and shortcomings coming and sacrifice my soul for the common good. I swear I could have this little cabin-raising thing of yours all over the internet in no time. We could get Jonathan to dress like Thoreau and put Sheila in an old-time outfit with a hoop skirt and a bonnet, post the two of them on YouTube all kissy-face at the cabin site, and it would go totally viral. Set a construction date and this place will be swarming with Luddites. People will be lined up all the way down the driveway just waiting to swing a hammer. We could have sixteen cabins built in no time. Hell, we'll have to franchise them out."

"'*We'll*' have to?" Derek repeated.

"What?" I asked.

"You just said '*we'll*' have to."

This time I was the one who scooted my rocking chair even closer to his.

Chapter 54

Attention! Atención! Achtung!

Luddites of the World, Unite!

Come one! Come all!

King Ludd respectively requests the honor of your presence at the following hugely hip happening:

THOREAU'S CABIN RAISING

Say What? Help us to timber-frame an exact (more or less) replica of the cabin that Henry David Thoreau (you know the dude: philosopher, environmentalist, critic of the modern world) built at Walden Pond in 1845.

Where Is This Awesome Event Happening? Udder and Gramps's Funny Farm, 253 Larch Row, Haydenville. Head down the hill to the orchard, and there we'll be.

When Should I Show Up? Saturday, August 12, 8:00 A.M.–???????

Can I Bring a Friend? Of course! Everyone is invited. No experience necessary. Bring your body, your brain, work gloves, any random *hand* tools you happen to find lying around (no power tools, please—we're Luddites, damn it!), food to share for a potluck, sun hat, water or drinks to share, musical instruments, sense of humor, and anything else you can think of. But please, please, PLEASE—leave the cell phones at home!

I'll Definitely Be There, But . . . Why Am I Coming Again?
Thoreau's spiritual quest for simplicity, harmony with nature, and rejection of a life of "quiet desperation" has inspired us to walk in his footsteps. We are building a replica of Thoreau's cabin that will be a gathering place for technoholics in recovery, Luddites, Luddite wannabes, nature lovers, and every chill person out there. Seriously! How awesome is that?

Who Can I Contact for More Information? You can text (no snarky comments about that, please!) or call us at 413-586-3063 or visit Thoreaucabinreplica.com. #thoreaucabinreplica.

Chapter 55

"Do you have your Scrabble board?" I asked.

"What the hell kind of a question is that?" Derek asked, furrowing his brow and scowling at me. "Of course I have my Scrabble board!"

"Weird. Very weird. You are one strange dude."

"Right back at you, darling," he said slyly.

There was that word again. I gave Derek a look.

It had been a long day. And now, with darkness settling in and the fireflies doing their thing, Derek and I were sitting in—wait for it—a newly constructed replica of Thoreau's cabin. Or at least the beginnings of it, more or less. It was nearly framed up, no siding or roof, one end a little lopsided and drooping precariously toward the orchard. But still, the clear outline of a cabin.

Miracle upon miracles, we had somehow pulled the whole cabin-raising thing off! Huzzah and hooray! Thoreau's cabin was up and running!

After posting on every social media site known to humankind, including my hastily constructed Thoreaucabinreplica.com website (believe it or not, I could do more than just text!), a shit-ton of people had shown up to help out. Hundreds. Thousands. Hundreds of thousands. Okay, about thirty-three, to be exact. But boy, were they the sweetest thirty-three people *ever*! Most of the softball team had showed, plus a good bunch of the NA'ers. Karen the Cat Killer, Jeremy the Goat-Roper, Peter the Porno—all were in fine form. But other folks had come as well. Ponytailed hippies, cool-as-cucumber hipsters, youngsters and old farts, a mom with a baby, Luddites and the Luddite-curious. Even Udder and

Gramps, arthritic as they were, had lent a hand and supplied folks with a never-ending stream of good, strong coffee.

It had been quite the happening. And best of all? A few folks showed who actually knew how to swing a hammer. All things considered, the whole kit and caboodle had gone pretty damn smoothly. No one was killed or even seriously injured, though this time I was the one who repeatedly hit Derek on the head with the two-by-four. There was no way I was going to let Sheila whack that boy around anymore. That job was for me alone.

A good time was had by all, and everyone was in unanimous agreement that it was clearly the event of the century. As fab a job as we did, thank goodness no one was going to live in the damn thing. As a symbol of Luddite love, it was a stunning success. As an actual place to reside in? I don't think so.

After a final group hug and a staged picture with my phone, Sheila and Jonathan, now inseparable, had headed back to his place. Being back to besties with Sheila was a huge relief. As crazy as that girl was, if she didn't have my back I didn't know what I'd do.

Udder and Gramps had gone to bed, and Derek and I were sitting cross-legged, face-to-face, in the middle of the cabin floor, the Scrabble board between us. I had just returned from walking down the road to that sweet spot where I could get service and post construction pictures on Facebook and the website, and text a bunch of congratulatory huzzahs and online high fives, fist-bumps, and smiley-faced emoticons to some of our newfound Thoreau cabin-building friends.

I know, I know—posting and texting right after Thoreau's cabin raising? Seriously? The sheer audacity of it. Poor King Ludd would be rolling over in his grave. And God only knows what good ole' Henry David would be doing. I was half expecting to be struck down by Luddite lightning and then fried to a crisp in the raging fires of Netaholic Hell. But hey, I had made a pact with the devil and, come hell or high water, I was going to keep my end of the bargain.

I took the bag of Scrabble letters out of the box and gave them a shake. "If you want to play, it's got to be by my rules," I told Derek sternly.

"Oh no," he said. "Don't tell me we're back to illegal *yoinks* again?"

I took a deep breath.

"Even better. Relationship Scrabble."

"What?"

"You can't play a word until you use it in a sentence having to do with our relationship."

Derek rubbed one of the numerous bumps on his head where I had boinked (or was it bonked?) him.

"But I thought we weren't—"

I put my hand over his mouth. "Quiet! Don't talk. Don't even think. Are you in or are you out?"

"This," Derek said, removing my hand but continuing to hold it, "will definitely be interesting."

"BOZO!" I yelled. "Thirty points. Yeehaw! Who's going to win! Me! *Me!*" I took the scorecard out of the box and wrote a big "30" in bold under my name followed by eighteen exclamation points, one for each year of my life plus another one for good luck.

A delightful breeze was blowing in from the orchard, and the firefly light show was in full swing.

"BOZO is not a word," Derek said. "It's a clown's proper name. It doesn't count."

"What are you talking about? Of course it counts. It means a foolish or stupid person. As in: I'm a BOZO for treating you the way that I have. And I feel really, really bad about it. Thirty points. Deal with it. Your turn."

Derek fidgeted and looked down at the board, his fingers fiddling with his letters. He was silent for a minute and then played a vertical YES, which gave him that word plus BOZOS.

"YES," Derek said. "There have been one, two, possibly even three bouts of extreme BOZONESS on your part. But let's face it, you haven't had a total monopoly on playing the fool. I'm going to go out a limb here and suggest that YES, at one time or another, we've both been BOZOS. Twenty-one points."

"ZOO," I played, barely hesitating and coming down from the Z with two of my O's. I had drawn four of them to start the game and was more than happy to ditch them. "Twelve points."

"Oh God." Derek groaned. "Do I really want to know how that word fits into our relationship?"

"How about this: There have been times when I've been around you that I've felt like a caged animal. Pacing back and forth. All of my faults on display for you and everyone else to see. Captive in a ZOO."

"Deep." Derek looked hard at me. "Very deep. And scary as hell. A BOZO in the ZOO? It makes me think of some teen slasher movie with chainsaws and clowns where all does not turn out well in the end. And all of this from the girl I'm so attracted to."

Blush, blush, blush.

"By the way," he continued. "When you blush your freckles stick out even more."

"Is that a good thing?" I asked.

"A really good thing. I have every intent to remain a certified freckle-holic for the rest of my life. Don't even try to get me into a twelve-step program for that one."

I blushed even more deeply.

Derek set down three of his tiles.

HOPE, he played, working off my last O in BOZO.

"HOPE?" I said. "Like you HOPE I'm really not a ZOOEY BOZO?"

"No offense, but sorry, I pretty much think that you've got that one locked up. Actually, I know it."

"Thanks a bunch."

"You're welcome. But I meant HOPE as in, you know, I really HOPE that everything will be. . . okay between us. More than okay. That everything will be . . ."

Long awkward pause.

"Wonderful," he finally said. "In a BOZO ZOOEY HOPEFUL kind of way."

"Don't you find it kind of weird," I asked, "that HOPE is only nine points while BOZO is thirty? That doesn't really seem right, does it?"

"'*Either learn to love thorns, or don't accept any roses.*'"

"Thoreau? Yogi Berra? MLK?"

"The magnet on my refrigerator," Derek said smiling.

It was my turn. It took me less than a minute to find the perfect word, one beginning with the first letter of his YES.

"YOINK!" I shouted. "Oh yeah! Double word. Twenty-four points."

"No way!"

"You better believe it, buddy."

"Okay then. Use it in a sentence. A *real* sentence. Go on. Do it." I could tell Derek's SAD (Scrabble Anxiety Disorder) was beginning to kick in.

"Way back when, after I played YOINK for the first time, you kissed my hand. I remember thinking to myself, damn, this guy could make offline . . . interesting."

That was a fastball right down the middle of the plate and it caught Derek totally by surprise. He calmed right on down.

"Interesting?" he asked, his eyebrows doing their up and down thing.

"In a totally BOZO ZOOEY HOPEFUL YOINKISH kind of way."

"That still doesn't make YOINK a word," he said softly.

"I could take it back and play POINK instead."

"*Wahhh!*" Derek whined. "Why do you always get all of the good letters?"

"Because I'm special. It's 66 to 30. I'm kicking your ass. You're up."

"All right Ms. Special. Take this. PENGUIN. Off the N in YOINK."

"PENGUIN? Seriously? For our relationship? Use it in a sentence."

"Ever since your Wednesday-night confessional at the netaholics meeting, I've been having dreams about being Mister PENGUIN. You know who I'm talking about. That little stuffie under your bed at home. The one you couldn't live without."

I gulped down another big swig of coffee, blushed so hard I could practically feel the freckles burning off my face, and reached down deep into the little cloth bag for another round of letters.

It was getting late. So late that most species of fireflies had gone to bed. But with the moon out and the light from my phone illuminating the board, we could more or less still see to play. Plus, we were both firefly-flashing like crazy.

The game was almost over and Derek and I were neck and neck. I had three letters left to play. An L, an O, and an E. I was six points behind Derek. Six measly points. The board had turned difficult and there was little room left to play on. If I could just use my three letters and go out, I'd win the game. Three little letters.

I stared hard at the board.

"Go!" Derek said. "You can't take all night."

"Quiet!" I scolded. "Let me think. Genius takes time."

Suddenly, just the way it sometimes seems to happen in Scrabble, a word popped magically into focus. I could use my three letters plus the letter V, part of EVOLVE in the top left corner of the board, and close things out.

I could do it! I could win the game with a final four-letter word.

V-O-L-E.

VOLE!

A vole was one of those little mouselike rodents that Gramps hated and chased with a hoe because they wreaked havoc in his garden. VOLE would win the game for me! Sweet sweet victory would be mine!

But how to use it in a sentence? Hmm . . .

If you were a VOLE in my garden, I'd use a have-a-heart trap and keep you as a pet.

Way too weird.

If you were a vole in my garden, I'd spare the hoe and spoil the vole.

Say what? Even weirder.

Then it hit me. An epiphany like no other. I almost knocked over the Scrabble board.

V, O, L, and E. There was another word that I could play with those four letters.

I looked up from the board and I stared hard at Derek. Between the two of us, we were practically lighting up the night sky.

I thought of all the things that had happened to me in the last couple of months. Gardens and softball, Luddites and insects, technoholics and Thoreau's cabin, Scrabble and . . . Derek.

And now it had all come down to a single four-letter word.

V, O, L, and E. Rearrange those four letters and they'd fit together even more beautifully than a furry little rodent.

I looked at Derek once more, held my breath, and went for it.

"Seven points," I said. "I'm out. That would make the winner: ME!" I got up and did a little twist and spin, my Quaking Shaker victory-dance move.

Derek sat stock-still and stared up at me with those big wondering eyes of his. Full lips quivering away.

"What?" I asked. "I just won! Fair and square!"

He pointed to the last word.

"What about it?" I asked.

"You've got to use it in a sentence."

"Come on!" I said, avoiding his gaze. "I win and you know it! Sweet victory is mine!"

"Use it in a sentence." Derek's voice, soft and gentle as it was, was still pretty forceful.

Once more I held my breath.

Lots of options here. TNTC—too numerous to count. How to use that most amazing, that most magical, that most spectacular word of all words in a sentence. Hmm . . .

I LOVE to see the look on your face when I make a triple play.

That was safe.

I LOVE it that you were such a BOZO at the beehives and fell into the electric fence.

I really did love that.

I LOVE the fact that when I walked down the road to text, you didn't give me crap and accuse me of being a sellout or a loser or weak or a very, very bad human being or anything mean like that at all. You just sat here and waited for me and watched the fireflies and let me do my thing.

Without too much thought I could have come up with all sorts of reasonably innocuous sentences like that.

I could have. I really could have.

But there was another way to use it as well.

This is it, I told myself. *The entire summer has all come down to this.* Who knows? Maybe my entire life. One four-letter word on a Scrabble board.

But boy, what a magical word it was.

"Go on!" Derek said, still staring at me. He had reached over and put my hand in his again. Nothing in the world had ever felt so good as holding Derek's hand. "You have to use it in a sentence. Otherwise I win."

I took one more deep breath.

Scooting over to him, I plunked myself down onto his lap and wrapped my arms tightly around his neck.

"Actually," I said, fixing my eyes on his, looking at him harder than I had ever looked at anyone ever before. "I was kind of hoping, really hoping, that we both just won."

"Use it in a sentence," Derek told me one last time. His voice was barely audible. Hardly a whisper.

"How about if I just show you instead?"

I pulled his head and his lips and his whole mouth toward mine.

And this time, this glorious wonderful time, huzzah and hooray, he kissed me back.